Praise for
Angelika Frankenstein Makes Her Match

"I was hooked the moment I read the first page, and I adored every delightful word of this book. It gave me *Bridgerton* meets *The Addams Family* vibes: a little bit spooky, a little sweet, with a wonderful, loving cast of friends and a creative, heartwarming romance that kept me on edge right up until the very end. I of course knew it was going to work out, but the *how* had me biting my nails! I absolutely loved Angelika Frankenstein, a heroine who is as confident as she is competent. The banter is world class, and I caught myself laughing out loud and staying up far too late to read just one more page. We need more wonderfully weird romances like this!"

—Ruby Dixon, #1 Amazon author

"After reading an early draft of *Angelika Frankenstein Makes Her Match*, we immediately emailed Sally's agent and called dibs. Okay, that's not a thing you can actually do in publishing, but this is the book we've been waiting for, and we can't wait to shove it into everyone's hands. Take everything you've come to love in a Sally Thorne novel—witty banter; a sexy, toe-curling romance; and a voice that practically pirouettes off the page . . . but add one part Tim Burton. Dear reader, that is what's waiting for you, and we are OBSESSED. This is Sally Thorne at her absolute best."

—Christina Lauren, *New York Times* and
USA Today bestselling author

Angelika Frankenstein

makes her

Match

ALSO BY SALLY THORNE

Second First Impressions
99 Percent Mine
The Hating Game

ANGELIKA FRANKENSTEIN MAKES HER MATCH

A NOVEL

Sally Thorne

AVON

An Imprint of HarperCollinsPublishers

P.S.™ is a trademark of HarperCollins Publishers.

ANGELIKA FRANKENSTEIN MAKES HER MATCH. Copyright © 2022 by Sally
Thorne. All rights reserved. Printed in the United States of America. No
part of this book may be used or reproduced in any manner whatsoever
without written permission except in the case of brief quotations embodied
in critical articles and reviews. For information, address HarperCollins
Publishers, 195 Broadway, New York, NY 10007.

HarperCollins books may be purchased for educational, business, or sales
promotional use. For information, please email the Special Markets De-
partment at SPsales@harpercollins.com.

FIRST EDITION

Designed by Diahann Sturge
Map by Jeffrey L. Ward

Library of Congress Cataloging-in-Publication Data has been applied for.

ISBN 978-0-06-291283-1 (paperback)
ISBN 978-0-06-327163-0 (hardcover library edition)

22 23 24 25 26 LSC 10 9 8 7 6 5 4 3 2 1

This book is for Christina and Lauren.
Your belief in me gave me a new life.

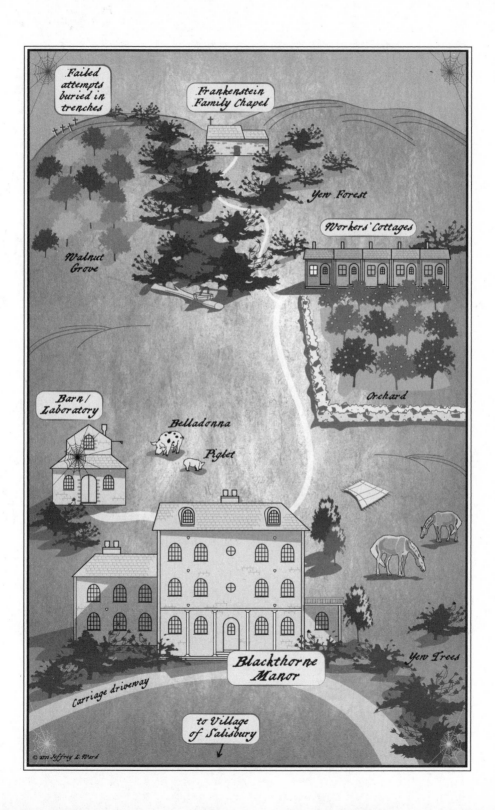

Angelika Frankenstein Makes Her Match

PROLOGUE

Here is a little-known fact: houses are proud of their observational skills.

A well-maintained house perfectly understands the weather, local gossip, who is an esteemed caller or an unwanted visitor, and, above all, they know their inhabitants.

A smart London town house on a prominent street will know the contents of love letters hidden beneath a pillow on its second floor. A humble cottage, with a clean-swept stone floor and a new log in the fireplace, knows what's for dinner next Tuesday. Will you need a coat today? Ask your house. Which chambermaid is in love with that soulful-eyed footman? There are no secrets.

But if neglect is involved, a house tends to grow sullen. And our story begins with a very disillusioned country house named Blackthorne Manor, owned by the Frankenstein family for ten generations. Located a brisk trot from Salisbury village, England, this house was built in a grand gothic style, with buttresses, arches, gargoyles, and stained glass aplenty. Blackthorne's windows had not been cleaned since Alphonse and Caroline Frankenstein died—that is to say, in precisely eleven years. Now, everything the house wished to know required a squint, and the surrounding estate appeared as a blur of yews, horses, a free-roaming pig, and apple trees growing heavy with fruit destined to rot. These views were not noticed by the occupants, and there were rarely any visitors.

A fresh coat of black paint on the sills was an outlandish, impossible daydream.

Blackthorne was suffering from weakened awareness, a general sourness of spirit, and it had very little of interest to observe, but perhaps things were about to change. Strange work past midnight had been occurring out in the barn— pardon, the "laboratory."

What were the last two remaining Frankensteins doing out there?

The older boy—no, Victor was a man now, and fond of his own reflection, and he raised his sister through her adolescence as best he could. He laughed at half of her jokes, teased her for every failing and flaw, tossed coins to her when she was sad, hugged her once a year, and informed her when he wouldn't be home at night. He used to come back stinking of ladies and liquor but now preferred leaning on doorframes, rereading letters from someone called Lizzie. Blackthorne had a notion that Victor was a "genius": a clever chap, who made sure everyone else knew it. He wanted to be remembered by history, or some such nonsense. Those genius hands would be far more impressive holding a rake, attending to those mounds of dead leaves on the northern wall.

The girl—Angelika, now twenty-four years old, and even prettier than the portrait of her dearly departed mama, Caroline—had turned plaiting her own hair into a meditative half-day activity, after which she would take a half-day bath. She had the talent of an artisan when asked to sew something, but she walked past the unraveled hems of the window curtains. Even with its capabilities diminished, Blackthorne Manor knew how badly Angelika suffered during those years when her brother rode off at dusk. She cried like a pup into her pillow, and she tagged along at his heels now. Unlike Victor, she had no one special to love her, and her longing filled the house like steam.

Blackthorne Manor knew this much: dearly departed Caroline and Alphonse Frankenstein had left their children too soon, and although the coffers were brimming with gold, Victor and Angelika suffered from the same neglect as their inherited house. Tender love and care were needed, as a matter of utmost urgency.

Things did not look promising, however. The Frankenstein children slept, ate, spent without thought, and acted very merry, but their lives were choked by ivy, and sadness.

"Orphan," Victor whispered to himself as he put on his father's coat.

"Orphan," Angelika whispered to her reflection, pulling her own hair tighter.

It would take something, someone, or a miracle, to change this present state of affairs.

CHAPTER ONE

Salisbury, England, 1814

Angelika Frankenstein knew what physical qualities her ideal man should have; unfortunately, she had to find those attributes at the morgue. She and her brother were in the doorway of the basement, like two customers about to stroll into a fruit market. Laid out on tables were around thirty corpses.

"I never get used to the stench," Victor Frankenstein remarked through his shirt cuff. "Be quick and choose."

"I'm always quick," Angelika replied into her perfume-soaked handkerchief. "Why would I want to linger?"

"Because you want to make sure you choose the best-looking."

Angelika was aghast. "I do not."

"What's the price tonight, Helsaw?" Victor asked the morgue attendant in a raised voice.

Helsaw sat outside the doorway on an upturned pail, biting his thumbnail in loud snips. "A shilling each," he said to Victor, then spat on the ground.

Victor considered it. "Any room for negotiation? Two corpses for a shilling?"

Helsaw nodded in the direction of their tied horses. "You both jingled when you hit the ground. Don't like it, go elsewhere."

Victor grinned. "All right. I'll pay anything."

"You're such a good negotiator, Vic," Angelika praised sweetly.

His smile turned evil. "Quiet, Jelly, or I'll send you to an orphan house."

"I'm twenty-four. They'll never take me." What would their parents have thought of these late-night activities?

Helsaw provided the siblings with a lantern each and heaved a sigh. "Bickering already. It's a long wait tonight, lads," he told the growing queue of medical students. They muttered and lit their pipes.

Inside, Angelika addressed her brother again. "I am only doing this to put my name in medical history, alongside yours."

"You are so terribly noble," Victor scoffed, picking up a corpse's arm to bend and straighten it. "You help me because you're bored out of your wits."

"You can't do this without me, and you know it." She waited for his nod. "I wish we were traveling again."

Victor gave her a narrowed glance. "Give up. I hate living out of luggage, with no laboratory. When Lizzie arrives, I'm home forever."

"Forever?" Angelika picked up a dead man's cold hand, and interlaced her fingers with his. Then, she rotated the wrist joint. She might be living without love, forever? She'd be a white-haired old lady, still living as her brother's ward? "If you had done your duty as older brother and guardian, I wouldn't be here right now."

Victor replied, "I've introduced you to every unmarried man I've ever met. I've struck up conversations in theaters with men you thought were your destiny. I've sat through fortune-teller visits. I've delivered anonymous love notes and objected at a wedding. I once helped you perform a spell under the full moon. It was absolutely unscientific, but I did it."

He did sound very close to tearing his hair out.

Angelika forged on. "My point is, you haven't helped me for a *long while*. The moment you saw Lizzie, you forgot about my goals. I think you forgot how to spell your own name."

"This, from a girl whose name is spelled with a *k* instead of a *c*. Here's a little suggestion for you," Victor said as he pressed around on a man's rib cage. "Men do not like being asked questions from a preprepared list. My friend from school, Joseph, said meeting you was like being interviewed for the position of junior footman."

"You praise my organization in the laboratory." Oh, dear. Victor had a point. Somewhere around the questions about *favorite color* and *happiest childhood memory*, men abruptly spoke of the late hour and the long road home. "Sometimes, I had the length of a cup of tea to make my choice. I need to know everything about a man, as quickly as possible."

Bending a corpse's knee up toward the ceiling, Victor replied, "For matters of the heart, you must go by feeling and instinct. Lizzie taught me that."

He had the smug glow of new love, and it sparked Angelika's temper.

"I would take this advice if I had anyone left to meet. I once had so many suitors, they were in a queue like that." Angelika nodded toward the doorway, where the medical students stood smoking. "I thought I had forever to find true love, the kind Mama and Papa had."

"You do have forever. There's no rush."

"Spoken as a man. I want to travel. I want my own house.

Especially as you are soon to be married, and you'll both want Blackthorne Manor all to yourselves. I'm quite sure I would be a bother."

"You would. I am hereby reinvested in your marriage project." Victor looked around the dark room. "Well? Does anybody here wish to belong to a selfish young lady who will keep you as a handsome pet and will refuse to compromise on anything? Make yourself known if you are indeed that fool."

There was a long, dead silence.

Angelika glared at him. "Is that how you would have introduced me at the military academy ball?"

"Are you still angry about that? It was weeks ago."

"Yes, I am angry that my brother refused to take me somewhere to dance with soldiers and to meet the new commander." She put her hand on her hip. "It's my fault I'm considered odd, and superior, and a bit witchy. It's my fault I'm unmarried. But it's your fault, too."

Victor ran a hand through his famous honey-red hair; the same color as hers. "I accept that I could do more," he conceded. "But I draw the line at country dances."

"Lizzie will want to go to them." Her brother's betrothed was currently packing her belongings, in preparation for becoming Mrs. Frankenstein as soon as possible.

Victor smiled at the mention of Lizzie's name. "Only she could drag me to one. Be proactive. Pick a chap here tonight, and if he survives, you can bring him tea trays in bed, wearing your prettiest gowns."

"Oh, certainly, much less effort than attending a dance." She held it in as long as she could, but then cackled at the absurdity. "All right, husband, please volunteer. I promise you do not have to tell me a single thing about yourself."

Victor was laughing, too, and gagging, in the unventilated

back corner of the room. "Other women order lace and hat trimmings. My dear sister is tailoring a suitor, right down to his cock."

"I hate you, Victor. So very much."

Sincerely, he replied, "I love you, too."

Angelika found a corpse she had not checked. Her pulse throbbed in her throat, and Victor's teasing faded into the background.

Here lay a beautiful man, frozen at the climax of the fight for his life. He appeared incredulous to have died. His brow was creased between the eyebrows, his jaw was gritted tight, and his hands were half-curled in fists. He had faced death like a gladiator, and when she rolled up one of his eyelids, there was such a direct challenge in his brown eye that she felt true fright and released him. "You fought hard, didn't you?"

She watched for his furious inhalation, which never came. It was terribly sad.

Tousling a gentle hand through his thick bronze-brown hair was very forward of her, but she could not resist. It was soft as tabby-cat fur. She noticed his smile lines and long lashes. He had neat fingernails, and all his teeth were present. "Beautiful, beautiful, beautiful," she whispered to him. "Would you like to be mine?"

She was inspired in a new way. She'd never been somebody's last chance before.

"Are you alone? Are you afraid?" She took a deep breath and had to muster her courage for this next question. "Can I do this for you? Do you wish to come back?" Her lantern flickered, and a breeze blew in, banging the door against the wall. Her skirts swirled around her ankles. Even Helsaw clutched his chest and barked an obscenity.

Angelika knew, deep in her bones, this dead man's answer was: *Yes, yes, yes. Bring me back.*

"That was eerie," Victor remarked blandly from where he was tapping his hands on a chest, feeling for evidence of fluid. "Who've you found there?"

She cleared her throat of sudden strong emotion. "Someone perfect. I won't change a thing about him."

"That's not the experiment," Victor argued. "My nemesis, Jürgen Schneider—"

She cut over him. "I know full well who your mortal enemy is."

"Then you know that in his exquisite German laboratory, he's reanimating entire men left and right." Victor could not think of the man without a tormented growl. "I must go bolder and exceed him, and do what he said is impossible. My achievement must be made of many parts, all sewn back together, to be better than Schneider's. Is everything present and accounted for?" He nodded toward Angelika's beau.

Angelika looked under the filthy scrap covering the handsome man's loins and considered what she saw. She had been reading a lot of anatomy manuals; possibly too many. What she saw lying on his lap was unremarkable. And upon closer review, his chest was trim and strong, but not the heavy padded muscles she preferred. "He looks . . . fine."

Victor came over to assess Angelika's claim. Bending the corpse's joints, he said, "He probably died only today. He's an excellent candidate, and his looks are almost as refined as mine." He searched around for a mirror, and then declared, "Keep his head, and we'll remake the rest."

She followed Victor to the next table. Then she glanced back at the handsome man.

He seemed alone, in a way the others did not.

She noticed something on the next man along, a stocky fellow in his fifties. "This one has a tattoo. 'Bonnie.'"

It was unlikely that Bonnie would approve of tonight's activities, and reality struck, harder than this imagined woman's slap. Angelika began defending herself out loud. "Surely a second chance is better than being tossed into a hole in the dirt?"

She wasn't talking to Victor, but he answered anyway. "If it's not us, it's them." He nodded to the doorway. "The difference is, we have a chance to reverse this. A few years too late, I suppose." He meant for their parents, and they both swallowed a lump of sadness. With forced humor, he continued. "Here, you'll like this one over here. Rippling all over with muscles, and a cock like a hog's hind leg. I think you've got a few options to work with here."

The shroud was pulled down to the knees, and she assessed the body part in question. The anatomy manuals had not prepared her. "Is it . . . too big?"

"Sister, I cannot advise you on such things," Victor replied. "Just get spares where you can."

It was good advice. Their laboratory smelled of burning hair.

This person's biceps did not give under her prodding finger, and his hands were black from coal, or metal. The body belonging to her handsome man had been refined and clean; this one was a brute. She faltered, looking back again. "I still like mine as he is."

"I think this was the blacksmith. Athena threw a shoe in the village last year. Shame." Victor slapped the man's shoulder heartily. "He put up with her biting very well. Don't look so worried, Jelly. We will make somebody who is ideal to you in every way."

Helsaw was leaning through the doorway. "What's taking so long? Heads are now an extra sixpence."

Victor ignored him. "I think this time's the charm, don't you, Jelly? We learned from the last three attempts. When I present my rebuilt man at the next Cerulean Order meeting, Schneider will cry himself to sleep." A cruel expression spread across his face. "I'll bring Lizzie along, to remind him of all the ways he has lost to me."

"'Urry up," a second voice said from the doorway, putting true fear in the siblings. It was their elderly servant Mary, tired of waiting with the pony cart. "What the bloomin' heck is the holdup? How hard is it to pick a couple of dead lads? You," she threatened Angelika with just a word. "*You.*"

"I'm finished," Angelika defended herself. "Why does everyone think I am slow?"

"I've told 'em," Helsaw gossiped to Mary. "There's twenty waiting. Any minute, the night watch might come around. Pick, pay, and get out." Against the wall, the queue of young men huffed in unison. "But there ain't no rushing these two."

"You don't know how hard my life is," Mary replied bitterly.

"We're done," Victor reassured her with a smile. "I bought you a fruit bun at market today, my dear Mary, and here is an extra shilling for your time, Helsaw."

Overcome by sudden adoration, both beamed at him.

Turning back to his sister, and instantly devoid of charm, Victor began to move the blacksmith. "Come on, Jelly. Get his ankles."

"I will pay you to carry for me." Angelika tried to bribe Helsaw, but he turned away with a sniff. "What is the difference between my brother and me? We both pay well, just the same."

"Does our heart good to see you lift a finger," Mary said. "Get a little sweat on that pretty brow, my lady." It seemed to be true for the entire waiting queue. They laughed and heckled, egged on by Mary, as Angelika helped to lug their first pick outside. She wouldn't lower herself to respond and kept her eyes trained skyward. It was a full moon tonight, and there was something different in her favorite constellation.

"See, I'm telling you. There's a new star."

Victor didn't even look up. "Scientifically unlikely."

"I've been looking at that constellation since I was a child. I know what it is supposed to look like."

Her brother shook his head. "Not now. One, two, three—" They hoisted the man into the cart. "Let's go back for your dream man. We can't forget him."

Angelika wished again on the new star for luck. "I couldn't forget this one if I tried."

CHAPTER TWO

The Frankenstein siblings worked most of the night, and the following day.

Angelika, skilled from years of needlepoint lessons, was able to make the tiny sutures that Victor insisted on. She remembered his joke in the morgue: *Other women order lace and hat trimmings.* Arteries were like the fine satin cord on a hat brim; muscle fascia was a textile suited to a cheap petticoat. Everything was silky with blood, but she was used to it. All night, all day, she sat in a seamstress pose, while the tailor watched over her shoulder, intolerant of one incorrect stitch.

Now her midday mutton stew was long digested, and the sunlight was fading from the room. She could not feel her thumbs. "I need to rest my hands."

"With your project fully stitched and complete, and my own in a hundred pieces." Victor gave her a mean look as he jumped up to grab the iron bar spanning the top of the door. Pulling his chin up to the bar with muscle-shuddering effort, he grunted: "Typical—Angelika."

She wasn't in the mood. "Look at all I've done, you ungrateful lout."

Another chin-up. "You—sad—little—spinster."

The locals said similar things to her turned back. *Un-married. Unwanted, unusual, ungodly.* Her hurt must have showed, because Victor dangled and added on a heavy sigh, "Sorry. I'm tired, too." He continued his chin-ups. Angelika knew he was expecting her to count his repetitions, but she never did.

"Nothing is stopping you from learning to sew, Vic."

"I've—already—tried." Many years ago, a handkerchief was ruined by his attempt, and his dots of blood. Victor had no tolerance for tasks that he wasn't immediately excellent at. Dangling and huffing, he added, "Anyway, I don't need to learn. I've got you. How many's that?"

"Just ten more," Angelika said cruelly, and picked at her cuticles as he performed many, many more of his groaning, trembling chin-ups. When he looked half-dead, she said, "Done."

Victor dropped to the floor, and through gasps he said, "I can't wait for Lizzie to see all my hard work."

"I do hope you're not referring to yourself." Angelika grimaced.

"I've noticed that ladies like muscles. He could have posed for Michelangelo." He gestured to Angelika's project.

The siblings sat on windowsills near each other. Fresh air was vital. "How long will you rest?" The strain was evident in Victor's voice as he leaned out to check the weather. "I can smell the storm. And they're starting to smell worse, too."

"I'll just take five minutes," she said, and her brother nodded, drinking from a flask of liquor. She put her hand out for it, sipped, and winced at the taste.

"You did such a good line of stitches there," he admitted in grudging admiration, getting to his feet again to study the neckline of Angelika's project. It was roughly as long as he ever sat still. "If he always wears his cravat, no one would know."

"Thank you, he turned out nicely." She looked at Victor's workspace. His scientific hopes and dreams were currently facedown in a metal bowl. She took another sip from the flask and handed it back. "I'll do yours as neat."

"Mine only needs to be functional." He produced an apple from his pocket, taking a huge bite. "Did you see your elegant stranger had a gold ring on? How Helsaw missed that, I have no idea. I took the hands for my project." Angelika put out her flat palm. Victor flicked it.

"The fingers have swelled; it's stuck. Remind me to get the tin cutters from the garden to get it off," Victor said, sitting back down, eating ravenously. "I think it is a type of betrothal ring. We'll look at it later."

Is anybody unwed? Voice rich with despair, she said, "How marvelous."

Victor cackled and got to his feet again, stretching. "You never had this jealous green look when working on your earlier three husbands." He nodded at the worktable and continued to rile her. "He might compare you to his beloved when he wakes."

"None of Schneider's men woke with memories."

"I am better than him." Victor was instantly crackling with annoyance. "I mean, I will be if these don't burn to a crisp. You are always asking me about what will happen when they wake up. I cannot answer you." He threw his apple core out the window with force. "It's an experiment. A single heartbeat will be a success."

"Where will they sleep? What will they wear? Do we keep them forever, or do they go home again?" She shrank under her brother's poisonous glare. "One of us has to think of the future."

"You live your life almost exclusively in daydreams about the future. We are doing this right now, in wild new territory. There are no rules that I can explain to you, because I do not know." Victor's composure faltered, revealing a rare glimpse of self-doubt. "You are probably worrying for nothing. I haven't succeeded before." He crossed to the completed man and looked down at him. "I've never tried harder than this, knowing how much you want him, Jelly. You deserve somebody to love you."

Her throat felt tight, and she returned with equal vulnerability, "Thanks, Vic. But I don't expect him to love me. He probably won't even like me. But if he stays, and convalesces here, maybe he will . . . get to know me."

Victor was uncomfortably earnest now, with his hand on the man's shoulder. "He will learn that you're stubborn, and ridiculously extravagant, and that you spend more money than humanly possible."

"Now say something nice."

Victor patted her creation. "He will see your world-famous beauty—"

"Stop," Angelika protested, smiling. "Keep going."

"And after he knows you, he will see your heart of gold. You surely have an expensive heart, just as he now has the strongest heart I've ever handled. Nothing spared," Victor said to the man. "Everything is of the best quality. She made sure of it."

Angelika felt her brother deserved some encouragement in return. "When you succeed, and the news travels the world, Lizzie's father will be boasting about his son-in-law. And yes, it pains me to admit it, but she will love your muscles."

"Oh, I know she will," Victor replied, before becoming so invigorated by joyful energy that he completed another set of chin-ups. He now lived like he'd learned a secret, and Angelika yearned to know it, too. Wouldn't it be wonderful to be in love?

She covered her sudden melancholy with a tease. "If she won't have you, Belladonna waits patiently in the wings."

"Belladonna is the one female I should never have encouraged." Victor snorted with laughter, dropping back to the floor and wiping his hands on his trousers. "When Lizzie arrives, there may be a murder at Blackthorne Manor. Rested enough?"

It was very late at night when Angelika laid down her needle and thread.

"It's time," Victor said, and he was right.

It was time.

Angelika's work was done, and she was not overly interested in the reanimation process. Victor directed. She sewed. He dealt with obtaining the afterbirth, the weather forecast, and the wire cabling attached to the spire on the roof. She took off her soiled apron while her brother dashed about, aligning the bodies in their individual chambers.

Rinsing her arms and hands, she said to Victor, "Something about tonight feels different. I should go and put on a nice dress." And a little cheek rouge, perfume, and a hairpin. Whilst she could not find anything overly objectionable in her reflection, and she had indeed been described many times as a beauty, there was something about her personality that was untenable. Unnatural. *Unlovable.*

"What if he convulses and burns like the last one? That's what you should focus on, not your appearance. Besides, you always wear trousers at home. He'll have to get used to it."

Victor poured the barrel of afterbirth into the first chamber, submerging his creation. Their sheep-herding neighbors no longer asked what they used it for, and laughingly referred to it as liquid gold. With a grunt of exertion, Victor diverted the barrel to Angelika's creation, and she watched as the translucent, smelly substance began to coat him. Then the flow weakened to drips. Victor banged the side. This triggered a new splattering, but not much.

"I thought there was more," he began defensively, but Angelika was beside the chamber in a blink.

"It barely reaches an inch up his side, and yours is completely covered." Her tone was plain: *It's unfair.* "How is mine to have an even chance?"

Victor pondered this. "We'll animate mine first, then put yours in. Don't fret, it will work out." Above, a rumble of thunder caught his attention. "The storm's almost here. We must hurry."

Maybe it would be for the best. Victor's creation could fail, he could adjust the technique, and hers would succeed. Everyone would be happy, and these months of late nights would be over. She dropped herself heavily into a nearby armchair to wait.

Victor was now in his creative state of flow and could not be interrupted. It struck her that Lizzie should see what he looked like right now, energized by the storm's crackle. Victor was spoken of by the village girls as *terribly handsome and rich, but oh so strange, and always eating an apple, and slightly bad-smelling.* It was all truth. He was up to his elbows in other men, all day and night.

Besides, the Frankenstein coloring was difficult to get used to. Red hair, pearl skin, and green eyes. On Angelika, these colors read as beauty, or sorcery. On a tall man such as Victor, it was . . . confronting. He was regularly given blunt assessments by strangers out of tavern doors and carriage windows. Several artists had asked him to sit, balming those stings. Seeing both siblings together? They could charge an admission price.

"You're doing well," Angelika encouraged her brother, but he was too focused to acknowledge her. She fell into a doze and had a short dream that she was lying on her back in a grassy field, beside a warm body she knew was a man's. His voice told her that he would be here soon. He'd fight to be with her. In her dream, she was reaching up to the night sky, trailing her fingers through the dark and stars, like a man's soft hair.

She was jolted awake by a crack of lightning.

Victor then howled, "It's alive!"

There was movement in the chamber—and it wasn't convulsions.

Angelika was now disappointed that they hadn't done hers first but covered it well. "How marvelous. Can he hear you?"

"Not sure. No, don't come closer." Victor was leaning over the chamber, trying to help his creation sit up out of the slurry. "I may need to scoop out his mouth." Not necessary: the man began coughing in earnest. "He's tall, isn't he, Jelly? Even seated. How did I make him so big?"

"You said, and I quote, 'No, Jelly, I want the long legs.' Let me help."

"Stay back." Victor spent a minute grooming his gigantic baby, wiping away the viscous gel while he blinked slowly, his slack mouth gaping and closing. "Welcome, my friend. I am Victor Frankenstein, and I have brought you back to life. You shall make me famous. Wait until Lizzie meets you."

A mournful groan was the only reply.

Angelika went to visit her beau with butterflies in her stomach. "Not long, my sweet."

He was indeed superior quality. She'd justified it thus: if she was being reassembled, she would hope her maker would select improvements wherever possible. And though she had felt a pinch of guilt as she passed off sections of his perfectly satisfactory body to Victor, she was deeply happy with what she saw now.

This was an unparalleled masculine specimen.

She really should be assisting Victor, but she could not stop her eyes from trailing down this body. The blacksmith's chest was padded out with muscle and corded sinew. His hard work was not wasted. Angelika continued her review of her own creation. She had decided to use the second-largest penis in their inventory. It had made her brother roar with mirth, and he teased her about her newfound economy, but the one she had selected would likely stiffen out to a good size, if he ever felt that way about her. She may never know. This late at night, with her dark under-eye circles, it felt like a very large *if*.

In the places where the afterbirth had splattered, his stitches appeared to be healing. "I need to transfer him into the full chamber," she told Victor. "Hurry up."

"All right then, come and help me," Victor barked. By the time she made her way around, Victor's achievement had both feet on the floor. As he began to straighten, slipping like a newborn foal, she could see the errors they had made.

"Those legs and that torso do not belong together." This man was straightening up to seven feet tall.

"None of it does," Victor retorted, in no mood for critical feedback. "Stand still, man. It's all right." The man howled; a terrible hurt sound that was probably heard in the village. "Jelly, come and see if you can calm him." Victor ducked when his creation swung out an arm.

"Shhh," she soothed, amplifying her feminine presence.

"It's all right. Angelika is here. You're safe." For a heart-stopping moment, the beast was silent, regarding her form with glassy eyes, lingering on her breasts and hips.

"Good. I shall begin my examination and interview—" Victor was cut off by screams so loud that the candles above dripped wax. This big man had apparently never beheld anything as horrific as Miss A. Frankenstein, and he began to struggle away to the door, evading his master's clutches.

"How rude," Angelika managed to say.

"He's gone wild," Victor shouted, exasperated. "And I'm abruptly sick of him."

"Do you need my pistol?" Angelika called, unsure if killing a dead man would be murder, but her brother waved her away irritably. The mismatched pair of nude creation and dandy creator struggled off together out of the barn doors. She could hear wet scrabbling, grunts of effort, and fading distressed cries.

"Right. Your turn," she said to her project, refusing to be daunted. "In you go, my love. The storm is overhead."

She slipped straps underneath his shoulders and around his waist and, with difficulty and a lot of dripping goo, used the wheel and pulleys to transfer him into the deeper tub. "This is an awkward way for us to meet. Just as I am your last hope, I think you are my last hope, too." She closed her eyes, and the truth of that statement sank in. "I refuse to be an old maid at twenty-four. Victor will marry Lizzie soon, then a baby will arrive, and I'll be their unofficial nanny, then governess. Then, a withered old aunt."

She'd be happy for her brother, but it would be hard to smile through the jealousy. In her dreams, for years, she'd heard the call of true love; a yearning inherited from her madly devoted parents.

"Hmmm. I'm not sure what comes next." Maybe she should have stayed awake more while Victor did this next bit. His notes were strewn around the benchtops, all in his particular shorthand, and were therefore useless to her. Now was her chance to prove she was a full contributor. "I will do my best."

Even though prayer of any kind was forbidden in their household, her next words sounded very close to one. Eyes closed, hands folded, she said:

"Dear sir, I will do anything for you. To have you, I will change what I must about myself. I will sacrifice and make you proud—" Here, her eyes welled up, and as she bent down over him, her tears dropped into the vat. "I will cut myself up into as many pieces as you are."

There was only silence in reply, but she felt like he understood.

Angelika took a few fortifying breaths. "I think I connect this here." She pulled a springy cord down from above and slipped a metal ring around his forehead. "And then I tighten it just so, and lightning hits the rod on the barn roof, and I wish myself luck, and—"

An almighty rumble of thunder drowned out her next words. There was a crack, everything went white, and then the world filled with sparkles and star-fire.

There was the smell of burning hair.

"Damn it all," Angelika cried out in anguish. "He was so perfect. I will never again have another so perfect." Those beautiful brown eyes would never gaze upon this world again. Loss nearly turned her inside out. Outside, her brother was roughhousing with his creation, but her own darling was burned. "Well, I'm alone forever," she said to herself as her tear-filled eyes began to readjust to the gloom.

Her heart stopped.

Wrenching himself upright in the chamber of gel was the most handsome man she'd ever seen. He was spluttering out mouthfuls of liquid, before inhaling some rough, crackling breaths.

"My love?" Angelika came closer, and all she could see was how well she'd done. Unlike Victor's man, her keen eye for sewing and pattern making had resulted in a truly excellent outcome. He was perfectly formed, with ideal proportions.

This was a body to live for, and a face to die for.

She came closer still, smoothing down the front of her blouse and plumping her bosom up. "My love?"

After an almighty coughing fit, the naked man managed to get out: "Where am I?"

CHAPTER THREE

Angelika had rehearsed a welcome-back-to-life spiel three times before this, but everything was now forgotten. "Oh, goodness. Sir, you are gorgeous."

"My arms feel strange." He tried to rub his face on his shoulder. "Oh, the pain. What has happened to me?"

Angelika took a handkerchief from her trouser pocket. "Let me help." She wiped his eyes clean, and when they opened and looked into hers, she could have sworn she felt another lightning strike. Star-fire was in her blood and bones. "You're alive. I cannot believe it."

The man winced and shifted, breaking the moment. He was busy getting his bearings, eyes wild and unfocused as he looked around the room and down at his own body. "Who are you? Where am I?"

"You died, but I brought you back. Well, my brother and I. I am your new . . ." She hesitated on the phrasing. Maker? Admirer? Friend? He was waiting for her explanation, so she went with: ". . . mistress, and my brother, Victor, is your master. You may live here with us now, as long as you like."

"But *where* is here?" The man reached out for the edge of the chamber and froze at the sight of himself. "This isn't me," he said in a daze to his arm, and began to struggle, clumsy like Victor's creation. "I'm all heavy and cold. It's pain like I've never known, piercing right through me. And you won't tell me where I am."

"Blackthorne Manor. Well, the laboratory anyway, which used to be the barn."

"That's not as helpful as you seem to think," he replied, and with a huge amount of placenta slopping over the edge, he hauled himself out of the chamber to stand beside Angelika, his muscles gleaming in the candlelight. She could not admire his body now. He shimmered with agony, and it made her sick to her stomach. She put a hand on his slimy elbow, but he shook it off irritably, looking instead to the window. He moved toward it with wincing, grunting determination, his ambulation stiff. Both of tonight's creations seemed hell-bent on escaping.

"No, stay here, it's raining," Angelika shouted. She noted his exceptional backside in an abstract way as he leaned out the window. But he made no further move to climb out, and when she came closer, she saw he was observing Victor struggling on the lawn in the sheeting rain. Victor had managed to loop a rope around the huge man and was wrangling him as best he could with the loose end around a tree for leverage. In the shadows of the house, a lop-eared pig was observing the commotion.

"That's my brother. Pardon me, Victor," Angelika called from the window.

"I'm busy!"

"Mine worked, too."

Victor's head whipped around in shock. His creation took advantage of his broken attention, untangled himself, and fled, pursued by the pig.

Victor roared unintelligibly. He was soaked and exhausted, with one boot missing.

"He's alive and talking." She pointed at the man at her side. "Let yours go, you'll never stop him. Come back inside."

Victor couldn't accept this. "He might hurt himself." He took off running into the night.

The man looked down at Angelika. "What did you mean, yours worked, too?" He was shaking badly with cold, his skin still an unhealthy hue. "Am I like that giant . . . thing? What did you do to me?"

"He's not a thing, he's a guest, just like you. I told you what I did. I saved your life. Come away now." This time when she took his elbow, he allowed her to lead him back into the relative warmth of the room. "I'll ask our servant to light us a fire and heat some water."

She pulled the lever marked MARY on the wall—another of Victor's great inventions—but summoning her this late at night was dangerous. "Come up to the house with me. Here, let me find you something to wear," she said, cursing her lack of organization. "Wrap this around yourself."

She passed him a long muslin cloth, and together they knotted it at his hip.

"I'm not going anywhere until you explain everything." His teeth were audibly chattering. "It's all a dream, nothing more. I've gone mad, that's what this is. I'm in Bedlam. I'm in hell."

"Everything is fine. You are in England. Blackthorne Manor is two miles outside Salisbury. I'll explain everything when you're in a nice warm bath."

A distant bang could be heard. A gunshot? Worse: Mary slamming a door.

"But I have no memories. Was it an accident?" He was looking again at his arms, thumbing a line of healing stitches. "Is this a sanitorium? I've been in a long sleep?" He began to beg. "Please, my name. Tell me my name."

"I don't know it."

A shadow darkened the room. It was Mary in her soaked nightgown, a scowl on her weatherworn face. Both Angelika and the man took a step backward.

Angelika recovered first, and said in her best mistress-of-the-manor voice: "Mary, my guest has arrived at last."

Mary had seen too many unusual things in this household to be shocked. "Fourth time's the charm," she said snidely. "When's the wedding?"

"Oh, Mary, what a joke," Angelika replied, blanching under the man's narrowing eyes. "We need hot water. Enough to fill two baths, at least."

"Do you know how old I am?" Mary began, before remembering she was a servant. She left the room, shrieking an obscenity when she thought she was out of earshot.

"I'm worried about Victor," Angelika said when the man would only stare at her. She went back to the window. "If you promise to stay in the bath, I might go out to help him."

The man joined her and looked at the lawn where the violent scene had taken place. He then assessed the stormy sky, and his wet hand slid around her waist and tightened. To Angelika, it felt like a husbandly, possessive touch, telling her to stay inside and out of danger.

Just as the pleasure of the moment rang through her body, he seemed to notice what he had done, and reacted in surprise. He pushed her away hard enough that she bounced off the window frame, her cheek smarting from the impact.

"I'm sorry," he blurted, his eyes darting. "I'm not this strong. My body isn't my own." To add to his humiliation, under the muslin cloth, his penis was growing erect. He looked at Angelika's waist, her thighs in trousers, and the situation became more prominent. "I didn't mean to push you. What is happening?"

The hotness in her cheekbone was a reminder of reality. This was nothing like her girlish daydreams, and she refused to lasso her creation as her brother did.

"It's up to you if you come with me now, but life will be hard for you with no clothes or money or shelter. If the villagers see you like this, they'll assume you've escaped an asylum and will beat you to death. If you come willingly, I will give you warmth, a bed, food, and answers."

Silently she left the room, and he followed her.

As she crossed the lawn that separated the barn from the manor house, he was still behind her, limping and biting back groans. She felt his attention on the rear of her body acutely. Apart from the involuntary circulatory response from his new penis, there was no indication that he found her even remotely appealing.

Only she felt a connection, and it was a familiar situation.

If Angelika saw a man more than twice, and could somewhat guesstimate where and when she might see him again, she fell into rapturous infatuation. The baker's pockmarked delivery boy had no idea that he starred in Miss Frankenstein's most romantic fantasies; ditto the neighbor's footman, the goatherd who used their back laneway, and, for a shameful time, Victor's elderly bookbinder.

Angelika had a passionate heart, but as she walked through the dark foyer of the manor and up the left-hand curved staircase, it finally struck her how unromantic this was. Instead of being patient and letting fate decide, in typical Frankenstein fashion, she had been too proactive.

"You've become rather quiet," the man behind her said. She

turned on the staircase and saw he was only on the second stair, struggling to raise each leg.

"It's difficult?" She went to his side and put his arm around her shoulder. "I'll help you. Lean on me."

"I think I'm dying." He was matter-of-fact about it. "I'm turning blue." He resisted her help for as long as he could, but then grew heavier against her, until the remaining stairs seemed to Angelika to stretch upward like a mountain summit. Not once did he complain, and she was in awe of his sheer strength of will.

Now that they were pressed together, she could hear a wheeze in his lungs. *I did this to him,* she told herself in a daze. *I have put him through this terrible agony, and for what? To have a handsome man around the house to have afternoon tea with? What was I playing at?*

"I'm so sorry about this. My brother is a bad influence on me."

Up and up they toiled, until they halted, puffing with exertion, on the landing, beneath the portrait of Angelika's mother. The expression of the painting changed, depending on the angle and circumstance.

Right now, Caroline Frankenstein was deeply unimpressed.

"I'm clearly doing my best, Mama," Angelika said up at the frame. "Come now." She steered the man left. "My bedchamber is at the end; we just need to make it that far."

"Your brother might not approve."

"A man in my bathtub will not be the strangest thing happening today."

His body leaned into hers, like it wanted her feel and scent. Against her hip, his member retained its rigidity. "Why does my body keep doing this?" He pulled back with distaste in his features and pushed at himself with his palm. "I want you to know, from the neck down, this is not me."

He was completely correct, but it still hurt her feelings.

"My hands want to touch you, but I don't want to, and my—" He focused downward again. "Everything is different. I have no memories, but I know this isn't me. What did you do?"

At the end of the hall, Mary appeared with swinging buckets, blessedly breaking the moment. She snapped, "Finally. You've been an age. Get him in. Don't waste my hard work." She marched off, grumbling.

The man watched her depart. "Should I help her?"

"As I said, you're my guest." Angelika marveled at his thoughtfulness as she led him into her bedroom, but he balked in the doorway. "Come on, you'll feel so much better."

He was assessing the room with a crease on his brow. He took in the four-poster bed smothered in fine silks and the jewels strewn on the dresser. He noticed the embroidered chinoiserie dressing screen, the 250-year-old Persian rugs, and the alcove by the window filled with a copper tub and potted ferns. "You're rich," he said in an accusing tone.

"Yes."

"You live alone here, with only your brother? Remind me of your name," he commanded.

"Angelika Frankenstein. It is Latin for 'angelic.' But my name is spelled with a *k*, not a *c*. Mama wanted to be creative, but I wish she hadn't bothered." She went to her bathroom and found a tin of salts. As she stirred them into the tub, she said, "You are right; I am a wealthy heiress, and an orphan. We lost both our parents very fast, one after the other, when I was thirteen." She coughed to clear her tight throat. "After that, Victor did his best to raise me, so my faults are his doing. These salts are from Paris. They may sting your stitches but will help you heal."

"Why do I even have stitches?" He could not resist the steam and came closer, his teeth still chattering. "I really shouldn't be in here."

"We'll tell Mary to clear out the guest room next. Victor has one of Lizzie's theater costumes lying on the bed. It's a big brown bear."

He was too overwhelmed to be interested in that. When he put his foot into the water, he let out a yowl. "It's too hot, it's agony, agony," he repeated grimly, even as he lowered himself downward. He lay back and looked up at the ceiling with genuine suffering in his eyes. They cut to Angelika, now in that same battle-fierce stare she had glimpsed in the morgue.

"If you did this to me, I hate you."

"Then I suppose you hate me." She went to the shelf to get a fresh bar of soap and a nailbrush. "That didn't take long. Perhaps it is my new record."

Mary had reentered, and this time her hearing had not failed her. "You hate her, eh?" She sloshed a bucket of water onto his face with no regard. "You'd prefer to be dead in the ground, dinner for worms? You're soaking like a lord in a manor house. One of the richest women in England wants to scrub your fingernails. Get a grip on yourself," Mary scolded him, and with effort heaved the second bucket onto him. "Count yourself lucky she hasn't sent you back where you came from."

Her words had an effect. When Angelika pulled up a stool beside the tub and held up the nailbrush, he gave her his hand with a contrite blink.

"I really was dead?"

"Yes. I found you in the morgue. We think you died yesterday." She began to scrub his fingernails. "Are you feeling any better, my love?"

He was reeling from this news. "Why do you call me that? Did we know each other before?"

"I call everyone that," she lied. "'Tis a habit I have." She gave him back his scrubbed hand, and he held it up for his own inspection. "You are right. You are made up of several men from the neck down."

He jolted upright and water sloshed out of the tub, soaking Angelika's trousers. "I knew this wasn't my cock," he barked, before sinking deep in the water. Angelika thought she could see the first glow of color in his cheeks. "I can't remember a thing, but I know that much," he said to himself.

She lied again. "You were mangled by a cart wheel. I had to improvise."

He charted his fingers over his body in a way that had Angelika blushing. "And this is the body you have made for me?"

She watched as the pads of his fingertips ran down the stitches around his neck, the shoulder joints, the heavy chest and ridged abdomen. He raised his knees and noticed an old scar the previous owner had. He had astonishment in his eyes when he looked back up at her. "You did this?"

"I did all the pattern making and stitching. It can be complicated with the arteries, and messy, but Victor's procedure is ultimately what brought you back. He's a genius."

"You're a genius, too," the man said with admiration. "If what you say is true, and I should be dead in the ground, then I must say thank you."

"You're welcome." She could not stop herself; she picked up a sea sponge and began to cleanse his face. "My love, you look so much better already."

He smelled infinitely better. His eyes closed in a way that looked like pleasure as she ran the sponge down his brow, cheeks, jaw, and throat. She repeated the pattern several more times, putting every bit of care and love into the movement.

His hand clasped her wrist. "But why me?"

"Why? We are scientists." She shook him loose and, to avoid his piercing brandy-brown eyes, she got to her feet. "Oh, I'm soaked."

This distracted him.

"I have never seen a lady wearing trousers." His pupils dilated wide, and he pushed the heel of his hand below the water at waist level. "At least, I don't think I have."

"I can't stitch men together as easily if I'm hindered by skirts." She felt self-conscious enough to want to retreat further out of his range. "I'll change my clothes. Oh, Mary, my love, there you are. Did you put heating bricks in my bed?"

Mary noticed the endearment and nodded warily. She then went over to the tub and assessed the water, ignoring the large man soaking in it. "He was so dirty and smelly this water is brown," Mary said snidely before reaching down between his feet and pulling the plug. "Victor's invention," she explained offhand as Angelika went behind her changing screen with dry clothes.

"Invention?" the man echoed.

Mary boasted, "Master Victor has a brilliant mind."

"Yes, just ask him," Angelika cut in dryly.

"He put in a copper pipe that empties the water outside the house. It's a godsend. Now if only he'd just invent something to carry water upstairs. I'm sure he will." There was a gurgling sound, and then Mary began refilling the bath. "Already a better color," she told him. "And we can see the blood's flowing well to your prick."

"Madam, it is out of my control," he protested.

"What's your name, anyway?" Mary asked him. "What do I call you?"

"I cannot remember," the man said.

"Well, pick a name, or I'll pick one for you. Hmm. You

came from the barn outside. Barney?" Mary gathered the empty pails. "Mistress is naked behind that screen. Don't you think about getting up for a peek."

"I would not," he retorted in horror. "I am not interested in her remotely."

"Ah, my lady," Mary said with deep regret. "I don't think this one will work out."

Victor was mostly self-sufficient, but his younger sister was nothing but hard labor. Mary could be heard muttering as she departed, something about *unwed* and *unbelievable*. And it was true. All true. Forever. She wrenched on a nightdress.

"I'm sorry," the man said. "That was rude of me."

Angelika's tears soaked into her fresh handkerchief in a steady stream. When she breathed in, she made an accidental sniffle.

There was a shifting in the tub. "Miss Frankenstein? Are you all right?"

She tried for a normal voice. "I'll get you clothes and have Mary make you a pack of supplies. I'll give you money and a horse. I will release you from my company."

"You're upset. Come back please, Angelika." His tone was kind.

"No," she replied with a louder sniffle. "I'm staying back here alone, forever."

"If that is your wish," the man said. "But I would like to know what you are experiencing."

"I feel pain. Of a different sort." She waited for the lashing that she deserved. *Spoiled, selfish brat.* It did not come. "I thought I was doing a good thing, but I now see you did not want me to help. I should have left you alone."

"I'm glad you did not."

"Do you remember what it was like? Being dead?" She hesitated, then asked the question that Victor would have forbidden. "Is there anything beyond?"

"Before I saw your face, it was just . . ." He fell silent, for so long that Angelika peeked out from behind the screen in alarm. But he was just resting, the candlelight shining in his eyes as he thought. "Before you, it was absolute darkness. I wasn't torn back from heaven. I'm sorry if that upsets you to hear."

"Not at all. Heaven and hell aren't very scientific." She watched as his expression darkened into a scowl. "Is that offensive to you?"

He sighed, and his face smoothed out. "I don't know what to be offended about. The only thing I know is what you look like. I can't even remember my own face."

This brought Angelika out from hiding. "I will fetch you a looking glass later. Trust me when I say you are extremely handsome. I will add more salts to your water. Does it sting?"

"Like you can't believe," he replied, eyes on her face, before breaking away to survey her nightdress in one quick slide, shoulders to toes. He was barely submerged now, and he had a relieving pinkish hue to his lips. "It was true. I smelled like death."

Angelika laughed in surprise, wiping her wet eyelashes, and he mustered his first-ever smile. It was a lovely thing. His teeth were even better than she remembered.

"Choose a name, until you can recall your own," she encouraged him, pulling her stool nearer his head. "I shall wash your hair."

"Thank you," the man said as she began to work suds onto his scalp. "I really don't know how I've gone from the morgue to this moment. My name," he pondered, eyes drooping closed as she began to massage. "List a few, and maybe I'll remember mine."

"George. Charlie. John. David. Francis. Edward. Liam. Ted. Hubert. Howard. Hugh. Horatio."

"Enough *H* names, that is not it," he ordered her gruffly, but telltale smile lines were by his eyes.

Angelika remembered the ring he had worn in the morgue. Was it still on the hand of the nude creation currently howling across the moors? It might hold a clue to his identity.

"More names?" he prompted on a sigh.

"Albert. Lawrence. Edgar. Chester."

"Chester? Do I look like a Chester?" His mouth still had a faint amused lift, and Angelika's heart fluttered and resettled in her chest.

"You look like a man who could be anyone he wanted to be."

Mary returned presently with more water. She was badly exerted by now, wheezing and coughing, her face glowing with sweat. When she put the pails down, she could not restraighten her back. It alarmed both Angelika and her guest.

"Sit down, Mary," Angelika said, at the same time as he said, "Be easy, please."

"Pour it in yourself. I'm going back to bed. Remembered your name yet, son?" Mary narrowed her eyes over him. "What about William? That was my husband's name. He can be Willy, or Will."

Angelika was surprised. "I didn't know that you were married once."

"You never asked, missy."

Angelika thought back to his body on the slab, to the defiance in him even then. "I think Will would suit him perfectly. He has shown me what a strong will he has. What do you think?"

The man was turning the name over in his mind. "Will. Yes, that will do, until I get my memory back. Thank you, Mary. You've saved my life tonight, too."

"Breakfast is at seven," Mary replied, but his praise had her smiling. "No funny business in here, understand?" She cast a suspicious look at the man, then, looking to Angelika, she mouthed a familiar phrase: *No hesitation, no politeness, run.*

It was an old code between them. It hardly looked like this man would attempt to overpower her. "Thank you, Mary, I remember well. Good night," Angelika croaked at the old woman's departing form, her face burning with humiliation.

Will's eyebrow moved. "I'm sure that's not what you resurrected me for. I would not be so vain as to presume." Angelika shut him up with an entire bucket of water on his head. Spluttering, he wiped his hair back. "Where are your other staff? It hurts to watch her struggle."

"It's only her. We require a great deal of privacy." At his incredulous look, she amended quickly, "But I will hire more if it pleases you. How do you feel?"

"I think I am all right. Very tired, but the pain is less."

"I will give you some laudanum and tuck you in, my love." She went to fetch a towel. Behind her, he stood up out of the water.

"No point in being shy, I suppose," he said to her back. "You've seen it all before. You put a lot of thought into my body."

He wasn't being flirtatious. When she turned, he was bent over and admiring the stitch line on his abdomen. The ever-present erection pointed cheerfully in her direction. "Whoever owned this penis was positively mad over you."

"I hope it wasn't Victor's naked friend," she said, making him laugh. "I didn't know that the different parts would have different feelings. Maybe they are retaining the memories of their owners."

"My old body was mangled, you said?"

Victor's rules on a reanimation to exceed Schneider's benchmark now seemed like a petty reason to dismember Will's original slim, tidy frame. But she couldn't tell his expectant face that. "Try not to think about it."

"But I need to know why you've done this. Please tell me, or I will not be able to sleep." He wrapped the proffered towel around his waist, and a yawn cracked his jaw. "I shall sleep on the floor."

"You can sleep in my bed; it's very warm. You must recuperate." Angelika ignored his shocked expression and left to look for some nightclothes in Victor's room. In truth, she had shocked herself at her forwardness.

In her well-worn fantasies, it would have been love at first sight, and he would have been laying her down in the coverlets for a night of exploratory passion, and Mary would have definitely been soaking a virginity stain in the morning. How had she been so cavalier about it all, and so optimistic?

She found some fresh nightclothes in her brother's chest of drawers. "Here," she said when she returned. "Dress yourself if you can manage." He disappeared behind the screen, and she allowed him his privacy to dry and dress.

She turned back the bedcovers, and he wordlessly climbed in, letting out a throaty groan that made her thighs quiver. Angelika gave him some drops of laudanum, and he shuddered at the taste as he sank deeper into the pillows.

"Here, look," she said, raising her silver hand mirror so he could see himself. "Don't you agree that you are very handsome?"

As he regarded himself, the drug unfurled inside him and his eyes went hazy.

"I don't believe I am as handsome as you think."

"I have seen every sort of man there is," she said, remembering the thousands of cursory assessments she had made in every crowd. "Your face is my favorite."

"I can say honestly," he said, exhaling slowly, "yours is my favorite, too."

Angelika finally understood the term *bittersweet*. "That's because you don't know anyone else."

"But look at you," he said huskily. "When I opened my eyes, I thought I was in heaven."

With effort, she resisted the urge to ask him to elaborate. "Sleep well."

"I permit you to sleep next to me, but I should warn you . . ." He trailed off, lost the thought, and his eyes closed. Then they opened again, with a startling intensity in them. "I'll tell you now, before I forget. You've seen all of me. I want to know your body in return. I'd touch you everywhere. I want to pick you up, to feel your weight. I want to test my body." His eyelids fluttered almost closed to slits. "Of course, I will resist. Lean down, closer. Closer. I will not bite."

She did, reeling from this sensual confession. It would take only one upward pull of linen for her to be naked. Was this to be her first kiss? He only tilted his face into her neck, inhaling her skin. He held that breath, before exhaling hot air into her nightdress.

"May I ask for something?"

"Of course," Angelika said, a little afraid, her heart throbbing in her throat.

"Could you help my hands? They are in such pain."

"Have you a cramp?" She took one of his in both of hers, and the size of it stunned her afresh. All she could think was: *He could easily pick me up, and where would he hold first?*

Flushing, she massaged his wire-tight hands, applying herself to the task so diligently he smiled.

"Why did you bring me back? Are you sure we were not in love?" He fought to keep his eyes on hers as the opiate dragged him under. "The way you care for me, and look at me, I think we were. I'm sorry that I do not remember."

"We were not in love," Angelika told him as he sank into sleep's black hold. "But I wish we would be."

CHAPTER FOUR

Victor limped into the dining room. He was filthy and still wearing only one boot. "Good morning," he said to Angelika and Will, who were partway through their porridge. "Mary says we are to call you Will. Nice to meet you. I haven't been up this early since I was a boy."

"It's true," Angelika said to Will. "I have breakfast alone. And sometimes lunch."

"I work late," Victor defended himself. "And what a wild night that was."

"I have to agree with you," Will replied. He had given no indication to Angelika that he even remembered his late-night confession, but she burned with it. Not noticing her pink cheeks, Will asked Victor, "Did you catch your friend?"

"Sadly, no." Victor dropped into his seat with a groan. "I nearly had him in the orchard, but he was moving uphill quite fast. I followed the screams for a long time, but it's rocky ground."

"Will you keep looking?" Angelika passed a basket of bread to her brother. "He's completely defenseless out there."

"I will find him. I just need to eat, saddle Athena, and find a new boot."

"There's a new pair in the bottom of your closet." Angelika gestured now to Will. "He's so handsome, he can make even your clothes look respectable, Vic."

"Thank you for the loan," Will said. Angelika noticed that he acknowledged every courtesy another person did for him.

Angelika sat up straighter, and when Mary came back through with a pot of butter, she thanked her graciously. She received a suspicious side-eye in reply.

Victor replied to Will, "The clothes? Don't mention it. Jelly will get us more." He yawned, but then refocused on his sister's face with sharp interest. His green-eyed stare, so similar to hers, was unnerving. "How did you get that bruise?"

Angelika glanced reflexively to Will, the bump of the laboratory's window frame a tender remembrance of his instant rejection.

Victor fixed him with a death glare, gripping his knife. "You did that to her?"

"It was an accident, and I'm very sorry, Angelika," Will said with genuine remorse. "I'm still figuring out this new body, and I was careless. What felt like a mild reaction became something stronger."

"It's those blacksmith shoulders," Victor observed, relaxing down in his seat. "Well, I hope you were gentle to her last night," Victor said, assessing Angelika afresh. "Was it everything you were hoping for?"

"Nothing happened." She transmitted with her eyes: *Drop it*.

"What are you hoping for?" Will asked.

Ignoring her glare, Victor said cheerfully, "You, my friend, were created purely for Miss Angelika Frankenstein's personal use. She was going to bonk you halfway back to the grave."

"Shut. Up. Victor." Angelika's cheeks were crimson. "I was not. You are contributing to scientific advancement, Will."

Will's complexion did not betray a blush, but his eyes darted between the Frankenstein siblings, trying to make sense of this teasing.

Victor continued. "Now that my own fantastic achievement is probably halfway to Glasgow, I might need to borrow you for a few scientific assessments." At Will's expression, Victor brayed heartily. "Don't get the wrong idea; it will all be proper. I have a nemesis named Jürgen Schneider, and he is about to become very depressed by my skill."

"Personal use?" Will was caught on that earlier detail. "I'm sure I misunderstand you."

Victor replied, "You understand correctly. Jelly, I will need a full account of how you resurrected him by yourself. We will run some tests. This justifies a new microscope nicely." He was beaming at the thought.

Will seemed to be grappling with this revelation when he looked at Angelika. His pupils were dilated, turning his brown eyes almost black, reminding her of last night and how he scented her neck like they were animal mates. "Why not just go down to the village and find a living volunteer?"

"She's tried that many times," Victor said with all the tact of a brother. "She has practically gone to Salisbury on market day and put herself into the livestock auctions. No buyers."

She begged, "Please, just leave it."

Will gave his observations. "Angelika, you are very fair, with your striking coloring."

"Thank you," Victor replied on her behalf, for he shared the exact same rippled waves of honey-red hair. "I once received an anonymous love letter, describing my eyes as 'celadon gateways into sunlit fields of sage.'"

"That's terrible writing and makes no sense," Angelika said, looking at her own reflection in a spoon. Even in daylight, with his decorum restored, Will still thought her very fair? Encouraging. "You probably wrote a love letter to yourself."

"Ask Lizzie. She'll tell you."

"I have no idea what she sees in you. And I don't wish to know."

Will continued to address Angelika. "You are clever enough to defeat the laws of living and dead. This grand house, and what I imagine is a fine dowry, would be an inducement."

"This is my house, unless Athena bucks me off into a wall," Victor said, biting into an apple.

It should have been flattering how bewildered Will was when he turned to her and asked, "How have you possibly remained unmarried?"

Instead, she imagined the subtext of the question was: *What's wrong with you?*

"She's got something about her," Victor said slowly, answering the unasked, and it sent Angelika escaping to the window at the far end of the room, with a pastry in hand. "Something that the local men do not respond to. They want simple, straightforward women. Childbearing candidates. Good churchgoing sheep. Bland fair maids who know how to cook cabbage and whatnot. My sister is exceptional in every aspect, and they sense it. They know they cannot measure up to her, so they choose to laugh, or call her spinster, or witch."

"Thank you, brother, how kind," she replied with a tight throat, and looked outside the window. She did not feel very exceptional. Underneath the window stood a sow. Belladonna was tawny brown, spotted, big enough to saddle, and had a permanently hopeful countenance. One solitary piglet—a runt, slow to wean—was rooting around in the fallen leaves behind her.

Angelika opened the window and leaned down to feed the

pig her pastry. "Victor, your secret admirer is here. The one who thinks your eyes are celadon gateways."

"Tell her I'm not home." Victor's voice had the animal's ears quirking up.

"But you are both wealthy," Will said, valiantly staying on topic. "Surely she's had countless suitors. Come back, Angelika, it's all right."

It was nice to be with someone who remained kind, instead of teasing like Victor. If she could, she'd sit on Will's inviting lap and rest her face in his neck. Maybe he'd rub her back, up and down, until the loneliness subsided. Then, she might sit up, and he'd put his hand onto her jaw, encouraging a kiss—

Victor continued. "Suitors have come from miles away, from different towns, countries, and continents. They arrive in carriages to call, and to work out the extent of our fortune. The ones who are fervently religious are quickly shown the door. Others bore me to death. It is incredible to me how many men take no interest in science."

"You aren't finding *yourself* a husband," Angelika reminded him dourly.

Victor grinned. "She then asks them very creative questions from a prepared sheet. They do not accept a second cup of tea."

"I'll take a second one," Will said charitably, extending his cup.

Victor poured, and spilled. "She's too focused on the end result of her love experiment. As a scientist, I tell her that unexpected things happen all the time. She'll find her match. Frankensteins always do." He considered Will at length. "Besides, she's the only one I trust to be my assistant, and she does everything to my exact requirements."

Will nodded. "I gathered that firsthand."

They set about eating and chewing, like two relaxed friends. Angelika decided to wait by the window until her red face faded.

"How are you feeling?" Victor asked Will.

"Like I've been drinking spirits. I have a headache. I'm cold now, though your sister kept me warm all night." Will said that last bit with a slice of humor. "I should tell you, I couldn't keep her out of my bed."

"*My* bed," she corrected him, smiling.

"Of course," he replied, sinking down lower into his seat. His countenance changed in an instant. "I believe there is no room for me in this house."

"Mary is making up the room across the hall from mine, like we talked about. That shall be yours." Angelika saw how he only relaxed when Victor nodded his assent. The man had a sparkle of sweat on his brow now. "We would not bring you into our home if you were not very much welcome."

"I am grateful for such hospitality," Will replied in a faint tone. So, this was a person who required his own guaranteed personal space? Angelika really should have slept across the hall last night, but the bed across the hall was unmade, cold, and had a bear costume on it. She'd slipped in on the edge of the mattress and stacked pillows between them to allow him some dignity.

They'd woken up wrapped in each other, the pillows thrown to the floor, her cheek tucked perfectly on his beefy shoulder. She'd looked up. Eye contact occurred next. Her nightdress had ridden up at some point, and her thigh was across his. His cock was harder than iron.

They'd rolled violently apart.

Like he was reliving the same memory, Will said to Victor in a whisper, "You're a doctor, correct? There's something wrong with my . . . It's private." He put his napkin back across his lap.

"Jelly installed that for you, so you'd best ask her what she did." Victor lolled back in his chair, cackling. "We are scientists, not doctors. I must say, I'm glad you're here. It's nice to have a new person to chat to. I'm glad you're not screaming through the forest."

Will laughed, too. "Angelika made a strong argument against it. I've got nothing. Not even my memory. I'm afraid I will need to rely on your generosity until I have my strength enough to leave."

"Leave?" Angelika was brought back to the table by this. "Where are you going?"

"To find my old life," Will replied. "When I see where I'm from, my memories will come back."

Angelika was aghast. "I forbid it. Here, try some ham."

Will recoiled at the slice of meat she forked onto his plate. "I cannot stomach it."

"Only yesterday he was like meat," Victor reminded his sister. "And it is his decision to make if he wants to leave us. Let's try to find some clues about you. You speak like you are educated. Here, what do you make of this?" He rummaged in his clothing and then proffered a discolored and well-folded piece of parchment.

Will narrowed his eyes at it, then looked up. "You carry your last will and testament in your breast pocket?"

Victor snatched the page back. "Grand, you can read."

"Perhaps I should have done the same," Will said, looking at his hardly touched breakfast.

Victor replied, "You had not a pocket upon your person. So, we have deduced you may be a gentleman indeed. But finding you at a public morgue for commonfolk leaves a question mark."

"I did not think you would be so interested in your past. Perhaps you could instead think of what the future might offer you?" Angelika looked around the dining room, seeing things through Will's fresh gaze.

They sat underneath a sixteen-candle French chandelier, with fine glittering ropes of beads that might break under the weight of a dragonfly. When hosting guests, Angelika's father, Alphonse, would often gesture upward and retell the delivery-day story. Eight people had walked thirty miles from the port of Bournemouth, carrying the chandelier's crystals in baskets. They were too fragile to withstand the rattle of a carriage or cart. Angelika opened her mouth, ready to share this anecdote, and then closed it again, remembering Will's concern over Mary carrying the heavy pails of bathwater.

She hardly knew him at all, but she thought Will probably would not like that story.

The dining room walls were stacked to the ceiling with frowning ancestral portraits. One painting of a great-great-uncle, nicknamed "Poor Plague Peter," stood ajar on a hinge from the wall. Behind it there was an open safe box, glinting with gold in the morning sunlight, and it had not escaped Will's notice. For a split second, Angelika felt fear.

Was he being truthful about his memory, and who he was?

There were another twelve hidden vaults throughout the house, from the basement cellar to the uppermost chimney on the roof, and now a stranger sat at their table. Hidden treasure, towers of treasure, dusty and forgotten treasure—enough for a hundred extravagant lifetimes at least—were all brought here by persons unknown, to be collected under the one black slate roof.

It was a fine upgrade from the morgue. Wasn't it, indeed. A swindler could be sitting here right now, with her mother's napkin on his lap. When she made eye contact with Will again, she saw no guile, no concealment, and she forced herself to let go of her gold-clutching terror. All she could do was hope, and trust.

Angelika put on a smile. "Could you start to make a list of things you would like me to purchase for your wardrobe?"

Will ignored that and replied to Victor's remark. "Maybe we could go back to the morgue. They must have a record of me. I could be home before nightfall."

"It is more likely that if you do have a family, they do not know where you are," Victor said carefully. "Or they had no option but to leave you, rather than bury you at the church. Come now, my good chap. Is this so bad?" He gestured to the table, and then the room around them, and finally, at his sister.

"I am grateful." Will's gaze lingered on Angelika's lips. "There is nothing bad at all."

Angelika saw his hesitation. "How do you think your family will react when you appear like an apparition on their doorstep? You're sewn together. They will not understand."

"I'll make them understand," Will said, taking a sip of tea and wincing, a hand on his stomach. "I'm sorry, but in the interests of science, I'll advise I am about to destroy a chamber pot. I'm afraid of what will happen just now."

"Mary will be ever so pleased," Victor said, after roaring with laughter. "Off you go. We will help you find your old life," he added with more seriousness when Will stood.

Will bowed politely. "I will do my best not to inconvenience you."

Victor wasn't done. He held a finger aloft.

"We are an unconventional household, but I must be old-fashioned about something. If you deflower my sister with that unpredictable knob, I'm afraid you will be stuck with her for good. I will insist on it, brother-in-law."

"There's not a chance of that," Will said, and left the room.

The look of sympathy on Victor's face was unbearable. "Don't say anything," Angelika said quietly.

Victor disobeyed. "I always thought that I would recognize your future husband when I met him. I walked in just now and saw you two sitting together at breakfast and thought: *Yes. That's him.* A patient, sensible constant, to counter your headstrong extravagance. Will is absolutely perfect for you."

Angelika's stomach flipped happily at the surety in her brother's voice. "I did make sure of it. And I knew it, too, the moment he sat up."

Victor was regretful. "But I'm afraid he will never know that he's your match. Give up on this particular dream, my dear sister."

"I don't want to."

"If you take that path," Victor warned, nodding at the hallway, "you will find only heartbreak. He is going home to his family. But you will always have me, and Lizzie, and you will be Aunt Jelly to our children. We will all live happily here, together, forever."

"But there's no room for me in this house," Angelika said, echoing Will's earlier assertion. "Where am I to fit into this life, once the children begin arriving?"

"I'll clear out a few inventions" was all Victor said in reply. "Now, let us return to the laboratory. We must write a full account of what happened last night."

"Please bathe yourself first, you smelly boy." Angelika drank from Will's teacup. Did this count as a first kiss? "And there is a question I must ask of you. You used some of Will's original body. Did you take the ring off his left hand?"

Victor looked at her in surprise. "I couldn't be bothered finding cutters. My creation is still wearing it. The engraving bears a clue, no doubt," he breathed, looking at the hallway. "I should go and tell him—"

Angelika was grim. "Your loyalty is to me, brother. When we find that ring, I want you to give it to me. Promise me. He's mine. I made him, and everything he has is also mine."

"You are wrong, you brat," Victor said in a warning tone. "He belongs to himself. Or to a pretty widow somewhere who is crying her eyes out. I do find this rather amusing. You have found the one man you cannot ask a hundred questions of."

She put her face in her hands. "I cannot believe neither of us could be bothered to look properly at his ring. I think we are a pair of fools."

"This is the sort of thing a man would be very angry to find out about."

"I'll deal with that if it ever happens. There is no point in raising his hopes. For all we know, your naked creation is shot dead by now, lying on a slab again."

"I should ask my colleagues to keep an eye on the county morgues," Victor replied, grabbing another apple from the silver bowl on the table. "You're a genius, Jelly."

CHAPTER FIVE

"Mary, where are my nightgowns?" Angelika asked the old woman on the upstairs landing. She held up a fistful of slippery silk. "These aren't what I wear."

Mary performed a slow, blinking grimace. "Mightn't hurt to try."

"Are you trying to wink at me?"

"For a week you've passed him on the way to bed, flannel nightgown buttoned up to your ears." Mary boomed it so loudly the entire house could hear. "These were your mother's negligees. I brought them up from the basement, to see if they'll move things along. I'll have you married yet," she said like a threat.

In her gilt frame, Caroline Frankenstein agreed with this new plan.

"He won't notice or care." She grimaced, imagining Mary in the black, dusty basement, then realized it was probably the first time she'd worried for the old woman. Mary had always seemed so capable. Angelika used her best mistress voice. "With Lizzie no doubt arriving soon, and Will joining us for as long as he's able, we need to hire you a chambermaid to supervise. We also need a footman, a cook, a stablehand, a groundsman—"

"Slow yourself," Mary said, but she was not displeased. "Maybe a maid would ease the load. Someone young to run up and down stairs. I could ask my older sister, who runs the boardinghouse, if she knows of anyone suitable who could be trusted to be discreet."

"An older sister?" Angelika echoed in horror, reflecting on how positively ancient she must be. "I didn't even know you had a sister."

"You never asked," Mary said, but she was smiling as she gestured to the silk nightgown. "Now, slink about in that, be a good lass."

Angelika shook her head as Will's door opened at the end of the hallway. "Please, Mary." Too late. The old woman had walked off.

"What's happening?" Will asked as he approached. He was in his nightclothes and an embroidered burgundy robe, his hair towel-dried and ruffled attractively. He smelled like citrus soap.

Angelika sighed. "Mary has decided to stock my drawers with only negligees in the hopes I could pique your interest. Utter nonsense."

"Very sly," Will agreed mildly, barely glancing at the silk she'd awkwardly hung on the stair rail. He'd overcome his spontaneous erection issues, because he stood easy in her presence. "Whoever furnished my closet did very well, thank you."

His praise was deeply gratifying. "It was me, of course. Victor doesn't buy his own clothes unless I drag him to the tailor. When Lizzie finally marries him, I'll have one less wardrobe to worry about." Her glum tone betrayed her. "Where is he?"

"He's putting his horse away."

"All of this endless searching. He will make himself sick."

"You'd leave me out there?" Will asked.

"Of course not." She could not resist folding down the lapel of his robe. "I would not come home until I had you."

She'd loved the task of shopping for Will and had spent half a day choosing shirt materials alone. She had paid handsomely for seamstresses to work night and day. It had felt like a wifely duty, and she'd pretended thus to the clerk, even as the thought followed her around the shop: *A lovely man like this is likely already married.*

He was an outstanding houseguest: unobtrusive, polite, and tidy. Any casual observer would believe him to be an old family friend. He turned every conversation deftly back to his companion. The way he listened was intoxicating. Victor had already declared him as *the finest fellow I ever met*, because he now had a captive audience.

Angelika smiled at him. "You will have to come to town, to be measured for your winter wardrobe."

"I won't be here by then." Will hesitated, and then said, "I still think I understand this situation incorrectly. Your part in all this, and why you . . . made me. It makes no sense. I can't sleep for thinking about it."

"I wanted my own project, to prove my skill to Victor, to make history, and to assist humanity—" She broke off when Will raised a doubting eyebrow. "And should he be a handsome man, even better. I like beautiful things, and trust me, you are everything I like best. But in terms of your *use*, I had no designs. I just thought that—"

"Please, speak plainly," Will cut in. "To not hate you for doing this to me, I need to understand."

"Hate?" But she did deserve it. "What have I done to you?"

"The pain is hard to bear. Imagine a wooden stake," he said, touching a finger to her shoulder joint, "pressed deep here, and here"—he touched her elbow—"here, here, here"—

wrist and two knuckles. "I feel every bend and every joint. Every movement is an agony, and I'm very cold."

She ignored the pleasure she took from his fingertip. "Would you like more laudanum?"

"I should work to become accustomed to this, or I might drink the bottle daily. Please, just let me understand why, Angelika." He allowed her to take his hand and watched as she began massaging it. The soft leather of his palm was familiar to her now, and his cold fingers uncurled as she worked with her thumbs, pushing, loosening.

Grateful for the busy task, she said to his hand, "I made you the way you are, so ideal to me in every way, because I thought you might be here awhile, recuperating, and we might form a connection. The last suitor to call was over a year ago, and Victor is no longer helping me. Time is marching on, and I found a wrinkle by my eye here—" She showed him, but he smiled, like she was charming. "And time drips by, slow as treacle, up here on this hill."

"Victor asked to—" Will stumbled on how to word it. "He asked to *use* me, to make Schneider jealous. A trip to Munich was part of it. I declined, and he accepted it without question. I don't understand why he didn't throw me out. I'm no use to anyone."

She changed to his other hand. "Your only occupation is to recover and rest. And if he tosses you out, I shall pack a bag and keep you company. He will want to have the house for himself and Lizzie."

"He would never toss you out. Is that a terrible outcome, to remain here? You will never want for anything."

"I will want."

Their fingers slipped together, linked, and squeezed.

"I am beginning to understand. Loneliness is a pain all of

its own." He seemed to be able to see straight into her most secret thoughts, and she felt them unspooling. She released his hand, and, leaning his shoulder on the wall, he invited: "Tell me more about your plans for us."

Was this her final chance to explain her offer? "I would dress you in the finest clothing, fill your pockets with gold pieces. Ships, and horses, and carriages. Spices, tapestries, wine."

His dark eyebrow lifted. "As someone who has been dead, then back again, I can say with certainty that I don't need those things."

She was hot inside her clothes, and her fingertips still glowed from rubbing his skin. "We would travel to every city and country I could think of, eating, drinking, and sleeping to excess."

He shrugged, nonplussed.

Irritation made her bold. "I was going to find out exactly what gave you pleasure, and I was going to give you that pleasure. I would never want for anything again." She saved him the awkwardness of a rejection and added, "But as you have said, you have no need of these things."

"I often do. Without my memory, I am only my body." He maintained his steady composure, even as he said, "My body wants you wildly, and it scares me." He offered his hand, seeking her attentions again, but then swiftly realized and pocketed it.

"I think you should seek Victor's counsel regarding this."

"I did. He told me to have a few good tugs to clear the system. Those are his words, not mine."

Angelika gaped. "And?" She grabbed up the silk nightgown on the pretense of shaking it out.

"It didn't help. I'm sure you can sympathize. Wanting

so much, as you do." He looked at the silk in her hand and watched her pull it slowly across her palm.

Did the moon fall from the sky, and did the candles dim? Was this hall always so dark and secluded? She tried to stay in the conversation. "I keep myself well-tended. If you had been keen, you would have been a nice big happy addition to my life, and bed. But I can carry on, as before."

He was adorably flustered. "I think we have struck upon why you are unmarried. No man alive can handle this level of honesty."

"That is precisely why I searched for a perfect dead man." To see what he would do, she shook out the negligee to admire the lace. "Do men even like such things?"

He would never give an answer. "Did you know there is a purse of coins on my dresser?"

"It's your freedom, to take, any time you want it."

He appeared skeptical. "So if I wished, I could pick it up and walk out, without a goodbye or any fuss? I've seen your brother searching so frantically for his lost creation. Aren't I your only proof of his technique?"

"We don't think of you as proof. You're our friend. And if you did leave, I would hope you would say goodbye first." Angelika was not sure if she meant it. If he walked away, she'd likely follow, if only to ensure he landed in a safe situation. But this was what she had agreed with Victor, and she quoted his words now: "We don't believe in caging up beings who do not wish to stay."

"Is that why you have a pig on the loose?" Will grinned at a memory. "I had the fright of my life when I saw it, up on hind legs, looking through the kitchen window."

"That's Belladonna. She's in love with Victor."

"She doesn't know he's engaged?"

"It will be a difficult conversation. That is what happens when you toss apple cores to a piglet, over and over. I imagine she is an unfortunate princess."

Will laughed. "Cursed forever and wanting true love's kiss." He looked toward Victor's bedroom. "Perhaps we should let her try."

Angelika was so glad he was a man who could play. "Exactly. She does have an intelligent stare, so we err on the side of caution, and she will never make the dinner table."

"Prudent."

"Make sure you close every door properly. She will come up the stairs." Angelika looked at the portrait of her mother. "Mama, perhaps I should vacate to Larkspur and leave this madness behind?"

"Where is Larkspur?" Instead of finding this strange, Will faced the portrait and bowed to it with elegance. "Madam, an honor to meet you."

"Caroline Frankenstein, this is Will. At least, he's Will until further notice. Larkspur Lodge is our lake house and has been closed up for many years. That house will be Victor's wedding present to Lizzie one day, just as Papa gifted it to Mama. Apparently that is now a family tradition. But it has only a caretaker and will be in a dreadful state."

He was eager. "That is something I could do for you both. I could go there and clear the cobwebs out of Larkspur."

"You were supposed to clear the cobwebs out of somewhere else, but we've seen how that worked out," Victor bellowed as he ascended the stairs.

Will laughed. Angelika growled.

"Speaking of cobwebs, look at the state of this place," Victor continued as he collected a spider off the stair rail. "My sister is talking of Larkspur, is she? I don't know why you adore it, Jelly. It has no laboratory. It's a dull life there, just lake swims and roses. And so many spiders," he added to his new friend, letting it walk across the backs of his fingers. "I shudder to think what state it will be in when I take Lizzie there for our honeymoon."

Angelika hated the distasteful curl to his lip. "Every good memory I have is of that place. Larkspur is heaven."

"We don't believe in heaven," Victor reminded his sister on a yawn. "I'm going to bed. I was only hours behind a sighting of a huge person who had been stealing from a field. Out the window you shall go, my good fellow," he said to the spider as he carried it off. "Good night. Remember, Will. If you bed her, she's yours for good."

He kicked his bedroom door closed behind him.

"I would be glad to never hear another door slam ever again." Angelika scowled, glad to hide her embarrassment.

Will was also annoyed with Victor. "You can believe in heaven if you wish to. He cannot police your beliefs."

"He doesn't." (He did. Often.)

"He thinks religion is thought control, but he does the same to you. You never argue back. You simply nod. And though I hardly know you at all, I know that this really does not suit you."

Angelika rode out a wave of defensiveness, biting her tongue until it hurt. Then she thought that Will had a point. "Sometimes I don't know who I am. Without Vic . . ."

Will gave his assessment. "Your true intellectual capabilities, directed solely to your own interests, would be a far more fulfilling use of your talent and creativity. What is your ambition, beyond spending money and pursuing the goal of being adored?"

She had no answer. It had always been Angelika and Victor, together all the time. He experimented, she assisted.

"Perhaps we are not so different," Will observed. "Please, allow me to go to Larkspur, to clear my head."

She made a huff to change the subject. "Every time you laugh at one of his awful jokes, I dislike you. The remark about cobwebs," she reminded him in a withering tone.

Will tried. He truly did.

But the memory was too much; his eyes crinkled, his shoulders shook, and he broke. Angelika screeched in fury.

"I apologize," Will spluttered, regaining momentary control, but he did not sound sorry. His gaze landed upon a feather duster that Mary had misplaced on the hallway credenza, and he laughed until he cried.

Cobwebs in her personal anatomy. It was the kind of joke the village folk would roar with mirth over in the tavern, exactly like this. She stormed down the hallway. To hell with it. Angelika was going to put on a negligee, do her hair, paint her lips, and loll around in bed reading a saucy book. She'd knock her own cobwebs out. She'd indulge in a late-night bath filled with expensive French oil. Mary would have a conniption, but until Lizzie showed up, Angelika was still mistress of this house.

A house Will itched to leave.

"He needs to clear his head?" she muttered to herself as she pawed around in the slippery nightwear that now took up hardly a quarter of her entire drawer. She then pulled black silk down over her head. "He's got a beautiful bedroom and a beautiful new wardrobe of the finest clothes I could find. He can go back to the morgue and really get his head cleared, right off his shoulders by a student of medicine."

"Angelika, I can hear you fuming," Will said through the door. "I shouldn't have laughed at Victor's joke." He had a smile in his tone.

"Go away." There was even a small pair of slippers with rabbit's tail fluff on the toes. "I'm having a pampering evening alone. Go chat through my brother's door."

Will said, "I forget that I'm a guest and not just a rude brother."

"That's exactly who you remind me of when you make those little jibes. You're spending too much time with Victor."

The mirror confirmed it: this lace negligee was scandalous, cut low front and back and reaching barely halfway down her thighs. It was so old and fragile, it would hardly withstand a nap.

Will confided, "I like your brother awfully. It's why I should go to the lake house, to get some perspective. To remind myself I am not going to be a part of this family."

"You don't seem to remotely resent Victor for his part in your resurrection. He was there, you know. He taught me what to do. And yet, you share lunch together and go for walks. But me, you cannot seem to get past my role."

Victor was her best friend, and he preferred another now. She called out for them to wait, but they were too busy talking and laughing to hear her. Will was right. Loneliness was a pain all of its own.

Will said, "If you had left me to nature, I would not be dealing with all of this . . . frustration."

She'd inconvenienced him by saving his life, whereas Victor was blameless? "You'd rather be dead than faced with the prospect of me?" On that stormy night, Victor's creation had screamed at the mere sight of her. Apparently, Will was only a tad more genteel.

Angelika wrenched open her bedroom door. "You wish to be an apple in the orchard, left to rot?"

Will looked down at her body, and his eyes almost fell out of his head.

CHAPTER SIX

She pointed a finger into his chest.

"My crime, in addition to body-snatching, is that I'm lonely. I'm aging by the day. Twenty-four, never kissed, never touched. I cannot travel without my brother, and unless the destination has a fully stocked laboratory, he is not interested. I have money I can't seem to spend because I am marooned on a hillside. I am a woman." She raised her voice. "And a woman needs certain things, even if society tells her she should not."

"I . . ." was all Will could reply to her negligee.

"Do you know what men call me in the tavern? My nickname that not even Victor knows?" Angelika paused and wondered if he might use it against her.

"You can confess it to me," Will said. "I will keep your secret safe."

"The barren-ness. A play on *baroness*. Because I am wealthy and barren, I suppose? But how could anyone know that? For all we know, I am infinitely fertile, given the proper treatment."

Will was having a personal malfunction. "I . . ."

"Apart from that night we slept together, I have never lain with a man. Now if you'll pardon me, sir, I'm going to lie on

my bed and sulk. Unless you'd care to join me. My final offer
to you, before I shrivel up and die from embarrassment."

His entire body shivered. He took a step toward her. The
pink of his tongue was obscene, licking at the corner of his
mouth.

Now he was blinking, realizing, and lanced through the
heel by reality. "I will be forced to belong to you. My pride will
not allow me to be kept like a stray dog. Or worse, a mutt, but
treated as a pedigree poodle. I am a man, and I am someone.
I just have to find out who that is."

Angelika thought that whoever he was, he had remarkable
principles.

"You could be Will Frankenstein, richer than your wildest
dreams. More exhausted from the previous night than you
ever thought possible."

"But I am not a Frankenstein. You can't just open your
home to a stranger and offer him everything like this. What if
I am a bad person? A dangerous one?"

"You are not."

"We don't know when my true nature will reveal itself. I
must find the life I left behind. Until I know who I really am,
I can make no choices for my future. You will not distract me
with your beauty, or how silk lays on your body." He closed his
eyes and swallowed. He appeared tormented. "You will not
distract me with your perfume in every room of the house, or
how you bounce up and down stairs."

"It does sound like I am rather distracting."

He saw her smile and turned dour. "I am quite resolved."
He turned on his heel, walked across the hall, and shut his
door, audibly locking it. Was he anticipating she might slink
in, during the night, as Mary had directed?

Her cheeks burned. "You didn't need to lock it!"

A door opened, but not the one in front of her.

"You two, shut up," Victor barked from his end of the hall. "Either bed each other or do not speak. Will, we are going to the morgue tomorrow night to sort this mess out, and maybe I will have some peace."

"And maybe I'll collect myself a new husband while I'm there," Angelika snapped back. Neither man replied. Louder she hollered, "Mary, fetch hot water. I am having a long, distracting, and very naked bath, with my door unlocked."

"Ugh." Victor recoiled in horror and slammed his door harder than he ever had before.

"You both will have to go to the morgue without me tonight," Victor said as he fastened his cloak with one hand, the other hand gripping the reins under the chin of his evil gray mare. "I'm sorry, but this sighting is too promising. Athena, stop prancing. Give me a leg up, Will."

Word had come via messenger that a seven-foot man with a waxy pallor was spotted several parishes west, stealing cabbages.

"I will be two days, possibly three," Victor said on a grunt as Will legged him up onto the horse. "Take care of my sister. The morgue is dangerous, but it's not the dead ones you'll have to worry about."

"He can go alone," Angelika said spitefully. "He has declared he has no need of me."

"You must go, too, Jelly," Victor said, circling his mount around them. "He has no proof of identity until I find my lost achievement. If Will gets into trouble, only you with your honorable Frankenstein name can keep him safe. There's been news of thieves and highwaymen. Every stranger will be under scrutiny by the night watch."

"Fine, I will accompany him," Angelika said. "Even though he wishes to be a stranger."

"So, in summary, I wish for you to look after each other," Victor advised them both, but his eyes were on Will. "You are in charge of protecting the house in my absence." Athena spun in rearing pirouettes, skittering gravel on their shoes.

Will was uncomfortable. "How could you let me have that role?" He looked back at the house, perhaps noticing its faded grandeur for the first time.

"Because my sister trusts you." And with that, Victor allowed some rein and galloped down the wide carriageway, arched over by yew trees. He called back, "My sister created you, and that counts for something, brother."

The impressive exit was slightly undermined by Belladonna chasing after him, tailed by her runt piglet.

"Brother," both Angelika and Will echoed cynically, but he did look pleased. Then he remembered something. "What did Victor mean just now? He said we have no proof of my identity until he finds his creation."

"I never know what he is talking about," Angelika evaded. The image of the ring flashed behind her eyelids, but it was soon blinked away as she noticed how handsome Will was in this fading afternoon light.

She wasn't the only one distracted. Will had not recovered from seeing her in a negligee. Every time they saw each other, he obscured his lower half. A hat. A bunch of carrots. A hunting trophy. Anything that came to hand, he'd utilize it. They'd had a bland discussion about the smoking fireplace in his bedroom while he stood behind the bust of her great-great-grandfather Leonard Frankenstein.

This much was painfully clear: Will's brain abhorred her, but his body adored her. It was a pity that his upstairs faculties always won out.

He tore his gaze away from her. "I should have accompanied Victor."

"We have no idea if you can even ride," Angelika reminded him.

"I've actually got a good seat. Victor gave me a fine gelding; it was most generous. And I am honored beyond measure that he, and you, trust me enough to remain here to man the house. Without you both I'd have nothing. Not even life. It's most humbling."

It was a fine apology, but Angelika did not want it. It had the first echoes of a goodbye.

He tried again. "You're a scientist. Surely you can understand the intense curiosity to know everything, rather than making assumptions?"

She had to confess a partial truth, because the urge to put hope in his eyes suddenly outweighed her own selfish aspirations. "The big man Victor seeks has your transplanted hands. You were wearing a ring when we found you. Now he wears it."

He was filled with energy now. "A ring. Describe it to me."

Angelika could anticipate what his reaction would be if she admitted the truth: that the Frankensteins were so careless with trinkets of pure gold that neither of them had paid it much notice. She had wanted to forget the possibility of a wife, and Victor had been too lazy to walk two minutes to fetch cutters. The possibility of a crest or engraving might raise his hopes, only to be dashed if it were gone forever.

"It was dark, so I have no idea of the particulars. That's why we are trying so hard for you, even though you do not realize it. Victor will locate his fine achievement and bring him home, and in turn, you may find a clue to your identity."

He nodded now, beaming. "I'm sorry I've been so difficult. So, could we try to be friends? And you'll help me tonight at the morgue?" When happy, he was illuminated.

"Yes," she said, thinking ahead. "If you'll take me to the tavern for an ale after. I've always wanted to. Saddle your new horse and we shall ride out at sunset." She smiled at the direction Victor had left by, hoping to appear cool and unaffected by Will's close presence. "Maybe I will have some fun at last. I'm not being facetious. I think I might search for a new husband while I'm there."

He didn't like that. "Where? The morgue or the tavern?"

"Don't you know me at all?" Angelika laughed and walked away. "I'll search both."

They rode their horses over the crest of a hill. Angelika pointed with her crop.

"I will give you a tour of Salisbury. It is a fine village, with much history. Victor says we are ideally situated, only a day's carriage ride from London, and we can easily ride to the plains to see the big stone druid temple. We can take a basket of food and a bottle of wine. It is a marvelous day out."

"I am sure it is all very nice," Will said. "You do not have to be nervous that I won't like your home. I already do."

They halted their mounts and looked at the village lanterns in the distance. The sky was peach and lavender. Turtledoves cooed in a hedgerow, and honeysuckle perfumed everything. The horses sidestepped, causing their riders' legs to brush. It was a moment steeped in romance, but only in Angelika's imagination. She looked sideways at what was indeed a fabulous riding seat. That horse was a lucky creature.

Will broached a new topic with care. "Victor used my hands for his monster, but you said my body was not salvageable due to an accident. Can you explain this to me, so I can stop wondering about it?"

"He is not a monster. I wanted to test my skills in transplanting body parts, and as a scientist, Victor needed to prove his superiority to Jürgen Schneider." Science was something Will rarely argued with.

"The way Victor rants about that man is unhealthy. I think he would gain peace if he could just forgive his past offenses. Whatever they are."

She shrugged. "It fuels Victor. It goes beyond science. Schneider was once a potential suitor for Lizzie. Victor is a beast when he is jealous."

"How did they meet? Please do not tell me that Lizzie is also . . ." He gestured vaguely to his own neck area, where his cravat hid his stitches.

"Goodness, no. Victor has been betrothed to Lizzie since they were children, but when Papa died, he forgot about it. He got drunk and wrote a manifesto of sorts, denouncing the institution of marriage. 'Opting Out of England's Elite Breeding Program' is what he titled it."

"I saw it on your dressing table. I read it. I've felt terrible for prying." Will did look guilty.

"Hardly prying, when it has traveled the world ten times by now. Victor has always wanted to be famous; now he most assuredly is. Lizzie's father was livid. Threatened to expel him from his secret society. We traveled to Russia to handle the situation. His grand plan was to be so boring that she rejected him."

"I don't think he could manage being boring for long."

"No, indeed." Angelika smiled. "Lizzie is a playwright, and funny, and beautiful. Anyhow, we went to let her reject him, but found ourselves in a caravan following her acting troupe through some very remote parts of Russia. Her first play is *The Duchess and the Bear.* She forced Vic to wear the bear costume, night after night, while villagers threw sticks at him on the stage. My job selling tickets was much better."

He let out a disbelieving laugh. "That bear costume in the corner of my room is his?"

"She's the duchess. He's the bear. Some things are just meant to be, even if falling in love with her was a catastrophe for him, on an intellectual level. To marry her, he has to declare himself a hypocrite. He'll be a laughingstock. The anti-marriage man takes a wife. But he doesn't care anymore."

"I suppose you are hoping for something that dramatic yourself?" Will now looked at her like he was afraid. "I feel I am quite a letdown."

"Please remember how we met and reexamine your statement."

"I feel quite sure that I am a dull person in comparison. I cannot see myself traveling with a Russian troupe."

"All my interesting stories feature my brother. I've merely invited myself along to anything I could. That is what it is like for a woman. I can't wait to get out from under his wing. But anyhow! We are having our own adventure tonight."

Will moved his mount closer to hers. "Your morgue outfit is quite special. That color suits you well."

It was a turquoise riding habit, with swirling skirts. Heinously expensive, of course. Angelika preened her sleeve. "I always dress like I have a date with destiny."

This was a reference to her husband hunt, and it did not

please him. "Do the villagers say anything about how you ride astride?"

"If sidesaddle versus astride is what occupies their pathetic conversations, then I feel sorry for them. Be glad it was me who experimented upon you, my love. The villagers would have used your body for target practice."

Will huffed in amusement. "Sometimes it feels like you do the same."

"Alas, I do not use you for any kind of practice. Come now, before the place gets overrun." She grinned at his expression and pressed her heels against Percy's sides, urging him on. "What did you name your horse, by the way?"

His smile faded. "I cannot think of a thing to name him."

They rode the rest of the way in companionable silence. She had a pistol in her saddlebag but suspected that Will would always make her feel safe. Victor usually rode on ahead, causing her horse to pull and fret, but Will maintained his mount level with her own and checked to make sure she had seen low-hanging branches or poor footing.

And the more truly *herself* she was, the more he looked at her. She had no need to pretend feminine incompetence, or to hold back a curse when Percy stumbled. A log in her way? She jumped it. He liked the wildness in her. She saw proof in the curl of his lip, and the glances he gave.

And one thing more: it felt like they were equals. They were a well-matched pair on some well-matched horses, riding in the falling dark through fragrant fields of cut lucerne hay. Being with Will felt like a dream she didn't want to wake up from, and she cursed how close the village was. Up above, her favorite constellation appeared normal. She double-counted the stars. "Victor was right, as always," she grumbled to herself. "I was mistaken on that."

It was only when they reached a fork in the lane and he looked to her askance that she realized he was riding by her side because he did not know the way.

Ah, Angelika, she said to herself. *Always making something out of absolutely nothing.* When they arrived at the morgue, they tied their mounts. Will seemed spooked and hung behind to needlessly recheck some part of his horse's tack.

Compassion swelled in her and she tucked her hand firmly into the crook of his elbow.

"You've been here before. Remember, not a word about the science that Victor and I undertake. We'll be locked up as heretics. To this man, we are trainee doctors."

Will pulled a face. "But that's going to make things very difficult."

"Be creative. Impress me with your quick thinking."

"Not you again," Helsaw said dourly when he saw her approach. "Ain't you got enough bits and bobs for whatever it is you do?"

"That's none of your concern." She put a lace handkerchief over her nose. "How's business, Helsaw?"

"Prices 'ave gone right up," he warned, glancing to Will behind her. "But I deal with your brother on that. Who's this geezer?"

"This is my good friend Will." They had not worked out a surname.

Will covered smoothly. "Sir William Black. I'm here to ask you some questions, if I may."

"You may not. You know I do not allow just anybody here, Miss Frankenstein," Helsaw spluttered, until Angelika held up a shilling. "You may ask me anything you wish, Sir Black," he amended in a much better tone. "If I know the answer, I will tell you honestly."

"Are you the man who brings the bodies here?"

Helsaw nodded. "That I am."

Will stepped closer into the bright lamplight. "Have you ever seen me before?"

Helsaw narrowed his eyes in thought. "Should I?"

"My identical twin brother died and was brought through here. We were estranged, and I have been searching for him for years. I tracked him down through Miss Frankenstein, and now I seek your records so I can bring the information back to our family, and to connect with his."

Angelika was wordless with admiration of his quick mind, his rock-steady nerves, and the way the moonlight cut a shadow under his cheekbone and jaw. She could happily remain with her hand tucked into his bent arm for the rest of her life.

"A twin. I've heard of those, never seen one." Helsaw thought over this explanation with one eye squinted shut. "I don't go looking at the faces. I don't keep records. I can't even read. This is where the poor come through," he explained patronizingly. "Your brother, if he was a gentleman, would have been held at his local church. These are working men."

Will had truly expected a ledger of some sort to be produced. "You know nothing of where you collect each dead soul?"

"It was a day after the collapse of the mine shaft," Angelika said to jog the man's memory. "I checked through the newspapers."

"Good thought. You're so clever," Will praised her, with a glow in his eyes that made her swell with pride.

Helsaw coughed and spat, spoiling the moment. "I didn't get any out of that mine. They just filled the hole in. But it does help me remember the time," he added as Angelika moved to put her coin back in her pocket. "There was a bunch of boys all died, up at Dunmore. Sometimes I wonder what they do up there," he added conspiratorially.

For Will's benefit, Angelika pointed in the general direction. "Dunmore Military Academy. I don't know what they do, except march around, looking handsome in their uniforms."

"They train, so they don't lose the next war," Helsaw clarified witheringly. "And they sometimes have gunpowder explosions."

"Angelika said my brother's body was completely mangled." Will winced for himself now. "Would that fit the theory he came from the academy?"

"The Frankensteins are my premium buyers. They'd have just moved on to the next table if he was too bad. I bury the real damaged goods."

"And would any of the bodies be wearing jewelry?" Will asked.

"Oh, sure, good sir. We dress our corpses with the finest gold and gemstones. Jewelry!" Helsaw looked at Angelika with eyes full of mirth. "Your new friend is not from around here, is he?"

"He's rather naive," she agreed acidly. "Well, we've taken up enough of your time. I might go down just to see if there's anyone I can't live without." The doors were folded outward and blackness was all that could be seen. "I'm after someone exceptionally handsome for my research."

"Of course," Helsaw simpered as he gave him his payment; enough to feed his family for weeks. "I could even home-deliver, for a small amount more. Watch your skirts down the far end, but you know that. Floor gets wet," he explained offhand to an appalled Will. "Take my lantern, my dear Miss Frankenstein."

"Are you coming?" Angelika said to Will, who looked like

he was about to mount his horse and kick it into a gallop. She thought of her bold brother and decided to impress Will with her bravery. She stepped in without expecting him to follow, but he did. He was breathing fast.

"Angelika," he gasped in horror as she raised the lantern high. "This is something from a nightmare."

She saw it through his eyes and had to agree. Without Victor's brash apple-chewing presence, it seemed far worse. There were rows of motionless bodies stretched out on tables around them, and rats were at the edges of her vision. Fear began to tighten her limbs, until she could hardly take a step.

"I'll be quick," she told Will, but her eyes were unseeing as she went to the first table. There was no other face she could be interested in when Will stood behind her so close. When his hands slid around her waist, her grip on the lantern shook.

"Don't let the candle burn out," Will cried in terror, clinging to her. "Don't leave me here."

She put her hand over his and squeezed. "Haven't I already proved that I will never leave you here?"

His arms hugged her, tighter-tighter-tighter. Was this emotion, or his newfound strength? To have someone hold her so desperately was worth having no air in her lungs. They fit together exquisitely, tall and small. When he spoke, it was with an endearment. "My love, show me where I was when we met."

"This table." They walked as a pair and then looked down at the mottled-gray middle-aged man laid out before them. "I saw you and I thought . . ."

"What?" Will prompted after seconds passed. He put his face into her hair and inhaled deeply. Proof of his ardency nudged her bottom. "Your hair smells incredible."

Romance happened in unexpected places for Angelika Frankenstein.

She continued after a swallow. "I saw your face and you looked so indignant. Like your final thought was *How bloody dare they!* I lifted your eyelid, and I thought you looked at me."

"Perhaps I did." Will sounded like he was smiling.

"I got the fright of my life and had to check you for breath. Victor's theory is you were not long dead, and that's why I got you back. That night I . . . asked you something."

"What did you ask?"

"If you wished to come back." She turned in his arms, the lantern swinging by their knees. "I felt like you said yes, somehow."

"Of that, I am certain I did. I finally understand the magnitude of what you did for me. I am indebted to you for the rest of my life."

He caught her chin gently in his cool hand, lifted her face, and pressed a kiss on her mouth. It felt like that moment all over again: a magical swirl of wind and a deep surety that this was right. *Yes, yes, yes. Love me back.* Just as surprise parted her lips, he broke their kiss and said, "Thank you for choosing me, when you could have anyone."

"You can thank your own handsome face for catching my eye. In all the trips I'd made here, you were the only one to take my breath away."

"I'm handsome enough to inspire you to make a husband? How kind." He gently wound some hair away from her face. The clean smell of his wrist was a welcome relief. "I apologize that your plan did not succeed."

How easy it must be for him to be so assured of her devotion, while simultaneously telling her that she meant nothing. He was standing very much like an adoring husband right now, when the fact was, he probably belonged to some other lucky wench.

Not noticing how stiff she'd become, he added, "Our trip was not a complete waste. Now we can investigate the military academy."

Not a complete waste? She'd just had her first kiss. The desire to hurt him made her say: "You weren't my first attempt at a suitor. You were number four."

Will removed his hands from her. "Fourth?"

"What does it matter?" She paced away, pinching her nose against the smell. He did not move to follow. "You thought you were my first and only, and it flattered you."

"I am fourth?"

"In reality, you are at the back of a long queue of men who would not take me on. You know that good feeling you just had? How nice it felt to be special to someone? Please realize I have never experienced that feeling in return."

Uncaring if he was following, she marched to the doorway to relinquish the lantern. There were several students leaning against the wall, waiting their turn. "Anyone good this evening, Miss F?" Davey Gurney asked around his pipe.

"There's not, for she carries nothing in her hands," the man behind him said bitterly. "The Frankensteins get first pick of everything." He fell silent when Will appeared behind her.

"I am going to the tavern. You may do as you wish, Will." Angelika untied her horse, wrestling with her emotions. "Leg me up." He did, and she had half a mind to canter off before he could follow.

"Careful, miss," Davey called. "Rogues out tonight in the village."

"They'd be more scared of her," someone shouted, and the entire queue roared with laughter. Angelika was near tears, and she pulled on her riding gloves. Will's words echoed louder in her ears. *Our trip was not a complete waste.*

"I daresay you should be frightened of her, for her intellect is more than all of yours combined," Will said, and the queue fell silent. "The things she can achieve will change the world."

"Seems like she's changed your world," someone said. More raucous laughter followed.

"Undoubtedly." Will mounted his horse, and in his profile, Angelika saw a well-bred, powerful man. "What a pathetic lot you are. Show some respect to Miss Frankenstein."

"Brave enough to court her, are you, guv?"

"I'm not remotely worthy of her. Nobody is." With that, Will overtook Angelika's horse and they trotted together for some time without speaking. "We are returning home," he said to her shortly. "I've had enough for one night. Do not even think about going to the tavern."

"Who are you to tell me what to do?" Still, she turned her horse to follow his. "Tell me more about your identical twin brother. Is he unmarried? Could I persuade him to kiss me, or would that be a total waste of an evening?"

"Ha," Will replied with no humor. "You like having a ready replacement."

"It hurts you to know you were not the first man I made," she told him as she pushed Percy to a canter. "Lie in bed and think about why that is."

"I lie in bed and think about you, wearing silk." His words echoed across the fields, but there were only foxes and owls to overhear him. Their horses, headed toward home, began to pull and increase their pace. Both riders loosened their reins at the same time, and now they were racing.

Whyever not? Angelika thought as they pounded up the laneway. *The horses want to run so badly, what's the point in holding them back? It's in their nature.* And it was exhilarating, taking the inside position on corners, letting her smaller, nimble mount gain strides in those sharp, dangerous moments. She was furious with Will. He'd kissed her mouth as though he'd done so a thousand times before, an unthinking, instinctive thing; and she wasn't even sure if he realized he'd done it. Her world had changed; his had not.

He was so measured, even in this dangerous race, it drove her mad. It was in the straights that Will's horse made significant ground. As they were galloping up the wide carriage drive to the manor, he overtook her, and Angelika saw torchlight in the bushes on the library side of the manor.

"Will," she called, reining her horse in. Everything was forgotten now. "There's someone at the house."

CHAPTER SEVEN

He slowed and circled, halting beside her, the horses blowing and snorting.

"Is it Mary?"

"She wouldn't use a fire torch. Looks like the thieves from the village have noticed our absence." Angelika unbuckled her saddlebag. When she produced her pepperbox pistol, the look Will gave her was a mix of horror and utter admiration of her self-sufficiency.

"What are you going to do?"

"We are looking after the house, as Victor charged us to do. Who knows, maybe my husband has delivered himself to me. I have six shots," she added, holding up the expensive weapon, engraved with *A.F.*, naturally.

"Shoot once into the air, to scare them. Angelika. Look at me. Promise you will not be rash."

"I promise. We'll ride behind the house, keep to the grass to stay quiet."

The drawing room window was open, with a young man standing beneath it, holding his arms up for a bag that was being passed down.

"Oh, hello!" Angelika called out in a friendly voice, raising her arm. "You're stealing from me, are you?" She shot into the sky and rode out Percy's sideways spin. When she was facing the house again, there was only the abandoned bag beneath the window.

A window opened on the upper floor.

Mary's face peered down at them. "Thank heavens you're here, Master Will," she said, completely ignoring the gun-toting Angelika. "There's still one downstairs. I'm locked in my room. Come on, hurry up, get 'em out. I've got to heat your bathwater." The window closed.

Will forcibly took the firearm from Angelika. "No more shots."

Angelika found it deeply vexing that Mary had not considered her a savior. Abruptly, she was sick of everybody. "You can go and be the man of the house, like Victor wanted." She scowled up at Mary's window. "But please know this. I am not a helpless maiden."

They dismounted and put up their stirrups. Will handed her his reins. "I could never think that. Stay outside, until I tell you it is safe."

Angelika unsaddled the horses and turned them out in the orchard as an apology for not rubbing them down. They bolted off, bucking and skittish. She sat down on the low stone wall, with their warm leather bridles hung on her arm.

She did not feel particularly concerned for Will. He had her gun, and the thieves looked to be barely in their teens. Indeed, if she sharpened her senses, she could practically hear the calm negotiations that would be happening inside.

He'll be explaining to our thief why he's done wrong, but that he understands why. Angelika pictured the unfortunate villagers of Salisbury. She hated riding through there; everywhere she looked, she saw a crying child, a sad-eyed woman, a man in rags. *He'll tell him that times are hard, and jobs are hard to come by, and the crops did poorly, and scarlet fever has taken even their strong ones. Stomachs are empty in Salisbury.* She wiped sweat from her temple. *If I know Will, he would think a bag of candlesticks and silver would make a suitable donation. And tonight, as I think about it, I'm inclined to agree.*

Angelika found herself having an odd daydream about what a silver candlestick might be able to buy. Warm bread, curls of butter, wedges of cheese? A bag of apples, like those ripening on the trees behind her?

"My goodness. I'm sitting here daydreaming about villagers' larders and not my own first kiss?" She tapped her knuckles on her temple. "What has happened to me tonight?"

She was preparing to stand, listening for Will's call, when she heard a stick snap behind her. With a dry mouth, she whispered, "Who's there?"

Silence was the reply, but she felt their stare on her seated body. She took back her earlier declaration: she *was* a helpless maiden. Rogues were out in the village, strangers were in her house, and there was someone behind her. Frozen, she could hear the slow press of footsteps approaching, and the trembling jingle of the bridle buckles on her arm.

"I'll give you what you want," she said to the night air. "Don't hurt me."

When a hand touched the top of her head, she closed her eyes and nearly lost consciousness. It was a slow stroke, from the crown of her head, down her back, to the tips of her hair. When it lifted away, she let out a whimper. "Don't."

It happened again. She was being stroked like a horse in a field. Man, or ghost? Impossible to know. The moment the touch lifted away was the worst part. Would the next touch be on her side, sliding around to her breast? Or hands, wrapping around her throat? She flinched when the touch resettled on her crown. Surely this was a joke, before the tearing of clothing began. Nobody in the village had any fondness for her.

"He'll come," she said through her clenched jaw, shuddering through the next downward stroke. "He'll come for me."

"Angelika," Will's voice called at a distance. The touch stopped. When Will walked up to her, he found her still sitting on the stone wall. "It's all over. The boy in the library was terrified. I gave him a coin, and we had a talk, and he promised not to come back." He took the bridles from Angelika and laid them aside. "Are you all right?"

"I'm not. I'm not. I'm not—" She began hiccupping for air, and Will enfolded her in his arms. "Someone was here, and . . ."

"Someone? Who?"

"They were behind me. Right behind me. And they were touching me." She felt the swell of horror in Will's rib cage. "My hair. A hand, stroking down my hair. It was the most disgusting thing I have ever felt. But it also felt like my mother." She gave a hysterical bark of laughter. "They could have snapped my neck, or cut my throat. And I just sat there."

"Come inside," he urged, and when she could not walk, he put an arm under her legs, lifted her, and carried her toward Blackthorne Manor. "At daylight, I'll go and look for footprints. Perhaps there was a third thief, hanging back. Or could it have been . . ." He looked toward the barn.

"Victor is chasing him, miles away. He's angry at us, besides. I'm sure he would not have been so gentle."

They were at the kitchen door now, and Will called, "Mary, help."

Angelika was still in a wheezing heap when she was laid

down on a bed and saw a sideways bear. This was Will's bedroom. "She's had a shock," Mary said. "I'll fetch smelling
salts, and whiskey. I've been telling Victor that there's someone in the orchard."

"Angelika," Will said, unlacing her boots. "Please, come
to your senses. Did he touch you anywhere else?" When she
shook her head, he let out a shaky breath. "I'm sorry. I was
intoxicated by the thought of protecting the house, but I did
not protect you. Victor should hang me."

When Mary came back, they urged Angelika to sit up and
drink several mouthfuls of liquor. "You're all right," Mary
said brusquely. "But what am I always telling you?"

Angelika's throat felt like it had closed completely. She
could not repeat the mantra that Mary had drummed into her
for so long, and the old woman said it now with angry force.
No hesitation, no politeness, run. Did you do that? Angelika,
did you do as I told you?"

"She was terrified," Will defended her. "She was frozen
solid. Don't be hard on her."

"Someone has to be," Mary returned. "She is a simple fool."

"I—" Angelika could not explain. All she knew was that
Mary's expression was full of deep disappointment as she left
the room.

"Don't talk," Will told her, closing the door. "Don't try to
talk. We will wash your hair."

It was marvelous, having someone understand exactly what
was needed in this moment. He guided her to his tub, prepared earlier by Mary. With shaking hands, they worked Angelika's riding habit loose, until she was sinking down into the
water in her muslin underdress. "Just like when we met," she
croaked, and Will skimmed the warm water over her shoulders, washing her with urgency. She was not the only one in

shock. Her hair was lathered and rinsed, and he applied the sponge to each of her fingertips.

"I'm so sorry," he told her, and his voice cracked with emotion. "You didn't deserve this terrible fright."

"It could have been worse." She closed her eyes and focused her breathing. And gradually, she sank back into her own body again, hearing the lap of water, and became aware that the wet muslin on her body must have been translucent. But she trusted him and the careful way he handled her body, and he repaid that trust. There was nothing lecherous in his eyes as he kept them firmly on her face, checking her mental state.

"I'm all right. I think I am myself again. What an odd experience." She blew out a breath, and a smile quirked her mouth. "I was sitting there, imagining you counseling the thief on the moral error he had made. I was right."

"It seems you know me well." Will thought about that for a minute, rubbing the sponge along her arm. "How you can know me when I do not know myself is a mystery."

"I don't know who you are, but I know *what* you are. You are good. And you make me want to be good." She raised a hand and touched his jaw, seeking his attention. Under her wet fingertip, she felt his pulse tick faster. "I thought of you, I waited for you, and I knew you'd come for me. You saved me." She didn't want a sponge all over, she wanted his hand. Was it the whiskey in her stomach? The fading terror? The wet cling of fabric, all over her body, tangling up her legs like vines? "I wish you'd kiss me again."

"I know what you want," Will said evenly. "You do not hide it. Your eyes tell me everything, all the time."

"I cannot hide much right now." Through the wet cloth, every freckle on her body was visible. "I have seen so much of you. I should let you see me. 'Tis only fair."

He did look at her body now, with such male admiration she felt her cheeks grow warm. "If our positions had been reversed, and I was making my dream woman, there is nothing I would replace or change about you, Angelika."

A fine compliment, but also a gentle rebuke. "Victor insisted on reassembling you. I'd been reading a lot of anatomy books, and whilst I said I'd have you as you were, he convinced me some improvements could be made."

He raised an eyebrow. "Is this your way of explaining I had a small cock?"

"You had a perfectly good cock, and everything else was lovely, too, but spoiled Miss Frankenstein went hunting around like a child in a toy chest to see if she could improve on perfection. I only thought of the musculature, not the spirit inside. And I want you to know that if I could go back in time, I would not change a thing about you, either."

"Even my hands, with a wedding ring?"

He'd known all along? "I was mad with jealousy. I had found my dream man, with a face that stopped my heart, and he possibly belonged to another? I know it was wrong to lie to you, but I want you to know this: She didn't love you like I do. She didn't try to bring you back."

"Not everybody has your resources or intellect," Will reminded her with quiet censure, not acknowledging her love declaration. "People love in different ways. Just because a wife with no scientific knowledge doesn't beat back death doesn't mean she is less caring."

"You're in my world now, and it does mean that. Why aren't you more surprised to be married?"

"You're just confirming something I have suspected. How else could I resist?" He gestured wryly in her direction.

"You've always known deep down that you belong to another. It's why you feel unfaithful. Pass me that soap bar, please." She pointed to the basin stand. The change of subject would head off the swell of bad emotion inside. "When Lizzie and I dragged Victor to Paris, we found this tiny soap store tucked into a laneway. They supplied Marie Antoinette."

"If it was good enough for the queen of France, and Princess Angelika, it's fine for nameless, nobody Will," he said, fetching it. "I shudder to imagine the cost."

"I have never smelled anything as divine as your soap." She cupped the cake in her hands and inhaled deeply. "I can smell you all around the house. I chose this scent for you, long before I ever saw you."

"That's why I am finding it hard to trust you now. If your first attempt at a husband had worked, you would have given him your favorite soap."

Angelika tried to picture it. "I'm quite sure I would not." But she *had* been infatuated many times before with total strangers.

He was patient. "I cannot know that it is me you love when you do not know me. I understand why you didn't tell me at first about the ring. But it changes things, and I now have to investigate new threads tying me to my old life. My death may have been a catastrophe for my family." He hesitated, then made an admission. "It made me sick to think of myself as your fourth. I want to kiss you again, too. But these thoughts are chased by the idea that I am not free to make a new choice. I may have children who depended on me, and now they might be stealing to survive."

Emotion swelled inside her because he was a very good man indeed.

She spilled the truth.

"Your ring has an engraving, but we were too careless to

even look at it. There, now you know everything. All of my terrible wrongdoings and lies. You were found by the worst person." She laid her head down on her folded arms and shivered as he cupped water across her shoulders. "We will follow that ring to the ends of the earth, and with it I hope you can unlock your entire past. Your family, your wife . . . You will go home to them."

She added some salt tears to the bathwater.

"I probably will. But don't worry yourself tonight. Lie back." When she did, he pillowed her head on his forearm. "My poor love, you have had such burdens, being so lonely up on this hill," he said with total understanding, and her tears came in earnest. After keeping these details from him, she'd expected a scolding, but now he just carefully washed her face, cleansing her tears like he couldn't bear them. "You were good to confess the full truth, and more so, I never had to press. You give me everything, at every chance you get. I love my new boots, by the way."

"I'm so glad." She reveled in his touch as he stroked the sponge across her face.

"This is what you did for me on that first night. I was in the most unspeakable pain, right through my bones. It was the way you washed my face that made me want to keep living. Who would think a sponge and warm water could be so soothing?"

She tried to lighten her tone. "The sponge is from the store in Paris, too. Only the best for you."

He wouldn't allow her to sidestep her emotion. "I felt how much you cared for me."

Maybe he was asking her to feel that now, too, so she closed her eyes, and it felt real. He was tracing and stroking the sponge across her brow, cheeks, lips, neck. Over and over.

This was forever love, till death parted them.

"I will tell you what I know now, in this moment. You are the most beautiful woman who ever lived," he told her with quiet certainty. "The most brilliant, the most witty, the most brave."

Angelika could not find a reply.

He continued. "I need you to know I am in awe of everything you are. Even the bad parts of you. But this resurrection pastime is not a game. You need to give life, and death, the respect it deserves. It is not up to you to make these decisions. You are not God."

Angelika was not used to such gentle censure. "I see it now completely, and I will be better. I promise."

He completed another pass with the sponge across her face. "I would like to see you make some changes in your life. Look around yourself. See your privileges. Find ways to help the people of this village who are struggling to survive. Show mercy and kindness to them, because you can afford to."

Angelika's voice was small. "I know I have lived a self-absorbed life."

"I know you will improve. I have faith in you."

Faith.

Somewhere along the way, the Frankensteins' distrust of the church had erased that word from their vocabularies. Will accepted all these good and bad parts of her, tended her near-naked body like it were art, and he was confident that she could, and would, do better. Angelika had dreamed of a declaration of love for her entire life.

This one felt monumental.

This felt like a preview of what their life together would be like: Riding through fields as equals on adventures, each supporting and saving the other. Bathing companionably, a debate, a laugh, then curling together in French linen sheets to lusciously defile each other. No other person could breach this little world they had created together, and no man could ever replace him.

And just as she was reaching for him, to put her hand into his hair, to bring him down to her mouth, he evaded her. "You do not hide what you want," he repeated to her. "But I wish you would. From the neck down, I do not believe we should wait. And I need to leave now, before I lose my head completely."

He was out of the room, closing the door quietly behind him, and she was left behind to soak in the freezing water in his bathtub.

CHAPTER EIGHT

Two days later, on the way to the Dunmore Military Academy, Will asked Angelika, "Whose carriage is this? Did you create these footmen last night in your laboratory?"

"Our neighbor lets us borrow it, in exchange for using our fields for his goats and sheep. It's a good arrangement. As you know, Victor is not fond of formal outings anywhere. Myself, I'd love a coach drawn by eight black horses to see the world in."

He had empathy in his expression. "I truly wish that for you. I wonder how Victor has gotten on. Will he send a messenger, or just arrive home?"

"He took a pigeon with him. He's trained them to fly home. They arrive and wait on the windowsill, with a note in a canister on their leg. It's frightfully exciting. Last time, he sent me this silver necklace." She hooked her thumb into the chain at her throat.

"How pleasant, to be so wealthy a bird can be trusted with such a delivery." He thought this over, and a brilliant grin spread across his face. "Another Frankenstein invention."

"I'm sorry you got caught up in our nonsense."

Will was seated opposite her, their knees sometimes brushing and her boots held secure between his. It was another of those *I wish this was forever* moments. In her instant day-dream, they were just married and about to crest a hill, the ocean below foaming against the shore. A ship was docked, ready to take them across to new worlds. She felt she could travel for hundreds—thousands!—of days, until the ache of being manor-bound had eased off. And she would do it gladly, holding Will's hand, with a tired ache in her thighs and his kiss on her mouth.

This much was true reality: now that they had touched lips at the morgue, it seemed impossible to stop staring at each other. Being left behind in cooling bathwater the other night should have been enough to chill Angelika's passion. Instead, she was in a constant sweat over him.

She attempted a joke to break the silence. "Buy me a carriage and horses when we are married. I promise to be very surprised by the gift. But—you do not seem comfortable?"

His hands clutched tight on the seat. His face appeared pale, and his Adam's apple was bobbing in swallows. "Something about this enclosed space is fraying my nerves," he admitted, looking through the lace curtain at the forest they were traveling through. "I feel like I'd rather get out and walk."

"Fresh air will help—breathe deep and count to one hundred." Angelika was gratified that after a minute of deep breaths, he turned a better color. "Perhaps this is a fear from your last life."

Now he was concerned about something else. "Victor mentioned there have been robberies on the roads. He says the military presence is the only thing keeping it checked."

Angelika did not want to panic him further, but it was true. "Carriages have been stopped or overturned. The passengers robbed or worse. There is no point in dwelling on it. I have my pistol. As I'm sure they do, too," she added, nodding up toward the drivers. "Everything is all right, and we are close to Dunmore, judging by how the road has turned to cobblestones. If we only have minutes, we should discuss our strategy."

"Strategy?" Will repeated, his eyes back on her face. "I haven't thought about it. You are beautiful today. You smell like lilacs."

"You are quite the connoisseur of flowers," she teased. "Please focus. You cannot utilize your twin brother story line again."

"Why not?"

She began checking her appearance in a small mirror. "Because you don't know his name. It's not remotely believable. These men at the military academy are a thousand times more clever than Helsaw at the morgue. They will want to hear the full tale and, my love, you have not devised one."

This had him panicking. "I see the outer gates," he said after putting his head out the window. "Whatever will we do?"

Most men would be too proud to ask for help, and she liked that about him. "I have devised a story." From her valise, she retrieved an heirloom. "This was my grandfather's medal. I am here to research it. I hear women nowadays fill their time researching their genealogy. This is my latest little project. I grew tired of cross-stitch."

Will rubbed a hand on the healed stitch line at his collarbone. "No one could speak to you for more than ten seconds and be convinced you fill your time with mindless needlepoint."

"You forget, my love. I am a rich lady. That buys me access to most places. And I have an appointment with the new commander of this facility. And while I am here, I will find out all about the tragedy that befell his men."

"You have an appointment. Meanwhile, what should I do?

Maybe I could go to the kitchen and speak to some of the servants, to find out what they know."

"No. Wait in the carriage." Angelika pulled her gloves on.

Will protested, "Why even bring me?"

"Because I love looking at your face, and I was hoping for another kiss." She leaned forward to quickly peck his cheek. "If you can bear the confinement, stay here, and do not show yourself. Someone might think they have seen a ghost."

Angelika's gray kid boots hit the ground and she walked off without a backward glance. DUNMORE MILITARY ACADEMY was written across the arch she was crossing beneath, along with a Latin motto she read as: *Duty Before All Else.*

Will would like that motto, she thought. *And here I am, assisting him to find his way back to his familial responsibilities. I am a fool.*

She did not have long to ponder that because she was being handed along by various assistants and underlings until she was left alone outside an enormous pair of walnut doors, at least twelve feet high.

"What a tree this must have been," she said, at the exact moment they opened.

"I do often think that myself," the man before her agreed. "Miss Frankenstein, I presume? I am Commander Keatings."

He was much younger than she had anticipated, and much better-looking: tall, fair, with remarkable cornflower-blue eyes and winsome smiling brackets framing his mouth. He offered his hand and shook hers firmly. He wore no rings.

And goodness, how remarkably neat his appearance was. There was not a single hair lying loose on his brow, and not a crease on his clothing. Angelika found herself searching all over for one singular flaw: a loose stitch, a crack in his thumbnail, a budding yellow pimple. She found nothing.

The old Angelika would have been wondering whether he found her fair or plain. The creases of his smile deepened, revealing lovely white teeth, but her heart did not flutter.

For the first time in her life, it was not love at first sight.

She had to explain herself. "I'm sorry to stare, but you are the tidiest-looking man I have ever met. My goodness, I do believe I could eat my dinner off your white collar."

He laughed in delight. "I do not know why I am this way; it is not through any particular effort. I do not so much as carry a comb."

Angelika gestured in the direction of the central courtyard. "You must inspire your men to turn themselves out nicely for inspection."

His grin widened. "In the limited days I have been here, I have caused them to despair. Please, come in."

Angelika could not ignore this realization: Commander Keatings found her very fair. This she ascertained without doubt or conceit. He was as taken aback by her appearance as she was his, studying her with an equal fascination.

She moved an eyebrow. "Did you imagine an old crone, hoping to find the names of some ghosts to pester?"

He laughed again. "I confess I did. I have a page bringing up the relevant record book. Take a seat, please."

He sat behind the desk, framed by the window and surrounded by militaria. Compared to him, the velvet drapes looked crumpled and sad. On the wall was the mounted head of a buck with impressive antlers.

"I hope you don't consider this impertinent," he began after she sat, "but you do not strike me as the type to sit indoors and write down the names of great-great-great-uncles and -aunts."

It was more or less what Will had observed about *mindless needlepoint*.

"Oh, but I am," Angelika countered. "I am trying to improve myself. According to my brother, Victor, I get into all sorts of mischief if I am not kept occupied at all times."

"I am sure, madam, that you speak honestly," Commander Keatings said with a look designed to make her blush. "Are your parents well?"

"I live alone with Victor, and we have no other family."

This grave news pleased him immensely. The commander was husband material, and from Mary's gossiping she knew he was unattached. He had a title, a history, a family name. They were getting along wonderfully, and eye contact produced a spark in her stomach. Even still, her heart pulled toward the man waiting outside for her, the one who'd leave one day without looking back.

Fate was a trickster.

"Are you quite all right, Miss Frankenstein?" Commander Keatings asked, leaning forward in concern. "You have gone quite pale. Here, take some brandy." He went to a cabinet by the far wall and poured her an inch of liquor into a snifter. "Your journey has tired you."

"How thoughtful." She sipped the glass as he sat on the edge of his desk. "You're right. I am a little tired. Please, tell me about your work, Commander Keatings."

"Call me Christopher. What do you wish to know?" He seemed amused. "I say, it's nice conversing with a woman. I spend all of my time with men."

She swallowed the rest of her brandy in a gulp. "What is it like being the commander? Is it *Duty Before All Else?*"

He enjoyed her clever use of the Latin motto. "Lately, yes. It's a lot of office work, writing letters, approving requests, and releasing funds. Very much like managing a large country estate, but instead of cattle, I have one hundred men to feed and water." He added, like he was unable to resist: "I am also fortunate enough to have my own country estate, where I like to spend some time out in the fresh air." He looked up at the glassy-eyed buck on his wall.

Angelika attempted to transition the conversation. "What sort of men train here? Are they all officers, like you?"

"It is a mix, like all militia," he explained, taking her empty glass. "A touch more, I think," he decided, going to refill it. "You are getting your coloring back. There are lower-ranking men reporting to officers. We train them here so they may be available for times of war. They live in the barracks."

"That must be difficult for those who are married," she prompted. "Having to live apart from their wives."

Christopher took this as a flirtation. "Many of us are married to this way of life," he said slowly, his eyes on her mouth as he sat back on the desk. "But I've been thinking lately that there is more to life than just work, and training, and maintaining an immaculate wardrobe."

"Well, don't tell them that." She nodded toward the grounds and he laughed again. *Stop being funny and lively*, she scolded herself, and then was astonished at the thought. *I am charming this man. How is this happening?*

"We have a row of cottages in Highgrove Street where the married officers live with their families. I live here, and I must tell you, Miss Frankenstein, this place is cold at night. And sometimes I hear howls, but I do not know what animal it could be."

"Sandstone produces the most frightful kind of cold." She attempted another subject change, but she was too abrupt. "Now, tell me of this accident they are speaking of in the village."

His expression lost all amusement. "What accident?" He

stood from his perch on the desk and went back to his imposing chair. "Whatever do you mean? Ah, thank you, put it here," he said to his page, who approached at that moment holding a huge leather-bound book.

Christopher took the opportunity to gather his wits as he fussed with turning the page to the correct record. "Frankenstein," he read out, his tone significantly cooled. "You will find your ancestor's information here. I will step out to allow you privacy."

Angelika regretted her tendency to speak without thought and leaned forward to put her hand on his. "I'm sorry. I spend a lot of time alone. I speak my mind without thinking. I had heard someone mention something terrible happening here, and I wondered if you were all right."

It was essentially the abbreviated truth. He heard her honesty and relaxed. "I was concerned there had been gossip."

"Not as such. Just a passing comment that I decoded. I am too clever for my own good, and my mouth is smarter yet. I apologize for being so direct about such a traumatic subject."

"No harm done. Yes, there was a training accident that went badly. I'd barely been here two weeks." It was a terrible thing to witness the sadness in his once-sparkling eyes. "I understand we lost some very fine men."

Angelika imagined that in her ear, Will's voice encouraged: *Look around yourself. See how you might offer to help another who needs it.*

Inspiration struck.

"That is why I was asking of their wives. I thought I might make up a condolences basket of fruit and pantry goods, if there was anyone recently bereaved. I must step up my charitable efforts in the village." Producing a notebook and a pencil from her pocket, she began copying down information on her ancestor to maintain her cover. She felt his eyes on her face but did not look up.

Christopher said softly, "How remarkably kind women can be."

She answered defensively. "Nonsense. Anyone would do the same. Should I prepare a basket?"

"Just one married officer was killed." He searched through his own notebook, filled with perfect handwriting. "Clara Hoggett. Yes, a basket is just the thing to do. I could assist you with the contents. My predecessor left some good Scotch here."

Off he went for a third time to the liquor cupboard. Angelika finished her refill. She took the unopened bottle that he presented to her.

"I should like to accompany you to present this to Clara." Christopher was sitting on the edge of the desk again. She wouldn't have left those thighs at the morgue. The obscene thought poured heat through her, like a teapot.

"You're a busy man." Angelika got to her feet. "'Tis simple women's work, like my genealogy project. You needn't bother yourself."

"I have neglected my duty in checking on her. As the new commander, I must go. As my new friend, you can ensure I don't get lost. Have you taken down the details you need?" When she nodded, he offered her his arm. "I shall walk you to your carriage."

Her traitorous hand grasped his firm biceps. Good gosh. "That's quite all right. You're busy."

"I'm really not," Christopher said, and he smiled broadly for the entire walk downstairs and across the grounds, making perfectly agreeable conversation and pointing out aspects of the architecture. Angelika ached to touch his porcelain-perfect shirt cuffs.

They halted at the carriage.

"Miss Frankenstein, may I call you Angelika?"

"Certainly, Christopher—as you said, we are friends now." The carriage stairs were against the backs of her calves. She prayed Will had followed her orders; he must be holding his breath inside. "I must thank you for all your help. And I will ensure the poor lady receives this bottle."

"I insist on visiting her home with you." Christopher took her hand in his, smoothing across the knuckles of her glove. "Pray, allow me a moment to be quite impertinent. I would be grateful to call upon you. I wish to introduce myself to your brother, given you were both unable to attend the ball."

"He is out of town at present, for another day or so." Giving in to the urge, Angelika laid her hand on his cuff. No magic, no witchcraft: it was regular fabric.

"I trust you have plenty of servants to keep you safe. There are many thieves and rogues in the village. And there are tales of something more unexplained. You haven't seen any monsters, have you?" He was clearly amused. "Something huge and barely human?"

"I haven't, but I wish I would." It sounded like Victor's travel was wasted.

"Please, do not ever go out after dark. We are commencing night patrols. I shall send a card to your brother, and I hope to see you again soon. Do you ride?"

She couldn't help herself. "Frightfully well."

"I'd like to know all the things you are frightfully good at." He wanted to hand her up into her carriage, but she couldn't risk his seeing Will. She backed up the tiny stairs, attempting to squeeze through a four-inch gap. "Allow me, please," he said, reaching past her waist and opening the door wide.

The carriage was empty.

"Thank you. Goodbye." Angelika settled herself into her seat and blew out a breath. She heard Christopher exhale in a similar way, long and slow. He'd held his breath? He needed air? Oh, but wasn't this a dark delight, knowing she would be in his thoughts as he lay alone tonight in his sandstone fortress—

A whip crack jolted her out of this forbidden thought. Flattery was a worse intoxicant than brandy. Where in the blue blazes was Will?

She drew the curtain on the opposite window and clutched her heart in fright. Will was hanging on the outside of the carriage, posing as a footman—a very irritated one. Quick thinking, but she still felt embarrassed that he had eavesdropped on that excruciating scene.

In contrast to Christopher, Will was thoroughly ruffled. He had hair falling on his brow, a clothing crease at every joint, and a sparkle of sweat on his brow. He was reassuringly alive.

Out the window, she hissed, "Get down from there."

"Not until we are past the gates. No one can see me on this side. What is that for? A parting gift?" Will looked at the bottle of liquor on the seat beside her. He scowled through the carriage windows back at the building. "He's standing there, watching your carriage depart like a lovesick youth."

"Don't be ridiculous. This is a contribution to the hamper I am making for the bereaved wife of an officer who was killed here ten days ago." She hated how Will's attention sparked up. "And before you ask, no, I didn't ask for his name or any further particulars. It would have been suspicious."

She pretended not to hear his questions until they were stopped safely down the road and he could climb back in.

"You didn't ask anything that could help further?" Will said with a bit of accusation. He sat opposite her, his knees caging her legs in. "You've been drinking liquor in his office, in the middle of the day. Probably being lively and charming."

Angelika put her palm in front of her mouth, exhaled, and sniffed. "Just a couple of brandies, and only moderately charming. I'm glad you did as you were told and stayed here."

"I didn't. I saw some gravestones down the side of the eastern wing."

He explained how he had run across and examined all of the graves that looked fresh, before evading an approaching groundskeeper and hiding in the small chapel until the footsteps faded. "They were all privates, low-level soldiers. None of their names made me feel anything. But being on those grounds gave me a strong echo of memory. It washed over me until I was dizzy."

Clara Hoggett's husband must be buried in the village, or indeed there may be an empty casket under his gravestone. "You are an officer, my love, I am sure."

She nearly said: *And I think I know your wife's name.* She'd opened her mouth to say it. But the fear that he would jolt back into himself, regain his memory, and ask for a lift to town was too much. She decided to keep him to herself a few minutes longer. By the end of this carriage ride, she would release him. In a voice designed to intoxicate, she cooed, "You're too refined and elegant to be a lowly private."

This did not flatter him. "Not as refined as your perfect Commander Keatings. He is planning to call on you."

Angelika's insides thrilled at the flat jealousy in his eyes. "You heard that, then."

"I heard it all. I heard how enchanted he was." He reached out and drew the curtains on one window, then the other. It gave Angelika a dip in her stomach, like the carriage was gliding downhill. "He thinks you are very beautiful."

"We can't know that."

"Anyone could see that you are."

"I'm not sure about that—"

"Your smart green eyes are always watching, calculating, changing. They turn dark, like green glass, when you look at my mouth. You fill that dress sinfully, and your lips are my favorite pink."

She felt hot. "Thank you."

"But no matter how beautiful you look today, I still prefer you in men's trousers. I know your true self, in a way he never will." He sat back, laid an arm along the back of his seat, and nodded in the direction they had left. "I know what that man wants."

Her heart leapt. "I prefer you."

"Then come and show me." He smirked at her shocked expression. "You have been unraveled since that kiss in the morgue the other night. I am boiling mad with jealousy right now, so come over here." He slapped his own thigh.

"I'm annoyed, too," she said as she moved to his side of the carriage, lifted her skirts, and slid a knee across his legs. "You walked out abruptly, leaving me wallowing in your cold bathtub."

"I was the one who needed to soak in ice water." The carriage rattled, causing each to clutch the other. Fingertips sank into flesh, and Angelika leaned forward. He put his cool hand on her face. She drew one breath, and then she was being kissed.

Her only thought was: *I chose him so well.*

He must have had residual lightning in his veins, because she was feeling it now, sparking at every press of his lips and the unexpected touch of his teeth. His forearm banded around her, grasping handfuls of her waist, testing and releasing her body.

He put his tongue in her mouth, his hand in her hair, and Angelika Frankenstein had never felt so alive.

He tasted fresh, and his lips prompted sensations into other parts of her body. It was of scientific interest, but also something alchemic that she did not want to understand. This was why humans courted and chased, primped and flirted. This was why there were groaning, shifting shapes in the alley beside the tavern and why humanity continued to produce new generations. She'd had one small glimpse with him before, but now, the experiment was complete. Kissing was absolutely, completely magical.

Together they made a sound: part groan, all lust.

Will lifted his mouth from hers, his thumb sliding down to her throbbing pulse. "I can say this with certainty: I have not had a kiss like that before. Is this acceptable to you, Miss Frankenstein?"

She pulled him back to her.

Their next kiss was gentle. His lips were barely on hers now. He was wordlessly repeating that question: *Is this acceptable to you?* She licked his lip, then his tongue, and his grumble vibrated through her body to the soles of her feet. "This is all I want to do from this point onward," she said when he let her take a breath. "You will spend your life kissing me."

"I feel inclined to say yes," he replied, pressing ravenous kisses on her neck. "If Victor doesn't hasten home, I will lie between your legs all night."

"And I will love it," she gasped, fisting her hand in his hair. She was no longer unkissed, and she was desperate to have everything. "I've studied the theory components of intercourse very closely. I have an ancient Indian book with so many drawings. I sometimes think I'm perverted, the things I want to try."

"I want to. I ache for you." His entire body shivered. "But . . ."

She caught him, right before he blinked out of the haze.

"It is just a game we play," she said, and licked into his mouth until he groaned. "A little make-believe, to pass the time on this dull journey home. We can make up any nonsense thing. It is your turn."

"When we live at Larkspur," Will said, and her toes curled in her shoes, "I will have you all the time. In every room, outside, daylight, midnight, I will see your body." He smiled at her frantic nod. "Your turn. Tell me all the times you've thought of kissing me."

"After breakfast and you'd taken my empty plate for me, or stoked the fire for Mary. It's your thoughtfulness and care that makes me sweat."

Now she had to break off, because the kiss was dominating everything. Breath, thought, existence.

But she tried. "If a shadow slid across your face just right, or I saw your tongue on your water glass—" She was heaving breaths now, her hips moving and encouraging. "It is your turn. Tell me when you've touched yourself, thinking of me."

He whispered in her ear, and she strained for every word. "I touch myself when I think of you naked in your bed. When I think about the life we could have, and the ways we would know each other. Closer and tighter than any two people ever were, and the loyalty I know you would have for me. Till death. Beyond death."

The carriage hit a bump, and their anatomy aligned in a new way, through their layers of clothing. Every dip, rock, or pothole was creating sparks. And this was a very, very poorly maintained stretch of road.

"I really feel you," Angelika confessed, and he bit his lip. "I really"—bump—"feel you."

"We should stop," Will said, but it was too late for her.

It was the idea of that perfect life that tipped her over the edge into a pleasure she'd never experienced, because it was shared with him. It was almost unendurable, endless tightening and releasing of every muscle in her body. And over her own heartbeat, Will said in her ear:

"You would never love another man. You would live and breathe for me. You would take me into your body every hour. I know you, Angelika," he impressed on her as she slumped forward, limp on his shoulder. "And I cannot wait for you to know me." He put his hands on her waist and moved her back to her seat. He was flushed and disheveled.

She stared at him, too stunned to be embarrassed. "Imagine what a really rough cobblestone lane in London could do to me."

"I would dearly love to find out."

"If we let the horses walk, we could make the trip to Larkspur take twice as long."

Realization dropped into his eyes like a screen. "Oh, Angelika. When I said—"

"Of course, it is just a pleasant story we tell each other in the moment."

They rode in silence for several miles. It was obvious that passion was clearing from his head, and he now deeply regretted what had come to pass. Several times, he tried to start a sentence, and all of them gave her a feeling of dread.

Angelika drew back the curtain. "We are nearly home."

When she picked up the bottle of Scotch, it caught Will's attention.

"The hamper you are making, for the bereaved wife of the dead officer . . . How are you going to deliver it to her?"

"I know the street she lives on, and her name."

The shadows cut across the carriage now, turning it chilly. The truth should have been something he would have had to crowbar out of her, but he held her strings like a puppeteer so effortlessly.

He didn't even have to open his mouth to ask.

"Clara," she said, and the carriage stopped in front of Blackthorne Manor. She didn't wait to be handed down, but jumped out without a backward glance, like she had done all her life.

"I think you have a wife named Clara. Does that spark perfect memories for you?" She hardly knew why she asked, because she ran inside before she could hear his answer.

CHAPTER NINE

W e should talk—" Will began at breakfast the next day, but Angelika clapped her hands over her ears. She still heard him finish. "—about other ways to investigate my past. If you are amenable, I might write letters to some investigators in London."

"I thought you'd want to talk about my discovery," Angelika confessed as she lowered her hands. Or did he want to discuss how she had dissolved from that kiss? She forced herself to speak. "You still don't feel anything when I say the name Clara?"

He shook his head. "I remember nothing about myself."

Mary dropped a basket of bread between them onto the table and put her hands on her hips. "Where is that girl? No point calling for her." She walked out after this nonsensical statement, seemingly in search of someone.

Will's brandy-brown eyes were steady and sad. "I don't deserve to stay in this house, after what I did to you in the carriage. I think I should prepare to leave."

Angelika was taken aback. "You didn't do anything to me. I did something to you. I climbed on top of you, and I—" She tried to think of how to describe it. "I accidentally enjoyed myself too much."

Now the look in his eyes was feral and black. It suited him. "Angelika," he warned, and the growl gave her a delicious shiver. "I acted very wrongly. You ran from me and hid all night."

"I was worried I'd gone too wild." She refolded her napkin, wondering how much to confess. "The minutes where the heartbeat slows are terrifying. You look at me like you've made a mistake, and I'm not a mistake. I'm your Angelika."

His smile was a relief. "You are."

They were interrupted by Mary. There was a second person, hanging back in the shadows of the hall. Angelika squinted. "Who's there?"

Mary turned and beckoned. "Meet your new maid."

A sturdily built tall girl of around sixteen years crept into the room.

"How do you do?" Will said. "What is your name?"

Mary spoke again. "This is Sarah, and she's as shy as they come. Barely says a word. I thought she'd be a good fit for this ungodly household, and will keep her mouth shut in the village about whatever she sees here." After Sarah nodded meekly, Mary went to the fireplace and began vigorously thwacking the burning log with a poker, releasing sparks into the room. "She's sent by her parents to find work, after they lost it all. Her father was a gambler and a fool. She's staying at the boardinghouse. My sister recommends her."

Angelika waited until the blushing, downcast girl chanced a glance at her. "How do you do, Sarah? It's quite all right if you are a shy sort."

The girl gulped and nodded helplessly.

"Is the boardinghouse comfortable for you? Is it warm, and are you given a hearty supper?"

Angelika regretted the question when the girl grimaced, rubbing her hands together as if in memory, and looked at

Mary's back. Of course she would not speak against her land-lady with her sister present. "It is too cold," Angelika surmised. "And the food is slop."

When Sarah made eye contact again, there was humor in her expression. She risked a nod before Mary turned back to them.

"Whilst not compulsory, reading and writing is a nice thing to do," Angelika continued. "Have you had those opportunities?"

Sarah spoke for the first time, soft and halting. "I went to school, until Father had his troubles. I have not kept up my writing and reading."

"Well, it is not too late to start again. You can borrow books from the library here," Angelika told her, and the girl nodded. To Mary, she ordered: "Sarah will have one hour, paid, after breakfast, to practice her reading and writing. You are not to make her feel guilty about it. Am I clear?"

Mary grumbled. "It's about ruddy time I had some help around here, now she takes time off? The messes I find in the morning! The library was ransacked last night."

"It was probably just how Victor left it."

"Hardly. I think we had another thief. And a message from the military academy arrived." Mary added in a bellow at Sarah, "Give her the mail. Are you heading to war, mistress?"

At that exact moment, a movement caught everyone's attention.

Angelika clapped. "Victor!" It wasn't her brother, but it was his pigeon on the sill. Angelika went to the little messenger and gave it a crust while she unfastened the leather tube from its leg. Sarah's mouth hung open. Unrolling the minuscule parchment, Angelika said, "Finally, we have some news. Victor will be here tomorrow morning. And Lizzie is also on her way and will be here by tonight."

Because she enjoyed secrets, Angelika decided not to read aloud his postscript: *Get Grandmama's big diamond ring out of your jewelry box and polish it, Jelly! I hope it's fit for a duchess's finger.* It made her grin. At last, a sister. "Where shall we put her?"

"We're running out of space," Mary said, but it wasn't her usual complaining tone. The mere presence of Sarah, with her youth and energy, had apparently lifted a weight from her ancient shoulders. "If Master Victor did not use so many bedrooms for storage, we could accommodate an entire wedding party."

Will volunteered in an instant. "Is there a bed in the servants' quarters? I'm taking up space that you do not have."

"No room upstairs, neither." Mary thought for a moment. "There's the servants' cottages on the hill past the orchard, but they're barely fit for Belladonna. Won't she be pleased to have Victor back? Never would I have believed that a pig could pine."

"Those cottages will be fine. I cannot believe I did not consider how many rooms were available. I'm very sorry," Will said. "What an inconvenience I have been."

"There is plenty of room," Angelika told him, walking to clasp his shoulders. He did look ever so rattled. When Mary and Sarah had left the room, she unfolded Christopher's correspondence. She'd expected a date and time to visit Clara Hoggett but was confronted by a full-page letter. "Of course his handwriting is this neat," she said, reading.

"What does he say? That he was positively enchanted by you?" Will said, downing his tea with a vicious gulp. He turned in his chair, and Angelika stood between his boots, stroking through his hair as she read.

"He was a little enchanted . . ." Angelika felt her cheeks

heating again under Will's stare. "But I've received letters like this before. It doesn't mean anything." At the foot of the page was a postscript about their joint mission to visit Clara in her time of need. "We are going to visit the widow tomorrow." She folded the letter back up and pocketed it.

"I wish you wouldn't find it strange that men want to know you," Will said. He held up his hand in a silent request.

"They're sore? And cold. My goodness." As she massaged, unbending his curled fingers, noticing his winces and hard blinks, she wondered if he would still experience these tremors of jealousy and possession if another had not appeared on the scene.

A dreadful thought occurred to her. "You should be warned that if you fall in love with Lizzie, Victor will drain your life right back out of your body. And I might help him."

"I won't," Will replied with a glint in his eyes. "It wouldn't be possible."

"She's young and lovely, and so very funny." She heard the worry, so patently obvious, in her voice. Rub, rub—she put her heat into his hands, until he took them both back, testing his fingers.

Gently, he repeated: "I won't. Thank you. They feel better." He reached up and smoothed both hands down the sides of her body in a long stroke. It felt like: *I could never prefer another over you.* Her head knew otherwise. Then those same comforting hands gripped the trousers tight on her thighs, making her look at him. "You're not to fall in love with Commander Keatings."

"Not until you've fully explored your options and found your way back home. I'm sure that's what you mean." She strode from the room. "Oh," she said as a bell rang out a loud *ding* above their heads.

Will, close on her heels, flinched at the sound. "What was that?"

"It's Lizzie, I think. She's arriving early. Mary!"

"I heard," Mary called back from the kitchen. "Gracious. Never a dull moment 'round here. Another teacup, Sarah."

Will was still confused by the bell above the door.

"When Victor and I were children, we invented a way of knowing if a carriage crossed into our drive. Copper wiring, buried alongside the road, connected to a pressure plate with a spring under the gravel. You'll hear a sound from that." She gestured up to the brass bell above the door. "We did it over the summer when I was eight."

"Must have been quite a roll of wire."

"We dug a trench for weeks. It was so hot, we did it at night." She caught Will's gaze on her face—that admiring, astonished expression he had when he thought her clever—and gave him a self-conscious look. "I've been creating solutions for a long time. It's typical Angelika. Again, I'm sorry you were caught up in it."

"I'm standing here breathing, so I don't mind."

"Mary only hears it now when she is standing close by. Perhaps I could make her life a little easier and hang a red scarf from the bell, so she might see it flutter."

"That would be most thoughtful," Will praised her. "I like you best when you are like that. I'm pleased you offered to help Sarah with her education."

They went outside and watched as the carriage grew closer. As the horses rounded the bend, Lizzie hung out the window, waving madly. She was leaping out of the carriage before it had even properly stopped.

"Jelly! I couldn't wait, so we set off early and traveled all night—have you been expecting me? Vic said he'd send a bird."

Angelika caught her future sister-in-law in her arms. "It must have been flying only a quarter mile ahead of you. Victor is arriving home tomorrow. I'm so happy to see you."

"I thought I remembered you wrong," Lizzie said with fondness, cupping Angelika's chin in both hands. She glanced at Will to involve him. "As the carriage turned the last corner, I said to myself, *She doesn't really look like a fairy queen.* But here she is, her hair both red and gold at the same time, and big green eyes full of naughtiness, and this magical beauty mark on her cheek that the late Marie Antoinette herself would have died to possess." This, Lizzie kissed. "You understand of course, sir, she's wearing trousers so we don't see up her skirts when she flies off."

"That makes perfect sense," Will replied.

Lizzie was not finished making her theatrical address. "I thought my future sister-in-law was a daydream."

"Just a girl," Angelika said, her eyes filling with tears.

Lizzie was tender. "But yet, I still reach back to find your wings."

"So shall I," Will said. The spell utterly cast, they each took a turn rubbing a hand between Angelika's shoulder blades, while she stood, overcome with every lovely emotion. Rather than declaring her mortal, Will concluded, "She will show us her wings when she is ready."

Lizzie clapped. "So you are in fact good fun, my dear nameless, handsome man. Jolly good. We must make our own theater out here." She raised her sparkling brown eyes up to the house. "Blackthorne Manor," she said reverently. "At last. What a house."

It was time for Angelika to make the introductions. "Lady Elizabeth Lavenza, this is Sir William Black."

"How do you do, Lady Lavenza, or should I call you the duchess? I am Will." He bowed formally.

"Oh, goodness. If another man called me *Duchess*, I think Vic would take him apart. Better call me Lizzie. Or my various noms de plume. Or, very soon, Mrs. Frankenstein." The women giggled and clutched at each other's arms. "He's lovely. You finally met your match, Jelly, marooned out here, without telling me?" She cast another look over at Will, clearly approving. "Where did you dig up such a handsome bachelor on this hill?"

Angelika had to laugh as Will coughed. "Will is my very dear, special friend and guest, for as long as he wishes to stay. I shall fill you in when—"

"When we are alone, and you can explain in detail."

Lizzie appeared tired from her journey but was still beautiful to Angelika. She was tanned gold, with that famous onyx hair. She had mischievous dark eyes, and the blackest eyebrows, permanently lifted in a questioning arch. Her mother was Spanish, and she enhanced her looks with jewel-tone clothes and stained her lips red. Judging by the trunks labeled COSTUMES and PROPS, ETC., she had interesting plans.

Lizzie noticed Angelika's perusal, then sniffed at her own armpit. "Well? Will I pass your brother's inspection? Oh, I stink."

"He thinks you're divine. The only star in the sky, and he speaks of no one else. Please ask him to stop leaving apple cores on the stair rail."

Lizzie's smile was bright. "Shall do. Oh, look—she enters, stage right: a lovely big pig to greet me. Good day, madam, do you bring word from London?"

They all turned. Belladonna's beady eyes surveyed the black-haired woman, the luggage, and the girls' clasped hands. Her head began to lower. A front leg lifted.

"Come now, Lizzie," Angelika said, grabbing her arm. "Inside, quickly."

Once safely in the foyer, Lizzie ran her hand on the stair rail like she was introducing herself. "I love this house," she said.

"I'm sick of it," Angelika countered. How lovely it must be to move into your marital home. In the midst of such excitement, her anxiety was beginning to build. She was likely never going to pack her trunks to leave for her own house.

Victor was right. She was going to end up hurt.

Will took Angelika's hand, like he felt the shift in her mood. "Whatever happens tomorrow," he said, referring to the visit with Clara, "we will deal with it together. I promise, I will help you through. Just as you have helped me so much." With that, his cold hand released hers, and he went to assist with the luggage.

"What's that about?" Lizzie asked.

"I'll tell you everything later. Stay in my room tonight. Goodness, so many trunks," Angelika said as they linked arms. "It looks like you are moving in permanently."

"Well, now that you mention it," Lizzie said on a laugh, and they both fell into squeals of laughter, hugging each other, and in that moment Angelika thought that she probably could bear what the future would bring. There was much fuss and ado in the foyer, and even more when the bell above the door rang again.

"He's a day early?" Angelika shrieked, and dragged her fingers through Lizzie's hair to tidy it. "Couldn't he give her a single minute to bathe, and rest?"

"That's my bear," Lizzie replied, panicking, too. "Please, please. I need a bath. A wet flannel would be fine. I can't let him smell me this way."

"I bought you some apple-scented soap. A joke a year in the making."

"Jelly, it's the strangest thing," Lizzie said as they ran up the staircase. "I know it can't be true, and I'm probably imagining things again . . ."

Angelika was startled by her serious tone. "What is it?"

"I believe that pig did not like me."

CHAPTER TEN

Angelika's eyes opened in the darkness, and she lay completely still with her blankets pulled up to her chin. Everything was now silent, except for her own heartbeat and breath.

She had fallen asleep to Victor and Lizzie's distant mattress rhythm. It was like being lulled by the creaking of a ship that periodically hit stormy seas. Occasionally there were the cries of a woman drowning. Lizzie would certainly be walking unsteady across decks in the morning, and she had been sternly warned not to venture outside alone. She had taken the news of Belladonna as expected: she'd laughed her incredible husky laugh until tears had streamed down her face. *Am I the other woman? Oh, what a play this would be.*

Victor saw no point in waiting for matrimony. *I'll be damned if that spotty old corpse they call Father Porter influences what happens in my own bedchamber. We are human beings, doing what humans do. It is natural science! I plan on fucking Lizzie senseless tonight, should she be amenable.* After such a monologue—delivered at dinnertime, as Lizzie choked on her drink, then nodded—it was confirmed that a bedroom shuffle was not required. Victor's door slammed so hard that it would have been heard in the village.

When told he would retain his room, Will had paced around and stood in his own doorway, struggling to explain himself. In the end, he could not. All he knew was he did not like it.

In the darkness, Angelika ran her fingers across her quilt. It was embroidered with thousands of little stars. For the first time, she thought about that unknown person who had labored over something she liked but also barely noticed. They were probably paid a pittance. Her thoughts then turned to the new chambermaid, Sarah, sleeping in a very cold and uncomfortable room at the boardinghouse. Angelika had no idea of how to ration coal.

She turned over, plumped up her goose-down pillow, and wondered at the randomness of wealth. It was her luck to be asleep in this ornate room, and her maid Sarah's misfortune to have a gambling father. It was clear which woman worked harder, and who had the greater difficulties to overcome.

Will was another example of how, in an instant, everything could change. Angelika tried to imagine waking up tomorrow, with no name, belongings, home, wealth, or options. How would she survive? She'd have to work underneath a cantankerous old Mary in some grand house and would certainly be thrashed for her incompetence.

She was either dozing, or more awake than she'd ever been. The house hummed with a new energy. A quick succession of memories began: every time she thoughtlessly paid a lot of money for something unnecessary. Over and over in a loop, her hand dipped into her purse to buy figs, chestnuts, soap, tapestries, gloves, and garnets, and grapes, and geraniums, and garters, and grosgrain, and gold rings, and—

"Enough," she told herself out loud. "I will be mindful from this moment on."

The air had a peculiar tightness, and when she propped

herself up on her elbows, she thought she heard a sound, perhaps downstairs. In the dark, she whispered, "Something's happening in the house."

After donning her robe and slippers (and noticing the fine quality of each item), she went downstairs and saw Victor standing in the open doorway to their father's study. He was shirtless and holding a candelabra, and there was an iron fire poker leaning on the wall beside him.

Victor had a tattoo on his shoulder, a letter *L*, almost certainly for Lizzie. When had he gotten it? Didn't they tell each other everything? Angelika thought of her brother as reedy and slim, but she could see now that he was an adult man, his body the result of roughly ten thousand chin-ups in the laboratory.

Disgusting to admit it, but Lizzie must have been *very* impressed.

Angelika refocused on the iron poker. "Vic, don't be rash."

In a hushed voice, Victor replied, "Shhh. Look, it's Will."

He held up the candelabra and they could see Will at the shelves behind their father's desk. The already-cluttered room looked as if it had been messily searched. There were drawers pulled out of the bureau, and a crate overspilling papers on the floor.

Victor indicated the fire poker. "I came downstairs ready to dash a thief's brains in. I found him like this. I have been watching for ten minutes, at least."

Angelika's heart was beating uncomfortably. It looked very much like her beloved was a nighttime thief. "What is he doing? Why isn't he turning around?"

"He's sleepwalking. Is this common for him? Does he talk in his sleep?"

Angelika gave her brother a withering look. "I haven't had the good fortune to find out. Does Lizzie?"

Victor rolled his shoulders in a stretch. "Lizzie is rendered utterly speechless for the rest of her life. Look, he's really turning the room upside down."

"I'll get him—" Angelika started over, but her brother blocked her.

"If you stop him, you won't find out what he's doing. Use your head, Jelly. This is his subconscious mind at work. His true self."

Angelika leaned on the doorframe. "Mary has complained about messes in various rooms, but I thought she was exaggerating."

"Then an apology is owed." Victor's tone was dry. "Will asked me the other day when she will finish working for us. I honestly never thought about it. She is well beyond working age."

Angelika winced. "We are lucky to never consider how we will live, or survive, or afford anything. We will never have to work until we are Mary's age."

Victor was open-mouthed. "I have never heard you speak like that. Usually, you are just at me for more, with your hand outstretched."

"It's Will. He's opening my eyes, and he makes me want to be . . . better. I want him to be proud of me. And I want to be able to wake in the middle of the night and know I am as good as I can be." She tensed, expecting teasing.

Victor just nodded.

"I am the same with Lizzie. And when I find my own creation, and bring him safely home, I think I will have a chance at being my best self. I care less about Schneider now. That poor wretch, lost out there." He paused, wincing, trying to choose his words. "I am very proud of you, for starting to think this way, and I shall do the same. I think we lost our parents before we could learn the importance of economy."

"And charity. And community. Will's always thinking about others. What is he looking for in here now, I wonder? He knows I'll give him anything he wants."

Victor lifted the candelabra higher. "We cannot wake him suddenly. The shock could be too much for him." They watched Will pawing in a pile of papers.

Angelika said, "I have heard of a technique called mesmerism, in which we could attempt to speak to his sleeping mind. I would want his consent first, and it requires further research before we attempt it."

Victor did not have his sister's ethics. "Let us see if we can gain a clue. Will. I say, Will." There was no reply. "It is not his true name, so he does not reply. I say, my friend, what are you searching for in there?"

The siblings winced as Will roughly pulled out drawers from their father's desk. It took a lot of effort not to intervene.

"Do you need money?" Victor asked him.

"No," Will replied in a lifeless tone. Angelika let out a squeak and hid behind her brother. He looked as though he had risen from the morgue on his own accord.

Victor began guessing. "A map. Parchment to write on. A keepsake from your past. A musical instrument. A favorite book." Will looked up. Victor seized on his last suggestion. "You want a book. Tell me the author. We will have it, or I can get it."

Will turned to the bookshelf, then began touching the spines of books in almost total darkness. They tried for several more minutes to engage with him. Every question that Victor asked was met with an irritated headshake, indifference, or that same flat *no*. They could not ascertain his name, his age, his place of birth, or his favorite fruit.

"Maybe he is searching for his estate's ledger," Angelika suggested. "Or a certificate of ownership."

The candle was burning lower, and Victor hissed when the wax began dripping on his hand. Enough was enough.

"You can't find what you're looking for because it's too dark," Angelika told Will as she stepped into the room. This got his head turning back toward them, his search forgotten. Her insides thrilled at how he responded to her presence, drawn closer like a moth to a flame, his dark eyes on her.

Softly she asked, "My love, are you quite all right?"

Will replied, "I'm all right."

Victor nudged her. "Don't pretend you don't want to hear his secret thoughts about you. I'll ask him. Do you know my sister, Angelika?"

"I know her," Will replied.

"We've found his favorite topic," Victor said, and continued: "And what do you make of her? Do you think she is beautiful?"

Will nodded, a serious crease on his brow.

"Is she smart, and funny, and talented?"

"She is all of those things," Will said.

(Angelika huffed modestly, and also hoped this line of questioning would never end.)

Victor grinned wickedly at his sister. "And would you like to make her your wife?"

"I cannot," Will said.

"Why not?" Angelika asked, hurt. The certainty of her feelings could no longer be sidestepped, and she could confess it safely, knowing he might not remember in the morning. "I love you, Will. I'd marry you if you asked me." When he said nothing, she pressed: "Do you already have a wife?"

Will replied, "I cannot, and will not, ever marry you."

"I understand," Angelika said. It was all laid bare tonight; she was a vapid, wastrel heiress, inured to her own privilege, up to her ankles in rotting apples while the village starved. She was not good enough. Tears welled in her eyes.

He saw them and moved closer, perhaps seeking to apologize or comfort, but fell over the debris on the floor. When he got onto his hands and knees, they could see he was now awake and completely disoriented. "Where—where am I?"

"Calm yourself. You were sleepwalking," Victor told him. "And we are going to use this development to find out who you are. Here, take my hand, I'll help you up. Wait, Jelly, where are you going?"

Angelika managed to hold back her tears until she was upstairs. Below, she could hear a bewildered Will asking, "What did I do to her?" She couldn't bear the look on his face if she explained, so she ignored Will's knocking on her bedroom door until he gave up.

Angelika thought that perhaps she should give up, too.

CHAPTER ELEVEN

Clara Hoggett, the widow of the deceased military officer, was crippled by grief. She had been shocked to find Angelika and Commander Keatings on her doorstep, then burst into tears. Twice she had gone to fill a teakettle, and both times left it abandoned.

Commander Keatings—*Christopher*, as he insisted on being called—took one look at the fireplace and went outside to cut some wood.

In her cramped sitting room, Clara moved from each pile of clutter, apologizing profusely. "I received the commander's calling card, of course, but I cannot remember the days anymore." She bundled some children's clothing into her arms but could not figure out where to place them. "I do not know if it is day or night."

Angelika was alarmed at the woman's increasingly frantic motions. "Please, rest yourself. You do not have to tidy up. I don't care if your home is pristine." She retrieved the armful of laundry from the woman.

Angelika was grateful to have left Blackthorne Manor. The sleepwalking incident had driven a splinter into her heart, and it pricked every time Will looked at her.

What did I say to you last night?
You said enough.

Christopher reappeared, interrupting the bad memory, with cut logs stacked on his forearms. Once the fire was crackling bright, Angelika could not see a single crease on his coat. He understood her perusal and grinned. His nature was thankfully not starchy. He'd be unbearable otherwise.

Together, they coaxed Clara to sit in the chair by the fire and made tea for her.

"You're the first visitors in . . . well . . ." Clara didn't need to finish her sentence. It was very obvious she was without any support. "I'm just glad my boy is sleeping. Thank you so much," she repeated again as she leaned down to creak open the lid of the wicker basket they had earlier presented her with. "I have not had meat in an age." Judging by the kitchen larder, she had not had much of anything.

"Our hogs are kept in our apple orchard, and they eat the fallen apples. It gives the meat a marvelous flavor, and they live so happily." Angelika sat down onto a low stool. She began attempting to fold the laundry, something she did not have much experience with. These were such small, oddly shaped clothes. Christopher would be better suited to this task. She held up a tunic. "How old is your baby?"

"He is just turned one. Do you have children, Miss Frankenstein? Oh, goodness." Clara went red. It was the first color they'd seen in her face. "Of course you do not, an unmarried lady. I apologize. I'm so muddled."

Angelika grinned. "It's quite all right. I'm overdue for one, I do admit."

"You must get organized on that front. If I can assist in any way, do let me know," Christopher urged her with an easy smile. The mood of the room depended on how Angelika would respond.

"Shocking impertinence," Angelika replied, and they all laughed. Christopher lightened the spaces he occupied; it was a surprise to realize she could, too.

While Clara resumed her grateful review of her hamper, Angelika tried to think of how to bring up the topic of her dead husband without ruining the new cheerful tone.

"I should like to see your baby, if he wakes before we leave."

"I've no doubt he will." Clara grimaced. "We moved here and I do not know many people. I was so lucky to have a husband like my Henry. He always woke in the night when Edwin cried. Now . . ." The tears were back in her eyes.

"Tell me about Henry, if you can. It might help to talk about him." Angelika felt ashamed of her underhandedness and applied herself to folding the remaining clothes as perfectly as she could.

Christopher filled the pause as Clara wept. "He was a fine man—though I only just arrived, I could tell that much. Excellent officer, I'm told, and always quick to laugh. At my welcoming ball he had our whole table in stitches."

Clara was smiling now, even as she cried. "He was quick, for sure. The house always felt lively." She addressed Angelika, trying to think of how to describe him. "He was a fine dancer. He was a great marksman who always brought home a goose or pheasant for us. We ate well. He was the only one who could stop the baby crying, and he didn't think himself above doing the household chores normally reserved for a woman. We had a silly made-up song we sang together. He was my greatest help, and my best friend."

Angelika thought about Will. He was quick and dry, ready to assist with servants' tasks, and she could imagine him holding court at a table of amused diners. She scanned the room again for any paintings of Henry Hoggett. There was no locket at Clara's throat. "And was he a tall, imposing man? Or short and stocky? Fair or dark? I wish to picture him."

"Unusually handsome," Clara said with feeling. "His coloring was striking. Wouldn't you agree, Commander? I'm sure it's what you noticed first about him."

Christopher nodded. "A fine fellow in every possible way. The church service was a very fitting tribute, do you agree? Father Porter paid great homage to his accomplishments, and I feel I knew him well now."

A shadow crossed Clara's expression. "It was fine indeed."

Angelika replied without thinking: "But you do not mean that."

Clara looked up, surprised to have been so easily read. "I wasn't able to say goodbye to Henry in the way I'd hoped." She took a minute to gather herself before she continued. "I'd asked Father Porter for a quiet moment before the proceedings, but he would not allow the casket to be opened. I begged, and got quite upset." She licked her lips nervously. "He said I wouldn't want to see."

It sounded like Father Porter did not have a body in that coffin at all.

Beside her, Christopher shifted in his seat. "Perhaps he was right—" he began, but was cut off.

"He was wrong." Clara's eyes were blazing. "Now I have to imagine what my Henry had suffered, and believe me, my imagination is supplying things that have me awake at night. I would have seen for myself and known, and kissed his cheek one last time, if it were not for Father Porter."

Angelika had once grandly declared to Will that his wife had not loved him, because she had not tried to bring him back. But she knew now that she was deeply wrong to dismiss the depths of another's love.

She leaned forward and clasped Clara's hand. "I wouldn't have been so polite as you. I would have pushed him aside." She made a mental note to visit the church to find out what kind of body-selling scam the good father was involved in. Her part in the trade now made her feel ill.

"I was hardly polite," Clara admitted. "He accused me of being hysterical. I do not know if I am welcome back."

Christopher said, "I saw Henry after the accident, Clara. He looked like he was merely sleeping. Not a mark upon his face."

This comforted her significantly, and Clara patted Angelika's hand before releasing it. She was exhausted by her outburst. "Father Porter also promised to call on me, but has not. No one has, except you both."

Angelika's lip curled with dislike. "Unless you have a gold coin in your purse for their collection dish, you are soon forgotten and left to your grief. I know that firsthand."

Clara's bleary eyes refocused on Angelika. "I'm not sure why you have been so gracious, considering we have never met?"

It was a good question, and Angelika reflexively thought of Will. Not of his personal mystery, but the words he had said to her: *I have faith in you.*

"I realized that I should be doing more good in our village, as my mother did. And whilst a basket is barely anything, I thought I should try to make you feel like you are not alone. I have been struck by unexpected loss myself and have felt alone many years, living up on the hill. It isn't nice. I don't wish for anyone to feel that way." Angelika was surprised by how easily this speech came; more so that she meant every word. "If you have need of a new friend, I volunteer myself."

"I am grateful," Clara said through fresh tears. "I haven't a single soul."

"You do now."

Christopher was ashamed. "I'm sorry it has taken me this long to visit. And as I said, Clara, you are able to stay here as long as you need; we are in no rush."

This comment put a great deal of worry into Clara's eyes now, but they were interrupted by a high-pitched squeal and then some wailing. "He's awake." Clara's eyes were on the door. "I'll go fetch him. He's the absolute image of dear Henry. It will be like meeting his father, in a way."

Angelika pictured Will's beautiful dark eyes, the copper glints in his dark brown hair, and wondered—would he put his stamp upon his progeny? She felt sure he would, and she braced herself for the pain she felt looming.

Christopher took advantage of Clara's absence and turned to Angelika. "Would you like to attend the tavern with me for a glass before we ride homeward? I promise, it is quite respectable."

Angelika felt a flip of energy in her stomach when he looked into her eyes, even as she felt guilty at the memory of Will behind at home, anxiously awaiting the news. But she had always wanted to go to the tavern, and life didn't hold many chances for it. And frankly, if this baby was proof of Will's former life, she'd want to drink every bottle they had.

She had no sooner said, "I should like that," when the door opened and Clara came through, holding a tear-stained baby.

Without ceremony, she handed the baby to Angelika. "This is Edwin."

"Exactly like his father," Christopher remarked, his eyes crinkling as a stunned Angelika took the infant in her arms. "Even has the same bright red hair."

CHAPTER TWELVE

Angelika and Christopher rode back to Blackthorne Manor in the dark, and rather drunk.

"I'm highly suspicious of Father Porter," Angelika told Christopher with a slur in her voice. She held her loose reins by the buckle and had not offered much input to her mount, Percy, who thankfully knew the path home. "I wonder what secrets he is hiding."

As they had admired the baby's milky skin, carrot-red hair, and periwinkle-blue eyes, Angelika had found herself repeating a reflexive prayer of thanks. To whom, she wasn't sure. She was just grateful to the universe. Clara was not Will's wife, nor Edwin his child, and she had enjoyed a surprisingly lovely afternoon. It was a respite from the tensions in Blackthorne Manor. To atone for that, she planned on ordering a crate of vegetables and meat, to be delivered to Clara on Mondays.

And apples. She would send her a bag of apples a week, saving them from their fate.

Drinking in the tavern had softened the wound of knowing that Will, deep down, completely believed he would never wed her. But now, under the rising moon, she was rallying her troops, to borrow an expression from Christopher.

She spoke to herself firmly.

Regroup, Angelika. You will not win Will by drooping and crying. Give him time. Think of the miracles you have already witnessed! A marriage proposal is hardly out of the realm of possibility.

Christopher brought her back to their conversation. "Father Porter is a man of God." Then he grinned and pointed skyward. "His big secret is that he has no real employer at all."

She nodded her approval. Another atheist. "If my own dear father had not been so manipulated by the church, we would have ten times the estate we have now. They bled him slowly over many years. And when Mama—" She broke off, emotion choking her.

Christopher wanted to know. "She died when you were young?"

"When I was thirteen, and Victor was sixteen. Papa was to bring a doctor to the house, because she had scarlet fever. Father Porter convinced him to pray for my mother's soul instead. It did not work, of course, and Papa died of grief three months after her. There is nothing I despise more than a thief, and that is what I believe Father Porter is at heart. He stole that last chance to save her. And so that is why Victor and I do not attend on Sundays. We will not be taken for fools. Heathens and witches, yes. But not fools."

"I have heard that he will be replaced soon. Hopefully by somebody younger and more progressive in their thinking."

She snorted. "He was ancient when I was a child, so someone younger would not be difficult."

"I'm sorry that happened. To lose your father to grief is especially tragic." Christopher sounded like he was uncertain.

She shrugged. "It is part of the Frankenstein temperament. We are passionate people. When my beloved dies one day, I expect that I shall die, too." She rode in silence for a few minutes.

If Henry Hoggett's body had been sold to the morgue, as she deeply suspected, who else had the good father cashed in on? She would pull on this new thread for Will. "I've got to be a glutton for punishment," she said out loud.

Christopher's seat in the saddle had loosened considerably these last few miles, and Angelika thought she might be about to witness a rare crease upon his immaculate person. That must be why her eyes kept returning to him. It was an undeniable fact: he had wonderful thighs. Absolutely marvelous.

"Not much further now," she said. "I can go on alone from here."

"After the story you told me, about some oaf in your orchard, petting your hair? Not a chance." His attention was completely on her. This had been the case from the time they sat down in the tavern, and the first and second ale mugs became the third and fourth. She'd gradually revealed more of herself to him; the parts that she knew were most unattractive.

Her habit of wearing trousers? He'd grinned.

Her interest in science? He'd asked her if she knew anything about chemistry. They'd discussed the various ways gunpowder could be unreliable, and the scientific papers she had read on the subject.

Her past suitors? Her impression of the elderly Swiss count had him crying in laughter.

And this is why I'm on the shelf, she'd concluded.

Some men can't handle serious weaponry, Christopher had replied, and Angelika had no doubt he could. But as they turned through the manor gates and she guided Percy over the buried pressure plate to signal her approach home, new feelings began to rise up. She'd missed dinner and whilst Victor would be kissing Lizzie in a dark corner somewhere, Will was probably overwrought with nerves. He fretted over the recent disturbances in the village, and the types of people who came out after dusk.

She moved her horse's pace up. "I've probably caused a bother at home. I should have sent a message. I can go on from here."

"I'd like to meet your brother."

Angelika arched an eyebrow. "Reeking of ale, with your shirt untucked?" She cackled when he reacted with violence, searching himself in vain, and then gave her a dirty look. "Calm yourself. I would wager my entire dowry that you don't have a single horse hair on your trousers. Victor is a complete mess, you are forewarned."

"I've heard enough of Victor to know he's terribly informal, and I shall like him a lot. I may be tidy, but I don't require others to be."

Angelika thought with despair that Christopher was very, very, *very* handsome.

More than his outstanding personal presentation, he was fun, masculine, and had been warm to the barkeeper and kind to a beggar. He had an outdoorsy sun-kissed glow, nice teeth, and a smile that should make her pulse respond. He was technically ideal. Where had he been even a month ago? It suddenly felt absolutely imperative to guard and protect and fight for what she felt for Will, lest Christopher's thighs weaken her resolve.

"May I ask a somewhat personal question?" Christopher carefully touched the back of her hand with his riding crop to get her attention. "Why did you cry when you held Clara's baby?"

She asked his legs, "Did I?"

Gently: "You did."

Angelika's memory of the moment was being shocked that a baby could be so heavy. The child defied physics. He was like a wet sandbag on her forearm. Clara had shown her how to hold him, and as she and Christopher chatted by the fire—something about Clara's cottage and how much time was left—Angelika absented herself to stare into the baby's eyes for an age.

Life and possibility glowed in little Edwin. His skin was perfect and had a smell she liked. His sticky starfish hand pulled her hair. She found herself bobbing from one knee to the other, and when Clara proclaimed her a "natural," it deeply flattered her, and embarrassed her speechless.

Her hollow insides ached.

It was that thing that Victor was always banging on about: natural science. A lever had been pulled. It was time. There was nothing connected to Will, or her hopes for a future with him, in this memory—it was just the feel of her heavy red-headed friend in her arms.

She needed to answer Christopher now. "I'd never held a baby before." And she hadn't wanted to hand him back. In fact, she had already planned in her mind the tartan cloak she would have made as a gift for him, of the softest lambs-wool. Perhaps a matching Scottish bonnet, topped with a pom-pom—wouldn't that look sweet, set upon his head? Angelika thought about the endless outfits a baby would need for the ever-changing seasons, just extravagant spoiling, for years on end. The finest fabrics and the loveliest colors. Corduroy dungarees with a patch pocket on the chest, in russet tones for autumn—

Cutting into the daydream, Christopher asked, "Do you wish for your own child?"

Angelika contemplated kicking Percy into a gallop in lieu of a reply. But she found herself saying instead, "I think I've just realized that I should absolutely love one. But I've been a bit disorganized on that front," she reminded him.

But he did not smile, and confided in return, "I have long given up on starting a family. I am rotated to a new post every two years to train recruits. It's hard to find someone adventurous who would want to start over in a new town, possibly abroad, again and again. I'm told I am intimidatingly well-ironed, which people mistake for a lack of humor. Also, I am thirty-seven." He admitted his age as though he were an elderly man.

"You don't look too old to me."

"Neither do you."

They regarded each other with curiosity. Then Christopher's eyebrow raised and they both howled with inexplicable drunk laughter, causing the horses to shy. When they finally arrived at the front stairs of Blackthorne Manor, the first thing Angelika noticed was that the house had had a haircut.

"Something's been happening out here," she said, squinting at the visible porch railings. There were leaves on the ground and some sacks filled with greenery. "I think someone's been gardening." She felt conscious of the old house's appearance. "It was so grand, once upon a time. These days, it just looks miserable."

Christopher was charitable. "It looks grand to me."

"Not in daylight." It was a black brick gothic mansion, three stories, plus basement and attic. It had arched windows, and the thick glass panes shone iridescent, like soap bubbles. Now that the choke hold of ivy and creeping roses had been loosened, the gargoyles might be visible again.

"Must be twenty-five rooms, at least," Christopher said. He had been counting windows and doing his sums.

"And every one of them is stacked up to the ceiling in curios and inventions. Believe me when I say I barely have enough room to store a new hatbox. The barn to that side has been converted into Victor's laboratory. Stables, orchard, and so on." She waved in the direction of the dark. "The forest is the stuff of nightmares. Who has been working out here?" she asked herself again. "The ground is covered in petals."

The next odd thing happened when a teenage lad appeared from the side of the house and grasped her reins as she dismounted. "I'm your new stablehand, Jacob. How do you do, Miss Frankenstein?" His voice was thin from nerves.

She shook his hand firmly. "Hello. Who hired you?" Angelika could not imagine Victor being bothered. He usually left the horses free to roam.

"Sir Black did. Is this Percy?" The lad produced a carrot from his pocket. He barely spared Angelika another glance.

She laughed at his eagerness to be acquainted with his charge. "Yes, this is Percy. He is purebred Arabian. He was brought here from Persia by ship as a colt."

As she said it, she heard it: the casual brag, and the privilege she had. Poor Percy; how frightening the journey must have been. He had suffered in order to be a birthday gift for a spoiled girl? She was wicked. She ran a hand down the animal's gleaming neck to say, *I'm sorry, so sorry.* "I have had him half my life, and he is precious to me. You must be kind to him. I'm sure you'll do a fine job."

"He's a good match for Solomon; they both have the same white blaze. Sir Black's horse," Jacob prompted when she looked blank.

"Will finally named his horse," Angelika said, beaming. "Please make his stable a nameplate."

"I surely will. Sir, I'll take him." He led away the two

horses, tying Christopher's nearby. As he walked off into the darkness, Jacob called out, "And, miss? I'm terribly sorry. For what I did." He was gone before she could question him.

"Has he already made a blunder?" Angelika pulled off her gloves. "More staff popping up around here. Probably a good thing."

"Who is Sir Black? An uncle or cousin to impress?" Christopher examined his cuff. "Never fear, I shall attempt it."

"He is my brother's colleague," Angelika said as the front door opened. "Ah, here he is now."

Will stepped out to join them, and the two men faced each other.

It was like comparing daylight to darkness. Christopher was a bright, blond sunny day; a creaseless sheet on a washing line. But Angelika had always been drawn to the calm, cool, and stars. She liked lightning strikes, and the tawny patterns in owl feathers. The intimacy of what she had done with Will—how she had created him and watched his first breath—could not be matched by any other.

The shock of the two men's juxtaposition blended into a new concern: this was a huge risk for Will to take if he had indeed originated from the military academy. But a bland silence followed.

"How do you do? I am Commander Christopher Keatings."

"Will Black. I am well, thank you. Very late to come home, Angelika." Will spoke like a chiding husband—a role he seemed to take on whenever it suited him. "You are not dressed well enough for the cold."

She would usually luxuriate in his concern, but it was not done for her benefit. "I'm not a child. Hiring stablehands for me, are you? And a groundskeeper?" She ran a hand over the tamed honeysuckle.

Will's stare intensified. "I live here, so I see where the household shortcomings are. You also have a cook starting tomorrow."

Christopher raised his eyebrow. "Hiring staff is a wifely duty."

Will did not take the bait. "All I want is for Angelika to live comfortably." The unspoken end to that sentence was *when I am gone.*

She bristled. "I've always been comfortable."

Will continued answering Christopher. "We don't rely on rank, and we all contribute. Men and women do things quite equally here."

"How modern," Christopher managed. The air between the men was now tense. "What exactly is your acquaintanceship, Angelika?" It was obvious to Christopher that the *brother's colleague* label did not fit. When she dithered on a reply, and Will offered nothing, Christopher decided to sidestep the foot soldier and appeal to the general. "I should like to meet your brother."

Before she could answer, a female voice above them said, "And to think, I'd been worried about the lack of theater in the countryside."

They all looked up to see Victor and Lizzie both hanging out an open window. He was shirtless, and Lizzie appeared to be wearing bedsheets.

Victor bit into his apple, and said with his mouth full, "So you're the commander. Jelly has been very coy about you. Handsome blighter," he added as an aside to Lizzie. "Bloody hell, not a hair out of place, and meanwhile, Jelly looks like she's waltzed through a hedge."

"Shut up," Angelika cursed him. "Lizzie, do I?"

"You look ethereal," Lizzie assured her. "Moonlight becomes you ever so much."

"You are truly lovely," Christopher confirmed.

Will crossed his arms, his face tight with displeasure.

"Hedge," Victor said again.

Christopher bowed to him. "Lord Frankenstein, it's a pleasure to make your acquaintance. I am Commander Christopher Keatings." Meeting a flushed undressed couple, one floor up, did not faze him. "And good evening to you, madam."

"Hello, I'm Lizzie. Almost-Duchess Lizzie Frankenstein." This earned her a ravenous love bite on her shoulder, and her husky laugh rang out across the gardens.

Christopher persevered. "I have escorted Angelika home safely. We were enjoying ourselves too much, and afternoon tea became supper."

"He'd like it to turn into breakfast." Lizzie's whispered quip carried beautifully in the night air. "Oh, invite him in, Bear. Let's all play cards." Then she whispered something, and Victor whispered back. Then they started kissing.

Angelika huffed at how socially inconsiderate they were. "Did you find that man you were searching for, Vic?"

"I didn't go out today," Victor said, after tearing himself away. He did look suitably chagrined. "I was . . . busy."

"Well, it looks like rain, so well done. He'll be wet and cold."

"Perhaps I could be of assistance," Christopher offered, glancing between the siblings. "Who is it you are looking for?"

Victor hesitated, and then appeared to make a decision. "Come for dinner, Chris, so we can get to know you. We could use some entertainment. Here, Belladonna." He dropped his apple core into the garden below, which prompted a great deal of rustling and grunting, but Christopher did not blink.

Victor said, "I shall send an invitation to you shortly."

"I should be delighted," Christopher said, but his eyes were on Will. "I'd enjoy the chance to get to know you all much better."

CHAPTER THIRTEEN

Shortly after Christopher's exit, Will had stalked off into the dark, telling Angelika only: "Don't."

An afternoon spent drinking had loosened the cork on her emotions, and she desperately needed an ear, but Victor's bedroom door was closed. Angelika knocked and called softly, "Lizzie?"

"Fuck off, Jelly!" Victor yelled breathlessly from within. "I am showing Lizzie something very, very, very important."

"Disgusting," Angelika replied, then cried at various points of the hallway: slumped on the railing, at the top of the stairs, then underneath her mother's portrait. Receiving absolutely no sympathy there, she slithered snail-like on her trail of salt water to rest against Will's doorjamb.

The thought of Lizzie becoming mistress of Blackthorne Manor did not specifically bother Angelika. She had no great affection for this house and had spent too much time in it. But Larkspur Lodge was like a forgotten sapphire in a drawer, and the prospect of losing it, even to someone she loved, pricked at her heart.

She thought: *Please, Lizzie, if I could have anything, it would be Larkspur.*

After more cathartic tears and a cold soapy rinse of her more urgent areas, and once she'd picked the numerous leaves out of her hair (Victor had been right as usual; how terrible), she remembered she was on Will Watch tonight. Given that he was now prone to walking all over the house and his penchant for books, she had earlier volunteered to sleep downstairs in the library.

"He will avoid me, even in sleep," she said to herself, dressing in one of her mother's silk gowns, plus a robe and slippers. "Poor Angelika, sleeping on the lumpy chaise," she grumbled as she went downstairs, dragging a blanket and pillow. "Poor Angelika, after the day I've had—"

She was startled by a dark shadow at the foot of the stairs.

"Oh, it's you," she said when she recognized the silhouette.

"It is I, your brother's colleague. Did I hear you correctly just now? Poor Angelika?" Will's tone was plain: he thought her ridiculous. She passed without a word, the blanket sweeping across his feet like a bridal veil.

He followed. "Poor Angelika? Don't make me laugh."

"You've finally come to ask me if you are a married man. I'm amazed you've restrained yourself this much." She went into the library and began to make her bed. "Well, go on, then. Ask me if you have a wife called Clara."

Will closed the door, then added fuel to the dying fire. "That's not at the top of the list."

Angelika sat on the chaise and crossed her legs. "Ask your burning question, then."

He turned his face to her. "How do you expect me to sit through a dinner with him looking at you like that?"

For the first time, Angelika felt afraid of him. She had no idea who he really was, and right now, he had fire in his black eyes. His hair curled into horns. He was demonic, and it was a further contrast to Christopher's angelic blondness. But he had the gall to ask her this, when he was actively trying to return to his original life?

"Victor hates formal affairs. Knowing him, we'll end up eating sausages in the garden, sitting on apple crates." The next reflexive thought surprised her: *What would Christopher make of that?*

Will read her mind, and his stare was blade sharp. "Poor Angelika. The woman who always has a ready replacement."

"Poor old Will, lounging around in a manor house. You don't even care how I might be feeling today after what I've uncovered."

He put a hand into his hair, raked it into a more civilized shape, and turned on her. "Yes. Poor Will, or whoever I am. Dragged back from hell to have to sit through a dinner and watch you be slowly seduced by that flawless man."

"I will make your excuses."

"Imagine how I've felt as the day wore on and you did not return. But you've had a fine afternoon, haven't you? I could hear you screeching with laughter long before your arrival. Christopher Keatings must be a funny fellow."

"He is." (And she'd drunk a lot.) "Come and kiss me until you do not feel angry anymore."

"Believe me, it is my first impulse. You're fortunate I didn't pick you up over my shoulder off the front stairs. But I didn't want to give you the satisfaction." Will braced a forearm on the mantel and stared into the fire. "When I heard you laughing in the distance, my first thought was that you had not met my wife today."

"So, what actually happened was—"

He continued, speaking over her. "Then a new thought occurred. After confirming she is my wife, you had a half hour of hurt feelings. Then you decided to move on with your next option."

"I will tell you everything. Clara Hoggett is—"

Again, he stopped her. "Just let me be yours awhile longer."

The anger blew out of the room like smoke, leaving them both in tired silence.

When she'd found him on the morgue slab, he'd still had fight in his brown eyes. When she'd dragged him naked up the staircase, he'd declared that he might be dying but still had that stubborn tightness in his jaw. Tonight, staring into the fire, he looked utterly defeated. Unbreathing, and unblinking.

Perhaps, in this one moment, he could not face a life without her?

"You're still mine." She watched him absorb her meaning. "Is that good news, or bad?"

"Good news. I should feel terrible for admitting it." He sat down heavily beside her on the chaise. "Angelika, I am at my limit tonight. My head aches. My hands ache. My heart feels even worse."

"Lie down," Angelika urged him, and after some coaxing, he did, with his head on her lap. She combed her hands through his dark hair, admiring the coppery glints, thinking that if she could have moments like this, she would be happy to never see daylight again.

"Is Clara all right?" Will asked.

"No, Clara isn't all right. But I will send her a crate of groceries each week, and her fat little baby Edwin has found himself a new benefactress. You should see his red hair. I've mentally designed an entire wardrobe for him." She reached for his hand, and he submitted to her tender rubbing of his fingers.

"You do get a lot of pleasure from spoiling people rotten. I should know. He's a lucky baby." The first hint of a smile touched his mouth. "I like when you spend your money on good things. Was this your first time visiting a villager? How was it?"

"I felt like a marginally better person. And now we know you aren't from the military academy, unless Christopher didn't meet you. But don't despair, I've got a new angle for us to follow, and it involves the church."

He glared up from her lap. "I never imagined you'd start actively searching for my origin. Would you like me to leave this house now, or in the morning?"

"Oh, stop these sulking theatrics. You know full well that if I had my way, you'd never leave my bedroom." She felt relief when he smiled again. "You're just overtired, my love. What have you been doing today?"

"I've been keeping myself busy."

She inspected his hand closer. "You've got some scratches." His skin was still so cool. She mentally added a new pair of goatskin gloves to her shopping list. "What has kept you so occupied?"

"I worked in the garden all day. Don't look so outraged. Today has been a sort of epiphany. I think I worked outdoors in my old life. I knew how to prune roses and move a beehive. I mixed a paraffin spray for aphids without even thinking of it. I'm hiring some local boys to help get this place under control. Who knows, someone may even recognize me. I have been making discreet inquiries as best I can."

"But you do not need to earn your place here. You're not my groundskeeper." She pressed kisses upon the damage to his hand. "You're my special one. Please do not hurt yourself." She tilted his hand toward the firelight and noticed two dots on either end of the wound, done with her brother's purple ink. "What did he do this for?"

"You notice everything." Will was irritated, and he took his hand back from her. "He's measuring the wound and the healing rate. Your brother has ordered that special new microscope, by the way. I am no longer a man, just a science experiment."

Angelika winced. "I'm sorry this is happening to you."

"Better than dead, I suppose. The sleepwalking is something new to worry about. Some mornings, I wake with dirt on my feet. What am I searching for?" He asked this of himself. "No wonder I'm so tired."

"I think you are searching for a book. That's why I am sleeping in here tonight. Please don't walk off and get lost." Angelika was alarmed at the thought. "Should I tie you to my bedpost?"

"It was only a matter of time until you suggested that," he replied, with a glance that flipped her heart clean over. When they made eye contact, each thought about the sheer possibilities of a few lengths of silk cord. Then, he sobered. "I've asked him to swear to keep anything to do with his studies of me confidential from you."

She scowled up at the ceiling, in the direction of her brother's bedroom. "I thought we'd just established that you're mine."

"Being of scientific interest to him is difficult enough. But to you? I couldn't tolerate it." He sighed, long and deep. "And yes, I am yours. For one more night, at least."

She searched his face for signs of illness. He looked very tired. "Are you unwell?"

"I am fine. Promise me, Angelika, that you will never look in Victor's files."

The way he repeated it made her nod, though it hurt to be left out. "I can't read his shorthand. He deliberately made it Jelly-proof. But even if I could, I would allow you your privacy. I know you haven't had much."

She traced her thumb down his throat and had a vivid flashback: asking Victor his opinion on the best way to reconnect these pounding arteries. They'd argued, insulted each other, roared with laughter, and she'd gotten on with it. It hit her anew. This breathing, blinking person was a miracle. This feeling of awe and appreciation was so overwhelming, all she could do to express it was to cup his cheek in her hand.

But he was looking up from her lap like he understood completely.

"You look beautiful today."

"Did you miss having me around the house?" She grinned when he huffed in exasperation and sat up. "You actually noticed my absence and wished to gaze upon my beautiful face. Pray, tell me exactly how lonely and jealous you were. Did the minutes drip by like treacle?"

"You are prone to overexcitement." He was gruff but smiling as she put a knee over his lap and sat on him. Inches apart, they regarded each other as the fire crackled and the world faded away. His expression grew serious again as he ran his thumb down her jawline. "I cannot imagine ever preferring another face to yours."

"I feel the same."

"Please know that you are more than beauty. You're . . . energy."

It was the best compliment Angelika had ever received. Her eyes filled with tears and her throat closed up, preventing any reply.

He continued.

"I watched from the window as you rode up to the door. You tipped this perfect face up to the moon and I'd never seen you as happy as that moment. You were free of the worry and sadness that you feel whenever you are with me. And yes, I am hiring people for you and trying to address some maintenance issues of this old house so that you can live easy. This is all I can do for you, and you should let me."

"Before you leave?" When she blinked, tears overflowed. She knew the answer.

"Before I find out what my next chapter is." He tilted his head, watching the tears run down her face. "Believe me, Angelika, I wish the rest of my story could be written with you."

In spite of the tears on her cheeks, she replied flippantly. "I'm sure there's enough projects at Larkspur Lodge to occupy you for the next fifty years. It has a very overgrown rose garden, riddled with thorns, but there are some rare varieties. It needs someone hardworking." Hope flared when she saw that the prospect tempted him.

"I thought it was Lizzie's wedding gift," Will reminded her.

"I was trying to play our make-believe game. The place in our imagination where we can be together, forever."

She tried unsuccessfully for a kiss.

He wiped her tears with his thumb.

"Did Christopher tell you about his life?" When she nodded yes, he continued: "His childhood? A few terrifically funny things that have happened around the academy? What he likes and is good at? How many times he presses his shirt in the morning?" Will put his mouth on her throat. She anticipated a bite, but only gentleness followed.

"Yes, he told me all sorts of things. But I only thought of you." Guilt pinched; several times this afternoon, she had only thought of herself.

In between kisses on her pulse, Will finished: "He is everything I want to be: A single, independent man of good standing. An uncomplicated being who knows himself. He is a good match for you, and he intends to find out all about me at this dinner."

"Tell him to mind his own business. More," she begged, and she felt his mouth smile on her skin.

"I will not have a single answer to any of the questions he will ask me. He will be inquiring with colleagues and acquaintances, attempting to find out who this mysterious stranger is at Blackthorne Manor. I will be gossiped about and closer to being exposed. I may have to leave quickly. You will need to prepare yourself for any possibility."

"We'll cancel it. I don't know why Victor is planning this."

"He's doing this to push me toward a decision," Will said, shifting her off his lap. He laid Angelika down on the chaise and tucked the blanket around her. "Maybe I can endure the dinner, remembering that you look at me like this."

She bit her lip. "Yes."

"And you want me like this." His thumb brushed her bottom lip, and she opened her mouth. She managed one taste of his skin, just one scrape and lick, before he retreated with a groan in his throat.

As he turned to leave, she said, "Your self-control is what I like least about you."

"I don't know how I have any left." He switched to a different topic as he leaned on the closed door. "What did I say to you, the night I was in your father's study? I know it was something so terrible, even Victor won't tell me. I wish to apologize for it."

"You told me you will never ever marry me. That is what you believe, to the very core of your being. And I am beginning to think I should listen to you. But please know this. You are my perfect match. Every inch and every stitch. Trust me, I made sure of it."

He looked like he wasn't sure if he should laugh or cry.

"I suppose you did. Good night, Angelika."

CHAPTER FOURTEEN

S o, please tell me if I understand this Will situation cor- rectly," Lizzie said as she lay on a blanket on the grass beside Angelika. "Well, not the part regarding where he came from. Vic has promised not to create any new love interests for you until the situation is resolved."

Angelika glared. "He took full credit for Will? Typical."

It was a warm afternoon, and both women were barefoot in their muslin underdresses. Even prim, proper Will had stripped down to his sleeveless cotton undervest long before they had set up their afternoon-tea picnic, and the heavy muscle definition in his arms had caused both ladies to squeak and giggle in unison.

Now the sweat was running down his body, the vest dark and clinging.

"Even better than I remembered," Angelika said, her voice garbled with desire.

"He's been working hard," Lizzie said, her tone deliberately bland, but she had eyes and was looking, too. Then she swiv- eled her head, scanning. "Are you sure Belladonna won't bite my nose off?"

Angelika patted the broom she had brought along. "I shall protect you."

Will was halfway through hacking away the ivy that had taken hold of the side of the house. In the background, a few local boys he'd hired were cutting, pruning, digging, and burning. There was even someone on a ladder, painting the window casings. From another open window, one of the new chambermaids was beating dust from a rug. From this exact spot, lying on the cut grass, Angelika could see the shape of the house reemerging, and it struck her as a kind of reclaimed dignity for the old building.

It also made her miss her parents.

"What's this old book?" Lizzie asked, picking up the leather-bound book that Angelika had brought outside. She read the spine. "*Institutiones Rei Herbariae* by Tournefort. Oh. It's botany." She gave the pages a cursory flip to admire the illustrations of blooms, buds, and pods.

"It's a present for Will. I'm taking a guess that it's what he's been searching for when he walks in his sleep. This is his passion." Angelika took it back before Lizzie could read her inscription.

> *To my love: One day I will write your true name here.*
> *With all that I am,*
> *I am always,*
> *your Angelika.*

Will bent down to gather vines from the ground, but when he straightened he put a hand on the wall, the greenery dropping back down. His shoulders were rising and falling on deep breaths.

"Are you all right?" Angelika called, but he shook his head in irritation and ignored her. "He looks like he's about to faint."

Lizzie nudged her back to the conversation. "I know Will

was your work, because Vic can't do what you do. You're more clever than you realize. Promise me if Belladonna trips me on the staircase and breaks my neck, you'll bring me back, too."

Will was still bent over and struggling in some way. Angelika laid the book aside and debated getting to her feet.

"There is a risk of total memory loss, be warned. You'd have to fall in love with Vic all over again. Maybe you'll choose someone more normal next time around."

Lizzie sniggered. "I doubt it. I could tell you things about your brother that would scar you. He is utterly . . ." She searched for an appropriate word for an uncomfortably long time, settling on: "Inventive."

"I beg you, please, do not ever, ever elaborate. I don't know how you bear to kiss his apple breath."

Angelika was lying on her stomach, propped up on her elbows. She was glad of Lizzie's company, which only seemed possible when Victor was riding his horse in the forest, searching for his creation. And even then, Lizzie just wanted to drone on and on about her brother. People in love were tedious.

She watched Will resume work. Her chest was still tight from fright; was he often feeling dizzy? "What else has Vic told you about Will?"

"I can see for myself that he is very handsome. Oh, don't get those sharp eyes with me." Lizzie exhaled heavily on her new diamond ring and polished it on her neckline. It was apparently a frequent impulse. "Are you sure you don't mind me having this?" She'd been awkward since Victor mentioned that the ring had previously resided in Angelika's jewelry box.

"Quite sure."

"Because I can give it back." Even as Lizzie said that, her hand curled into a fist. It would be cut from her cold dead finger.

To Angelika, that ring looked like a lump of glass. She had no idea why Lizzie loved it so. "Since the moment he met you, it's always been yours. It looked hideous on me, and perfect on you." She smiled as Lizzie leaned against her in silent thanks. Larkspur Lodge flashed behind her eyes when she blinked. "Back to the topic. Will is desperately handsome, and perfectly endowed. I made sure of it."

Lizzie snorted. "He thinks you are rather beautiful, and he's right. You glow with a new magic, fairy queen. I have never seen you look so well." She rubbed a hand between Angelika's shoulder blades. "The gardening lads think so, too."

Angelika reapplied herself to shredding dandelions into sour-smelling piles of yellow. "Yes, he does find me fair, but he doesn't remember any other women. I am his current and only favorite."

Lizzie kept going. "You are of marrying age."

"Maybe too old."

"You're not. When he kisses you, you feel like pulling his clothes off." Lizzie tossed a dandelion in Angelika's face.

"Definitely yes."

Lizzie revealed her point: "And you are spending your time attempting to find his wife. I don't understand it. He should be crawling on hands and knees to win you." She raised her voice on this last part, and Will's head turned. "Good, he should listen," Lizzie grumbled, putting her forearm across her eyes.

Angelika bristled with protectiveness. "Leave him be."

"I hate seeing you this way, Jelly. You are in your old pattern of falling in love with men who will never notice or return it. Don't think I've forgotten that ancient bookbinder."

Angelika screeched, "You swore we'd never speak of it!"

A boy up a ladder dropped his paint tin.

Lizzie continued. "Will is a handsome, polite man, but I

don't see any fire in his heart. You need someone who will fight to the death for you, and I'm sorry, my dear, but I think that person will be Commander Keatings."

"It was *your* idea to invite him to our grand dinner." It was confirmed when Lizzie's lip curled. "You wench. Mary's having conniptions over it. Sarah is polishing all the silver, looking like she could cry."

Angelika dropped down to lie flat on her stomach and closed her eyes, feeling the warm sun on her back and the wool blanket on her cheek. "It's not going to be grand, though, is it, with Victor running the show. It's going to be odd, and Christopher will know we are . . . odd."

Lizzie sounded thoughtful. "You care what he thinks. He must be the first suitor you've had that you did."

"Christopher is not my suitor. Will is."

"So, if I am understanding you right, Commander Keatings is the first gorgeous man in your entire life you didn't fall in love with at first sight? He is the exception. Isn't that interesting? If I were Will, I would be very worried."

Angelika sniffed. "He doesn't have to worry about a thing."

Lizzie kept pushing. "I want you to know what it feels like to be desperately wanted. That is what love is, Jelly. Knowing that he will fight for you—and I do not see Will fighting. Do you know what Vic would do if another handsome man was sniffing around my skirts at a dinner?"

Angelika considered the question. "He'd most likely break his own hand in a fistfight, and then I wouldn't see the pair of you for two days."

Lizzie's dark eyes flared with energy. "Three days. I don't see that passion in Will. I see him calmly trimming overgrown ivy and being polite at breakfast."

"All love is different." Angelika could still feel the squeeze of his hand on her waist and the indecent rock of the carriage. "He doesn't kiss in a polite way."

"Why should he even get to kiss you?"

"His situation is complicated. I revived someone with no memory but very high morals and ethics. Anyhow, is this how engaged ladies occupy their time these days? Entertaining themselves with their friends' affairs?"

Her temper was hidden cleverly in this little jibe. Will burned for her; she knew he did.

Lizzie said, "I want us to be married at the same time, then waddle around with matching stomachs. This time next year, we could have our babies lying out here with us, and we could learn how to be mothers together. Believe me, Vic is hard at work on that project." She exhaled strangely and grew flushed. "I wish I could tell someone about what goes on between us. It's too much to keep to oneself."

"Please be quiet."

"Everything is such a theatrical production. Oh, and his muscles. His. *Muscles.* He took off his shirt, and I could not speak for ten minutes. He's absolutely—"

"Please don't confide," Angelika said with her hands over her ears. "Tell the pig, not me."

"But you're my best friend." Lizzie was frustrated, and scowled in Will's direction. "Can he even have children? Or were his nice big bits dead for too long?"

That was a question that kept Angelika up at night as she found herself stroking her pillowcase. Silk was soft . . . but not as soft as a baby's cheek. Even if Will did give her such a gift, the child would not have its father's beautiful amber eyes. Absolute sadness hollowed her out, and she knew she deserved it.

"We have no idea if it's possible. I hadn't thought that far ahead."

Lizzie leaned back on her elbows, closing her eyes to the sun. "If Commander Keatings fully applies himself to courting you, I want you to let him try. Remain open to that option. You'd have a herd of neat blond boys in no time. Imagine their nursery. The little blighters would keep it spick-and-span."

Angelika imagined it. Then she pictured a quieter child, with messy hair, and an affinity for plants.

"I think you forget who you are, Jelly. You're the most eligible young woman in this county. Men should be fighting over you." A shadow fell across them both. Lizzie said in a different voice, "Oh, how very sweet."

Angelika rolled onto her back to see Will, hot and sweating, standing over her with loose flowers in his hand. Some still trailed roots and dirt. She was touched that he understood her so well, and was gratified to have Lizzie as a witness.

"Did you almost faint before?" When he said nothing, she prompted, "I will always prefer wildflowers over hothouse roses. Oh! I have a gift for you in return." She held up the book to him, and he took it and read the spine with a dawning recognition in his eyes.

"I think . . . I know this book," Will said, looking disturbed, holding the now-forgotten flowers tighter. With some difficulty, he opened the cover and flipped straight to the illustrations. He read out loud as he turned pages, "Momordica . . . Pomme de Merveille . . . Xylon . . . Coton . . . I know these drawings."

"Jelly, you clever little thing," Lizzie praised her. "I have to say, you are the world's best gift giver. I need more of that apple soap; it drives Vic wild."

"Hmm," Angelika hummed noncommittally, glum that Will hadn't noticed her heartfelt inscription.

Will looked up from the page. "Yes, this is a book I have owned, I am certain of it. I can read this."

"French and Latin. Excellent." Lizzie beamed. "We are narrowing down your background, and you are undoubtedly educated. Perhaps you were a botanist. Is it exciting to star in this mystery role?" She picked up her notebook and began to jot. "A play about someone with no memory. Intriguing. Do I have your permission to be inspired?"

"If you think of an appropriate end for my character, please advise me." Will closed his book like he was reluctant to stop reading, and to Angelika he said, "Thank you so much."

"You're so very welcome. Anything and everything you could ever want, I will give you." Angelika really wanted her flowers now. "Are they for me?"

He appeared to be greatly embarrassed, glancing to Lizzie. He had overheard her earlier words. "They are not a fitting return gift."

Angelika frowned. "They are from you, so of course they are."

"They're not mine to gift. They belong to you, like everything here." Ignoring her outstretched hand, he laid them on the blanket beside her, in the same way one might put flowers on a grave. He was gone before another word was said.

"Poor man," Lizzie said with empathy. "He tried his best."

Angelika gathered up her flowers. "He picked each one thinking of me. Can't you see that is something that cannot be bought? All I ever wanted was someone who thinks only of me and will let me spoil him. I was right about the book. I think he can rest easier now."

As she sorted the blooms into a bouquet, she noticed there were dozens of rich purple larkspurs. She wondered if his subconscious knew it, or if it was a sign from the cosmos.

It was time to do something scary.

"Lizzie, I want to talk to you about something important to

me. Something that probably belongs to you now." Lizzie was already clutching her ring in fear. Angelika rushed to clarify, "Larkspur Lodge."

"I don't know where that is," Lizzie said, perplexed. "I haven't heard of it."

"It is our lake house, six hours by coach. It is terribly overgrown and unloved and has been sitting out there alone with only a caretaker for many years. I can relate to it very well," she added, trying for humor. She didn't quite succeed. "I am possibly destroying a very large surprise, and I do apologize."

"A surprise?"

"When you are married, it will be your gift that you can rightfully accept, but I want you to know that I love it desperately, and it is the only place where I think I can decide what to do with the rest of my life. Becoming a scientist is Victor's ambition. I want to use my talent," she explained haltingly, "for something that is mine."

Lizzie patted her notebook, titled *IDEAS FOR PLAYS*. "When you find your role, the rest of your life will fall into place. I promise you."

"I don't like to ask for anything, but if you should decide that six hours is so very far away—"

"You wish to have Larkspur." Lizzie clasped her hand on Angelika's. "I will talk to Victor. It would be my honor to see that gift go to you. But in exchange, I wish for you to be open to being courted, by either man. Let them compete. And think of what meaningful occupation you will take up in your new home. That is our deal. Promise me."

With larkspurs in her hands, Angelika found herself saying, "I promise."

CHAPTER FIFTEEN

Angelika knew her brother very well, because as soon as their dinner guests finished eating dessert, Victor threw down his napkin and said: "Let's go outside. My colleagues have told me there is a high chance of star showers tonight. It is too dull to sit indoors like our fathers did. Ladies, too. Get your cloak, Lizzie." At the doorway, he hollered, "Mary! I say, Mary!"

"Already bringing it," Mary said with a bottle of liquor under each arm and a tray of crystal tumblers. She knew Victor well, too.

"I shall light a bonfire," Victor told the small assembly. "I have some Chinese firecrackers, too, and a huge piece of cheese. We shall make up ghost stories and have a laugh."

As they all pushed back their chairs, Angelika watched Christopher. If he found this outdoor sojourn odd, he didn't show it—except for a flicker in his eyes that might have been frustration. He had probably been counting on adjourning for brandy as an opportunity to corner and cross-examine Will.

Angelika watched Christopher, and Will watched Angelika.

The entire evening had been both pleasant and tense.

Christopher had arrived early with an enormous bouquet

of flawless hothouse roses that Angelika had dutifully admired for approximately one second before looking back to the carriage, where her other dinner guest, Clara Hoggett, was emerging, with a very important package.

"Give him here," Angelika had begged, arms up, and the bouquet was completely forgotten in favor of the baby. Luckily, Christopher had laughed good-naturedly, saying, "She's mad over this little chap."

Will leaned against the porch in shadow and did not initially come over to admire Edwin. When pressed to do so, he had offered a tense half smile and let the tot hold on to his finger. The heart-stopping, womb-squeezing moment was merely an illusion, but Angelika snatched it and sewed it into a momentary reality, one where she was also a good person.

Inviting Clara had not been an act of kindness, but one of selfishness.

Angelika forgot everyone in the room except Edwin, She talked only to him, in cooing nonsensical prattle. She had sat with him on her lap for the entire first course, kissing his head while he played with her spoon and her soup went cold. The smell of his flossy hair was a drug stronger than opium. He was heavy and humid, and she loved him to distraction. At some point, he'd started to sob, and Clara took him away to change him and let him nap in his basket in the drawing room. Angelika had almost cried herself.

When she blinked herself out of this haze to be fully present for the first time, she noticed that things were not going as she had planned. For example:

She had arranged the seating to keep Will and Christopher apart; but someone (Lizzie) had switched them to be sitting opposite each other like chess opponents, with Angelika between them at the head of the table. Christopher had taken on

the burden of keeping conversation running and had repeatedly tried to engage Will in various topics, but his answers
were short.

Christopher: "What county did you grow up in, Sir Black?"

Will: "I shouldn't think you'd know it."

Christopher: "And your parents? Are they still with us?"

Will: "Both passed, sadly."

Christopher: "The roast beef not to your liking?"

Will: "I do not eat meat."

Christopher: "Any particular reason?"

Will: "It smells like death."

Clara had been quiet and deferential, staring around the
enormous dining room with worried eyes, and she tried to cover
as much of her threadbare dress as possible with her napkin.

Lizzie and Victor had drunk too much. They frequently
dropped their voices to a whisper, then broke into dirty
chuckles. Victor was distracted by Lizzie's low neckline, and
she knew it. He never finished a sentence, and twice left his
seat to look out the window because he thought he'd seen bats.

The Frankensteins were not good hosts. But it was not too
late to turn things around.

Now, as they all put on warm clothing to go outside, Clara
approached Angelika. "Thank you so much again for inviting
me. And thank you again for your kind deliveries. The ham
is as delicious as you said, and your apples are the best I've
ever had."

"Think nothing of it, but I hope you aren't leaving just
yet?" Angelika replied. "Thank you for loaning me your lus-
cious little baby. He's very quiet, no? I might just quickly look
in on him."

Mary said in the foreboding tone of a jailor, "Sarah's sitting
with him now. Attend to your guests, Miss Frankenstein."

Clara smiled. "It was nice to give my arms a rest. As you know, he's frightfully heavy. And it was a nice diversion to dress up and enjoy a lovely meal. I feel almost like my old self tonight. It reminded me of when Henry was here; we always went to balls and dinners. Your house is very grand." Clara smiled up at Christopher as he stepped forward to help her tug her cloak around her shoulders. "It makes the homes for let I have seen seem very shabby indeed."

Angelika was perplexed. "But why are you looking at new homes? Your cottage is very snug, and I'm sure Edwin likes everything just so."

Clara smiled, but she was sad. "My cottage belongs to the academy. Commander Keatings has been most patient. And he was also very kind to collect me in his carriage."

"It was my pleasure," Christopher replied. "Come, shall we see what adventures await outside?" Gallantly, he offered Clara his arm. Holding those muscles would be another fine treat for her tonight. He added, "I do hope it will not be too cold for you, ladies."

Behind Angelika, Will said in a dry tone, "Victor builds his fires too large. I think you shall be overwarm in minutes."

"That's true," Angelika agreed, surprised that Will had noticed this trait. "You know him like a brother, I think."

As Christopher and Clara walked outside, Angelika noticed they looked quite fine together. It prompted a hot, quick emotion that she did not have time to examine because Will was wrapping her velvet capelet around her shoulders.

"My thanks," Angelika said absently, watching Clara's face turn up to Christopher's as they stepped out into the night. Even in her mourning grief, Clara would have to notice he was exceptionally handsome. Angelika itched to follow but remained in the frame of Will's arms as he tied the ribbon at her throat. The scratches on his hands were not yet healed, she noticed.

The garden now looked marvelous, and the house was shining like a black button, but at what cost?

She asked him, "How are you feeling lately? Any more dizziness?" Mary was gone, and they were alone now in the dark hall.

With a heroically small amount of censure, Will replied, "I am finding talking about myself very dull."

She turned to him and smoothed the lapels of his beautifully tailored coat. "I'm sorry I left you to fend for yourself."

He frowned in the direction of the courtyard. "You don't need to fend for me. But I would have at least expected some help from Victor in managing the conversation." His tawny eyes were wry when he looked back at her. "It's clear what came over you. Fat, tufty hair, rather whiffy at one point—does that assist your recollection?"

Angelika winced. "I wish I had a mysterious temperament."

Will sighed heavily. "Your commander is presently testing a theory that I am a fortune hunter, here to drain you dry. I'm out of ways to deflect." Now he was slowly, gently pressing her flat against the wall and lifting her chin with his palm.

She said on an exhale, "He is not *my* commander."

"I should hope not. And you are not his." Will considered her face, but instead of the kiss she was anticipating, he said, "It is a shame that he does not know the truth about me."

"Why?"

"He thinks you merely beautiful, and rich, and unmarried. He doesn't even know your full intellect and capabilities and what you have achieved. I am the proof."

"That's kind," Angelika began, but his lips moving on her earlobe stole her breath.

"And he definitely doesn't know what your mouth tastes like, or how you look up to your neck in bathwater. He doesn't know how your breath catches in your throat when you're about to come apart, and how easily you can."

Now he bit down on her earlobe, and reality melted.

Her only thoughts were fantasies of him: the angle of Will's thighs as she knelt between them, her reflection in the shine of his leather boot, his knuckles against her nape, his hands deep underneath her bedcovers, touching between her legs.

This hold on her ear was a reminder, and a warning: *Do not notice other men when you know what I can do for you.* The gentle bite he held her with now was soothed by the touch of his tongue, and when he released her, she let out a gasp that echoed around them.

"He doesn't know you like that, does he?"

Now Will put his mouth on her throat, and every kiss on her pulse wrought more gasps, though she tried to quiet herself. She felt him inhaling deep, greedy for the scent of her body.

The doorway to the courtyard was open, and she could see a long, neat shadow.

She managed, "Only you know me."

Will kissed her lips now, quick and desperate. His mouth opened hers, and they were pulling at each other's shoulders. Slip of tongue, edge of tooth. His erection pressed into her stomach, and it reminded her body of how empty it was.

When they broke off their kiss, Will said, "I feel sorry for him. He'll never know you like I do. *Never.*"

"But he wishes to." She captured Will's chin in her hand, like he had done to her. She maintained her bravery when she saw the dangerous jealousy in his eyes. "I made a promise to Lizzie. For my entire life, I've loved men who do not love me back. You give me such dazzling compliments that you must believe me to be worthy of admiration. So, I will allow it. You and Christopher must compete. If you do not wish to, then do not."

Will was taken aback. "I am to compete with a successful man who knows everything about himself? Whilst simultaneously trying to find my old life? It is absolutely unfair. And as each minute passes, you notice his eligibility and are slipping away from me, just as I am from you."

"I'm not slipping away," Angelika said, puzzled. "You have significant advantages over him, as you have just outlined. I already love you. And you have a choice in whether to participate."

Will appeared to be shocked. "You—love me?"

"Of course." She watched the emotion in his eyes change. "I thought I was supremely transparent. You've told me that I am, several times. I loved you the moment I saw you."

"I love you, too."

"For how long? Forever? Just nod," she urged. "Just lie to me."

"For as long as I can."

"The real you may never come back. Have you had any memories?"

He did not answer that. "You have no idea what it costs my pride when I think of what I lack, and how he is superior to me." Will swallowed, and his entire aura dimmed. His next words seemed to slice and stick all the way up his throat. "I have talked to Victor at length. We cannot guarantee that I will be able to have children. There is no precedent. And I know that is what you want, more than anything in the world. Don't deny it," he said when she opened her mouth. "It is obvious, and you do not need to be ashamed. You are ready for that, and I am a catastrophically large risk for you to take."

She stroked his jaw. "You are not a risk. You're my love."

He blew out a breath. "I seem to be talking myself into thinking Christopher is your better choice. If you had attended that welcome ball for him, what might have happened?"

"I would likely have taken a sunlit path, that much is true. But you found me first."

Will was amused. "You found me dead."

"Then we each had perfect timing. I am beginning to see that each person has multiple paths, with choices and cross-roads. And for you, I will take this dark forest path. You once told me something, after you had seen both the bad and the good in me. I will tell you the same now, and I want you to listen, because it's important."

He prepared himself. "Tell me."

"I have faith in you." She kissed his cheek and slipped out of his hands.

A strange, cozy scene had formed outside. A huge bonfire was blazing, licking the stars above. Chairs with cushions and lap blankets were placed around it. Clara and Lizzie were seated and talking. Victor was holding a bitten apple in his mouth and was struggling to break a large branch over his knee.

"Trust Victor to casually ignite an inferno." Angelika shook her head at her brother. "That's enough, I think."

"I'd best not sit too close to the orchard," Victor said after swallowing his mouthful. "You never know who might come forth to touch my hair, which is even more irresistible than yours, Jelly." The party only heard his joke, but Angelika knew he was deeply rattled by the incident.

Christopher was waiting for Angelika like a groom at an altar. She walked to him and before he could speak, she asked at full volume in front of everybody, "Are you intending on courting me?"

"Yes," Christopher replied, steady and unflustered. "But I wanted to give your brother the courtesy of that conversation first."

"Kwertesy," Victor repeated scornfully with his mouth full of apple again, grunting with effort as the branch broke at last and he threw it into the fire. Bite, chew; he decided it was too sour and pelted the apple into the darkness. "It is only Angelika's opinion that matters. But fine, I'll play old-fashioned brother. I shall ask you three questions."

Christopher nodded. "Please do."

"Make them count, Vic," Lizzie urged him with a saucy grin. Clara was either delighted or disturbed.

Victor held up one finger. "Are you a good, God-fearing Christian man?"

Christopher would not fall for this trap. "No."

Victor was surprised, and he had not prepared a follow-up question. He thought for a moment. Two fingers went up. "Are you a gambler or a thief?"

"No."

He held up three fingers with a grin, and Angelika knew they were in for trouble. "Are you especially talented in the bedchamber? I ask that as a favor to Jelly."

Christopher answered him without so much as a smile. "Yes."

Victor doubled over laughing.

Angelika's stomach did a strange thing, even as she looked for Will. He stood in the shadowed doorway of the manor with his arms crossed. Angelika thought he turned to leave, and she could understand why he would. But when she blinked, he was walking over. She thought she saw him forming a fist. He wasn't. This firelight was playing with her vision. Energy was radiating from him like a thundercloud.

"Sit down, Jelly," Lizzie said. "You look a bit peaky."

Victor held out his hand like a deal was struck. "All right, Chris. You may feel free to court her. I hope you do not live to regret that decision. Now, she's cantankerous, especially on an empty stomach."

"You make this sound like a horse sale," Angelika protested as they shook hands.

"I am not your average man," Christopher said, without any boast in his tone. "I am ready for the challenge of an exceptional woman."

"Well, I'll say she is. She's a temperamental little mare," Victor continued, "but if you gain her respect, she'll try her heart out for you."

"Wait," Will said, and everyone's laughter died. "I want to say something. I do believe you have noticed my evasiveness tonight, Commander."

Christopher nodded. "I have."

What Will said next surprised them all. "I am not Victor's colleague. If we sit down, I will explain everything."

CHAPTER SIXTEEN

W hat are you doing?" Angelika hissed at Will as they moved to the bonfire.

"It's the only way," he replied. When everyone was sitting and leaning forward in their seats, Will began what sounded like a ghost story.

"It was about one month ago that Victor and Angelika were out riding at night and they found me on the roadside. I was beaten and wearing not a stitch of clothing. Everything I might have had was gone. They brought me back here, and when I woke up, I had absolutely no memory. Angelika's was the first face I saw." His expression softened with affection as he looked to her. "She was telling me her name was Angelika, and I was at Blackthorne Manor. I was quite rude to her."

She laughed. "He was, it's true."

"How utterly frightful," Clara said to him with alarm. "My goodness. Have you recovered?"

"I have, but I don't have my memory. And I need to know who I am."

"What do you know about yourself so far?" Christopher asked without so much as a blink of surprise. Adaptability was an attractive trait in a man.

As he cut a wedge of cheese, Victor replied, "He's educated, can read and write, with good manners and a fine mind. Good teeth. No pox scars. Knows Latin. He can navigate by the stars, and I'd wager he could tell you the botanical name of every plant in this courtyard. He can ride better than I and load a pistol. I believe him to be a gentleman of excellent standing."

Christopher plainly did not like this assessment. "Right."

Will noticed, and continued his explanation. "The Frankensteins have been doing everything in their power to help me find out where I came from, and they have given me the very shirt on my back. But I think we need your help, Commander."

Christopher's expression gave nothing away. "What do you imagine I could do?"

"You have resources that would be invaluable to my search. You can discreetly speak with magistrates, the night watch, military men, the church."

"We have tried to investigate to the best of our ability," Angelika agreed. "But it isn't enough."

"That's why you first visited my office," Christopher said slowly, turning to her. "You asked me if there had been an accident. Surely you know we would not leave an injured officer behind, and not on a forest road. Is this why you made my acquaintance? You could have just asked me directly in that first meeting, and I would have done all I could."

"I know that now," Angelika said quietly. "But it was confidential, and strange, and I didn't know you then. Please don't feel that I have used you."

She could see that he did.

"I would like to know the exact date and location. I will visit it tomorrow." Christopher's voice had changed, and now he was every inch a military commander. "Was there a coach overturned? Any debris, any signs of a scuffle?"

"Not a thing. Just Will, lying there looking very much naked and dead." Victor coughed after a pause. "We did locate a ring with possibly a family crest on his person, but it has since gone missing."

Will explained, "We have followed what leads we could, but so far we have not been able to find any promising local events of violence."

"You haven't tried hard. The village is overrun," Christopher exclaimed in disbelief. "There's dozens of places you could have come from. This village is placed upon a trade route, and the inn is where horses are changed and travelers stay overnight. There have been merchants robbed at knifepoint, a group of tramps set up camp in a ravine near the high road south, a horse-stealing ring that has spread to the neighboring five counties—"

"Already, you are proving you can help us," Lizzie said, producing her notebook and a shard of lead. "I will begin writing these down. We are all part of this investigation now, and we must all swear to never tell a soul. We are now a secret society."

Clara exclaimed with a smile, "How utterly exciting." Then she went red and amended, stammering, "Except it is a t-terrible circumstance."

"It's all right, it is exciting," Angelika told her.

Victor said sagely, "I am already in three secret societies. It's not as interesting as you would think."

Christopher gestured in the direction of the academy. "On my desk, right this moment, I have a bulletin of missing persons and criminals wanted. I don't completely understand why you would risk that possible outcome. Why not just continue living here?"

Will replied to him, "I am living in luxury that is unearned. I sleep in the room opposite Angelika's bedroom, but I could be anybody—a thief, a scoundrel, a murderer—and it disturbs me. Until I find out if I am even worthy to be in her presence, or if I am free to court her, we are at an impasse."

Christopher was caught on one detail. "You sleep opposite her bedroom?"

"You mentioned you are not a gambling man," Victor pointed out to Christopher. "But I think you would take this bet. What are the odds that a man of this age, appearance, education, and apparent good breeding is unmarried? The ring we found was on the wedded finger."

Christopher stared at his handsome rival. "May I be forthright?" Will gave a nod. "I believe there is a possibility you are lying to these generous people. You have not lost your memory, but instead you are here to milk what fortune you can out of this situation. I have known swindlers in my time, even handsome and well-bred."

"That's not it," Victor said. "I absolutely guarantee that is not the case."

Christopher was unwilling to accept this. "You cannot know for certain."

"If that were the case, I would already be married to Angelika, and I would be presently draining the accounts dry, with her enthusiastic blessing," Will said gravely.

He left a long pause for her to issue any type of denial. The flames crackled and Angelika cringed under everyone's stare. She had been so brazen.

Then Will continued. "It is something I worry about. The way the Frankensteins trust so openheartedly? It terrifies me. What if I am a low-born criminal, someone cruel, someone who would indeed take advantage of kindness?"

"You are not," Angelika said. "You are the best of men."

Christopher heard her tenderness and straightened his spine. Two flyaway hairs on his head floated like insect antennae, illuminated by the torch at the back door. It was as close to disheveled as she'd ever seen him. "I am to understand that I am at a significant disadvantage in this scenario."

Will laughed at that. "I said that to Angelika merely moments ago, but about myself. You are at a great advantage, Commander. You know who you are."

"But Angelika knows you. You are around all the time, and she is clearly fond of you." Christopher made a decision. "If I assist you back to your old life, and your existing family commitments—"

Will finished: "I will be content knowing that Angelika will be able to move forward with her life, her reputation untainted, and she can be wed to a man of high status." The pain in Will's voice was evident to the group. "I would not ask her to marry me, even if it were what she wanted."

"I, apparently, have no input into this matter," Angelika said dryly. "The horse sale has become an auction."

Lizzie gave her a warning look, and mouthed, *Larkspur.*

"This is natural science," Victor informed the group. "In nature, the males compete for the female. Here we have two fine peacocks, posturing for the plain brown peahen."

"I was a horse and now a peahen? I hate you with all my heart," Angelika told Victor. He threw a piece of cheese at her in response. She ate it.

Victor continued. "I will tell you a well-kept secret about myself, Chris. I am not a formal, snobbish type of person." The group let out an identical guffaw. "If Will is revealed to be a street sweeper, but he proposes to my sister and she accepts, I will not stand in their way. It is Jelly's choice."

Christopher replied, "All I ask is that I am considered fairly. I want to get to know you, Angelika. I feel we have an interesting attraction. Do you deny it?"

The fire crackled more.

"You are allowed to confess it," Will told her. "I will not be angry."

Angelika took a deep breath, hating herself for this betrayal. But the truth was required.

"I do not deny it. Christopher, you are dreadfully handsome. I like your liquor cabinet selections, and you are a laugh. Since the second I met you, I have ached to scrunch up a handful of your perfect shirt in my fist."

Christopher's eyes gleamed in the firelight, and a new kind of energy passed between them. "I would not object. And how I wish we had met at the ball."

Angelika decided to be brazen once more. "But I will be clear on one point: I prefer Will. He is the one who has my heart."

"You prefer a nameless man," Christopher pointed out. "I am willing to wait until all is revealed to see what your final choice is. I do believe I am still a good option."

"That's all we've ever wanted for Jelly. For her to have a choice." Lizzie was writing in her official secret society notebook. "I undertake to be a neutral umpire in the courting of the fairy queen."

"I would put everything I have into this," Christopher threatened Will. "None of you know this, but I am a renowned hunter. There is nothing and no one I cannot find: foxes, stags, missing horses, or absconding officers. I have found everything I've ever hunted for. The very first thing I will need is a likeness of Will."

"I think I could help with that," Clara blurted out, surprising the group. "I'm—I'm rather good at . . ." They all leaned forward. She finished weakly: "Drawing."

"Excellent," Lizzie praised her. "Come back and we shall have Will sit for a portrait. Do you use charcoal, lead, or oils? We shall get what you prefer."

"I haven't used anything in a long time," Clara replied, worry returning to her features. "Perhaps I am not as good as I was. Someone else would be better."

"Nonsense," Angelika encouraged her firmly. "You can do it. Could you possibly have a better sitting model than Will?" She saw Clara's eyes flick back to Christopher. It was clear which man she'd prefer to commit to posterity. "Bring Edwin, of course. We will send the coach for you."

"I think we have a deal," Will said, but he was addressing Angelika when he asked, "Are you also in agreement?"

All eyes turned to her. She hesitated. Then, she firmed her resolve. Did they all think her so easily swayed? She would love Will no matter his past. Was he a thief or a trickster who would take advantage of them? If he were, she could reform him. If Will turned out to be a beggar, she would have him. If he were a gutter drunk, a shyster, a wealthy snob, a lowly pauper, she would have him.

"Well?" Will prompted.

The idea of a baby was the only thing to give her pause.

"It is the way for this uncertainty to end, my love," Will said to her softly, as if they were alone. "I am suffering. I cannot rest. I have nothing to offer you. This is the only way to guarantee that you know what your options are, and to end my torment."

Angelika nodded. "I agree. And I demand absolute confidentiality from this entire group. Christopher, do you promise to guard Will's secret with your life?" He nodded gravely. "And, Will, do you promise me that you will tell me the moment your memory returns?" He also nodded. "Then I agree."

Lizzie and Clara applauded.

"My deal with you has a caveat," Christopher cut in, addressing Will. "You are out of this house. You can have full board and lodging at the barracks. It is more proper." His meaning was clear as he glanced at Angelika.

Will offered no resistance and pointed in the direction of the orchard. "I am aware that the house is at capacity. I have already been clearing out one of the servants' cottages up on the hill. I think it will suit me very well."

"It's all settled," Victor said, slapping his hands together so loudly they all jumped. "What a host I am. This is a dinner for the record books."

"How so?" Lizzie inquired with a laugh as he pulled her onto his lap.

"Jelly has one and a half suitors. Will shall soon reintroduce himself to us. Chris has the look of a bloodhound. Clara is a secret artist. You have founded a secret society. I am a genius. When I find my proof . . ." Victor lost a little of his swagger and looked out at the dark fields surrounding them. He then seemed to shake himself. "Let's set off the crackers to celebrate." He lifted his voice and roared, "I say, Mary—"

"Already bringing 'em," Mary said from the doorway, holding a wooden crate. "But these will wake the baby."

"Oh, what a shame," Angelika said with patent relish, and everyone laughed, except Will.

He hung back as they all tipped their faces to the sky, dazzled by the starbursts. Angelika turned around to exclaim to Will, but he was gone, replaced by the silhouette of a sow, skulking along the wall.

"You'll miss it." Christopher put his hand on her lower back, facing her forward. His fingertips pressed so warm and firm, she felt a pop-fizz of utter splendor right down to her bones.

She could not deny it.

CHAPTER SEVENTEEN

Blackthorne Manor was dead quiet.

"Hello?" Angelika called, walking through the house. "Where is everybody?"

It had been almost a week since the night of the secret-society formation under the stars, and as always, Victor was right. Being in a secret society was not very exciting. Nor was being courted by two competing men. She hadn't seen Christopher since that night, and Will was occupied fixing up his new cottage.

"Angelika Frankenstein, the woman who managed to secure two suitors, only to never see them again," she said out loud to the portrait of her mother. "Mama, I think they both have forgotten about me."

Caroline didn't appear to care.

Desperate for some conversation, Angelika went to Victor's bedroom, where the door stood open. The poor bed was crooked from the wall. It was a good thing he was giving Lizzie a break from his ardent natural science activities; unless they were somewhere else. Lizzie would surely be with child soon. Angelika felt a terrified pulse run through her whenever she thought of that. She was being left behind.

Wouldn't it be nice to be so passionately occupied herself, in a lake house as the roses bloomed? What worried her was this: in her nightly erotic dreams, the face of the man changed without her permission.

Angelika halted at the window and watched as Jacob worked Percy on a long lead in a circle, trotting him over ground poles. The animal gleamed, and his ears were pricked forward.

"Everybody is occupied today, even my horse. What would I do with my time if I lived completely alone?" Angelika asked herself out loud. "What would I do if I could do anything?"

Her new awareness of her various privileges told her this: she was already at that decision point. She did not have any strong urge to go out to the laboratory. But she did remember her mother's fabric and trimmings in the trunk at the foot of her bed.

"Perhaps I will try making Edwin something new to wear," she decided aloud. It felt like a good, cheery thing to do, and she went off with a new purpose, to find a sharp pair of scissors. "I could pay the tailor to give me lessons to refresh my skills. I could embroider my own quilt."

Technically, Will was the last project she had worked on, and his comment about *mindless needlepoint* did echo in her mind, but he was whitewashing the walls of his new address; was his pastime any better? He was pulling away rapidly and had seemed so eager to leave the manor house he'd practically run away. She'd resisted the urge to visit him at least fifty times.

She repeated her mantra aloud now:

"Let him make the effort. I must have an invitation."

The search for scissors brought her to her father's study, where she found Sarah, diligently completing her hour of required reading and writing. She sat knock-kneed on a small stool in a dim corner, with a book on her lap and a slate abandoned by her foot. She flinched when Angelika's shadow fell across the page.

"Hello," Angelika said to her. "How are your studies?" She didn't need to wait for Sarah's reply. The girl looked wretched. "Don't sit slumped on this stool. Come, sit at the desk. Show me what you are working on." She wrote out the alphabet, and they read and wrote for an hour.

Angelika felt a corresponding glow in her chest as Sarah worked, and how with each passing minute the girl was growing in confidence to speak and engage. Doing good things for people felt marvelous. Wouldn't it be a fine thing for Will to walk in during a study session to witness this good deed? He usually only witnessed her dismal failures. She remembered the boardinghouse.

"I could buy you a bag of coal if you like. How much is it?" Angelika patted herself for coins.

"I am warm from my walk back in the evenings; it is no matter."

Angelika regularly saw Sarah at bedtime and lighting the fires at dawn. She pictured ravines full of bad men. "And how far is this walk?"

This interrogation was causing Sarah to grow increasingly uncomfortable. "I am not complaining." She got to her feet and backed around the desk. "Mistress, please do not think I am unsuited. I can work harder. My parents need me to work."

"That's not what I am leading toward. I am very happy with you." Angelika could have kicked herself for her carelessness. Sarah was her responsibility now, as long as she was mistress of Blackthorne Manor. "Where's Mary?"

"She had another one of her turns. But don't say anything, please. I must go help with lunch." Sarah rushed out of the room, turning in the direction of the kitchen.

"Someone has made that girl skittish, and I think I know who." Angelika scowled and began the long trudge upstairs. And trudge she did. By the time she took her last step into the servants' quarters in the attic of Blackthorne Manor, she was short of breath and wheezed for an embarrassingly long time against the stair rail with her heart drumming in her ears.

"And to think—Mary makes this trip, every day." Once she could breathe again and the beads of sweat were wiped from her brow, Angelika felt composed enough to discuss Sarah's living arrangements. She just had to muster some courage.

She had probably ventured up here once as a child, but was brutally chastised by Mary. She could feel the gusts of wind through the dark slate roof. One leap of excitement and Mary would crack her head clean through.

There was only one door, painted a dark maroon, with a silver horseshoe nailed to it. Angelika knocked meekly. There was no answer. One knew instinctively not to go into a sleeping bear's den, and it took courage to push the door open a crack. The scent of wet wool was released.

"Mary," Angelika said. "I must speak with you." There was still no answer. "Are you ill?" She pushed the door open wide and stood there, completely astonished by what she saw.

Mary's tiny home was how Angelika imagined a mouse might live. Every wall surface was decorated with . . . scraps. The old woman had apparently kept every offcut of fabric, discarded garment, pretty soap paper, or decorated parchment. Similar colors were overlaid and grouped together in a pleasing harmony, and in the dim light from the one dormer window Angelika could appreciate the artistry applied.

"A lifetime of Frankenstein refuse has been repurposed," Angelika marveled quietly. Had she ever thought to buy her a gift during her trips to Paris? The old woman would have been in raptures over a few yards of silk, or gold fringing. "This is something we have in common. I, too, am passionate about fine fabrics." She ventured in further, but could not stand at full height. "Is this why her back is so bent?"

A dish of glass marbles was glowing on the windowsill, beneath a drying row of ancient undergarments that Angelika would not see fit to wipe Belladonna's face with. Doll making must have been her hobby, because she had a row of simple creations made of wooden clothespins, each with a little gown and a painted face that made Angelika smile.

There was no sound or movement deeper within the room. Fearing what she might find, she stepped closer to a pair of curtains and peeked through.

Mary was lying on her back, mouth open wide and skin sagging over her skull, and Angelika's heart almost leapt out of her throat. But then she made a crackling inhale, and everything was all right again.

"Mary," Angelika said, sitting gingerly on the edge of the low bed. "Mary, it's me."

The old woman jolted awake. Confusion gave way to slow recognition in her watery blue eyes, and a fearsome scowl spread across her face. This was a monumental intrusion, and Angelika's inner child was screeching at her to run for her life.

Mary asked, "What time is it?"

"Just lie back. You are unwell?" Angelika shook her head when Mary attempted to rise. "No. Stay still, I order you. You have had a turn?"

Mary sank down against her pillow, expression mutinous. "Who told you that?"

"I guessed. What type of turn, and how often do you have them?"

"That's my business, missy."

The two women stared at each other.

Seeking to calm her, Angelika said, "Sarah and the cook have lunch in hand, and besides, everybody is busy. There may be no one to serve today."

Giving in to the urge to retreat, Angelika tied back the bedroom curtains and went to the window. She bent low beneath a holey gusset to peer outside. "I can see Will's house from here." It was the first in a row of five stone structures. She could even make out a cheerful wisp of smoke rising from his chimney. "Perhaps I should come up here to spy on him."

A grand, optimistic idea struck her now: when she accepted his eventual marriage proposal, Will could give his cottage to Sarah. She turned to Mary to suggest it, but the old woman had a hard look on her face.

"I have not seen either of my suitors in an age. Maybe they've changed their minds," Angelika joked with a half smile, expecting her to agree. But Mary just lay with her hands folded on her stomach, regarding her with an inscrutable expression. "I wasn't sure what to expect," Angelika said, polishing Mary's window with her sleeve. "But I thought being courted would involve more romance."

Silence. Perhaps turning the conversation back to Mary would be better.

"How old were you when you met your own husband, William?" She picked up a peg doll and waggled it at Mary. "This is rather sweet."

"Was there a reason for your visit, beyond idiotic chitchat? If not, I want you out." The old woman crackled with anger now. "What makes you think you can just walk in here?"

Angelika had to swallow down a retort that might go something like *This is my house.* Some of that sentiment was admittedly in her tone when she replied, "Yes, as a matter of fact, there was something I wanted to discuss with you. It's plain that you're no longer able to keep up as you once did." She waved an arm at Mary's supine body. "If you are having health troubles, it is time to let the new staff take over."

Mary said incredulously, "What?"

"It is ridiculous to hear that you are having turns and feeling so unwell." They weren't friends, but surely it wasn't something Angelika should have to find out about from another servant. "I'm saying we must discuss how much longer you will be working in your current role."

Mary echoed, "How much longer?"

"And I wanted to discuss Sarah's living arrangements, but seeing as you're in a foul mood, that can be separate."

"I've worked here since before you were born."

"I can see that," Angelika said, looking around. She was about to think of how to tempt Mary into considering retirement—more time for doll making and looking at this view?—when Mary rolled off the bed in an incredibly nimble movement and folded Angelika's arm behind her back to hustle her out.

"Ouch," Angelika cried out.

"I started working for your grandfather," Mary hissed. "I watched your father meet your mother and marry her. I saw Victor being born, then you crying the house down for years. I've kept every secret, when I could have had you taken away in irons."

"You're hurting me!"

"And now you come up to my private quarters, touching my personal things, to tell me I am no longer required?"

Angelika protested with her cheek on the doorframe, "I didn't say that. Things will be changing, that is all, and we don't need you for the difficult work. Lizzie will be mistress soon, and Will has seen to it that we almost have a full staff again. I thought you'd be pleased to hang up your duster and sleep past the rooster crow. You know we will compensate you generously for your years of service."

Mary ignored that and instead asked, "Who will be head housekeeper?"

"You're already training Sarah." If everyone accepted the girl's meek shyness and allowed her to grow in confidence, she could see no reason why it shouldn't work out. With a noise of utter contempt, Mary pushed Angelika out.

"I always knew you were heartless, Angelika Frankenstein. Good riddance. And by the way"—she pointed a finger in her face—"I pray for the poor soul who marries you."

The door was slammed, and Angelika was left stunned on the landing, rubbing her burning wrist and rotating her shoulder.

She probably did sound like a fleeing child as she took the stairs. She'd certainly had this kind of red, tight, upset feeling before, and she'd clutched a doll in her hand, both then and now. How had she so utterly botched that conversation?

Angelika ran below her mother's portrait but kept her eyes down. "I should have asked Lizzie to broach it with her. It is practically her house now, after all. Dammit, I should have just left it."

Angelika ran through the kitchen, where the warm cooking smells made her feel sick, and headed down the path to the laboratory, but it wasn't Lizzie she sought. Approximately once a year Victor afforded her a genuine hug. Perhaps she'd be in luck.

As she climbed the stairs to the laboratory and walked across the landing, she sharpened her hearing in case she was about to walk in on a passionate scene she would not be able to erase. Then she heard Lizzie say, "And when are you going to tell Jelly?"

Victor: "Nothing's certain yet."

Lizzie said, "But if you had to make a prediction?"

"It's not certain," Victor repeated, but now his tone was different. Bleaker. "We are in entirely new realms of science. He knows that."

"She deserves to know. This is her entire future. She cannot make a proper choice without knowing it."

"Inevitably she will work it out; she's a clever little monkey. But let's begin again with this formulation. I need to train you well if you are to be my very special new assistant. Let me tell you exactly how I like it." Victor's tone became velvety.

Angelika wrinkled her nose. She'd better make herself known, and fast.

"I deserve to know what?" Angelika's voice caused them both to jump. Lizzie dropped a glass tube and it smashed at her feet. "Is it Will?"

"Jelly, don't sneak." Victor picked up Lizzie and sat her on the bench, and then bent to scrape together the glass fragments. "How long were you there?"

"Long enough to know that secrets are being kept. It's about Will's fatherhood prospects, isn't it?" She belatedly remembered to dash the tears from her cheeks with the back of one hand. "It's fine, he told me already. And I've just had a row with Mary."

"That statement could apply on any given day," Victor said.

It was not a hug day. At least, not for Angelika. Once he straightened up, he stood between Lizzie's legs and put his arms around her. On the floor was an open crate, and on the bench was the new microscope. Victor hadn't even come to tell her it had arrived.

Lizzie wore Angelika's work apron. "Are you all right, Jelly?" she asked. "You look like you've seen a ghost."

The sight of her wearing that apron hit in the way the dia-mond ring should have; it was a jealous-lonely-loss type of feeling compounded on top of the feelings Mary had just instilled. She could see on the opposite bench that a simple chemical experiment was laid out, one she had learned many years ago.

There was steam rising from her regular mug, and her pen-cil was behind Lizzie's ear, and the apron looked better on her. Mary was not the only one retiring today.

"Jelly? What's the matter?" Lizzie asked again.

"You're officially his new assistant?" Angelika asked, try-ing her best to smile and sound normal, but it was clear from their faces that she was not succeeding. More tears fell. "I'm sure he'll keep you terribly busy, just like I was. Make sure you don't make him repeat himself, or he'll positively shout at you, and don't ever drop a glass tube again. That's the only one you're allowed to break for your whole life."

"Jelly." Lizzie said her nickname like an apology.

It was time for another escape—as dignified as she could—this one made worse by Victor's disgusted voice. "She's seek-ing attention, as usual." He was right, of course. He always was. "Let her go."

Angelika fled the building. "Let me go," she chanted as she ran across the lawn in the direction of the orchard, Will, any-where but here. She felt like she could run all the way to Lark-spur Lodge, to lie on her true childhood bed, until she worked out her new place in this world. "Let me go, let me go—"

Then, she saw him, on the edges of the forest, with a gold glint on one hand. The last man she ever expected, and he was looking right at her, and she imagined she saw compassion in his look.

It was Victor Frankenstein's missing creation.

And because she did not know what else to do, she lifted her hand in a wave, and walked to him.

CHAPTER EIGHTEEN

I t made perfect sense in the moment.

If she could just get Will's ring from this man's hand, things might turn out all right today. Even better if she could end this day with this big chap tucked into a bed in the manor, full from a hot meal. She indulged in determined daydreams as the lawn turned to meadow, and then tussocks, then rocks.

Tonight, the entire secret society could regroup by the fire to study the ring. There would be a pat on her shoulder from Victor and a grateful look from Will. Christopher would be speechless at her bravery. Clara would exclaim, *I say!* Angelika and Mary would exchange apologies in the hall, and Angelika would bring a cup of tea to her for once. Lizzie would catch her sleeve later and say something like, *I could never replace you.*

It was all going to work out.

If Angelika could manage this one little thing.

"Hello," she puffed as she hiked over the difficult terrain. "Do you remember me? I'm Angelika." The sun was at an awkward angle above, casting such a black shadow line between the forest and clearing that she had a terrible feeling she had simply imagined him. She shaded her eyes, squinted, and saw he'd retreated further into the trees.

He was bringing something up and down into his mouth. It was a deeply familiar action.

"You're here for some apples." She stepped across the shade line, and once in the cool dim light, she could study Victor's friend properly.

The size of him took her breath away. While Angelika was choosing the most handsome body parts, Victor was sorting through for the biggest. This man was clothed, and what a good thing, too. He wore stolen garments, with the pants calf-length and stiff with mud. His peasant shirt was designed to be worn loose in the heat. On this man, it was a vest. He wore no shoes or hat.

He was in a distressed state; equal parts dirty, tired, hungry, and hopeless.

Also, wordless.

"Can I please assist you?" Angelika asked, wincing at the sight of his feet. They'd covered many hard miles. Her advance frightened him; he shook his head and backed against a tree, furiously biting the apple, even chewing the core. Juice and seeds ran down his chin. "It's quite all right, do not rush. Please, be easy. Sir, do you have a name?"

He said nothing but looked down at her boots. She did, too, and saw an apple by her toe.

"Here." She picked it up and held it out. He was a color she did not think would wash away: ashy gray, with bruise-purple tones around his eyes and mouth. She tossed him the apple, but it dropped into the grass uncaught.

Those hands were Will's hands. She found herself staring at them intently as he fell to his knees to search in the grass. They were beautiful, despite the filthy nails and deathly tone.

Oh, to travel back to that moment, alone with Will as he lay on the slab. She should have fought Victor more vigorously and kept him utterly perfect just as he was. She deserved to lose her own hands for what she had done to him.

Victor's man was eating the apple on his hands and knees now. His bunched fist was right there, adorned with a thick band of pure, glowing gold. The insignia was tantalizingly close. Angelika had once purchased a tiara out of another woman's hair; this should be even more straightforward. She ventured closer, spooking him.

"Can I see?" She touched a fingertip to her opposite hand. "Sir, please can I see your lovely ring?"

This man uttered his first vocalization, and whilst it wasn't a word, it was definitely a no.

"I would like to buy it from you."

No.

They both heard a shout far away: "Angelika! You found him!"

"Ignore it," she urged the man as he flinched and gathered himself into a low crouch. "Come, take my hand, I will help you to your feet."

He managed it on his own, towering over her again. He was deeply suspicious now, his eyes darting over her shoulder, cupping his ring protectively. He was twice her size, and the fact he thought her capable of forcibly removing it gave her a shameful rush of power.

"I understand it is your one true possession, and I'm sure you love it dearly," Angelika said, stepping closer. "But I will pay more than it is worth. I will give you a cottage, and I will ensure an entire wardrobe is tailored for you. Food. Apples. New gold rings. Anything you want. Just name your price."

"Angelika!" another voice shouted, closer; it was Will.

"Angelika!" Victor again. "Keep him there! At last, my friend!"

"No, no, go back," she shouted in response, then said to the startled man soothingly, "Ignore them. I can see you will not negotiate. If you could just let me look at the ring, enough to draw a sketch of it, you can keep it. And I'll help you create a comfortable life. Just come with me. You can have a bath, and we are cooking lunch."

She got a hand around his wrist, and he was as cold as death.

With an almighty scream of surprise, he flung out his arm and Angelika was weightless, and the tree canopy spun like firecrackers. There was a moment that rattled every bone in her body, and the air in her lungs was pressed out by the impact.

Black. No dreams.

When Angelika opened her eyes, she was in a bed in an unfamiliar room. The first thing she saw was oak beams across a white ceiling. There was a sharp, bad smell. She tried to raise a hand to her forehead, but her arm was floppy and she grasped the pillow instead. The light was different now, a blue evening tone. Time had moved on without her.

"What happened?" Her voice was hoarse. No one replied. "Did I die?"

She could hear distant male voices arguing. When she rolled her head to one side, she saw an object that made her instantly orient herself. It was an old leather book, with *Institutiones Rei Herbariae* printed on the spine, set on the nightstand like a Bible.

"Finally, I'm in Will's bed," she croaked, then laughed, and regretted it.

She could find no wound on her scalp, only a lump. She pushed back the blankets and sat on the edge of the bed, holding her spinning head. She took in Will's cottage in short glimpses, in between closing her eyes and swallowing back vomit.

It was bright and spartan. The smell was the fresh white-wash. The floor was made of dark brown flagstones, scrubbed clean, and the fireplace was stacked with fresh kindling await-ing a match. A washbasin and ewer were on the wide window-sill, along with a single bar of her special French soap. Some shelves were inset in a corner, revealing a small collection of food baskets, a loaf-shaped cloth, and a jar of preserves.

Other belongings included a knife, a single wooden cup, a row of apples, and an upside-down bunch of herbs on a hook. His clothes were hung from a rail, wedged between the fireplace and wall. Everything about this place was the exact opposite of her opulent bedroom. If this was how he preferred it, she could now understand why he felt so uncomfortable in the main house.

"Would he like just one small tapestry?" she asked herself between gulps and groans.

"You're awake," Will said from the doorway before kneeling between her feet in a dizzying movement. "How do you feel?"

"Dreadful," she said. "How are you?"

"How I am does not matter," Will replied shortly, cupping a hand at her throat and encouraging her to lift her head. "An-gelika, what were you thinking?" He didn't expect a reply and she gave none. "Victor has gone mad. He's running around searching for Mary. She's the one who will know what to do."

"We had a row; I think she's hiding. I just need water." She managed to drink a few mouthfuls before patting Will on the cheek and crawling back into his bed. "You live like a monk," she told him, before she fell back into the black place.

CHAPTER NINETEEN

Angelika stayed in Will's bed, and clung to it when they tried to remove her. Every time he, or her brother, attempted to question or scold her over the events in the forest, she pretended to be sick and closed her eyes.

But it wasn't pretending.

Her bones felt bendy and the room became unfriendly; the beams on the ceiling were sickening, and she asked for air more than water. The shutters stayed open throughout the night, with a candle sputtering in the cold breeze.

Everyone was in the room: Lizzie on the edge of the mattress, Victor on the sill, Will leaning a forearm on the mantel. Belladonna's piglet was asleep by the hearth. "I'm all right," Angelika said at one point, causing them all to start in surprise, but their simultaneous movements and questions were too much and she fell back under the oily black pall.

When she woke again, she called for Mary—surely one of her divine cool compresses would make her recover—but she did not come, and Angelika felt hopeless. It was painfully obvious to her now as she lay back shivering. Mary was, for all intents and purposes, her grandmother, and Angelika felt her absence as keenly as grief. The memories and fragments she dredged up were all miscolored: running to Mary's open arms as a wobbly tot, being carried and fed, being tucked in too tight, and all the while, Mary despised her?

"Don't cry," Lizzie said.

"Tell her I understand why she hates me, and it's all right," Angelika insisted to Victor, before vomiting into a bowl on Lizzie's lap.

It was an endless night. The worst night. But like anything terrible, there were a few bright spots if one knew where to look.

Will took a turn on the mattress edge, and he read to her from his book of plants. Surely heaven would feel like this, his hand occasionally stroking her arm and his soft whisper alternating between French and Latin. She knew he was probably telling her a list of fungi, but she could believe he was saying anything she wished, as long as she lay with her hurt head on his pillow.

"Is that one of the bigger toadstools?" She tried to make conversation. "Or is it one of the smaller varieties?"

"Come and get me if she wakes," Victor said to Will, hoisting up a snuffling, sleepy Lizzie in his arms. "If she's still rambling about mushrooms in the morning, I shall send for a doctor. I'm going back out into the forest to search for him. Not now, Belladonna. Shoo."

"Take him some food, he's starving," Angelika urged. She lay back down and dozed.

Before dawn, Will asked in the silent room, "What possessed you?"

"Your ring," Angelika replied.

"You were planning on marching down there, to that big wild man, and taking it from his hand?"

"Yes."

Will let out a huff of disbelief. "What is it like, moving through the world with the confidence of an empress?"

"It's nice." She looked around the room with her eyes only opened to slits. "What's it like, living as a pauper?"

He echoed back, "It's nice. You really would do anything for me, wouldn't you?"

"I will prove it, again and again. Why aren't I in my own room?"

Will hesitated for a few moments. "I was half out of my mind with worry. I . . ." He looked sideways, wincing at a memory. "Victor could barely get a hand on you. I gathered you up from the ground and was growling and guarding you like an animal. I brought you here."

"You don't lose control often. I wish I'd been conscious," she said teasingly, but he remained serious.

"I was no more civilized than that giant beast. You must never do that again."

"But—"

"Do you understand me?" He was kneeling by the bed now, his lips moving on the back of her hand. "Not for that ring, not for me. Never. You could have been killed. He flung you like a doll. There was a rock on the ground beside you. Six inches was the difference between you lying in my bed rambling about toadstools and you lying on a slab in that nightmare morgue."

"Victor would have brought me back."

"Not with a rock clean through your skull. What if he had sought to take vengeance on Victor? Men do terrible things to women. He could have taken you deeper into the woods and . . . hurt you. I could not survive it."

Mary's old advice ran through Angelika's mind: *No hesitation, no politeness, run.*

He was shaking as he kissed her hand and then began speaking. Latin became English, and it was crystal clear: he was praying. They were words from her childhood; he was asking the Lord to keep her safe, to watch over her and keep her.

On Frankenstein ground, it was absolute sacrilege. Lucky Victor wasn't here.

Will didn't even seem aware of what he was doing; a long-held script from his past life was being recited. A devout husband could prove to be a very big problem.

"You shouldn't do that." She eased her hand away. "How did you find me?"

"I was walking down to invite you to dine with me. My cottage is finished now, as you see," Will explained shyly. "I saw you from across the orchard, fleeing the laboratory. Then you stopped in the most peculiar way and waved like a child, but not at me. The way you walked toward the forest made the hairs on my body stand on end. I ran for you."

She remembered the tenuous moment with the stranger, and their shouts ruining it.

"And now we've lost him. I wish you'd just let me deal with it by myself."

He heard her grouchy tone and smoothed her hair back. "I will never leave you to deal with things by yourself. When you face monsters, I want to be with you. I'm sorry I wasn't there to catch you."

"He isn't a monster. He is lost, and suffering, and oh, his poor feet. I'm sure his hands don't work properly. He needs me to massage them. We need to find him and help him. I feel like I can never be comfortable again, knowing that he is out there, and Sarah has a cold room, and Mary bends in half underneath the eaves to not hit her head."

"Empathy has found you later in life, and I think life's cruelties will burden you more than most. What happened with Mary?"

"I suggested that she consider retiring. She took it badly." Angelika looked around the cottage again. Could the other four vacant cottages be made this lovely with some hard work? "How do you feel about having an irritable old neighbor?" She thought about the people in her employ. "Add Sarah, so two neighbors? Or three, if Jacob wants to live closer to the horses? Four, if we persuade Victor's big friend to stay?"

"Now there's my Angelika." Will was deeply pleased with her. "Generosity is the garment that suits you best."

"Jacob apologized to me when we first met. I didn't understand what he meant." Angelika closed her eyes and the truth came to her, knowing Will as she did. "He's the boy from that night, isn't he? The thieves in the house. He's the one you scolded and let go."

"Yes."

Her past self would have been furious. She would have run to the stables, to check her valuable horse, and to order the thief to never set foot on her land again. But now, she just nodded her head. "Fine."

"His family has not been able to survive—"

"It's fine. I forgive him. I'm sorry things are bad for him."

He pressed a kiss to her temple. "Feeling sorry is one thing, but being practical is the better solution, in view of his family's poverty. He is paid handsomely to muck out the stalls and untangle Solomon's tail."

"You did well." She stretched against him. "Is my invitation to dinner still current?"

"Let's wait until your eyes are not big strange stars." He was quiet for a while.

They were interrupted by a distant howl. Animal or man, they could not ascertain.

"That poor man. His arm was absolutely ice cold." Angelika put her hand on Will's wrist to demonstrate what she meant, then recoiled, and patted him all over. "You're rather chilly, too."

She searched his face intently, relieved to note his skin still retained its healthy glow.

"It is very cold. The window is open." He pulled the blankets more snugly to her chin. "What was wrong with the man's hands? You said they don't work."

"It looked like he had no ability to make a fist or use his hands properly. He had trouble picking up an apple. Are you worried the same will happen to you?"

"It's natural to worry about the future." He allowed Angelika to gather his hand into hers. The rubbing massage was a ritual now between them, and she needed the contact just as much as he.

She kissed each cool knuckle. "Can you feel this?"

He continued his thought with a small smile. "When you have stepped outside of the natural progression of things, as I have, every day is a blessing, and each night a terror. I'm glad you're here. The hours before dawn are the hardest for me."

"I didn't know that. I will stay all night."

"I've always thought it would be difficult to get you out of my bed." He curled her against him. "I will remain above the blanket, of course, to maintain propriety, in this race to win Angelika Frankenstein's heart."

"You already won it," she told him, tired now. "It is my turn to win yours. Besides, I don't think Christopher is still in the running. He's forgotten me."

"You're wrong about that. Some men would be repelled by

this type of competition. He is invigorated by it. He's out tear-ing up the countryside, hunting for my shadow. He will want you more than ever before."

"I'm not sure you're right."

"No one could forget you. Besides, Victor sent word of your ordeal to Christopher, in case he required the academy's doc-tor. I think you will be receiving a visit soon."

"I wasn't talking about toadstools that long, was I?"

"A very long time. And you thought you were speaking Latin," he said.

They lay together, holding hands, utterly respectable and chaste, until the sun came up and it was time for her to leave.

CHAPTER TWENTY

Clara had increasingly requested, in a variety of polite ways, that everybody not stand behind her while she worked on her portrait of Will. At each single mark she made on the page, someone uttered an encouragement.

"Marvelous." "A clean line, that one." "A gift, if ever I've seen one." "The artist is officially at work." "Brava!"

It wasn't until she became so flustered she broke her lead, and then hit her head retrieving it, that Will jerked his thumb and told the audience: "Out."

The following spectators exited in a subdued file: Victor, Lizzie, Christopher, Sarah, Jacob, and the new junior kitchen maid, Pip.

Mary was still gone, and without her, housekeeping limped along. No one knew where anything was kept, or what time things should be done. Clean undergarments were a rare luxury. But Angelika was glimpsing moments of Sarah taking charge.

"Out," Will said again, in a kinder tone, to the last two remaining onlookers.

"We don't have to leave, do we, Winnie?" Angelika said to Edwin, dancing him around the room in a waltz, his hand clasped around the base of her thumb. "We are allowed to stay and watch." She was recovering from her ordeal, and the lump on her head was smaller. But on the next twirl she grew dizzy, and she halted before anyone could notice.

Angelika adjusted the cuff of Edwin's new flannel trousers. Sewing baby clothes was one of the only ways she could take her mind off Mary's disappearance. She had an idea that if she could prove she had been usefully occupied, Mary would return and be impressed.

Clara was at her wit's end. "Miss Frankenstein, I cannot think with you twirling about, let alone put my lead up to ruin another fresh sheet. Will, please," she appealed to him.

"No exceptions," Will told Angelika.

"I have told you repeatedly, Clara, call me Angelika. Hmm," Angelika hummed to Edwin and carried him to the seated Will, allowing the baby's feet to kick his shoulder. Perhaps he'd boot a little paternal instinct into the man. "I suppose if it means this face is captured for all time—"

"In a rough sketch for the magistrate," Will cut in wryly.

"Then I can allow being evicted. Clara, can I commission you to commence an oil portrait after this? And do you paint lockets?" Angelika was jealous of how Edwin mewled and reached for his mother, but she handed him back.

"Lockets?" Clara echoed in despair over her son's head. "You have seen no proof of my talent to warrant a further commission." The sheet on the easel had a one-inch line.

Her arms now horribly empty, Angelika went to Will. "My love, you are so terribly handsome, I would have your portrait painted inside the lid of my casket." She tidied his thick dark copper hair, aware of Christopher's ice-blue stare through the door crack.

"Dreadfully flattering," Will advised her. His composure

broke at her silliness, and he laughed. "You are so extravagant with praise, my love. Now, kindly leave this room before
I must get stern."

Angelika winked. "Ooh. All right, come along, Winnie."

Clara said, "Edwin will sit and play down here by my feet,
and you simply must go and sit with Christopher."

"But—"

Clara cut her off. "The man's absolutely desperate for a
single glance from you." Did she just sound very, very angry?
Angelika studied her face, but any trace of temper in Clara's
eyes was gone in a blink. "I'm sorry. I'm worried I will fail at
this task. Let us talk about an oil or a casket lid once I get
through this."

"She tends to put her faith in people in ways that come with
some pressure," Will told Clara as Angelika left the room.
When she glanced back, he was looking down at Edwin. "But
we can only do our best."

Standing alone by the far window, Christopher did a good
job at pretending he wasn't waiting for her. He maintained it
for five seconds, then he half jogged the length of the hall to
her elbow. "Angelika. How I've longed for a moment alone.
Are you quite sure you are recovered?"

"I am fine."

He stepped closer and risked a touch, taking her hand. His
was pleasantly warm and dry. "I will find the man who did
that to you."

"When you catch him, please don't injure him or frighten
him." She winced at how poorly equipped she had been when
she approached the man that day, and she reached up auto-
matically to feel in her hair. Some tenderness remained. She
also had a pinch in her rib cage and some frightful bruises.
"He's a simple man who doesn't know his strength."

Christopher's temper flared. "Tossing a woman onto the ground like that? And you, of all victims? He'll be lucky I don't slit his throat, if the locals don't find him first. He's been stealing what he can. The village talks of nothing but the huge beast lurking in the forest. They haven't decided if he's a madman or a ghost."

"Neither. He's a poor soul who needs help. Just get the ring he took from Will in the least traumatic way possible, and I will compensate him for it. A finder's fee, if you will."

"I cannot imagine how you would know such a person. Is this one of the thieves who has been here? Or the man in the orchard who touched your hair? Please explain your connection."

She ignored the request. "Promise that you will treat him as my personal friend and guest."

Christopher relented with a nod. "With those eyes you have, I feel like you could make me promise anything. I am sorry I have not been able to court you as you deserve. I have been hard at work, trying to solve the mystery that might clear my path."

He looked past her at the room they had left. A rare crease appeared on his brow.

She knew his worry. "To be frank, I thought you both had forgotten I exist."

They began to stroll down the bright, sunlit hall to the drawing room. Victor and Lizzie had vanished, and Angelika prayed they could not hear their mattress from here. Sarah was setting down a tray of tea and interesting miniature cakes, courtesy of the new cook, Mrs. Rumsfield.

"Thank you," Angelika said to Sarah as she served them both. "Still no sign of Mary? She's not back in her room?"

Sarah shook her head. "Not at the boardinghouse, either."

"What is it?" Christopher asked, puzzled, after Sarah left. They made themselves comfortable on opposite ends of the peacock-blue settee. The chair squeak was vaguely lewd. After all that had happened, being alone with a man on a single piece of furniture was enough to boost her pulse?

Angelika replied, "Just having some housekeeping issues with my staff. My oldest servant—and I mean that figuratively as well as literally—has absconded. Possibly with my mother's emerald brooch, which is now gone from my bedroom."

"More theft?" Christopher blasted indignantly, but Angelika waved it away, choosing a pretty lilac cake.

"We had such a row that in all honesty, I owe her an emerald. If I see her again and she's got it pinned on her shawl, I shall not say a word except sorry."

Angelika played it cool now, but truthfully, when she had noticed the gap in her jewel box, she had temporarily reverted to her most primitive self. Her vision had gone red; she'd snapped her hairbrush in half, pelted a perfume bottle into the fireplace—creating a pungent fireball—and, to finish the tantrum, she'd screamed like a banshee so loud that Will had come running from across the orchard. "You've lost an emerald," he had wheezed, leaning on the doorframe. "Your problems are enviable."

She hadn't worn it for years, but now that it was gone, Angelika loved it more than anything else she owned. It was definitely Mary who'd taken it. She'd always remarked it was the finest jewel in Angelika's collection. It had taken some deep breaths, and the patient counsel of Will, to come to terms with the spitefulness of the crime.

Funny how Will coached her through her worst moments for Christopher to witness her at her best. She sipped her tea and said to him now, "I shall consider it a retirement gift."

"How extraordinary to simply accept this sort of news," Christopher said, crossing a leg over the other. "You once told me you hate thieves."

"I don't think I do anymore. Everyone has a reason for what they do."

Those thighs were twin works of art. Angelika bit so slowly and deeply into her cake whilst staring that he flushed pink. The man was so clean she could smell soap and starch.

Being alone felt like a bad idea.

After clearing his throat, Christopher said, "You see the good in absolutely everybody. I feel like I need to protect you from that aspect of your personality."

Angelika looked into her tea and pondered this. "If you had met me a few months ago, you would have said I was a young woman who only ever saw the bad in people, and probably would have hung someone for a ring or brooch. You wouldn't have liked me. Nobody did."

"What has changed?" The answer came to him immediately. "Finding Will has set you on a new path. Are you sure it wasn't he who stole from you?" Despite his smile, he was serious.

Angelika dismissed this with a haughty look. "The man is a saint."

"No man is. Believe me." A frisson of energy vibrated through them both, and Angelika's cup rattled on its saucer. Christopher's eyes were now the same dark peacock blue as the chair. "We have no idea if he is a sinner or saint. What will you do if I uncover him to be a thief?"

"I'll forgive him."

"Or he's a swindler? He's faked his entire memory loss to escape his debts? Married with his own brood?" This last one hit its mark, and his eyes gleamed like a hunter's. "You are madly in love with someone, and that is certain: Edwin

Hoggett. You will be an exceptional mother. And that requires the input of an exceptional father."

Nobody had ever made the word *input* sound quite that filthy.

"Do you actually wish for a baby?" Angelika asked him skeptically. "Or are you attempting to form a side negotiation with my female organs?"

"Well, that would be improper." He grinned, cutting a look at her waist. "Yes, I want a lot of babies, and I believe I want them with you. I promised to get you organized on that front, remember?"

"I definitely remember. And now I feel like we require a chaperone."

"Do you?" Christopher was intrigued and balanced his saucer on one heavenly leg. "I have made the bold, brave Miss Frankenstein blush? Now that makes me pleased with myself. Should we perhaps take the opportunity to see if we have a viable connection? A kiss, that is what I ask," he added quickly when seeing the look on her face. "I ordinarily would not be so outrageous, but—"

"You're in a rather outrageous household."

"Exactly."

He deserved the full truth. "I promised my hand to Will, virtually the moment he opened his eyes, whether he wanted me or not. I felt a sense of destiny, finding him the way I did. We have a connection I cannot possibly explain to you. It feels like he is mine. Like we are family."

"Your loyalty is a commendable trait. But you were not in possession of all the facts about him. He might not be of good standing. Meanwhile, I am a good match for you in every way. Here's what I know. You are bored and unstimulated here in the country."

"I cannot deny that I am bored at Blackthorne Manor." But she was never bored at Larkspur Lodge.

"I promise you adventure. At home, in private, you may remain as unconventional as you please, and I hope you do. For formal duties, you shall have the latest dresses and be the envy of all the other military wives. Do you hunt?"

"Frightfully well." Angelika looked down at her trousers. "You wish for me to change myself."

He rushed to reassure her. "No. I wish for us to be successful. You're clever, and you know how to play the society game. It would be fun, wouldn't it, having our secret life together, after the day is done?"

He did have a point. She could hardly stride into a military banquet dressed like a soldier, and she did wear dresses into the village. He was hardly asking for a major concession. "Where would we live?"

"Every few years we would move to new places and make new friends. Oceans, mountains, plains; they will be the views from our window. No more boredom or loneliness, ever again, for either of us. Balls, dinners, dancing."

His offer gave her a flashback to the moment she had with Will, outside their bedrooms, dragging her mother's silk through her hand. She had offered him ships, horses, carriages. Spices, tapestries, wine. He'd replied, *I don't need those things.*

She found she had the same reply on her tongue now, though she did not express it.

Christopher let her consider this for a moment, before continuing. "All I ever wanted was to find someone who made me laugh, and think, and lust. When I moved to Salisbury, I never imagined I'd find you, tucked away in an old manor on a hill, like a forgotten princess." There was such admiration in these blue eyes, her heartbeat skipped.

"Should I consider this a proposal?" She found herself terrified of his answer.

He relieved her. "Not just yet. I am restraining myself, and it will be far more romantic." Christopher looked at her mouth. "Are you brave enough to try this with me? No one will know."

Angelika had almost certainly had fantasies like this before, and he was reading from a script that should have worked very well for her. But Will was down the hall, and portraits did not take forever—

Christopher put his teacup on the table. In a quiet voice that would inspire a weary soldier to take one final charge, he urged:

"Kiss me."

CHAPTER TWENTY-ONE

It was remarkable how some words hung in the air longer than others. These two—*kiss me*—hung like a puff of pink smoke, and Will and Clara walked right through it. In this quiet house, Christopher's voice would have definitely carried.

"I was just hoping for an opinion," Clara said faintly, bouncing Edwin higher on her hip.

Christopher did not attempt to wave away the lingering moment. He sat there, marvelous legs splayed out, and stared back at Will. The air seemed to leak out of the room. Edwin chortled at everyone's discomfort.

"Just hoping for an opinion on my sketch," Clara tried again, fainter yet. It was her embarrassment that knocked Christopher back into himself. He made a visible effort to concentrate, and addressed her with warmth.

"It's ready? That barely took you a minute. Grand. Let's see it, then."

"You told me to keep it simple." Clara gestured backward. "I left it on the easel, in case you think it is not a good likeness."

The four (plus Edwin) went back to the library to look at Clara's efforts.

"It's beautiful," Angelika told her honestly, and with a lot of relief. "You have drawn him well. I'm sure eyes are not easy, but you have got him exactly right." There was something she didn't like about it. The sketch of Will had a haunted quality; a tension to the jaw and in the direct stare. "I'd much rather a happier portrait, though," Angelika added. "If I could ask you to sit a second time for Clara, that would be grand."

"She has depicted my stress levels accurately," Will said with a hand in his hair.

"Should we talk outside?" Christopher asked him in a polite threat.

Angelika sighed. "Stop it, both of you. You forgot to sign it," she said to Clara. "Artists always sign their work."

Clara inscribed *CH* at the bottom of the piece.

"I will be meeting the local magistrate tomorrow morning," Christopher said, rolling up the drawing and inserting it into a leather portrait case. "I will send a message afterward to let you know what the outcome was."

"Can I have it back when you are finished with it?" Angelika asked.

"No," Christopher told her evenly. "Clara, would you and Edwin like to come back in my carriage?"

"I think that would be wonderful," Clara said, grabbing up her belongings, clearly wanting a speedy exit. Angelika watched the men walk on ahead, and relaxed a fraction as they began what looked like a civil conversation.

"I should like to pay you for your work," Angelika told Clara as they walked through the house.

Clara was surprised, and offended. "I thought I was an equal part of the secret society."

"You are, and you have performed an integral part. I want you to be compensated as my valued consultant."

"I don't like feeling like one of your staff."

Angelika had anticipated this argument. "Men are always paid for their work and talents; it is important to me that women are, too. Edwin demands that you say yes. The things he likes best in the world cost money."

"His favorite toy is a pine cone."

Out of her pocket, Angelika took the folded envelope she had prepared earlier, with ten pounds inside and sealed with the family crest in wax. She made Clara take it. "Just open it later, and feel happy that you are so very talented. You have earned this by doing something none of us could achieve. I am hereby requesting a further commission, in oils, and I will pay ten times what is here."

Clara very nearly said no. But then Edwin chirped and reached for the envelope, causing them both to laugh. "I never expected a thing. I was happy to just feel included in something. Thank you." She hesitated. "Who would the oil painting be of?"

Without thought, Angelika replied, "Will, of course."

Clara was rightfully puzzled. "I thought you hadn't decided upon him."

"I shall let the winner fight his way into the gilt frame in my bedroom." Angelika slowed her step, forcing Clara to dawdle with her. "Who loves me best, do you think?"

"Edwin," Clara deadpanned, unwilling to give her the satisfaction.

Angelika grinned at that. "And I'm mad for him in return. Did you find new lodgings? I am sewing a few more pieces for my little beau, and I will personally deliver them to you."

"That's kind, thank you ever so much. He's growing at a cracking pace." Clara reluctantly tucked the money away. "And this will help the house-hunting cause. I may have to go back to my hometown. Here, the properties are of two qualities: pigpen or manor house. The village is no longer a safe place, either. Would you believe the women are afraid to go out past sunset? They say there is a monster in the trees." Clara hesitated, and then added, "But I feel like you already know about that."

This was why Victor kept them isolated for so long. The more people coming into this house, the greater the chance of exposure. Just as Angelika began to panic, Clara added, "I was making a joke. You and Victor lead such adventurous lives."

Angelika changed the subject. "Should I speak with Christopher for you? Perhaps I have some influence to let you stay in your cottage."

Christopher and Will were now talking by the carriage. She heard one of them laugh. No explosive fistfights today, then.

"Thank you, but no. It is only right that the cottage be turned over to a military family. I will find something soon." Clara smiled faintly down at Edwin. "I never realized how fortunate I was until one day, everything changed."

"Despite your hardships and loss, you are lucky right now. You have something money cannot buy." Angelika kissed Edwin's cheek goodbye, loving how he clasped her face in his moist little hands. "You have this angel. Aunt Angelika adores you, Winnie."

Would this fatherless baby boy grow into a desperate teen, forced to break into manor homes to survive and support his mother? Her heart turned sorrowfully in her chest. How black and white her life had once been.

Clara still had her sad look. "Things change, and regret is forever. A mistake might hang on your wall and haunt you all your life."

Angelika heard her warning but chose to answer cheerfully. "If you need some help looking at houses, I can accompany you to help forge a good deal. I'm quite a fearsome negotiator."

The men heard Angelika's boast as the ladies made their way to the carriage. "Look out," Christopher joked. "What I wouldn't pay to witness that conversation between Angelika Frankenstein and a landlord. It would be better than theater."

"I can picture it myself," Will said. "She'd be standing in the chicken coop inquiring after the servants' quarters and croquet lawn."

"Perhaps the carriage would have room to turn if the outdoor privy were relocated," Christopher added in a mock-thoughtful tone.

Will pointed to a half-dead shrub. "This may be formed into the shape of a swan, with a little skill."

Clara decided to try. "Is the upstairs of the cottage located elsewhere?"

"Ha, ha, aren't you all just a hilarious group of people," Angelika said as everybody roared heartily at her expense, even Edwin. "I'm so glad my *haute bourgeois* can be so amusing. You'll see, Clara. I can be useful. I will say goodbye on behalf of Victor and Lizzie. It's a shame she wasn't here to enjoy this dramatic performance."

"Where did they disappear to?" Clara asked, puzzled.

Will fielded that. "They are reading poetry." Angelika scowled. Her brother was taking increasingly long "rest breaks" in between his searching of the surrounding forests and ravines. She made a mental note to push him harder on it.

Christopher took Angelika's hand and kissed it. "Thank you for such a lovely cup of tea. Think about what I put to you." The touch of his lips on her skin stirred the sparks between them. "Should you ever desire to read poetry with me,

I am your willing servant. Here, Clara, let me take Edwin while you step in."

He opened the carriage door and sat the baby on one forearm. Then he turned to let Angelika see how the future might look.

"A dirty military tactic," Will told him.

"All's fair," Christopher replied.

"Good to know," Will said. "See you the next time you can fit a visit up here into your busy schedule. Happy hunting, Commander." They watched the carriage depart.

"You heard him, didn't you? Asking me to kiss him?" She caught Will's elbow, forcing him to turn.

"I did." He was bland, and remembering his laughs with his rival sparked her temper. Imagine if Lizzie had been here to witness that quickly fizzling jealousy.

"How I'd like to see some goddamn fire from you."

Will stopped. "What were you hoping for? A violent fight in a house that is not mine, with furniture smashed, and bones broken? In front of your guest, a very nice woman with a baby?"

She gritted her teeth. "No, of course not."

"You want to be flattered." Will's eyes were sharp on hers. "You want to witness how badly two men want you. You would watch us bloody our fists, pretending to be offended. Typical Angelika, wanting to be adored by a lover beyond sense."

The flippant words said to Clara hung in the air like mist. *Who loves me best, do you think?*

"I will begin to think you do not care for me. Show me! Fight for me in your own way!"

"You think I am not?" He took a few steps toward her. "It costs me dearly to deal with every moment of my new life. I take these types of feelings and I place them somewhere deep, where they cannot bubble out. I do this because otherwise they will kill me."

"I did not realize—"

"I am not speaking figuratively, Angelika. I believe I have a limited amount of life force running through my veins. Everything costs me. I have to control myself more than you will ever know, and having your husband number five walking around this house, looking at you like he'd devour you whole, is draining me dry."

She thought of his dizzy spell while gardening. "Have you talked to Victor?"

Will sneered. "Any ordinary man would thrash him for what he asks in the name of science, but of course, I am anything but ordinary. Or am I? And now I find myself in a romantic experiment, one I have apparently failed today, because I had the decency of controlling myself and trusting you to not be tempted by perfection incarnate."

She was frustrated with his evasion. "Is your health growing worse? Answer me."

"I grow tired of being a test subject. I can no longer endure it."

"You didn't answer the question."

"And I shall not. I am going to the village, to continue trying to find out about myself. I am only disappointed at how little empathy you have shown for me. I hope you had a pleasant time today." He turned and walked toward the stables.

Angelika was left behind to sit on the front stairs, alone.

Angelika had an apology burning in her chest, but because she could not cough it out, and nobody wanted to hear it, she went into the forest at sunset.

She took with her a basket of fruit, bread, a sausage, cheeses, and a knife. Over her shoulder she carried a waterskin, and her arm ached from the weight of a wool blanket. She went to the clearing where she had first found the huge, lost man.

As she was setting out her gift on a fallen log, she noticed something.

On the ground, where her body had disturbed the golden leaves, was a wilted bunch of flowers.

CHAPTER TWENTY-TWO

The duchess is asleep," Victor said when Angelika entered the laboratory. "So do not clatter about." He proceeded to clatter about himself, knocking over a dustpan, and Lizzie stirred in the armchair. The siblings stood frozen as she made a sleepy grumble, and then resumed her deep breaths. Her lips moved silently.

"She dreams she is performing to an audience," Victor said with amusement. "Did you know she wants to build an amphitheater, to put on plays for the villagers? I suppose it would still work out cheaper than your soap habit."

Angelika watched Victor put his eye back to his microscope. "What are you doing?"

In a tone he'd used since childhood, he replied: "Using—a—microscope—Jellybrain."

She gritted her teeth. "For what?"

"See for yourself." He usually made her try much harder to use his equipment. It felt like a trick, but Angelika stood up on tiptoe to look through the eyepiece.

"What am I looking at? Bacteria? Bile?" Another world was teeming on this glass slide. Angelika adjusted the view. "Some sort of lice?"

"Spermatozoa," Victor replied. "A sample that Lizzie collected for me a few minutes ago. Say hello to your nieces and nephews."

Angelika recoiled. "Chemicals to wash my eyeballs, I beg."

The fact that he wasn't laughing was a worry.

"Be more mature," Victor chastised her. "I am only doing this for your benefit. This is selfless research."

"Oh, certainly. Did Lizzie obtain the sample with a needle?"

After a violent shudder, Victor continued his noble speech. "I seek to understand what Will's chances are of fatherhood. Whilst I do not flatter myself as the perfect specimen, I'm the only baseline I have easy access to. This new microscope is marvelous."

"This is what he meant about your unendurable requests," Angelika said slowly as the full scale of the experiment dawned on her. "You asked him for a sample, so you could compare."

"I did, and he reacted like I had offered to tug it out of him myself." Victor hunted through the mess on the bench and proffered a glass beaker. "Sterilize this, then see how you do. Make sure you bring it to me at once. Doesn't matter if it's the middle of the night."

"He said no." She crossed her arms and refused to take it. "So I will not even ask."

Victor insisted, "It's the only way we can know. Our other comparison subject is my friend out in the forest, but that would be a challenge I'd rather not attempt. Unless you're up for securing a third suitor."

The grin on his handsome face was infuriating, but it also put a happy bubble in her stomach. This felt so much like old times, bar a snoring Lizzie behind them.

"I think we've done enough to him."

Victor looked through the eyepiece at his sample again.

"I'm thinking about bringing a dead ram back to life as a possible alternative." His brow creased as he thought about it. "The things we do for science, eh?"

"Just leave it. This is one thing we can leave up to—" She mindlessly almost said *God*, but quickly finished with: "The mysteries of nature."

"And can you make Will your final choice, without knowing?" Victor leaned an elbow on the bench and they both watched Lizzie sleep. "She's with child, thanks to my spectacular efforts."

Angelika knew this was inevitable, but still felt stunned. "Are you sure she is?" A flash of envious, guilty, scrambling desperation coursed through her. The race to lie on a picnic blanket with their babies had now officially begun. "Are you absolutely sure?"

"She's tired, and is very picky about her food, and hates bad smells. Her courses were due two weeks ago. Check the slide again if you doubt me." He gestured to the microscope. "I am a very productive person. I should be the one asleep."

"Your greatest experiment begins. How wonderful." Angelika saw his smile did not quite reach his eyes. "Are you not happy?"

"I'm very happy, but it is creating friction between us. According to her, we have to be married as soon as possible."

Even in her sleep, Lizzie was pinching her engagement ring. "She would marry you today. Yesterday, in fact. I do not see the problem." She tactfully did not glance at the printed anti-marriage treatise tacked to the wall, riddled with knives and darts. She didn't have to.

"I am famous for my stance on it." It was amazing how Victor could still wince. "It won't die. It's multiplied and spread, like a germ. Every time I walk into a room, I hear titters."

"You're being very brave, facing your fear of worldwide ridicule."

"I'm not brave. She will only marry me in a church, to please her parents."

"Ah."

"I did not think it through completely, when I gave her the diamond ring. And now she is bitterly disappointed that I am being so difficult. Every time she looks at me, it's frustration and sadness and . . . doubt. We Frankensteins are risky propositions."

He moved away to the open window, leaning his elbows on the sill.

Angelika joined him, and copied his pose. "Can you not just endure it?"

"I cannot, Jelly. I cannot go and stand before the old man who told Papa to simply wish for Mama's health to return."

"Pray," Angelika corrected with equal bitterness. "He told our father to pray."

"Wish, pray, think very hard—it is all the same. Praying cannot cure scarlet fever." His fingers flexed on the sill. "My child will have no grandmama or grandpapa. You will be married and gone by then."

"Maybe not. The one I love looks at me with doubt and sadness, too."

Victor had an idea. "I need you to ask Mary if she would come back to help us when the baby arrives."

"I never told her to leave."

"Tell me exactly what you said to her." He listened as Angelika recounted the exchange. "She believes you dismissed her that day, Jelly. You did not say to her that she was to remain here for the rest of her days?"

Angelika audited the memory again. "I thought it was so

obvious. You need to understand, she was horrid to me." She told him about the strange decorations, the dolls, and the terrible underwear.

"She felt awkward having you in her personal space. Then you told her that Sarah would be the new head of housekeeping. She packed her bags and is gone forever, unless we get her back."

His tone was kinder than she'd expected. Was this Will's calming influence on Victor?

Quietly, she said, "She has hated me, from the moment I was born."

"Nonsense. She'd cut out her heart if you needed a new one. She was hurt and upset, but she'll forgive us. It's also my fault. I did not make circumstances clear to her." He was quiet for a while. "I should like her to be there when I am wed; she's all the family we have left. But Mary will also insist on a church wedding."

"Could we travel to another parish? Somewhere that doesn't know us? You could just pretend, and say the church words, and later on make your own private vows to Lizzie."

"I don't think she would feel well enough to be jiggled about in a carriage. I thought about asking Chris to use the chapel at the academy, but even if that's an option, I might open my mouth and no words will come out. I feel a rising sense of panic whenever I picture it."

Angelika so rarely saw him vulnerable. "You just need some time to adjust to the idea. You're Victor Frankenstein, and I am always at your side to assist you in inventing a solution. Thank you for not shouting at me, for mucking things up with Mary."

"I don't want to wake Lizzie," Victor replied, but he was smiling. "I know you do your best. I'm sorry I made you run out of here the other day. I forgot that I'm your best friend. I still am, you know. You scared me. If anything happened to you . . ."

He left the words unsaid, but she knew what he meant. They bumped their shoulders together.

The sun hung above the hill, preparing itself to slip behind, and when it did, the entire property would be plunged into an icy blue. It was a melancholy time. Angelika leaned further out of the window and asked impulsively, "Do you ever think about the terrible things we have done, and regret them?"

"Well, when you put it like that," Victor drawled, but then saw she was not joking. "We saved Will. He was dead. Now he's having a nice cup of tea and a biscuit."

"Please. We did not do it to be altruistic. You showed up that Schneider nemesis of yours"—here Victor grinned widely—"and I picked Will's individual parts like a vapid heiress, hoping he would fall in love with me over time. And even if he is having tea and a biscuit, he lives in the worst kind of mental torment and physical pain that he keeps hidden. We are *terrible* people."

"Yes, we are. But I've been observing you since that night we saw Will sleepwalking in the study. I know you've been tutoring Sarah, and helping Clara with food, and doing things for her baby. You're changing. It's like witnessing a moment in an experiment, when the most unexpected reaction takes place. All it took was the addition of Will." Victor mimed using a chemical dropper. "When I think of my creation, lost out there, and how I cannot find him—" Victor's voice broke a little, and he put his face in his hands. "Yes. I am a terrible person."

"What more can you do to find him?"

Victor hesitated. "I would need more people to help me.

Searching on my own is not working. But a well-paid group of men could easily turn into a mob, and a violent end is the last thing I want for him."

"You are going about it all wrong. You need to draw him to you. I feel his presence," she said, and they looked across to the site of her accident. "He's here, close by. Same with Mary. We just have to find what they need most, and bring them home."

Despite saying this, she still found herself hesitating to reveal her nightly meal deliveries into the forest. Just once, she'd like to show Victor that she could solve a situation alone. Besides, her brother would just barge in, ruining the delicate trust she was attempting to build.

"I believe he may try to kill me," Victor said suddenly. "And I would not blame him."

"When you find him, you will put this right. Are you going out again?"

"Nightfall seems to be when the villagers glimpse him. I will take Lizzie up to the house, set her down with some dinner, and ride out." He smiled at his sister wryly. "Be glad you coaxed Will inside on that dark, rainy night with the mere promise of a bath."

"You asked me if I can make my choice, being uncertain of his . . . reproductive viability. That will be my price to pay for my part in this if he asks me to marry him." She hesitated on this next thing. "He said something about his health. He believes he has a limited life force. I don't know what that means, but I don't think it's just his fatherhood prospects that plague his mind. It's something more serious. His hands, Vic, unless I massage them several times a day, they curl and turn cold. I worry about the future."

Victor answered with halting care, "I am not at liberty to discuss him."

"I know. I'm just telling you I'm worried. Are you ever afraid that they cannot survive the things we have done to them in the name of science, and love?"

"I am sick over it. That's why I need to bring mine home." Victor's expression was stark. "I'm worried also about something different."

"What?"

He dropped his voice to a whisper. "I do not know how to be a father. It's not in any of the literature."

"Maintain your faith in natural science. Human beings have been fathers for countless generations. And I have seen how you have searched for your lost man. He has awakened a protective instinct in you, I think."

"That is true," Victor replied, cheered up. "Speaking of instincts, I never told you about what happened when Will found you flat on your back in the forest."

"He told me that he turned a bit uncivilized that day."

"When he saw you in danger, he stepped out of his present form and became something I have never seen before. His true feelings. I saw a man violently in love."

Angelika's heart flipped, then sank. "But he cannot easily show me this side of himself. If he knows one emotion, it is guilt, and I don't know why." She had a sudden intrusive memory: dark stone, an ivy-covered building, a white porcelain cross. "What about our chapel on the hill? Get married there."

Victor was surprised by her change of topic. "I think it is where Belladonna births her piglets." He leaned further out the window to point halfway up the hill. "It would be a total ruin."

"But Will could help us repair it, and you could be married at home. You've seen how nice his cottage is now after a bit of hard work." Angelika was determined to make her brother happy. "I will go and assess it. If we can make it something lovely, and pay someone to be as unobtrusively religious as possible, would that be a good option?"

"It would be nice to do something so difficult at home. Thank you," Victor said, and when they stood up, he opened his arms. That blue-moon hug was being offered, and it was wonderful. He smelled like apple and arsenic.

Above her head, he said, "Do take a glass beaker with you. You never know what you may get if you let him adjust to the idea."

It was this thought that stuck with Angelika as she walked toward the wisps of smoke from Will's cottage. Sometimes, a person just needed a little time. When she saw the big man in the forest watching her, she waved to him and kept on walking.

CHAPTER TWENTY-THREE

W hen Will answered the knock at his door, he found Angelika holding up the specimen beaker. His expression slackened with dismay. Before he could say a word, she took some flowers from behind her back, and turned it into a vase. After blowing out a long exhalation, he said, "Thank you."

"I'm sorry he even asked you." She dithered awkwardly. Was he still unhappy with her, after their altercation in the driveway?

"Are you sorry? I thought you would have supported it," Will said, turning back into his cottage. From the doorway she saw him add water to his flowers. "Don't stand out there. Come in."

She came in, relieved by his easy aura, and stared around at his décor. There were not many more objects than last time, but somehow it was perfectly snug and comfortable. By the fire, she noticed a flat basket padded with a folded blanket, and an empty dish.

"Do you have a cat?"

"Not exactly."

"I do not mean to intrude. But if I may offer a suggestion? One tall oriental vase in that corner, filled with peacock feathers, would make this space perfect."

"How could you intrude into a place that is yours?" He positioned the flowers on his mantel, looking as content as she'd ever seen him. "It's perfect now. A beaker full of larkspurs was all it wanted."

"This cottage isn't mine, and I will never enter without your invitation. This place is yours, for a lifetime if you want it. I have to tell people exactly what they are entitled to."

He noticed her grimace. "What happened?"

"I accidentally dismissed Mary, instead of telling her she is a valued family member who is to live out her days with us. Typical Angelika."

"I'm sure you will come up with an ingenious solution. That is also typical Angelika." His bed had a compression mark on the blanket, and his cheek was creased.

"Were you lying down?"

"I am tired in the afternoons."

"The sleepwalking?" He nodded. "I was going to see if you wanted to come for a walk with me. I have a project to assess, up on the hill. We are thinking of marrying the duchess and the bear at home. But I can go alone if you're tired."

"Walking alone in the forest doesn't go very well for you." He sat down to pull on his boots, and Angelika roamed around, admiring his belongings. The leather-bound book *Institutiones Rei Herbariae* was still in pride of place beside his bed. She flipped it open to reread her inscription. *To my love: One day I will write your true name here. With all that I am, I am always, your Angelika.*

"I really can't wait," she said to him. He didn't understand. "To write your name in this book."

"It would be sacrilege to write my name in such a special book. So, where are we going?"

It was another love declaration gone unnoticed by a man she

blindly adored; there was a trail of similar gestures through-out the years. This was the first that was permanently inked. Imagine his gentle pity when he noticed it. Perhaps he would have to hide the book from his wife, or tear out the page.

Angelika tried to sound cheerful, even as her cheeks warmed and her throat tightened.

"We always went to church in town, but the estate origi-nally had a chapel. I haven't seen it since I was a child."

Will looked up, startled. "I know where it is."

"Does it still have four walls and a roof?"

"I've never seen it in daylight, but I've woken up there three times now. We should make sure to get back before nightfall."

Angelika nodded. "Yes, I have something I need to do be-fore it gets dark." She'd asked Mrs. Rumsfield to make some small vegetable pies; it would be nice for Victor's man to find them still warm. Like Will, he would not touch meat, and the sausages she had left in his baskets were tossed into the leaves. "Did you make any progress on your mystery when you rode to the village?"

"Christopher's information on the travelers' inn was useful. I went there and met with the landlady but found it too diffi-cult to explain myself. The story of my twin brother is increas-ingly unbelievable." He put his hands on his knees and stood with a groan. "I have walked around Salisbury long enough to believe I am a stranger to the village. But sometimes I see a maid look at me a second time, and I begin to doubt again."

Angelika's eyebrows lowered. "That is because you are ter-ribly handsome. I will come with you next time."

"Jealous," he chided, but his eyes glowed with pleasure for several minutes as they began their walk. "I think I might have to expand my search for myself to London. I don't sup-pose you feel like accompanying me on my trip?"

"I would follow you anywhere," Angelika replied, and she did, into the darkening forest.

The path up the hill was roughly laid with crumbling stone stairs in some places, and in others it was nothing more than deer tracks traced into the fallen leaves. They fell into a companionable silence as they walked, and it was a good thing, too, because Angelika soon found her fitness was not up to this incline. "I'm hoping—it's in a reasonable state—Victor and Lizzie—" She bent over, hands on knees, and huffed unintelligibly about marriage.

"I know how Victor feels about churches. I suppose he wants to hide away up here to wed her." Will was unaffected by the terrain and stood patiently until she regained her breath. "Take my arm."

She gladly obliged, pressing her cheek to his biceps as they pressed onward and upward. A noise caught her attention; she looked back and saw a solitary piglet trailing them. "Is that Belladonna's runt?"

Will was sheepish. "It's terribly friendly."

"This is exactly how it starts. A basket. A water dish. An apple core, here and there." To distract herself from the incline, Angelika said, "Tell me what trees and plants I have here on this hill."

He began to name them. "These are blackthorn shrubs, but don't even try to taste those berries. They're only good for gin, but I have made a syrup to treat rheumatism. I'm not sure how I knew to do it, but I did." He patted her hand. "When Mary returns home, I think it will help her immensely."

"I'm sure it will make her feel better." The rabbit holes and slippery leaves were easy to traverse when she had both of her arms wrapped around his. "Maybe you are a doctor, my love. They have to know a lot about herbs. You certainly have the calm disposition, and you cared for me perfectly when I hit my head."

"It is a possibility." Will pointed out more trees. "You have hazel trees up here on the ridge, and walnut down in the grove. These huge, twisted trees are called yew, but I think you knew that."

She did. "I just like hearing you talk about what you love."

He patted her hand and continued the lesson. "Yew trees represent immortality, but also death. I rather relate to them." He put his hand on one as they stepped under its low branch.

"Perhaps you are a teacher. A botany professor."

"One could go mad wondering." It was a quiet warning to drop it.

On the steep slope, these mossy yews hugged the incline, casting their branches in fairy-tale shapes. In several places on the estate they formed tunnels. They were horrifically beautiful. Angelika asked, "Why do they mean immortality?"

"They're ancient. These would be hundreds of years old, and I could show you some that look like they could be a thousand. They regenerate themselves. Inside the old hollow trunk, a new one will grow. Then the old trunk will fall away. Your grandchildren will have reborn yews to walk beneath. That is the nature of their immortality."

He did not say *our grandchildren*, and the pang was acute. "And why do they represent death?"

"Many folktales exist, but mainly because they are poisonous. The Romans believed yew trees grew in hell."

Angelika was despondent. "Guess what type of wood my bed is made from. I suppose my nature makes sense now."

Will tried to jolly her. "Must be why I woke up that first morning after we met feeling regenerated."

"You couldn't wait to escape my hellish, poisonous bed. I

need to rethink my boudoir. Rosewood sounds more feminine."

What kind of tree would Christopher be? A solid, uncomplicated oak that shed its leaves in one pile and acorns in another. Why did he have to sprout in her thoughts so often?

"That brings us to these elder trees; these ones that look like cork." Will paused at a different trunk, pressing the springy bark to show her. "Elder supposedly keeps the devil away. Perhaps they balance each other out up here." He looked back for the piglet, and they waited for it to catch up. In the distance, they could hear distant hoofbeats.

She sighed. "That will be Victor riding out. He's so tired. I think we should plant a ring of elder trees around the house. And the laboratory. Maybe one in my bedroom." She was gratified by his smile. "But of course, I forgot. We do not believe in the devil, or in hell."

"I believe." He helped her over a log.

This time, she noticed that his hand was very, very cold. Had it ever been warm, as long as she'd known him? She brushed the thought away. "Did I tell you that the apples Victor eats are his own invention? He grafted two varieties together when he was ten. They are his exact preference."

"I'll have to ask him how he did that. What does he call them? I'm sure his invention has a name."

"Conqueror apples."

Will was quick. "Ah. Because he's the victor. Did you make your own tree?"

"As usual, I just helped him." She took a deep breath. "I thought about what you said to me, some time ago. That without Victor I would achieve my full potential. I think you are right. It is time for me to leave this place. But I don't know what my potential is."

"Your potential can be found in the places where you can

make a difference in this world. It is your duty and your privilege. I would like to suggest that you think about the apple harvest. You still have time to plan it ahead of the season. Mary told me that it all goes to waste, but I think you know now that it's not too late to start again."

Angelika was tired of talking about the future and trees now. "Apples are not my forte. It's more Victor's area of expertise, but he is riding out so often to search. Could you sort it?" Immediately she winced, and amended, "But you are not my groundskeeper, so I shall sort it myself. And don't make some allusion to the fact you may be long gone by the time the first apple falls to the ground. I cannot bear it."

They walked in silence until Will pointed. "There."

Angelika was both overjoyed and dismayed when they walked to the front of the Frankenstein family chapel. "The forest has tried to eat it." It was impossible to see if it remained intact. The ancient stones were barely visible underneath the ivy. Angelika tried to imagine a wedding party making the hike up this hill to find this structure. "I don't think this will work."

"The fairy queen, able to grant resurrections, is ready to quit before she even steps foot inside?" He had a point. She kept any further opinions to herself as they trod through red-spotted toadstools to the door. It was painted the same maroon as Mary's door, and it screeched as she pushed it open.

Once inside, she turned, taking everything in. "I remember it being so huge inside, but it's tiny, isn't it?"

The beamed roof was as sturdy as the day it was built. At the far end, stained glass was darkened by the ivy outside. Above the altar hung a porcelain cross, still as white as bone. "It's really not as bad as I thought it would be. Have you cleaned up in here?"

"Perhaps when I was asleep. But I don't think so." Will sat on the narrow pew and watched her investigate. "When we cut the ivy back, the sun will shine through that window at sunrise. Wouldn't that be nice?"

Angelika snorted. "You know that Victor barely makes it to the breakfast table."

Will gave her a faint smile. "For Lizzie, he will do anything. Even wake up early."

She stood at the altar and tried to picture how a ceremony might look, minus the piglet.

"Lizzie will stand here, and Victor here . . ." She turned to the blank space where the obligatory officiant would be lurking. "I suppose the church will charge us triple to send someone up here. How I wish I were qualified. Let's try." She took the priest's place and made a book shape with her hands. "You do? You do? Grand. Now kiss."

She waited for Will's grin, but he looked away with a tight jaw. "It's only a joke. So, how would I look if I stood here in a white dress?" She changed her hands to hold an imagined bouquet.

"You deserve to be wed in a cathedral, not this." He gestured up at the cobwebs. "You limit what you want for yourself, because of your brother."

She couldn't face what he kept trying to show her. "But how would I look?"

With his eyes full of affection and patience he replied, "Like the most beautiful woman who ever lived. Don't I tell you enough?"

Angelika beamed. "No."

"You're energy." He pressed that compliment deep into her heart. "You're warmth, and youth, and so very clever. And yes," he amended when he could see she was not satisfied, "you have the prettiest, most unforgettable face. It has been a privilege to stare at you so much. I wish I could, until the very day I die."

"I'd marry you right now, right here. You do know that, don't you?"

"I do," he returned solemnly. "Your heart is sewn on your sleeve. I know everything you want, beautiful girl."

Angelika sat down beside Will and tucked her hand into the crook of his elbow, letting herself imagine for a moment that they were an old married pair. "I need to apologize to you."

He covered her knuckles with his wintery palm. "No, you don't."

"I sat alone with Christopher, knowing he would lay out his offer. And he did, most comprehensively." She tipped her head sideways to look at him, but he kept his eyeline on the white cross.

"I forgive you." A scowl formed, before he blinked it away. "You should hear all of the options available to you. You still have a choice, and you always will."

"I always thought romance would be something like two men fighting in the dirt for me. But I realize now that being trusted, the way you trust me, feels a lot more romantic. Thank you for teaching me that lesson, and I'm sorry."

"Are we confessing to each other?" Will waited until she nodded. "You will not like what I will tell you now. I am religious."

Her heart sank, but she was not surprised. "How do you know? Do you remember something?"

"I feel angry when you and Victor make your little remarks about God, and those who believe. Like just before, you told me you do not believe in hell or the devil. Or now." He nodded toward the altar. "I don't like jokes like that."

"We don't mean it," Angelika protested. "We don't really care who thinks what."

"I think I wake up here so often because it is a repressed urge that I cannot express in your home."

"There's a church in the village. You can go there."

"A stranger suddenly appearing will only fuel gossip. They will all want to know who I am."

Angelika could imagine the stir he would make amongst the young unmarried ladies, and their mothers. She very nearly offered to accompany him—it would be an occasion to wear extravagant outfits and hats, and to hold his muscled arm—but the offer died in her throat when she imagined her brother's mocking. "They can mind their own business."

"That's not how it works in small villages. I thought you would be furious about this. We cannot tell Victor."

"Mary is a Christian, and she lives with us. Lived," Angelika corrected awkwardly. "She lived with us for so many years, and we let her keep her beliefs."

"You *let* her. Because she emptied your chamber pots and you did not wish to do it yourself. And she was like family. I am neither family nor servant. You surprised yourself earlier, tasking me with the apple harvest. I do not blame you. I feel like I live in a crack between worlds, and sometimes I feel like I might die inside it." He sighed, and added softly, "But when you are with me, I go quiet inside."

"You're family. I promise you." She flexed her fingers on his arm. "I was telling Christopher how I feel about you. I feel like you and I are connected. Do you agree?"

The sun was setting behind them, and shadows were sliding in like the tide. With his devout eyes trained on the cross, he replied, "Yes."

"When I made you, I imparted a lifetime of wishes into the

very fibers of your being." Angelika picked up his hand and entwined their fingers. "Your emotions pluck at a violin string inside me, and it vibrates and resonates until I feel what you feel, too. We are connected at a blood level."

"It feels the same to me. And it scares me sometimes." Will continued to stare up at the cross. "Because what would I do without you?"

"You won't be without me."

He paused, then asked haltingly, "And what would you do without me?"

"I'm a Frankenstein. I'd most likely die. Now we know what book you were searching for. I will give you my mother's Bible."

"That is most generous. I'd like to pray now. Would that be all right?"

"Of course."

Angelika knew she should be looking straight ahead, but she couldn't take her eyes off Will as he leaned, clasped his hands together, and exhaled like he was falling asleep. His lashes on his cheek pierced her heart. What sort of things did he wish for right now? If they were this connected, surely she could feel what he wanted so badly that his knuckles were white?

Angelika closed her eyes, too. On her lap, she held her own hand.

At first there was nothing; just the sound of leaves outside, a creak of wood, and an uncomfortable strain in her hip joint. There was the piglet's faint snuffling. But when she concentrated harder, on the sound of her companion's breathing, her own voice rang in her head.

Dear God.

The unfamiliar words startled her. Her eyes flew open, and

then she tried to resettle. Will's steady presence gave her the courage to try again.

Dear God. Please put warmth into Will's hands and warmth into Sarah's bedroom. Help everyone who lives here. Give the apples sweetness. Give my nature some sweetness. I know I have done such terrible things, and I should pay for them.

She had tears on her cheeks.

Help Will back to himself. I love him enough to let him go, back to his old life, if it would mean he is free of suffering.

And dear God, most of all, please bring Mary back to me safely. I need to look after her as she grows feeble, just as she did for me, when I was a spoiled little girl.

I'm trying to grow up.

Amen.

When she opened her eyes, Will was looking at her. "We are connected, because I could feel the goodness in your heart. I'm proud of you."

He put his arm around her, and before she could ask if kissing was allowed in a chapel, it was happening. His hand was on her jaw, she smelled the woodsy musk of his skin, and now they were tasting each other.

Was this the kind of kiss he would give her at the altar, after the forever words were said? She could only dream. He was reading her mind, because his mouth smiled on hers, and she felt the soft touch of his tongue. He was safety and kindness; like a husband.

A husband who knew how to deepen a kiss, demanding more of her attention and heartbeat, reminding what he could do for her later.

He increased the intensity, until she only thought of what she would do for him.

A dark shadow fell across them, but when she lifted her lashes, the only thing she saw was gold light. She sighed, closed her eyes, and sank back into languid fantasies. In the simplicity of his cottage, she would strip down to her skin, and he could kiss her just like this, all over her body. The lick of his tongue now caused a powerful squeeze, deep between her thighs.

It happened again: everything dimmed, then turned back to gold. Maybe it was the price she would always pay for being with him, and she should take these golden moments when she could. She savored him until he shivered, and she was ready to leave the world behind for him.

The pew gave a passionate groan when they turned toward each other a little more, making them both laugh.

He said, "I think we should go home, before I do something sinful. Would you like to have dinner with me, in my cottage?"

"I would love to. I've been waiting for my invitation."

"Is that why you've been avoiding me? You've been waiting? Poor girl." He saw how she searched his expression now. "What is it?"

"I'm just waiting for the little bit of pain that always follows a kiss." She closed her eyes when he put his palm to her cheek. "You're not about to tell me that you've made a mistake, or that you will never be mine, or that you're quite sure you have a family of ten children to return to?"

"No, my love."

"Just tell me that we shall never go to Larkspur, and I can complete my scheduled wince."

"I have been inconsiderate so many times. Forgive me." He smiled when she rubbed her cheek further into his hand. "What would you like for dinner?"

"The cook is making vegetable pies. I'll bring some up once I—" She stumbled on her words now. She didn't know if she would receive scolding or praise for the deliveries she was making to Victor's friend. The atmosphere was too delicate for her to risk, and she loved his smiling eyes so much. "Once I go home to change."

"Oh, please, yes. I will expect a fine gown for dinner in my cottage. You recall I do not have a table? We'll be sitting on stools at the windowsill." He stood and offered her his hand. "You're tired. I'll carry you home for a while. Unless you would like to unfold your wings."

"Lizzie's so silly." Angelika couldn't hold back her smile. "But I love being her fairy queen."

"I hope you are also mine. Here, climb on."

She balked when he stopped at the bottom stair. "I think it would use your energy. Your life force," she amended softly when he looked over his shoulder at her. "I would like you to explain it to me, so I won't have this dark pit in my stomach."

Here came that feeling that could only be delayed for so long.

He turned, composed himself, and looked at her with utter regret. "I don't know how I can explain it, in a way that won't make you panic."

CHAPTER TWENTY-FOUR

I can handle it."

Her attention was abruptly split, because Victor's man was visible to her. He was against a yew tree in a shockingly effective camouflage, and his eerie yellow stare was on her face. "But don't tell me if it's private," she amended to Will with the barest stutter. "Tell me later."

"I suppose you deserve to know," Will said as he toed gently at some moss on the stair she stood on. "And of course you can handle it. You will always be able to handle whatever comes in this life."

"I hope so," she said, swallowing. The hidden man's eyes were changing, and he was beginning to look angry. He was probably starving, and she was dawdling. "But you are right, I am tired. Could we talk more once I have completed my errands, and we are inside, by the fire?"

"I feel it," Will said to her, searching her face now. "You're so frightened of what I am about to tell you. But I don't want you to be scared. You should know the truth."

"Let us walk and talk." She looked back at the tree, and the man was gone. It took another few seconds to locate him, and he was closer. His graying complexion and tattered clothes gave him the appearance of a yew tree come to life. Victor had told her of Will's violent transformation when she had been threatened. What if there was a fight, and he was hurt, or worse? It would be her fault.

"Angelika, wait," Will spluttered as she marched past him and took the trail at a blistering pace. "Don't run away when I'm trying to tell you something."

"I just need to get back," she replied. The line into the clearing behind the house seemed like miles away. The slope sucked at her shoes, dragging her downhill.

"You'll trip," Will said, scooping an arm around her, forcing her to halt. "Shh, it's all right. Listen to me. I don't know if I am going to live as long as a normal man."

The way Victor's creation moved through the trees was soundless and frightening. Had he followed them up the hill, casting those shadows as he passed the chapel doors, circling, watching the two kiss? What was his motive? Food? Jealousy? He was radiating the same malevolent energy as the trees, and now he carried a short, thick branch like a club.

Will ducked to catch her eye. "Did you hear me?"

"It's fine," Angelika said airlessly.

"It's fine?" Will was stunned. His arm around her weakened. "Did you hear what I just said?"

She was juggling twin horrors. One must be prioritized. "I said I wanted to talk by the fire, but you didn't listen to that, either."

"I'm trying to tell you that I think I'm dying," Will shouted, and the birds roosting above them exploded into flight. "I am losing sensation in my fingertips. I am not healing. I am cold. I am fading away, Angelika."

Angelika wrenched her eyeline off the man who had been so effortlessly stalking them. "What?"

"Don't block this out." Will cupped her shoulders and gave

her a gentle shake. "This is not something you can fix with money, and according to Victor, it likely can't be fixed with science or medicine. This is happening to me, and I'm afraid, and I would very much like you to say something real in reply."

She opened her mouth, but the only sound now was a growl from the trees. Will's hands on her shoulders clamped harder, and comprehension dawned on his face.

"It's all right," Angelika told him from unmoving lips. "We just have to get to the clearing. He won't follow us there."

"Let her go," Victor's creation said, in a voice hoarse from lack of use.

Will released Angelika and whirled, blocking her with his body. "Leave us."

"You leave," the big man countered. "She is afraid of you."

"Of me?" Will was incredulous. "She is in love with me."

How pleasant it must be to be so sure of another's love. Angelika's voice faltered when she said, "I didn't know you could speak."

The man scratched at his neck with a curled hand. "At first, my throat felt . . . not quite right. Then, someone helped me to remember how."

There were kind souls in the world. "I'm glad. Do you remember your old life? What is your name?"

He did not answer, but shrugged and refocused his eerie yellow stare on Will. "I have seen you before. In a dream. A bad dream."

"You woke up before I did in the Frankenstein laboratory. We were lying side by side. We are like brothers."

This shocked the man. "But you are a gentleman."

In response, Will drew down the neck of his shirt to show his line of stitches. "You were made by Victor. I was made by Angelika, his sister."

"I thought I was yours," Victor's creation protested to Angelika. "I thought that was why you visited me."

Angelika confessed to Will, "I take him a basket in the evenings, with food and some essential supplies. Candles, soap, things of that nature. That's why I wanted to hurry back. We will give you vegetable pies tonight—will that be all right?"

"That will be all right," the man echoed. "We want more candles." He was preoccupied with Will's revelation. "Why are you a gentleman, and I live out here?"

"I'm not a gentleman," Will said. "I was spoiled initially, but I now live very modestly, in the cottage near the orchard."

"You can live there, too," Angelika offered. "You ran off so suddenly, I didn't have enough time to treat you well. You are both gentlemen." Her words did not ring true, because this poor soul was barefoot and dirty, and Will was in tailored clothing and boots. "I know you have suffered. But it is not too late to turn everything around. You must return with me now, to wash, and rest. We want to take care of you."

"I've heard about your big black house," the man replied to her. "I've heard you are not so nice, sometimes. You throw people away."

She was so horrid that even a friendless forest dweller knew it? Her reputation preceded her so? "I do not. You ran away. There's a difference."

"You only keep the useful ones." He was about to elaborate, but then noticed Will's interest in his gold ring. "It will never come off. It is too tight." He swung the club menacingly. "She tried to take it but learned her lesson."

"You hurt me that day, and I could have died," Angelika scolded, and to his credit, he ducked his head and looked guilty. "But I found your flowers, and I know you are sorry. Stop swinging that."

Will made a second revelation to the man. "I am only interested in your ring because you have my hands. They gave them to you. That ring was mine, once."

"It's true," Angelika said, but she hurriedly added, "But you do not need to give the ring back. That is not what we are asking of you."

"Keep it," Will agreed. "But I am hoping it holds a clue to my identity. I don't remember who I am. Does it have an engraving?" The man was unsure and shuffled his feet. Will tried another way. "Does it have a picture, or words, or a crest? An insignia? A carving?"

The man assessed his opponents, eyes narrowing over them, suspecting a trick. They both raised their hands and retreated six feet. It was only then that he lifted his hand and scrunched his face in concentration. "I do not see well up close now. There is a shape pressed into the gold."

"Feel with your finger," Angelika suggested.

The man rubbed his fingers over the ring. They did not straighten from their bent shape. "I do not feel things well. These are bad hands I have now."

Will asked, "How long have they felt that way? Did they start feeling cold, and the thumb joints hurt at night, then tingling in the fingertips?" He held up his own hand. "That is what I am feeling."

"It will get worse," the man said, with evident regret. "Until they are no good. Maybe we are brothers. I am not . . . very well. I heard what you told her," he said in a hushed, confidential tone. "I am dying, too."

Angelika could not hear another word. "I think you will be just fine if you allow me to keep you warm and fed. I will prove it by how well I take care of you both." Now she decided to ask the obvious question. "Can I come over and look at your ring, sir?"

"No," Will barked, scaring even himself. He put an arm around her waist, holding her tight to his body. "No, no, no."

"Release her," the man invited with a faint smile. "She can come to me."

Will was incredulous. "And will you give her back?"

"Her hair is soft, and she smells nice." It was not an answer that inspired confidence. He added, "Nicer than Granny, with a nicer voice."

"That was you, stroking my hair?" Angelika put a hand on her hip. "You frightened the wits out of me."

Will was bristling. "Angelika is mine, and you won't take her."

"I am bigger than you, little brother," the man reminded. Angelika's old daydream of two men fighting over her was on the cusp of becoming a reality, unless she acted fast.

"Here's an idea. If I get the candles for you, could you press the ring into some warm wax, and leave it for me? Perhaps your granny could help you." The man considered the unexpected request, but ultimately nodded. "Where do you live?"

His smile was sly. "Somewhere clever."

Angelika could see the military academy in the distance, and she pointed at it. "I want you to know something. There are soldiers looking for you. Have you seen them? They would be in uniform, on horses, and the commander riding at the front is fair and handsome." She watched the man think, and then nod. "You must stay far away from the village, and especially from him. He is angry for what you did to me, and I've told him not to, but he will kill you."

"Another who wants you." The big man observed Will's hold on her. "A fine lady, worth killing a wraith like me."

She shook her head. "No one will kill you on Frankenstein land. Do not cross over the gray stone walls."

"We won't," the man said. "I am so close to you sometimes, but you don't see me. Angelika"—he said her name slowly, like an experiment—"pretty Angelika. Maybe you should come and live with me."

She kept her composure. Will's arm around her waist was tight. "Follow us now, and I will get your dinner basket. Do you ever see my brother, Victor? He is searching for you, too. He has the same color hair as mine, and his horse is a gray mare."

"I see him everywhere. Every day."

"You see? We never threw you away. We have been desperate to find you."

The big man swallowed with emotion in his eyes and followed them for a silent minute. Then he said, "Granny is hungry, and she is angry with me all the time. She doesn't like how I eat. Or how I breathe, or smell." The way he winced was all too familiar.

The last rays of sun filtered through the leaves, and then everything became illuminated. "Please ask Granny to give you a name," Angelika told him. "She's good at that."

Will had not connected the dots. "Who is this Granny? I would like to meet her."

It was apparently the last question the man could tolerate.

"Why? So you can take her, when you already have the pretty one? Brother, you are always trying to take and steal!" Swiping his club against some branches, he stormed off into the yews, invisible in five seconds. The forest fell silent.

Will was bewildered. "What just happened?"

Angelika said wearily, "He's got Mary."

CHAPTER TWENTY-FIVE

Once upon a time, Angelika Frankenstein yearned for adventure. If her past self could have seen her now, she would have let out a cheer. *Finally, something is happening!*

Action. Excitement. Romance.

She was astride Percy, cantering down the long manor drive toward the village, flanked by Victor and Will, with her silk-lined cloak flowing behind her. It was a dramatic production, directed by Lizzie. She had waved them goodbye, and then vomited pitifully into an urn of geraniums.

Angelika had never felt as determined, or alive. It was worth noting that her mirror had also confirmed she looked very well indeed today, despite her patchy night's sleep.

But the gnawing worry in her gut over Mary ruined the moment.

She knew that the horseback tableau was impressive, because Christopher was waiting astride his horse at the front gates, and his expression was something like disbelief. As she reined Percy in, Angelika asked Christopher, "What is it?"

"I'm just surprised, every time I see you. I always think you can't possibly be as beautiful as I remember, and then you appear and . . ." Christopher made a helpless gesture, like he was out of words. His shyness made her heart quiver.

She understood how he felt. She could look at Christopher all day long.

When Angelika glanced to Will on her left, she could see he was irritated. "I see her day and night. She is always this beautiful." His voice had not lost its possessive growl from the hillside the day previous. "But beauty is only skin deep, and not an achievement. There is more than meets the eye when it comes to Angelika."

Christopher opened his mouth but was cut off before he started speaking.

"Yes, yes, very good," Victor said loudly. "Courting, complimenting, competing, et cetera. Can we return to that later? We have a family emergency."

Christopher still had the note from their messenger in his hand and held it up. "Your servant has been taken by the beast. I rode after breakfast, with no men, as you have specified."

"He is no beast, but a man, and she is the closest we have to a grandmother," Angelika corrected. "She is out there somewhere with the man, probably living in the forest, or in a cave somewhere."

"Is she the emerald thief?" Christopher asked, and Angelika was forced to shrug and nod. "Are we sure they have not colluded?"

Victor answered that. "Until we speak to her in person, and make sure she's all right, we are not sure of anything."

"We all need to be aware of a new fact," Will said. "That man is thinking about taking Angelika; he told me as much. And if he does, it will be hard to stop him."

Christopher's only reply was to lift one side of his jacket to reveal a pistol.

Will shook his head. "That gives me no comfort, because he can hide, and stalk. He blends so well into the trees he could be here right now and we would not see him." This statement caused them to all look around themselves, and the horses grew spooked.

Victor covered his fear by saying, "He'd give her back within the hour."

Will was not amused. "He told Angelika that he has been watching her, sometimes from close range, and thinks she is pretty, nice-smelling, and has soft hair."

Angelika tugged fussily at her suede gloves. "I don't like to brag."

Victor stood up in his stirrups. "I think he meant 'pretty smelly-looking.'"

"This isn't a joke," Christopher said, clicking into his military persona. "So, he will look for opportunities where she is outdoors and alone. Probably nighttime, when he can blend in. What else do we know?"

"He won't eat meat," Angelika volunteered. "He's got quite a few survival supplies by now: blankets, French blackberry soap, candles, a knife, a flint, a waterskin, a copy of *Paradise Lost*, and a nice book on oriental woodblock art."

Christopher asked, with strained patience, knowing the answer: "And how does he have those things?" He looked to Will now. "Another man who does not eat meat. Very strange. I've only ever met one in my lifetime. Now two?" His crystal-blue eyes narrowed.

Angelika stepped in. "I think we should consider another option, rather than hunting him. I've thought about this all night. I'm the only one he trusts, and I think—"

"No," all three men said together.

"If I go with him, he will take me to Mary." She appealed to

Christopher. "You are a hunter, so you know we need bait. I'm nice-smelling, and he will absolutely come for me. Then I can talk my way out of it, or pay a ransom, and bring her home."

"No, you little idiot," Victor said with feeling. "Absolutely not. Chris and I are going to ride up into the chapel area, where you saw him last. I am going to talk to him and convince him to take us to Mary."

"And if he won't be convinced?" Christopher's hand went to his pistol again like a reflex. "You both believe you can talk, or pay, your way out of anything, but take my advice. Things rarely work out that way in the moment."

"I agree with you there," Will said.

"If you shoot him, Mary might never be found. Look at that mountain." Angelika pointed to the peak rising up from behind their black manor house. "She is up there right now, possibly injured, and certainly irate. He could have her tied to a tree."

"Here's a plan," Christopher said. "Angelika will put out her gifts for him"—here his voice stiffened in disapproval—"and I will be in a deer hide, watching. I will follow him."

"You aren't listening to me," Will told him bluntly. "I have seen him in person. No one could track him."

Whatever emotion Christopher was feeling caused his mount to stamp the ground. "And you weren't listening when I said I can hunt anything. This man is finally a worthy adversary for me, and doubly so because I will be protecting Angelika."

"Enough, peacocks." Victor was weary. "Chris, let's set off to search the forest behind the house. Will, you stay with the bait while she undertakes her errands in the village."

"Errands on your behalf. I am going to arrange your wedding," Angelika said with a nose-wrinkle.

Victor tipped his hat. "Much obliged."

Angelika explained to a concerned Christopher, "I will be fine. He promised me he would not leave Frankenstein land. He will not cross over the walls."

"Promises don't mean much to desperate people. How vast is your land?"

"There's almost two thousand acres to search, so I could use some assistance." Victor circled his mare, Athena. She pinned her ears back and bit Percy's rump.

As they all reshuffled positions, Victor's eyeline was on Will. "Look after my sister," he commanded gruffly. "We'll take a route through the walnut grove. Everyone, reconvene for supper. Catch me if you can." In an unnecessarily showy gesture, he lined Athena up to the wall and jumped it.

Christopher grinned as he watched, despite the gravity of the situation. "Look after Angelika," he told Will.

"I have looked after her longer than you've known her. You're being left behind."

They held their reins tight as Christopher succumbed to the swirling excitement; he, too, put his horse to the stone wall and jumped it with easy competence. In the distance, they heard Victor whoop in exhilaration.

"They will have far too much fun hunting today," Will observed with a headshake. As they began to trot their horses in the direction of the village, he asked, "Are we going to talk about what I told you? Last night, you grabbed Lizzie and vanished."

"We were in my room. Hardly hiding." But she hadn't exactly emerged from her room, either.

He now held his reins tied in a knot, with his wrist fed through the loop; just like someone who was having difficulty with their hands might. Once she found a solution for this current crisis, she would explain to him very firmly that he was not dying. He'd told her that on the very first night as she half carried him naked up the stairs. He was wrong then, and wrong now.

"We really need to talk," Will repeated.

Angelika sat deep in her saddle, and pushed Percy into a canter.

The village of Salisbury was even more shabby and depressing than she remembered. Most of the shops were boarded up. A ruddy-faced maid had her skirts tucked into her underwear as she tossed a bucket of excrement into a ditch. Every eye catalogued her clothing, horse, and tack.

"Here, little sweetlings," Angelika said, tossing coins down to the children. "The church is along this left street, and we will ride past Clara's cottage. Let us call on her. I might even get to hold Winnie if he's awake."

Will nodded. "Of course."

As if she had conjured them with her thoughts, Clara walked into view down the crossroad and turned in the opposite direction, lugging Edwin on her hip. Her friend looked like any one of these poor folk, with mud on her hem and an exhausted aura. In addition to her boy, she was struggling with heavy string bags of groceries.

"She needs help," Will said.

"Where is she going? Down this horrid alley? But she lives this way."

They had to halt to let a pony cart pass, and by the time they trotted to catch up, Clara was at a wooden door, and was struggling to open it.

"Clara!" Angelika halted Percy. "Do you require assistance?" She noticed a sign: WINCHESTER BOARDINGHOUSE. A bucket was emptied out a window. A cough and a spit followed. They could hear a man shouting, and a woman's placating tones. A bang. A cat yowl. Everything stank.

Angelika was agog. "You've left your lovely cottage to live . . . here?"

Percy sneezed.

"Hello, Angelika, Will," Clara said, turning around with great reluctance. "How do you do?"

"Surely I misunderstand?" Angelika prompted from her seat in the saddle. "You are visiting an acquaintance?"

"We have lived here almost a week," Clara said, hoisting Edwin, who twinkled up at Angelika. "I am well aware that it is below your standards"—here she paused as a second bucket was emptied out—"but it will do for now."

"You cannot find anything more suitable?" Angelika held down her crop for Edwin to grasp and they played a gentle tug-of-war. "This place looks horrible."

"Better than the street." She cowered as a scowling woman poked her head out of yet another window. "I'm so sorry, Mrs. Winchester. We won't linger."

"No visitors." Mrs. Winchester had a face like a smacked behind, and she narrowed her eyes at Edwin. "No crying, neither. Did I just hear you say my fine establishment looks horrible, missy?"

"I haven't set foot inside, but I wouldn't board my pigs here, you rude old wench," Angelika told her with ringing honesty, and the window was slammed. Will scratched his jaw to hide his grin.

"Thanks ever so," Clara exclaimed. "She already hates us. Last night Edwin wouldn't settle, and she took the doorknob off my room. I had to beg to be let out this morning."

Angelika's indignation was rising. "Does Christopher know that you live here?"

Clara's reply was carefully worded. "He knows that I have vacated."

Will looked at Angelika. She nodded and said, "Come and stay with us until you work out your next move. We will not leave you here."

Pride had rendered Clara speechless, and colored her red to the roots of her hair. Then, the audible argument in the boardinghouse reached a pinnacle. There was a sickening slap, the woman began crying, and Edwin clutched Clara's dress, his chubby face twisted in distress.

Will assured Clara, "The whitewash in the cottage beside mine was dry when I checked it this morning. You will have your own privacy." He dismounted and tied Solomon. Gently, he put a hand on Clara's shoulder, bringing her back to the moment, and hung her groceries on the railing. "There is room for you."

Faintly, Clara replied, "Are you sure?"

He nodded. "Give Edwin to Angelika for a moment."

Angelika dismounted and bounced the smelly boy on her hip, singing him a song: "Disgusting place—not fit for pigs—is it, my darling Win-Win?"

It did not take long to pack Clara's belongings. She reappeared with a bulging carpetbag and Edwin's basket, and Will held a crate. His knuckles were bleeding. He had apparently found time to rescue the woman in distress, and she fled at speed with her hand to her cheek, mouthing a thank-you.

Angelika clicked her fingers, and a driver halted his cart. It was drawn by a one-eyed mule and was full of dirty vegetables, but beggars could not be choosers. "I'm hiring you for a private trip to my manor. I'll take a pumpkin, too." The driver nodded, and she put a coin in his palm.

"Angelika," Clara began, but found no more words.

"It's my pleasure. Will shall escort you home." She handed Edwin to his mother. "I'm going to the church, and then I'll ride home. Leg me up, please."

Will did so but was clearly torn by the decision he had to make as he loaded Clara's luggage and groceries. "I am not meant to leave you alone."

"I can take care of myself in the village. I've done so all my life. And they cannot." Poor Clara looked wretched, hugging her son tight. "Ask Sarah to fill a bath for them."

Will nodded. "Come straight home, my love."

"Of course." She waited until they were on their way. As she turned her own horse toward the church, the window opened once more. It was Mrs. Winchester, spying on Clara's departure.

Angelika flipped her a penny. "Invest in a new attitude." Percy lifted his tail and deposited a steaming heap.

Without Will by her side, she did feel vulnerable as she continued riding. Word had spread that the lady on the shiny horse dropped coins, and children trailed her like bees. Men leaned on doorframes to watch her pass. Percy was fretting for Solomon and wouldn't stop neighing.

It was the first time in her life she'd sighed with relief to be riding up to a church. She tied Percy to a wrought-iron railing near the rectory and loosened his girth-strap. "You're a foolish nag," she scolded him, and he began stripping leaves off an untidy hedge. She found herself unable to leave him and sought the attention of a sweaty young man sweeping the path in religious garb.

"I will pay you a shilling to watch my horse for a short while. The villagers look like they'd steal the shoes clean off his feet."

The disciple snorted a laugh, then looked skyward to mentally apologize. "If you donate it to the collection plate, consider it done."

"You need a groundskeeper here," Angelika remarked as she took off her gloves. "I know from experience that if you let ivy creep an inch, it will smother everything."

"Our work is never done," agreed the young man. "We almost did engage a groundskeeper, but we have had to make sacrifices. Father Porter is inside, if that's who you are here for."

Everything was arranged. She was here at the very place she had avoided for weeks. Years. Inside was a man she had not seen since the worst moments of her life. But if she could arrange this wedding, Lizzie would smile again, and Victor would perhaps increase his hugs to biannual.

There was nothing else to do but enter the big dark doors.

She had a premonition.

She was walking to her doom.

CHAPTER TWENTY-SIX

Angelika walked through the church with both arms across her stomach in a tight self-hug. Victor's voice kept her company, albeit in her imagination.

Walking down the aisle at long last, eh, Jelly?

Look out. The bearded man in the sky will throw a lightning bolt at you.

Those stained-glass panels look new, don't they? Lambskin upholstery on the pews. What do you think those cost? Father Porter is no better than a common grifting thief.

I will bet a thousand pounds he is wearing a jeweled ring the size of a quail's egg.

"Hello?" Her voice echoed and was not answered, so she stopped when she reached the fourth-row pew. On this lefthand side was where she once sat with her parents. She found she could not walk another step without sitting down in her old place.

Every Sunday morning had felt like an eternity in this seat, and she'd winced through every moment, hyperaware of Victor's incredulous expression and barely concealed scoffing at some of the priest's claims. It was now clear that she had wasted that time.

"I miss you, Mama, Papa," she said to the empty seats beside her. "I should have known that sitting with you regularly was my privilege." She whispered to herself now, "Typical Angelika. You've got to start noticing moments with other people, because they do not last forever."

"Miss . . . Annnnnn . . . gelika . . . Fran . . . ken . . . stein," an elderly man said, scaring her silly.

She tried not to gape, but Father Porter looked like he'd been buried six feet under since she saw him last. He was nothing but bone and blue-veined skin, and cloaked in robes fit for royalty. How he had the strength to bear that thick gold rope around his neck was anybody's guess.

She heard herself ask: "How old are you?"

"The good Lord has given me my ninetieth birthday," Father Porter replied.

"NINETY?" Her horror echoed around them like *ninety-inety-inety-inety*. She hurriedly got to her feet. "What I mean to say is, congratulations, and nice to see you again."

He bore that same shrewd smile she remembered. "You have not changed one bit."

"Thank you. I am here on business, to arrange wedding services."

He blinked. "Congratulations are due in return, then."

"For my brother, Victor."

"Ah. Victor. The young man who told me I was never welcome to call upon him again. The young man who I hear such strange, unnatural things about." Father Porter's stare was difficult not to squirm beneath. He finished coolly, "I would ask you to speak to an aide. But we are fully booked."

"This is a special request. Victor has a deep attachment to our family chapel. We wish for the service to take place there. If you could make one of your more—ah—nimble associates available, we will pay handsomely for the convenience. It is a fair hike, all uphill."

Serene, he replied, "There is only myself, my child."

"Oh. What about in neighboring parishes? Could a colleague be arranged?" She was beginning to feel panicked. Could he ride a mule? "Whatever will we do?"

"A donation may help bygones be bygones." Father Porter's rheumy eyes had a new gleam. "He may marry here, should that donation be sufficient. I will ensure he can pick his date, depending on the size of the affair."

He folded his hands on his midsection. As imaginary Victor had predicted, Father Porter wore a ruby that could have fit in a nutcracker. It was a stunning stone, but the memory of children swarming in the dirt for coins was too fresh to admire it.

Angelika forced a pleasant smile. "The ceremony we have in mind will be five guests and will probably take five minutes. But we really are set on him marrying at home."

"You have avoided this place a long time. Come." Father Porter was apparently tired out by simply standing there, and he gestured for her to follow.

They took a door to the left, then walked to a vestry office. It was one short hallway, but by the time he took his seat at his desk, Angelika was sweating from witnessing his arduous journey. He appeared close to falling several times, and she had taken his arm out of necessity. She collapsed into the seat opposite his own, so thirsty she'd willingly drink from the vase of roses behind him.

He let her sit for a long time in silence before saying, "You think me quite ancient, don't you, my child? I suppose you have not known anyone who has grown old. I still pray for your dear parents."

She masked her flare of temper. "I confess I did not think you would still be working at your fine age."

"I cannot retire."

"Oh, is that against the rules?"

"I cannot retire," he repeated with increased enunciation, making it clear she had interrupted, "until my replacement is sent."

"He'd jolly well better hurry up," Angelika said, then sank two inches in her seat when his lips thinned. "I'm sorry."

"Every thought comes out of your mouth. You really have not changed." Fingers creaking into a steeple below his chin, he stared at her. "You do not visit your parents' graves."

"We pay to have them maintained."

"It is not the same thing." He continued his staring.

She remembered how she'd strode toward the man in the forest with her eyes on his ring. *Diplomacy, Angelika. Tread carefully.*

She changed the subject. "I do not visit the village often. I was shocked to see how miserable it looks."

"Poverty is a cycle that is hard to break." He said this with utter sincerity as he sat on a small upholstered throne beneath a framed Botticelli. His hand lay flat on the desk, like the weight of the wine-red gem was too much.

His eyeline moved to a silver salver in front of her.

Angelika understood and took out her purse. She placed the shilling she had earlier negotiated onto it. Father Porter kept staring until she added a second shilling. Then a third. And a fourth.

He blinked and reanimated. "I have always said you possess a generous heart. I am surprised you are not married yet yourself, Miss Frankenstein."

Thoughtlessly she replied, "I will be. Soon, I think."

"And who is your intended?"

"You would not know him. He is from another town."

"Sir William Black," the father said, causing a chill to run down her spine. "A mysterious man, with a name that we cannot find in records. A man with no past, known by nobody, and rarely seen. Those who have seen him remark he is a fine-looking man; I pray a handsome face has not swayed your . . . generous heart."

"How do you know that?" She answered her own question immediately. "Everyone knows everything in a small village."

"I promised your dear papa that I would keep an eye on you." And he did, for another agonizingly long minute. "Are you quite sure about this man? What is his standing in society? What is his fortune, his estate? Who are his parents, what is his annuity?"

Angelika puffed up. "These are all his own business. Not yours."

His laugh cracked painfully. "The Frankenstein family is not for just any man to marry into, and I would venture that Victor has not done his due diligence. I should like to meet him, to assess his suitability. Why do you not attend Sunday services?"

"We have our chapel at home."

"A chapel with no priest." Father Porter now folded his hands in an ominous way. "I think we should pray together."

"I would love to, after we sort out Victor's wedding. He is marrying Elizabeth Lavenza, the firstborn daughter to Gregor and Isabella. Her mother hails from Majorca, Spain, although they have a country estate in England and Lizzie was raised here. They are dreadfully wealthy and not after Victor's fortune. Her hobbies include writing and directing theater plays. I hope the entire village will enjoy the merry entertainment she will provide."

She withheld that Lizzie's plays were not always suitable for children. Gory violence, gory kissing, and almost always a ghost, or a disturbing creature visiting from the stars—but these were editable details.

"You are able to give me your sister-in-law's pedigree, but not your own beau's."

Staring back was her only defense at this point.

"Victor marries here," Father Porter said to the shillings, "or not at all. He's a stubborn boy, but explain those two options to him as best you can. I will also require resumed weekly attendance at my services, and a long-overdue apology, and, naturally, an appropriate donation."

Angelika showed her teeth. "May I ask what our donation could help achieve?"

He did not surprise her by how readily he answered. "Beneath the main altar is a deep crack, and it requires refurbishment. The opportunity should be taken to exchange it for white marble, instead of the present green, in keeping with the new frescoes. Should you be especially generous, our statue of Christ requires repainting. The artist is Italian, and his services are quite out of reach in our present budget."

Marble, and a holiday for an Italian.

"And for the villagers? What would our donation afford them?"

He blinked like a toad. "I just explained that, my child."

Angelika knew when she was beaten. "I will speak with Victor when I return home. Our next order of business is that we seem to have lost our dear old servant, Mary. We are afraid she wandered into town and succumbed to some foul play or accident."

He was leaning forward to take the shillings. "I will pray for her."

"Could you tell me if you have received anyone dead who was unaccounted for?"

The coins were put into the pocket of his robe. "Try the morgue. I hear your brother knows the way there."

Rattled by his all-knowing tone, she stammered, "I did, and they told me that sometimes their dead start off here."

This time, he didn't blink. If he was selling bodies to the morgue to line his own pockets, he was a fine actor indeed.

"Families bury their loved ones here, as you are well aware. If the body is unclaimed, then yes, that would be usual that they be sent to the morgue."

Angelika's appointment was now ended, apparently, because Father Porter was rising to his feet. He said, "Perhaps you would like to visit with your parents."

He went to a side door, struggled with the handle, and then they were stepping outside. Angelika was relieved to spot Percy, still tied, and the church assistant continuing to sweep. Slow and steady, they toddled to the graveyard.

"Here," Father Porter said, and Angelika was reunited with her mother and father.

"Our money has not gone to good use," she said critically, meaning the moss and unkept grass. Noticing these details kept the squeeze of emotion at bay; there was nothing as terrible as seeing a loved one's name and dates carved into granite.

She didn't know what Father Porter wanted. Tears? Hands folded in prayer? "It is a fine spot," she remarked. From where he was tied, Percy let out a piercing whinny.

Where would Father Porter select for himself? She began to wander along the row, trying to guess what was premium real estate. She came upon a length of lime-green baby grass on a new grave.

"I told you I have been waiting for my replacement," Father Porter said behind her, "and sadly, here he lies."

Angelika raised her eyes, with a doomed feeling smothering her, and read the name:

FATHER ARLO NORTHCOTT

"A terrible shame," Father Porter said, and now Angelika was sweating from every pore. The date of death, it was—

"Six weeks ago, but I'm sure you heard what happened."

She whispered, "No, I didn't hear. How did he die?"

"His carriage was overturned by highway robbers, as they often are these days."

Angelika swallowed. "Did he die . . . quickly?"

"No. The drivers took a strange route, and the carriage was found in a ravine." Father Porter appeared to be genuinely saddened. "He was brought here alive and fought very hard through the night. Sadly, he returned to our Lord too soon. You can see he was very young."

Angelika did the sums. "He was thirty-three. That's very young to be a priest, is it not?" She found herself arguing vigorously. "There must be some mistake. How could he possibly replace you, being so young himself? That seems absolutely out of the question. It's ridiculous. I cannot think of anything more ludicrous than a thirty-three-year-old priest." She wiped her temple.

Father Arlo Northcott?

"He was, by all accounts, devoted to his studies, and lived in uncommon devotion and abstinence since boyhood. He led an exceptional life, though far too short." Father Porter sighed. "A great loss to the church, and this village. I should have liked to have met him, to talk, to understand his faith and his planned direction for the parish. Now we must wait for another replacement to be found."

"And he is definitely right here."

"I don't quite understand your meaning," Father Porter said, his tone sharper—perhaps defensive. "Do you see a grave before you? I conducted the final rites myself."

Angelika shook herself. "I just cannot ever accept the death of one so young."

This is a coincidence. Won't this be a laugh? A fine story, told in a lively way, by the fire?

"I see you are very moved. Would you like to light a candle for Father Northcott on your way out? We could pray."

"I think I might like that." Angelika really just needed to sit down again. She really *would* pray, that Father Arlo North-cott was another man, who had traveled from a wide world teeming with other people. But at that moment, a gate squeak announced someone's approach.

It was a man walking toward them, with his tawny-gold eyes locked on her face as though she were the only woman he would ever seek. He was tall, very handsome, and dressed as if someone with unlimited funds and a fine tailor loved him very much.

It was, of course, without a doubt, her love.

It was Will.

CHAPTER TWENTY-SEVEN

Angelika," Will said when he grew closer, "I am here to escort you home." He appeared flushed and slightly out of breath. "I met Jacob and some of my gardening crew heading back to Blackthorne Manor. They were plenty enough to escort Clara, and I didn't want to leave you alone. I galloped the entire way back."

She took a half step back, and he noticed the diminutive Father Porter for the first time.

"Forgive me, Father. I have interrupted."

"Please wait with the horses. I will join you shortly." She attempted to turn Father Porter with a hand on his elbow, but he was raising his eyeline up, squinting against the sun, and slow recognition dawned.

Father Porter looked sharply back to the gravestone, and so did Will.

"Father Arlo Northcott," Will read out loud, and the priest's eyes rolled closed.

Angelika managed to catch him. "Oh, God. Oh, hell." She lowered his head carefully onto the grass, then folded her shawl into a pillow. "Father, Father. Can you hear me?" She patted his cheek and saw his eyelids moving. "He's not dead."

Will croaked, "He recognized me."

"Don't you dare faint, too," she threatened when Will stared back at the headstone with glassy eyes. "Keep your wits. Go into that side door there. Help, help!" She waved an arm at the sweeping staffer, who dropped his broom.

To the gravestone, Will asked, "Is that supposed to be me? Father Arlo Northcott? Father? I'm a priest? I'm a priest?" He was fast approaching hysteria.

Angelika had to shout to get through to him. "We know nothing until we have proof."

He shouted back, "How? Angelika, how?"

"Go into that door and lock it behind you. Search the office as quickly as you can for anything bearing the name of Father Northcott. Files or letters. They may be locked in a drawer."

She felt in Father Porter's pockets, found a ring of keys, and tossed them up to Will. His hands did not grasp properly, and the way they landed in the grass reminded her of Victor's wretched man, dropping the apple. She passed the keys back up, and compressed the feeling she had in her gut. "Will, go right now."

Will backed away from the scene and managed to get inside before the aide from the front path sprinted up.

"What happened?"

She was truthful when she replied, "He looked like he saw a ghost."

"So, let me get this straight," Victor said, grinning. "You went to arrange my wedding but almost killed the priest? Typical Angelika."

The members of the Frankenstein Secret Society had reconvened in the library of the manor that same evening. They were eating bowls of stew off their laps, dipping into it with crusty bread. Christopher was the only one who looked somewhat elegant doing it and showed no signs of having ridden in a forest full of spiderwebs for ten hours.

Victor, on the other hand, most certainly did.

Christopher was subdued and apologetic to have come home without his quarry and kept heaving sighs as he stared into the fire. It wasn't his fault. He had no idea that he was essentially hunting a huge forest sprite.

Angelika addressed her brother haughtily. "Father Porter is ninety. A strong gust of wind could have killed him. And as a matter of fact, I saved him. He swooned into my arms like a lady." She was lying on her back in front of the fire, with her bowl scraped clean and Edwin sitting astride her stomach. She bounced him up and down. "I caught that nasty old man, didn't I, Winnie? Didn't I catch that old bag of bones?"

Edwin let out a belly laugh.

Will leveled a flat look at Victor. "Typical brave, generous Angelika, cool under pressure, and saving people left and right." It was a comment designed to defend her, but it also made Clara drop her gaze back to her stew.

"Sowwy, Jelly," Victor said with his mouth full.

"Do you know why he fainted?" Lizzie asked. She was sitting on the floor, leaning on Victor's leg, and patted the rug to get Edwin to crawl to her. He headed in her direction with cheerful determination. A competition was brewing between the two women. Lizzie looked up frequently to see Victor's reaction to the little boy; he was too busy stuffing himself with stew to notice.

Hopeless, Angelika sighed to herself. To Lizzie, she replied, "He fainted almost certainly because he is ninety. He was

roused after a few minutes, so we felt sure he would recover."
The moment his eyelids had fluttered, she'd left him in the
arms of his aide, rushing to find a frazzled Will pacing near
the horses.

Clara was happy to share her son and sat with her feet
tucked underneath herself. Sitting beside Christopher, she
looked like his relaxed wife, and a rather pretty one at that.
It was amazing what a bath, and an afternoon nap, could
achieve. It was the second time Angelika had noticed they
looked like a well-matched pair. She stared at the distance on
the chaise between them, and calculated the width of her own
behind.

Angelika continued. "I have also considered the possibility
that he grew light-headed from trying to wheedle some new
marble from the Frankensteins."

Victor was scornful. "Marble? What does he want with
that?"

"He'd like white marble for the altar, to give it a fresh new
look. And his Italian artist friend needs to come for a working holiday, to touch up Christ's eyeballs." The word *artist*
inspired Angelika to reach over to the bookcase for a blank
journal. Wordlessly, she passed it up to Clara, Lizzie passed
her a pencil, and after a minute, the young widow took the
hint, and began to sketch.

"He can keep dreaming," Victor said. "If he says it's a
choice between marrying there or not at all, I'm sorry, Lizzie,
but we're having a bastard."

She did not laugh, and the entire room went silent.

"What grand adventures you have had today, Angelika,"
Clara said to break the tension after processing that statement. "Tell me again what you told Mrs. Winchester. The part
with the penny."

Angelika grinned up from the carpet and mimed flipping a coin. " 'Invest in a new attitude.' I forgot to tell you this part: at the same moment, Percy grunted out some dung on her doorstep. It was the best moment of my entire life."

"What a frightfully good line," Lizzie said, writing in her *IDEAS FOR PLAYS* notebook. "I'm stealing it."

"I'm happy to be a muse." Angelika patted the floor and Edwin came scuttling back, quick as a crab, his blue eyes bright.

She was wrong. This was the very best moment of her entire life.

She was surrounded by her friends, full of good food, warm from the fire, and a baby was pulling her hair. Sitting in the church pew today had reminded her to notice every moment with those she loved, no matter how mundane.

She looked up at Will. He was withdrawn and rattled by the day's events, but oh, to witness the firelight in those eyes was an honor. The entire moment was unforgettable. If only Victor would start to think this way. He was blithely unaware of Edwin's presence, and equally unaware of how much it must hurt Lizzie.

Clara wiped away tears of mirth. "I would have given anything to see her face."

"Don't worry, I'm sure I'll offend someone else again soon, with you on hand to witness it. That's typical Angelika."

"A penny and some dung was too generous for that woman," Will said from his armchair. He was not served beef stew, and had only picked at the vegetable pasty that Mrs. Rumsfield had made for him. Christopher still found his dietary choices deeply odd, judging by how many times he glanced at the plate.

Saying the name *Father Arlo Northcott* aloud had not jolted

Will back into himself, if that was indeed his identity. He was still the same person she had rode to the village with, and on the ride home he was quiet, and also empty-handed. He had found nothing in the office. Overtired and pale, he had returned to his cottage alone, only reemerging for supper.

They had agreed to keep it a secret for now, given the presence of Christopher and Clara. But Angelika wondered if she could make use of her well-connected source right here and now—discreetly, of course.

"Christopher, did you hear about the new priest who was killed on his way to this parish? Father Porter told me about it. What a shame."

"It was my second troop that found him," Christopher said, using what Angelika now thought of as his Commander Voice. "Terrible business. The horses were cut loose, drivers killed, carriage ransacked, and Father Northcott was left for dead. He was too thirsty and feverish to last much longer." It was a strong, dramatic retelling; it was no wonder Lizzie was taking notes, and Clara turned the page to begin a new sketch.

"How long do you think he remained in the carriage?" Will asked faintly.

"Judging by the, er, condition of the drivers, the priest had lived for a number of days after they were killed."

Will did his best to mask his feelings. "Why didn't he break free?"

"The carriage had been tipped over. It slid down the ravine upside down and was pinned against one of those big yew trees. The windows were too small to ever climb out of. But I'm told he tried so hard to kick out, the sole was off the bottom of his boot." Christopher's voice rang with admiration.

"A fighter," Angelika observed.

The pieces fit too well. Charity-minded. Always providing

good, character-building advice. Uncomfortable in confined spaces, like during the carriage ride to the academy. Stubborn, and with an exceptional will to live. So uncommonly devout and abstinent, he felt he was unable to ever, ever wed her, let alone bed her. When she looked at Edwin, she swore the baby winked at her.

Christopher was on to Will. "Do you ask so many questions because you think you may be connected?" He assessed him for a beat. "You'd make a fine footman."

"The timeframe fits well," Will admitted.

"Nobody made it out of that alive. Trust me on that." Christopher finished his wine in a large swallow. Will was brooding into the fire. Edwin was tinkering with Victor's boot buckle and hoping for his attention.

Clara asked as she continued to draw, "Why would someone do this to a Christian man?"

Christopher explained, "A priest traveling to his new parish would be carrying a great deal of personal effects. Cash, jewelry, clothing, books, plus the extra security would have flagged it as a lucrative prospect. One of the drivers could have been in on it, judging by the strange route they took into the village."

Now he gave Will a stare.

"I don't feel safe living in this village anymore," Clara said quietly. Her pencil strokes slowed, and shyly, she displayed her page to the room: a steep incline, the shape of an upturned carriage, and the trunk of a tree. Everything was rendered quickly, but somehow captured the desolation of the moment. Her skill in one minute of work was astounding.

"Very good," Angelika praised her. "I want you to fill that book." She regretted her thoughtlessness when she saw Will turn his face away from it.

Christopher patted Clara's knee. "I must say, I'm glad you've decided to live up here. The villagers are growing desperate, and food is in short supply. I'm even wondering if it was our big forest monster who caused this tragedy."

"God works in mysterious ways," Victor said out of nowhere as he laid his spoon down at last.

"Vic," Lizzie gasped. "What a thing to say."

"That's horrible," Angelika hissed at him. "Victor, I cannot believe you."

He was defiant. "I'm just saying, maybe there are no more vacancies for talentless men who care more for marble than their parishioners. They all need to get a real job."

"You have no idea if he was like that." Angelika resisted the strong urge to look at Will, but she felt his helpless anger. "You simplify things in a way you should be ashamed of, Victor."

"And I'm saying, just among friends, that if I had my way, they'd all be tossed out into the street with nothing, so they could experience what their worshippers endure." Victor was stroking his fingers through Lizzie's shiny black hair, and nobody but Angelika noticed how Will's hands were clenched with the effort of staying silent.

That reminded her. "Are your knuckles sore? I am not the only one who did a little rescuing today. Will saved some poor woman from a beating."

"He did," Clara said, so admiring that Angelika was now juggling a two-way jealousy. "He kicked in a door at the boardinghouse, punched a man, and left, in as long as it took me to tell this story."

"He's nothing if not efficient," Angelika agreed. "I bet that woman is telling a story about the handsome stranger who saved her in her time of need."

Her jealousy expanded and threatened to eclipse her civility.

Will was cupping his right hand. Was that why he hadn't eaten anything? He couldn't hold a fork? Angelika sat up from the floor. He read her expression and shook his head at her. A fuss was the last thing he ever wanted, and also the one thing she liked to do best.

It was her house; she'd fuss if she liked. Will sighed, knowing it was no use resisting.

Christopher observed the entire wordless communication.

"Show me." She put his plate aside and sat on the arm of Will's armchair. He gave her his hand and she winced over the splits. There was a hint of warmth in the swollen joints. She curled his hand around hers and began a slow rubbing. "Poor, poor thing. Far too gallant. Far too brave. Now look what you've done. Are we telling Victor what we know later?" That last part was a whisper, and he shook his head.

"I think I will return home now," Christopher said abruptly. "Thank you for dinner."

Angelika was guilty over her inconsideration and tried to pull her hand back, but Will held on to it with newfound strength.

Victor glanced down at Edwin tugging at his trouser leg before addressing Christopher. "It's dark now; stay the night. Your horse is put away. We could set out early and go up to that clearing where you saw the footprints. I will rescue Mary if it's the last thing I do."

Edwin chirped for attention; Victor drained his wineglass. Lizzie stared at her diamond ring like she was debating hurling it into the fire. She was dramatic enough for such a gesture.

Angelika decided her brother was quite dim for such a smart man. "The roads are teeming with criminals, so perhaps you ought to stay, Christopher. The room across the hall from mine is still empty."

When Victor looked at her, she mouthed, *Pick up the baby.*

Victor blinked, rechecked his calculations, and realized he'd made a grave error.

"What is it, my good man? You wish to speak to me? Very well." Victor picked up the lad, seating him on his knee like a sack of flour. Experimentally, he bounced him. Edwin screamed with joy, and Lizzie laughed. The diamond ring remained firmly in situ.

It was Angelika's last good deed for the day before she went to bed.

CHAPTER TWENTY-EIGHT

It felt strange, knowing Christopher was in the room opposite her own. Angelika had locked her door before she got into bed. She could not say she liked his presence, because she still thought of it as Will's room. Now Christopher was using that tub, sleeping in that bed, and erasing the last traces of his rival's presence. Male cats rubbed against things to mark them as property. She could picture it now.

She'd slept soundly for around two hours, but was now awake, tossing and turning. It felt like a waste of time to be asleep when the house and grounds were so full of interesting guests and Mary was out there somewhere. Thunder cracked in the distance. Would she be kept dry? Did the big man have enough sense to keep her warm, and somewhat comfortable?

Angelika could not see Will's cottage from her window, but she was absolutely sure that he would be awake. She could feel a pull from him. He must be so hungry after not touching his meal. She pulled on a robe in the dark and put on her boots. In the kitchen, she found some leftover cheese and bread, and lit a lantern. She needed to see Will's face one more time, to ask for a hug, and to decide if the name Arlo suited him.

It was only a quick shortcut through the orchard.

During the day, she could agree to the men's terms, and they seemed reasonable. Stay close to someone, and be guarded by them. But what were the chances that in the next three minutes she would intersect with the huge man's path? She hardly flattered herself that he was so taken with her that he was waiting right now. She preferred the more likely outcome: she would soon be lying in Will's arms on his narrow bed, in his monastery-white room, listening to the storm rolling in.

Taking a calculated risk was typical Angelika.

The air outside was perfumed by approaching rain clouds, and something else strange that turned her stomach and made her hungry. She swung her lantern and walked through the first rows of apples, past the Conqueror variety, picking one out of habit. Biting it, she found it to be the same flavor as always: sour and sweet, the taste of childhood. It made her think of her brother and that day with the spade, and how Will had asked if she had planted her own tree. "I should have," she said out loud to herself to cover her nerves. All this talk of monsters and kidnapping couldn't help but affect her. "I am going to start creating things on my own, without Victor, no matter what he says."

She could hear a crackle. Was it rain?

"I'm going to get married in the Notre-Dame in Paris," she said, breaking into a jog.

In the far distance, up on the hill, there was a light glowing in Will's cottage. Perhaps it was a candle on the sill, burning for her like the star of Bethlehem. "I'm going to wear a dress that will employ ten seamstresses for a year, and I am going to have to increase my fitness to walk down that long aisle—"

She burst through a row of trees, and what she saw and smelled had her heart sinking into the earth.

It wasn't Victor's big man. But it *was* men. Men from the

village, four, five, huddled around a campfire, and they were not the regular gardeners. They had sacks of apples around them. It was theft, but no matter. She saw liquor bottles, and a rabbit cooking on a spit. In the heartbeat that they all stared, she saw them look at her nightgown, her loose hair, and the fact that no protector stepped out behind her.

"Hello, luvvie," one said, and his smile and tone were all the warning she needed.

Mary had drummed the following into her during her adolescent years:

No hesitation, no politeness, run.

Angelika swung her arm in a full circle, throwing the lantern into the middle of the group, and she began to run through the rows, faster than their rabbit. Behind her, she heard the roar of confused outrage. Her head start would last only as long as it took drunk men to get to their feet.

"Will!" Her scream pierced the air. "Will, open the door for me!" If he was asleep, or the cottage was further than she thought, it would be too late for her.

Never had she had such a profound empathy for hunted animals as she did now; she could feel every footstep behind her, could hear every branch snap, grunt, curse, and oath. At times it felt like she was miles ahead; other times she felt the pluck of fingers on her clothes. Her ankle turned and she lost a boot, just as her brother had on that fateful night when they created their masterpieces.

"Angelika!" Will's faraway shout was coming from the wrong direction. She had somehow gotten turned around, and she was in the green apples when she should be surrounded by russet red.

Her hesitation cost her.

Hands grabbed her upper arms and lifted her clean off the

ground. She smelled liquor and sweat. In her ear, a stranger sneered, "Where're you off to?"

Everything hung suspended in an odd moment, then time spun faster, and she began kicking her feet. The guttural sounds she heard behind her were horrible. Snarling like a wolf, growling like a bear. The hard grip was wrenched away from her body, and she fell down to her hands and knees. She could hear Christopher shouting, even fainter than Will. Rolling onto her back, she looked up to see her attacker having his neck broken very efficiently by Victor's huge man. The next one who blundered into the fray met the same fate.

Her rescuer tipped back his head, and let out a howl that echoed off the mountain.

He grabbed at a third man, who uttered his final foul word before joining the growing pile. "No! That's enough," Angelika panted, and they let the others flee into the night. Now they were alone.

Gasping for air, she asked, "How did you find me?"

"I think I always will," he replied.

Her nightgown was up around her thighs. She pushed at it, but her hands were covered in dirt. He knelt over her, brushing at her ineffectually with his unusable hands, uttering a *tsk*. He radiated nothing but protective, brotherly concern. Her breaths were sobs of sheer relief.

It was this tableau that Will and Christopher both crashed in upon, from opposite rows of apples.

CHAPTER TWENTY-NINE

Dirt, thighs, tangled hair, and tears.

Angelika Frankenstein lying beneath a monstrously huge man.

That was all Will and Christopher registered in this scene. They stepped over the dead men without even noticing them. All she heard was them saying her name, over and over.

Her savior roared to silence them, and Will put his hands up in a placating way.

"I'm all right," she told them. Then she saw the gun in Christopher's hand. "No, don't!"

He fired a shot. Whether it was designed to miss was unclear. Now he had no second shot prepared, and the man was getting to his feet. "Fuck," Christopher said in his cultured voice. He looked up and up, until the man was at full height. "Cover your eyes," he told Angelika, and then threw a handful of sand up at the man. It did not blind him, only landing mid-torso. Christopher scanned around on the ground for a weapon.

"He just saved me," Angelika said, scrambling up. She put herself in front of her rescuer. "He just stopped those—those—" She gestured, and they finally noticed the dead men.

"They were going to— I think they were going to—" Her teeth were chattering.

"They were going to take off her nightgown," the huge man said, his voice rumbling in his rib cage. "I smelled what they wanted to do. Filthy creatures, chasing Angelika, making her all dirty." She felt his icy hands curl around her shoulders. "Now I find two more chasing her?"

"You know Will, and Christopher is my friend," she assured him. "They were trying to save me, too."

"What are you doing out here?" Christopher's fear was converting into anger. "Why didn't you turn around? The house was closer than Will." He put a hand into his hair. "I was closer than Will, goddamn it, Angelika!"

"She was coming to visit me, because she was lonely," Will replied, but he was explaining to the man holding Angelika. "And she still wants to come to me, don't you, my love?" He said it slow and easy. She nodded. "We've talked about this, brother. She loves me, and she is mine."

"Brother?" Christopher echoed, opening the chamber of his pistol to see what he might do. "Let her go at once."

"Who is this?" the voice above her head asked. "Is this the man you said wanted to kill me? Drop it," he added, and Christopher had no choice but to cast the pistol away. "You have been searching for me in the forest, with my father."

Christopher sneered. "Father? Brother? You are mad. Let her go."

"How's Granny Mary?" Angelika tilted her face around. "She's all right, isn't she? What did she name you?"

He had a hint of a smile underneath the long-suffering expression. "She named me Adam, after the first man created. And also after her baby, who died. Granny Mary is quite all right. Don't," he added in a warning when Christopher stepped closer, itching to wrench Angelika away. "No closer."

"Let them talk," Will told Christopher in his calm tone. "No harm will come to her, clearly." He indicated the pile of men. "Step back a little with me."

"I cannot." Christopher was unraveling before their eyes. He raked at his perfect hair, he rolled up his cuffs; he was creased and crumpled within an inch of his life. He turned on Will viciously. "You coward. You'd walk away from this? Look at her, and the size of him. Angelika. Tell me to fight, Angelika, I beg you!"

She shook her head. "There's no need."

His sense of purpose denied, he deflated.

Will told Christopher, "This is out of our control now. It is up to them to decide how this ends. She can handle this." He took Christopher's arm and dragged his unwilling frame back a few yards into the line of shadow.

"They both love you," Adam whispered close to her ear. "But one loves you so much more."

Angelika turned in his hold and put her hands on his fore-arms. "Do you need anything? Food, clothes? I can have things made for you. Anything you want."

"Granny Mary told me to ask you for a pair of glasses. For me. Not her. Her eyesight is still perfect, thank you very much."

Angelika laughed. "I miss her so much. When can she come back and visit?"

"Whenever she wants to," Adam said, puzzled. "But she said not until you're scared to death and have learned your lesson."

"Consider this to be that moment." Angelika took his hand in hers. She turned it over.

Pure gold is unmistakable and irresistible to fairy queens. Even on a clouded night, with hardly a moon, gold has a glow that has fueled empires and inspired unremarkable men to do extraordinary things. The ring on Adam's beautiful, deathly hand (Will's hand? Arlo's?) was just that pure.

"I'm not stealing it," she told him as she rubbed her thumbs across it, feeling the lines.

"I know now that you won't," Adam said, and he sounded so tender. Will continued to watch, but Christopher could no longer bear it and went off to pace the rows of apples, pulling at his hair, ranting to himself about how unbelievable and untenable this situation was.

"I can't see it." Frustration began to build in her. It was just too dark, and her lantern was currently smoldering in the distance near a rabbit carcass. "Adam, I can't see."

"There's a candle on my windowsill," Will offered. He turned and walked away, giving them the dignity of his trust. They followed, and he heard her begin to limp on her bare foot. Will stopped and bent low for her to climb onto his back.

"Come on, Adam," Angelika said, wrapping her arms around her love's shoulders. "Let's take a look at this ring."

The cottage came into view, a white cloud in the dark. The next thing they saw was Clara, wrapped in a coat. "Christopher, thank heavens," she cried out, and ran the short distance to him, her breaths jarring in her chest. "I heard the most dreadful noises."

Her desperate eyes were locked on his face, not seeing anyone else, and it reminded Angelika of herself, running to Will. Adam had performed his trick of melting into the shadows and shapes of the night.

"It's all right." Christopher was gratified to hear one woman cry his name. He put out his arms and she burrowed gratefully into him. "Don't cry. Will's got Angelika. Everything's all right. Let's go inside. Now, next time, you need to stay inside with your door locked."

They really did look so nice together.

Will sat Angelika on the windowsill beside the candle and leaned beside her legs. He seemed depleted, and his breathing was heavy. "Adam?" he asked the night.

"Yes, brother?" Adam made them both jump by how close he was.

"Please, let me see your ring."

A hand began to slide into the candle's circle of light. There was the first spark. Gold this pure was magical. It dazzled their eyes. Adam stepped closer, and now it was done. The reflections off the gold slowed, then stilled, and everything became clear.

Well, sort of.

Angelika was initially stumped by how blank the crest was. It was just four unevenly sized squares, with nothing punctuating the smooth gold. No gemstones, no Latin engraving. It was plain and wasn't what she would have chosen for Will at all.

But then, she followed Will's tracing fingertip.

Dividing the ring were the two deep lines of a cross.

CHAPTER THIRTY

Angelika preferred Will's cottage to Blackthorne Manor.
It had everything she could want: a comb to fix her
hair, a little soap and water for her hands and legs, a clean
shirt from Will's doll-sized closet, and a tiny nip of his home-
made blackthorn gin. It ran down into her stomach like medicine and cured her of the pain in her wrenched shoulders.
The bed in here was a mere fraction of the mattress acreage
she normally enjoyed, but it meant that they had to cuddle
close together, knee bones clinking. One shared pillow would
always be enough for her.

But it wasn't the aftermath of her fright in the orchard that
they were dealing with right now.

"My love, that ordeal was too much for you." Angelika ran
her hand through Will's hair. "You're scaring me a little." He
felt as heavy as a corpse in his bed—and she would know.

"I did tell you," he replied on a long sigh. "I only have so
much energy in my body." He moved his fingers in slow, lazy
circles on her arm. "I hope Adam considers taking the cottage. I can have it fixed up in no time."

Angelika pursed her lips. "He wouldn't even venture in past
the threshold. And let's face facts: it's far too small for him. I

think he secretly liked it, all the same. He had a little smile as he disappeared into the dark." Angelika had already made a mental list of things she could do to make Adam's home comfortable, and the little luxuries she could procure for Clara and Edwin. "We could make it so nice for him. And Clara. And Sarah, and Jacob. My own little village, right up here. Conqueror Lane."

"Now that you have glimpsed the good you can do in this world, I believe you will be unstoppable."

A grumble of thunder was heard.

She put her forehead against his. "Were you awake when you heard me scream?"

Will nodded. "I was already at the window. I had the strangest feeling. We are connected, remember?" He considered this statement. "Maybe Adam feels that same connection to you, too."

Hearing his voice in the dark, saying things like *We are connected*, gave her another image. She became even more aware of her bare legs and no underwear. "There's something wrong with this picture."

"What?"

"I generally sleep naked."

"What just happened was a terrifying ordeal for you. The last thing you would want is that." His arms found enough strength to cuddle her closer.

"Mary was the one who truly saved me," she said into his chest. "She has trained me for this my whole life."

Tension ran through Will. "What do you mean?"

"She said I would one day be in a moment with a man I didn't know, where I would have to act instantly. She said I should trust my instincts, no matter if it turned out to be a misunderstanding. His feelings would not count. She always made me repeat after her: no hesitation, no politeness, run."

"And you did." He kissed her temple, and exhaled a quiet "Thank God."

"I never asked Mary why she had that advice for me. What has she lived through?" Frightening images began to plague her mind. Angelika put her hand up the back of Will's shirt, and his smooth skin grounded her in the present moment.

She was safe, with the person who loved her the most.

He said, "When I see Mary again, I am going to thank her most sincerely. She helped raise a woman who trusts herself. I am so proud of you."

"Mary's advice also applies when I find myself with the right man. The one I choose, and would have into my body, if he wanted me that way." She tipped her face up and saw his eyes watching her. "No hesitation, no politeness. Trust my instincts. Run to him."

"It was my name you screamed, not Christopher's, and I'm sure you noticed how deeply that cut him. You still choose me tonight, despite the doubts that hang in the balance? Are you positive?"

"Yes." She rubbed her hand on his side. "And your feelings count very much, and I know you have found out something about yourself today that will change everything. I understand this may be our only night together like this."

What would daylight bring? Might he wake, and remember his past, and leave forever?

He lay thinking in the darkness, his fingertips swirling on her arm in endless loops. "But I am not that person. Not yet, anyway." The touch was giving her goose bumps. "You know that Father Porter will come for me. This is only the beginning, and it may be something you cannot talk or pay us out of."

"But I talk and pay so well." Her reply was cute, but she

knew he was right. A dead man could not just walk up to his own grave with no repercussions. "We're going to have to tell Victor."

"That's what worries me most," Will said to the ceiling. "I know you'll love me no matter what"—he squeezed her—"but Victor's reaction is unpredictable. If he finds out he has been sheltering a clergyman, he may toss me out on principle."

"He loves you as a brother." She paused. "But he hates contradicting himself and making exceptions. But you are correct. I will always love you, exactly as you are. What do you want tonight?"

Her new life philosophy was to try to notice the lovely moments she was living in, knowing how quickly it all could end. His body was aroused, his hands were on her, and the hem on her borrowed shirt was riding up.

"I want to use my hands on you." He began to unbutton the shirt she wore. He struggled with the task, but she lay patiently. "I am losing sensation in my fingertips, and I think soon I won't feel anything at all. And to think I might never—" The sound he made in his throat was choked and emotional. He folded away the fabric, and passed his palm down her spine. "I want to feel you, while I still can."

"Is my hair soft?" she asked. "Am I sweet-smelling, and pretty?"

He huffed a laugh. "Adam tells the truth."

She tipped her face up to kiss his throat. "Am I completely naked in your bed?"

"I'm not sure."

"You'd have to use your hands to find out." She felt him go still. "Forget what we have ahead of us. Forget the morning. We have tonight, and we still have your fingertips, don't we?" Her own hands were beginning to stroke him: the satin of his shoulders, the line of stitches at his neck. His hair felt like owl feathers. "Can you feel me tonight?"

"I feel you," he said with a tremor in his tone, sliding his finger along her collarbone. "Do you feel me?"

"Since the moment we met."

"Say my name," he said in the dark, and he began using his hands in earnest. "I want to see how it fits."

It took the brave, bold Angelika Frankenstein a few moments to muster the courage.

"Arlo."

The spell was not broken. His hands continued to move, cataloguing her shape and smoothness under his bedsheets. The way he touched her was like a reverent savoring, like he was committing every rib and curve as memories he would hold sacred.

"I'm not sure," he said, and put his mouth on hers in a kiss. "I'm not sure it suits me."

This was the kiss that had hung between them in the air for every taut moment, retort, admiring glance, and endless night. Being trusted had imbued Angelika with power and pride; being loved like this did the same. There was no doubt for her. There was no one else. In a world full of options, where she could dip into her purse for anything and enchant any unwed military man, this was her only choice.

She would bring him back to life. "You say I'm more than beauty."

"You're energy," he said, reading her mind, understanding her in a way no one ever had. "And you're all I will ever need, for the rest of my life. I promise you."

Kissing was a wonderful way of sharing this close, connected sense of destiny that was enfolding them now, but touching was just as nice. "Oh," Angelika said when he swirled a palm across her nipple. "Arlo. Will. There's a lot of things I want to try."

"Really?" he said in the dark, pressing his lips onto her, dragging his tongue, finding her tight twisted part below her heart. "Really? Tell me." He tugged, and teased, and nipped words out of her.

She told him everything.

"Behind, I crave it from behind, bend me over things and step in between my feet and just—" She flexed forward, and now her thighs were curled against his arousal. He wasn't finished, and she gave him more. "Outside, I've always wanted to be licked between my legs under the stars—" She only caught her breath for as long as it took for him to kiss across to her other nipple. "I want to stay naked. In your bed, just like this, every night."

"What about Larkspur?"

"I know big houses make you jumpy and depressed. I'll live here with you, ah—" Now he was stroking her thighs. Now he was asking her to part them. "I'll be happy here in this little white house as long as you keep sliding your fingers up higher, until you find me right—"

As she gasped and groaned, he said, "Oh, dear. Now I'm never getting you out of my bed."

He began a maddening, off-kilter pattern that she couldn't get enough of, but also could not build on her pleasure. It was his way of asking her to relax into it, to enjoy for touch's own sake.

"Now, if you could do this under the dinner table while I eat my dessert, I would be inspired to treat you in return." Her hand found him, and twisted him, and pulled up until his hips followed.

Now down, pressing down, until he melted into the bed.

"This life you have planned for us sounds rather exhausting," he said with amusement, even as his breathing was increasing. "Even though you'd have me in bed constantly, I might be too tired to function."

"Functioning is not going to be high on our list of priorities." She felt ready. Was he? Did he want this? "What do you want me to call you?"

"Will. Arlo. I really don't know." Pause. "You could call me sir, when you're on your knees. That might be a new dynamic we explore, once we've worked out our hundred favorite types of regular lovemaking." He was starting to not cope with her rhythmic pull-press-pull. "What I'll really enjoy with you is the nuances, the mindset, outsmarting that quick brain of yours, making your body bloom only for me . . ."

He shivered, but did not go over.

"Start immediately," she suggested, but he had gone still in the dark. "My love?" Her heartbeat was tapping insistently in her chest. She needed a release, and she needed to know him in these new ways. "Please, if you want to, put yourself into me."

"I never have before."

"How do you know?"

"Because I found a letter from myself." He did not let her passion wane, but rolled her onto her side, and lifted her knee up onto his. As he began to explore her, gently, competently, using his fingers to test her softness in deep new places, he said, "I lied to you."

"I don't care."

"I found a letter in Father Porter's office, and it said I was a good young man who had never put two fingers into a woman's wet body like this. Or three."

She choked a laugh, even as her eyes closed in pleasure. "What else did it say?"

"I'm a virginal, abstinent man," Will said, rolling her onto her stomach and kneeling behind her. His hands pulled her hips up, and now he was positioned. The broad head she had personally selected was notching into place, and he was asking her, "Are you ready? Do you still want this?"

"Please," she said facedown into their pillow. "I don't want to be a virginal, abstinent woman. Give it to me." He did, and oh, she felt every slow inch of this moment. There was no pain, no agonizing ripping of her body to shreds. Natural science; that was what this was.

No, even more: it was a trance.

They knew what to do. Angles, and speed, and resistance, and a touch of gravity; nothing required any thought. Will was both careful and powerful in his movements, drawing out, pushing back, causing her to gasp, groan, and tingle. He began to pull her back firmer and firmer onto him.

Just like pure gold, Angelika's orgasm was unmistakable when she saw it start to glimmer on the near horizon. Will saw it, too, and folded his body down, caging her in with his arms. He bit down softly on her neck, then put a hand down to touch and help her. It was a claiming; a gentle, hard, rocking, thorough fucking, and just like the gold ring dazzled her eyes, her body tightened up, the enormity of the sensation feeling like panic and then—

Ecstasy, utter, decadent, blooming ecstasy, drawing cords through her limbs to pull and loosen, jerking and easing. He was in the exact same moment. They shivered and pressed and held still, his brow on her shoulder as he rocked in slowing spasms. The human body was capable of miracles, soaked in sweat and salt.

"I love you," he told her. "I have, from the moment I first saw you."

"I loved you before you took a breath."

Laughing giddily at this absurd competition, they slumped and rolled into each other's arms. "Are you all right?" He tipped her chin up with his thumb. "Was I too rough?" There was blood, but not much. "Mary would be furious to see this sheet."

"She did warn you. I felt you being careful in every moment. I am fine. Better than fine. Why do novels always make virgins out to be fragile little things? I feel . . . powerful. Don't you?"

"That's good you feel that way," he said. "Because I'm not done with you."

Will, Arlo, her love, whoever he was, diligently began work on his goal of one hundred.

She had no idea where he got his unlimited energy from.

CHAPTER THIRTY-ONE

D ear Father Porter,'" Angelika read aloud as she lay on
her stomach naked.

Will was kissing down her spine. "Such erotic words."

"We have been in bed all night, and a full day."

"We have."

"Well, I would have thought your inspiration would run dry
hours ago." The light was turning evening blue. "I need to get
Adam's dinner ready soon." Her own stomach growled.

"Just read the letter before we return to real life."

She began again. "'I am writing to introduce myself. I
am Father Arlo Northcott, and I am delighted to be selected as your replacement after your distinguished forty-
two-year tenure as priest of the parish of Salisbury. Whilst
I do not consider myself worthy of the appointment, given
your reputation and service, I hereby conduct to do my very
best—'"

"Apparently, my ink was not in short supply," Will interrupted. He was kissing the small of her back. "You can skip
the dull parts."

Over her shoulder, she said with humor, "So can you."

"I haven't found any yet," he said, and continued to prove

he meant it. She didn't know that her hips held such sensitivity, or that he liked them so much.

"It's a well-written letter," she defended, back to the task at hand. "And if it was indeed you who wrote it, I say well done. But I will skip over these sentences where you kiss Father Porter's derriere." As soon as she said it out loud, she realized what she'd invited. "Oh, no," she giggled as the first kiss was pressed slowly onto her buttock.

He invited, "Please, keep reading."

She tried to focus. "Here's where it gets to a proper introduction. 'Whilst I am only thirty-three, I believe I am fulfilling a calling to God that I first felt when I was six years old. I was fortunate that my dear parents saw my propensity for religious study alongside academics.'"

She had to stop to take some breaths.

The whisker-scratch kisses on her backside were unsettling, and delightful, and he knew it. "I knew you were a fine young lady who occasionally needs a little kiss on the backside to feel properly appreciated." He moved lower.

"No, no, I'm ticklish there," she begged, but his hands held her tight as he slid his mouth down the back of her thigh. "Oh, oh, stop!" Struggling was futile. He was very strong, but he always held her in careful ways.

He reached up to her buttock, squeezed it, then smacked it. "Keep. Reading."

That felt rather nice, especially coupled with an order.

"I think I've forgotten how to read." There was something in this letter that he obviously wanted her to get to. She fixed her eyes on the letter and concentrated on the handwriting. "It's technically very good penmanship, but it has a nice quick feel to it. The little flicks of the letters as the sentences run on . . ."

Now she'd done it. Will's tongue made its own little flicks on the inside of her ankle as he held her feet in a tight grip.

"It says here that you, or Arlo, lived in a seminary from the age of eight until the date of this letter. That's a very secluded life." She mustered some courage. "Do you remember anything from your past yet?"

"I remember things from last night," he said with seductive intent, moving off the bed. When she looked over her shoulder, he was kneeling at the foot of it. Her stomach flipped in anticipation.

"So I'm not really defiling a priest if you can't remember, am I?" It was a thought she'd swatted away throughout their varied, and filthy, couplings.

"I thought you wanted to know everything about me, but you keep dallying when the letter holds so much."

"But we still don't have absolute proof that you are Arlo Northcott."

"It is a high probability; Father Porter recognized me, plus the ring I wore. I think you will agree with me if you just keep reading."

She maintained her dignity as he took her ankles in each hand and began dragging her. As she slithered facedown across the sheets, she craned her neck to keep summarizing.

"You have a special interest in providing quality confessional services, and spent months attending wards for recovering scarlet fever patients. That's nice of you."

"I'm a very nice person," he said when her knees reached the end of the bed. "I really do hope you believe that I am." He rolled her onto her back, and now she was expected to do the impossible: keep reading. The words shimmered on the page.

"You're the nicest person I've ever met," she said with honesty. To feel him smile between her legs? She would never recover from this moment. "There's a big paragraph here about your views on the future of the Church of England, which I'm going to skip—"

She got distracted for a long moment, luxuriating and stretching, flinging her arm out straight with a paper-crumple sound. "I don't want to read this letter anymore. I have a new resolve to live in the moment more fully."

"Fine. But the last paragraph is really the only one you should read. Keep your temper," he warned, and she glared up at the ceiling. How on earth could he have known that frustration dipped her in ice water? "Be good and I will reward you."

"You'll have to do this every time you want me to do something," she said, relaxing her body, and he spread her thighs wide with his palms. "The final paragraph—let's see what's so important."

As her exhausted body received pleasure, she read:

"'In summary, I am delighted to make your acquaintance, and to learn how I may serve the parish of Salisbury in what I understand are socially and economically trying times. And on a personal note, I was also pleased to be informed that the rectory boasts a garden famous across the counties. My passion is—'"

(He showed her.)

"'My passion is—'"

"Read," he growled, and she felt the vibration.

She whimpered out the last sentences. "'My passion is all forms of botany, and gardening was the labor I gladly undertook at the seminary. I cannot think of an earthly pleasure more exquisite than putting my face to the petals of a rose.'"

"Indeed."

"How sweet and innocent you were," she said to the ceiling. "What have I done to you?"

"Concentrate on what I'm doing to you."

She obeyed, and this time when she unfurled in rapture, she said his name with more conviction: "Arlo."

Memories of his old life were returning to Arlo Northcott, in snips and pictures and smells, but it seemed a shame to worry Angelika about it. She was happy tonight, and for the first time since he'd known her, she had no apprehension in her expression.

She looked at him like she was rapturously in love, but then again, she always had.

Arlo's cobbled-together body never felt hungry, but he made sure to eat enough dinner to not arouse concern. Angelika noticed his every mouthful—again, she always had. And while Victor told a lively story about a goose hiding in a hedgerow that had caused Athena to shy and himself to fall, Arlo allowed himself the luxury of staring back at Angelika, noticing how the firelight cupped her cheekbone like a warm kid glove.

(Arlo's father—whose name eluded him still—had owned a pair of kid gloves, and the fingertips were oily-looking and worn smoother than baby's skin. When they were left on the table by the door, they remained curled in disgusting phantom fists.)

There were surely only a few days left before Arlo's fingertips dipped into unfeeling, oily shadow.

"Jelly," Lizzie said around a mouthful of bread, "after you were accosted in the orchard, where did you disappear to, for an entire night and day?" The naughty girl knew exactly where, and her dark eyes were sparkling.

"I was busy," Angelika drawled, then bit her lip to hold in whatever she was thinking now. It was for the best.

"I don't want to know," Victor advised from his seat at the head of the table. "Anyhow, it's a pity Chris insisted on the night watch removing the corpses. I would have reanimated them all, just to kill them again myself."

"Your huge representative handled it," Angelika replied. The memory made her reach for her glass and take a gulp. They were both their usual sardonic selves, but Arlo had seen the siblings embrace in the hall.

Victor was monitoring Lizzie's plate. He was similar to his sister; they both loved so ravenously. "Eat up, Lizzie. The chicken is succulent. Sorry, Will," Victor amended to Arlo. "I hope your vegetables are just as good."

"They're fine, thank you," Arlo replied. He could pick the exact moment Victor made a mental note to question his diet during his next examination. It would make a change from the same questions over and over: *Are you still fatigued? Are you healing? Is your pain any less? Can I trouble you for a sample of your seed?*

Yes, no, no—and absolutely not.

"Well, I want to know what's been going on. Tell me later," Lizzie told Angelika on a whisper, and the table fell silent.

Arlo scraped his knife and fork on his plate to keep up appearances. When the big green eyes opposite turned back to him, he forked up a hearty mouthful and chewed. Satisfied, Angelika wrinkled her nose at him fondly. Arlo imagined her questions later: *Was your dinner nice? Are your hands all right? Are you feeling so much better?*

He answered now, in his mind. *I will lie to your beautiful face and tell you what you want to hear, because I would die to make you happy.*

Perhaps I should rephrase that thought.

He didn't think himself so clever that he could guess her every question, because in bed she'd asked him things that had left him floundering for a reply.

(*When you do that, can you put your fingers in me . . . here? If I touch you there, would that be all right? What about if I suck you while you lick—*)

"They've both gone glassy-eyed again," Lizzie complained. "It's like sitting with a pair of corpses. No offense, Will."

Arlo laughed. "None taken. Eat a little more," he encouraged Angelika, and felt a new glow in his chest as she took a bite. Who looked after her, really? With Mary gone, it was up to him now. "Are you cold?"

Angelika shook her head, and pointed her fork at Lizzie, then her brother. "Now you can see what you pair have been like to live with." (They were suitably contrite.) "I am perfectly entitled to sit here in an exhausted puddle and replenish my strength. I'm surprised that Ar—my love doesn't need a second plate."

Nobody noticed the slipup with his name. She'd made Arlo swear to keep his news to himself, but it felt like a pressure in his chest. How could he transition from *I'm your blank-page houseguest* to *I'm a missing, presumed-dead priest*? Would he even live long enough to deal with the consequences of it? Some days he felt like he'd live to see his sixtieth birthday. Other days, next Sunday seemed optimistic.

He knew one thing: he was an asset that the church would seek to recover.

"Will, you know what I told you that very first day," Victor said in a warning tone, and Arlo's stomach made a nervous flip. Then he grinned. "If you deflowered my sister, you would be stuck with her."

"Oh, he's stuck with me all right." Angelika rolled her gaze over to Arlo, and with her second blink, her eyes were full of remembering. She'd done just as much deflowering as he had.

She occupied her exhausted puddle in the most delightful way, with her blouse slipping off her satin shoulder. He fancied he could see the lines his fingers had made when he ran them through her hair; and right there, at the nape of her neck, he'd wrapped it around his fist like a honey-red rope. It made her gasp and shiver. What audacity to put a wealthy girl on her knees.

"Corpses again," Lizzie said in a dark tone.

Angelika looked around, preparing to make an effort, then jolted with surprise as she remembered something. "Where is Clara?"

"She is very tired, and perhaps a bit unwell," Lizzie replied. "She is eating in her cottage. Don't worry, the cook mashed up something for our little friend. He's a big eater, apparently."

"Smashing lad," Victor chipped in quickly. Lizzie passed a hand down her stomach and smiled.

"He'll be asleep by now," Angelika replied on a sigh. Her appetite was abandoned and she put her napkin on her plate. She was fighting her way out of their bedroom fog. "What a fine host I've been. And Christopher? When did he leave?"

The man's name had always given Arlo's stomach a pinch, because Angelika's voice had a throaty catch whenever she said it.

Never mind his own fate amongst the earthworms; if those two had met a month earlier at some country dance, she would now be Mrs. Angelika Keatings, and she would be dining in a post-sex stupor beside Christopher's fireplace, with a swelling belly.

"I really should have said goodbye to him," Angelika added, staring into the fire. "Was he very angry with me?"

"His heart and pride are very injured," Lizzie said. "But all is not lost."

Arlo handled his base emotions with care, like a man removing a snake from a box; otherwise, he could find himself poisoned and exhausted. But tonight he wasn't deft enough. The fangs sank deep, and jealousy spread outward from his heart. Next came the doomed grief that he felt whenever he saw Angelika with the baby. But this time, the bad emotions were smothered by a new sensation. It took him a moment to identify it.

Smug, male, fist-tight possession. It might be time to take her back to bed.

"Don't ask about Christopher anymore," Arlo told Angelika with the new feeling in his tone. "It is not your concern when he comes and goes."

"He finally said it," Lizzie said with admiration and a laugh. "Jelly, I do believe Will has claimed you once and for all." She turned her dancing eyes back to Arlo. "Correct?"

"He has," Victor confirmed in the short silence that followed. "Remember? Stuck with her for good." The man was prompting him again for a reply, and Angelika was running back through the last minute or two in her mind, searching for a confirmation he had not made.

His new memories were of himself as a young boy; would tomorrow bring him his teens and his early seminary life? By next week would he be repeating Scripture under his breath to delay himself as Angelika begged his body for faster, harder friction?

"We should talk," Arlo said to the table at large, and received a kick on his shin under the table.

"We shan't talk," Angelika said, huffing herself up straighter in her seat. "Until you tell us all that you are going to love me until the day I die."

Arlo pondered, "Why must everything be until death in this household?"

"Because that is how we Frankensteins love," Angelika told him. "We love until death parts us, and then we die of sadness."

"Terribly dramatic," Lizzie said with a smile, but Arlo did not miss the chill of fear in her eyes as she looked at him. Victor, too, averted his gaze with tight lips. Only Angelika sat oblivious to the truth that was sitting across from her now: Arlo was a man running out of time. Fast.

"You're about to find out if you can survive a second death, Will," Victor said after an awkward cough, observing the fraught tension between the two new lovers. "Answer us now, or I will invite Christopher for dinner tomorrow. He's starting to look at Clara's rear end whenever she bends down for Edwin, but we can nip that in the bud."

Angelika's knuckles went white on the tablecloth, but she did not blink. "You are stuck with me."

Arlo did not know the future, or most of his past, but there was only one honorable thing he should say in this exact moment. "Angelika, please marry me."

She did not scream joyfully. With a solemn mouth she replied, "Why?"

"Why?" Arlo echoed in confusion. "Why ask you the one thing you've wished to hear from the moment we met?"

She said too quietly, "You've just been prodded by everyone to ask me."

Infuriating. "You wish me to beg on my knees?"

"I know you are asking me because you are obligated to. You can't see a way out of it." She picked up her wine and swallowed the rest in a gulp. "No, I want something heartfelt. Not just something my brother forced you to say at the table, over our empty plates." Her eyes glowed with temper as she gestured in front of her. "Don't I deserve a little more than bones and scraps?"

Lizzie backed her friend. "It was rather lackluster, Will." Her favor had always been with the commander. "Vic proposed to me on a cliff at sunset."

"A romantic story to tell our children," Angelika said with new resolution. "That's what I want."

"You want a lot of things," Arlo countered. "And what you always forget is that I have nothing to give you. May I speak plainly? There may be no children. We all know it."

He hurt his own feelings with this statement, because witnessing Angelika hold a baby made his bones ache with want. But still, he forced himself to add another horror: "And we wouldn't even know who that baby looked like."

"We'll see, won't we," she replied, her complexion white. She stood abruptly, her expression tight and her eyes averted. "My courses are due in sixteen days. You may count each day as a prison sentence, if that is how you feel."

She left the room, and Arlo remained motionless under the twin stares of Victor and Lizzie.

"My friend," Victor said with equal parts kindness and warning. "Now is the time to choose."

"I don't believe I can."

Like it explained everything, Victor told him, "You are alive."

Arlo replied, "For how long?"

"I don't know if tomorrow another goose will jump out from a bush and I'll fall from my horse, and that will be the end of Victor Frankenstein. Don't you understand this? *No one knows.* You have already lived through death, and you are living a bonus life. It can be anything you want. And dear

God, please decide it is a life with Angelika, or she will never recover."

Victor's entreaty to God went unnoticed by all except Arlo.

"Would it be cruel to marry her, only for me to die, weeks or months later? It will destroy her." Arlo asked the next question he feared. "Will she die of grief, just as your father did?"

"It would be cruel to not let her have you for the hours, days, months, and years you may have remaining," Lizzie said. "Whatever happens, we will take care of her. But for this moment, that is up to you. She needs you. Find that romantic story inside yourself. Never have I heard of one so extraordinary."

Arlo rose from his chair and threw his napkin aside. He didn't utter any polite good-evenings, but instead pushed through several mahogany doors until he was at the stairs. It made him think back to that first night, when Angelika had half carried him into her bedroom. In every step he took, there was a blade-on-bone kind of pain, and a thousand little deaths. The automatic thought came to him now: *I think I'm dying.*

Stubbornly, he rebutted it. *I think I'm living.*

The portrait of Caroline Frankenstein glowered contemptuously down at him as he climbed. Her look was, *You believe yourself worthy of my daughter?*

"I am not, fair lady," Arlo replied out loud, "but I am who she wants, and I allow myself to be chosen." It was a waste to spend another moment without Angelika. "I wish to marry her. I need to marry her. And I don't want to die."

Admitting this, no matter how undeserved, gave him the boost he needed to take the stairs two at a time. Light-headed, breathless, cold, and in agony, he was about ready to push through her bedroom door when Sarah appeared behind him bearing two heavy buckets.

"I'll take them," Arlo said. "Thank you, Sarah." The girl blushed red, of course, but she was happy enough to put the handles in his palms. His hands were fading by the moment—how many more pails of water? How many more strokes of his love's skin? *Forget all that*, he told himself firmly, and pushed open her door.

"I'm here," he said.

Angelika was sitting in the half-filled tub, her arms around her knees. "What do you want, Arlo?"

He poured the first pail of water in at her feet. "I beg you. Please marry me."

A sigh was the only reply.

The second pail went in, and he was also pouring his heart into the crystal-clear warm water. She did not lift her head to see him unbuttoning his shirt. Perhaps she heard the fabric moving, but his bride was stubborn, and that porcelain cheek remained on her forearm.

She definitely felt the shift in water as he put one foot into the tub, then the other, then he sank in behind her. The flawless expanse of her back, and the curves of her neck and waist, had his cock as hard as iron. He put an arm around her collarbone and eased her back from her braced position.

He used his hands to stroke her, wash her, pleasure her . . . but she did not reply.

"I'm not afraid anymore," he explained. "I will be married to you, and I will be your husband, until I die. It is the only thing I want from this new life."

Her breath shuddered out, and her spine softened, and she grew heavier in his arms. He watched his hands touching her: wrists, the bends of her elbows, the heavy palmfuls of breast, and the flat stomach that he would try to stretch full, in time, if miracles did exist. He ignored the knowledge that his fingertips were fading like the stars at dawn; right now, in this exact moment in time, he could still feel the wrinkles at her nipples and the hollows of her collarbones.

"This is only what your body wants," she countered in a whisper.

She was sad, even as she pressed her bottom against him. He knew the signs that she was becoming restless with need; her chest was blushed pink, her thighs were squeezing and relaxing, and she dropped her head back on his shoulder to give him access to her throat.

"I am my body, and my soul," Arlo countered as he kissed. "All of me wants to be your husband. Please allow me this honor."

"I want to be married in a cathedral," she said, and his heart soared with hope. She hid how serious she was with a flippant "But I suppose you would not want that."

"That is what I want." Scandal, gossip, his background exposed, jokes at her expense . . . nothing could touch them. "I will be there with you, and that is what you shall have."

She pulled away, and his hopes began to falter . . . until she got to her knees, turned, and straddled his lap. The bathwater was now an ocean. Between their bodies, his arousal was hard, and her tight fist squeezed out his breath.

"I want a honeymoon that lasts a year," Angelika told him as she lifted her body, aligned him, and began to sink.

"Fine," Arlo choked out.

"I want to see the world. I will be extravagant in every regard, and I am a ridiculous traveler."

"I already know that."

She leaned herself back, to find the angle she liked best. "But I do not suppose you would enjoy that type of life, being taken everywhere with me, put into my bed, and bought anything I think you will enjoy. Ships, horses, carriages. Spices, tapestries, wine." She was losing her breath. "Then, we shall return to Larkspur Lodge, where I will have our first baby."

"That is all I want."

He was having trouble thinking, but she deserved so much more. He angled his pelvis, and focused. "I was too much of a coward to say everything I want, because I feel like I could lose everything again. But it is no use; I simply must have you. All I have to give you is this, my body"—his breath stuttered in his chest as the water crested—"but even as I become completely myself again, I will still love you as I do now. Fiercely, violently, in ways that scare me. I vow to you that I will not change."

He felt his composure begin to break down. How had he been so slow to reach this surrender? "I will kill for you. I will live for you. I will allow myself to be spoiled by you. From this moment on, you are my wife."

"Father Northcott, performing his own wedding vows?" Angelika replied with a pinch of sarcasm and sweat on her brow.

She still did not believe him.

He did not know where the strength came from, and there was no longer any pain. He stood up slowly, feeling her gasp, and her body clutched him tight everywhere. With strange ease, he stepped out of the tub, and now there was the sound of rainfall and a cold chill. They did not notice. The windowsill was a promising height, and he didn't lose his deep seat inside her as he put her down and crowded into her open thighs. His world was narrow and tight, dripping wet, and he felt himself changing.

Beyond this leadlight window was the forest where he'd found her on her back, sleeping as if enchanted, having

cheated death by inches, and he was becoming that wild creature that had fallen to his knees, terror in his heart.

"I'm going to keep doing this until you say yes," he said,
moving his hips, and she uttered a rich, desperate moan. "I
will spoil you in ways you cannot imagine."

Her eyes rolled closed, but he did not feel that vise-tight
sensation that usually gave away her overloaded passion. He
put his hands under her knees, and continued pushing and
pulling her. "I want to have you like this every day, showing
you how I love you, how I am desperate for you. Every blink
of your eyes, and every tart reply, makes me store this up for
later, when I take you to our bedroom. Do you want that life?"

Her hands were slipping on his wet shoulders. "Yes. I want
that. Harder."

He put his hand to where they were joined, and added a
new tension to her next moan. When they made eye contact
again, everything turned desperate.

Words were not possible any longer, and now he used his
body and his lips to explain to her what she meant to him;
that she was exceptional in every way, the most gloriously gorgeous, rightfully vain, brilliant person he would ever meet.
Memories of her began to splinter in his mind as he thrust
again and again, and she began to break down in ecstasy.

Trousers tight on her thighs, a sea sponge in her hand, the
fall of her loose hair on her shoulder, biting into an unusual
apple, the spark of light in her green eyes, and how she always looked at him: like she loved him beyond any sense, side-
stepping the natural order of the universe with a grin and a
quip . . .

Now she was traveling into that private landscape of ecstasy, her limbs jerking, her pulsing and pulling causing him
to follow. He clutched her to his heart, and he felt like a wild

animal. "I love you." It was the truest thing he'd ever said, even if it was growled. "Marry me, for God's sake, give yourself to me."

He lifted his head as his body took care of his orgasm, tripping him back into jerks of sheer pleasure, over and over. He looked into her eyes, and she smiled.

"Yes. I consent to marry you, Arlo Northcott. But I have a complaint. This is not a story we can tell our children."

She put her hand to his cheek and kissed him.

He'd never felt relief quite like this.

CHAPTER THIRTY-TWO

They belonged to each other now, forever, until death.

In the first rays of dawn, as Arlo swirled his hands on Angelika's skin, he committed the sensation to memory. If his hands would not work, he would use his mouth to feel this otherworldly softness. He would adapt and change and live the life they had charted out together, in the quiet moments in between the breathless couplings.

He allowed himself to feel excited about Larkspur Lodge; she had described it to him so vividly that he had fallen asleep and dreamt he was walking the corridor, lined with ancestors' and foxhunt paintings, toward their opulent bedroom overlooking the wild acres of garden.

The future glowed so bright it terrified him.

"I want to live," he explained as she kissed his tears away. "The thought of dying now, when I have so many days and nights ahead with you . . . I cannot bear it."

"I will keep you safe," she replied, and because she'd proved it every other time, he chose to believe her.

Angelika was now lying across his body just like that very first morning, when he'd awoken in this rich girl's bedroom with a mind like a blank slate. Thigh over his lap, cheek on his chest, she fit against him like a missing piece, now fully restored. Arlo closed his eyes, exhaled, and felt complete peace.

"I love you," he told her, and although she was sleeping, she smiled.

And then, the bell above the front door downstairs rang. *Ding.*

It interested Arlo to watch Angelika don her armor: that of a practically royal lady who held the power in every situation. She was apparently unfazed by the dawn visit and left the magistrate, the church aide, and Christopher to languish in the drawing room for going on a full hour as she readied herself for her day. Humming, she uncapped a bottle of perfume and breathed it in.

Arlo lay in bed with the sheet pulled up to his waist, feeling quite depleted, and decided to borrow a little of her self-assurance. His trousers lay in a damp heap by the bathtub, and he wasn't keen to put them on. Like a rich man who cared for nothing but his own body, he stretched, enjoying her mattress and pillows.

"Are you nervous?" he asked, knowing what look she would give him in her mirror.

She scoffed with an arched eyebrow. "Me? Nervous? This is my house. They are lucky to even get a glimpse of me before breakfast."

"As am I."

She smiled, and Arlo's heart shimmered. "You've seen everything there is to see of me. Good grief, I have never reached ecstasy so many times in my life. Not even on my most inspired night alone in that bed." She pressed a pink cosmetic onto her lips.

Arlo's body began flooding his cock with blood. It was a display of impossible tenacity.

"It will be nice to see Christopher's face as you stagger into the drawing room with your lips all swollen," he told her. "I like the man, but I'm fairly sure I could kill him for the way he looks at you."

To his relief, this comment didn't pique her interest.

"No need," she shushed, and began an enjoyable sequence of dressing; this time choosing an impressive uniform of stays, garters, silk stockings, and drawers. "These are from a store in Paris that is busy with whores and dancers. It's absolutely scandalous. You will come with me and choose what I buy."

Now there was a five-minute diversion.

Pink-faced, she dressed in various layers of petticoats, a sumptuous violet dress, and a diamond necklace fit for a princess. The tiara was a bit too much at seven in the morning.

Arlo, naked, penniless, the luckiest man imaginable, knew himself even more.

"I was such a shy child," he told her out of nowhere as he realized his tongue-tied sensation was a familiar one. "I liked church because that was the one place where I could either sit quietly with no questions asked of me, or I could sing and knew the words."

"At least you knew the words," Angelika replied, turning on her tufted dressing stool and crossing her legs. "Victor and I used to just warble along like birds. You were shy? I can imagine that. You have a reserve with those who don't know you well."

They were interrupted by Sarah's rhythmic knock.

Angelika went to the door, opened it a crack, and had a

whispered exchange with Sarah, taking a stack of clothes. Closing it again, Angelika sniffed haughtily. "They want to know how much longer to wait. All I can say is it shall be even longer now."

She gave the clothes to Arlo—a fresh outfit for him, how scandalized poor Sarah must be!—and resettled on her fancy stool. "Back to where we were. Can you tell me about your parents?"

Arlo had an image in his mind: a hard-faced pair, unhappily married and trapped together in a house that did not suit the size of their family. "John and Frances Northcott. My brother is the eldest, also called John."

"I never understood why families do that," Angelika complained. "Two Johns would always come running when called. It's impractical."

"I also had an older sister, and two younger brothers and two younger sisters. That's . . . seven children."

"What else do you remember?"

Arlo began to dress, his mind lost in the past. "Our house was too small, and we lived cheek by jowl. I think that's the true reason for my training at the seminary. There was no room for me." A big swell of ancient hurt prevented more words, and he pulled on his pants and buttoned his shirt in silence.

Angelika said, "There is plenty of room for you here."

He found he wanted to argue back. "That's what bothers me about you, when you say such things, or buy me such nice things. Like these trousers, for example."

"They look marvelous," she said with her eyes on his crotch. "Tailored to within an inch of their life. Italian cloth from a particular wool mill in Milan. Don't you look nice, my love."

He sat on the edge of the well-used bed. "There really is no room for me in this house. I'm not used to being treated this way."

"Treated like you are worth treating exceptionally well? That makes me sad." She came to stand between his feet. "You have found your place in this world. Beside me. There is room right here."

At his eyeline, the material of her dress glowed a rich indigo, shot through with a glimmer that only came from pure silk. Like the finest ceremonial robes, worn by priests. He plucked it between his fingers, rubbed it, and could no longer feel any sensation from the fine grain.

He closed his eyes as the memories began to flood him. There was no possible way to summarize each for her, except to say faintly, "I didn't choose any part of my life."

She held his face to her chest, and he wrapped his arms around her waist.

"I want to tell you of my old life, but there is not much to tell. I was eight years old when I was sent away, and homesick enough to vomit when I arrived at the seminary. I'd said to Mother, 'Don't leave me here,' but she didn't listen."

Angelika was quiet for a long moment. "You used those very words when we visited the morgue together. You said, 'Don't leave me here,' with such a raw note in your voice. Poor pet."

Arlo couldn't stop now.

"It was such a narrow world, reading the same texts and Scriptures, debates on theological concerns, and manual labor in the name of the Lord. It was my job to scrub out the huge pot that the dinner stew was boiled in, and the stink of it. Metal and meat." He shuddered. "I was never sure if I was praying correctly, because it seemed a little uncomplicated— just thinking quietly—but no one could give me a definitive answer."

He pressed his lips together to stop the torrent of memories. He must sound mad.

Angelika said the right thing. "Don't stop. Tell me everything you want to."

"I had a best friend named Michael at the seminary. He was so witty, he had me crying with laughter. He found the absurdity in it all, and he helped me gain my confidence and to see that the place we lived was also a game we must play. He loved pigeons, and he bred and trained them up in the loft of the barn." Arlo was surprised now. "I think Victor's pigeons reminded me of my long-ago friend."

"Perhaps we could go together and find Michael."

Arlo could only now think of a plain white cross. "He died of consumption. We were around fifteen, I think."

"Oh," Angelika said with heavy sympathy. "The only true friend you had died?"

"I was crippled by the grief. I cried into my pillow, and during the day I had to pretend I was all right with the apparent fact that he was in heaven, and it was his purpose. But for me, his purpose was to make my life livable."

She ran a gentle hand over his head. "How did you live without him?"

"I went outside and pulled out an entire flower bed of weeds. It gave me a momentary release." The clock in the hall chimed. The real world grew impatient, one floor down. "The garden saved me. Just like you saved me."

She was smiling. "Well, I am dressed like a rather large violet." She gave a small curtsy in his arms.

"Like a little larkspur." Arlo stood, and let her fuss as he knew she wanted to. His collar was fixed, his buttons tweaked, his cravat retied. It was how she demonstrated her love, and when her eyes glowed with pleasure, he realized this was something he could do for her. "Could they make me a topcoat in this wool?"

Now she was very happy, and they kissed slowly, with smiles on their mouths. But when they pulled apart again, she had a new realization in her expression.

"You still had no choice, did you? You woke up here, and you were mine. You know that if it was what you truly wanted, I would let you—"

He didn't let her finish, and kissed her until she was smiling and convinced once more.

When they broke apart, Angelika said, "Come along, let's get these men out of our house. Victor might be still asleep, which would be for the best."

Arlo followed her down the hallway, then put an arm around her waist and stepped in close. Against the back of her ear he said, "Don't forget who you belong to."

"I never have," she replied breathily. She allowed him to hold on to her and it was at the top of the staircase that he halted her again, his arms tighter.

"Don't forget that you are marrying me."

The diamonds at her throat shimmered. "I could not forget."

Now he had to ask her something, and it was not very manly or brave, but he knew he could. "Don't let them take me."

The portrait of his mother-in-law, Caroline, had a smile dimpling her cheek when they looked up at her.

"I never will."

Angelika swept ahead of him into the drawing room, and Arlo tagged along behind to enjoy the drama of her imperial bearing. It would have made Lizzie grab for her notebook. "Pray, tell me the meaning of this early visit," she said the moment she was in the room. "Explain yourselves at once."

The three men sitting with empty teacups all jolted.

"Angelika! Are you well?" Christopher's eyes darted from her throat and creamy bust back to her face. His expression soured when Arlo stepped beside her and put an arm around her waist. "I believe you should unhand her, sir."

"I will not," Arlo replied, strengthened by Angelika's calm power. Christopher was still a very handsome, well-connected man, but he no longer had any chance of winning her heart.

"We are here to ask Will some questions," Christopher answered her. "There is a strange matter to reconcile, down at the church."

The church representative looked to Arlo and made his own introduction. "My name is Robert Thimms, and I am Father Porter's personal valet. He wishes you to meet with him as a matter of urgency. We believe a miracle of some sort has occurred." A smile split his cheeks unexpectedly.

Christopher addressed Angelika. "Father Porter believes that this is the priest who was sent to replace him." Miracles did not occur in Christopher's line of work; only mistaken identities and nefarious motives.

She did not so much as blink. "That man died in a carriage hijacking."

"That's what I believed, but apparently not," Christopher said, narrowing his eyes up and down on Arlo. "Until we can all sit down and sort this out, we need you to come with us, Will."

Angelika puffed up in outrage. "He goes nowhere."

Arlo squeezed his arm around her waist in wordless thanks.

Christopher turned his frustration on Arlo. "You remain silent, as you often do. This is the magistrate, Mr. Samuel Carter. He has accompanied us in his official capacity, until we can clear up what I'm sure is a misunderstanding. Let us depart now for his offices." The threat in his tone was unmistakable.

"How do you do, Mr. Thimms, Mr. Carter?" Arlo gave a polite bow. "I truly can only think of one way to completely clear up this strange matter, and I propose we reconvene at the church at my convenience; that is to say, nightfall. We must ask you to leave now."

"At your convenience?" Christopher echoed with a sneer and yet another reflexive glance at Angelika's dress neckline. "Nightfall?"

"Angelika has not eaten her breakfast. I am asking you again to leave. I am not being taken out of here all of a sudden, like a criminal." The words gave him a pinch, and brought back the memory of being a small boy again. But with his greatest advocate beside him, he felt unmovable.

"And you are not a criminal," Mr. Thimms placated, giving Christopher a hard stare. "We believe you have had a significant trauma and your circumstances have been . . . most unusual, but God has been with you. Please, we would be most grateful to allow Father Porter an audience with yourself."

Christopher was irritated and said to Angelika, "Where is Victor? We told your servant to fetch him, but she grew so flustered she could not explain to us where he was. Utterly tongue-tied, she was. She is a nice girl, but you need someone more suited to this household."

"Victor is asleep," Angelika guessed, "and my housekeeping staff is absolutely none of your business. Sarah is perfectly fit for the role, and I appreciate her many skills and abilities." She could go from bland to razor sharp in a blink.

"What's your proposal?" Christopher asked Arlo, turning his icy blue glare back on him. "When we meet at the church, how can everything be cleared up?"

"I'll bring a shovel," Arlo replied, and the three guests fell back in their seats in shock.

It was at this exact moment that the front door banged open. Huffing, puffing, a shirtless Victor Frankenstein appeared, gleaming in sweat. An apple was in his hand.

"What are you doing up so early?" Angelika was aghast. "Where is your shirt?"

"I've got nothing but early mornings in my future; I am adapting myself in advance." Victor leaned in the doorway and raised his eyebrows in greeting at Christopher, carelessly ignoring the other two visitors. He bit his apple and spoke with his mouth full. "Do you ever run for fitness, Chris? We could go together."

Arlo wasn't invited. He understood why. He still felt sad.

"We are here on something serious, Victor," Christopher replied after a shocked laugh, masked as a cough. "Perhaps you ought to take a seat, so I may introduce your guests and we can explain it."

"After a quick wash," Angelika pleaded wearily, knowing when she was beaten. "Please, Victor, you absolutely stink."

CHAPTER THIRTY-THREE

This feels a little extreme," Victor said from above as Arlo shoveled dirt up beside his boots. "I can't believe you, of all people, agreed to this, Chris."

"It was his idea," Christopher pointed out, putting his shovel into the ground and leaning on it. "And if it puts this nonsense to rest, then I'm all for it." He resumed digging, but his pace was much slower than his first couple of hours when he'd glanced up at his beautiful onlooker with every repetition.

Arlo was *this close* to knocking him on the back of his blond head and reusing the grave.

"How are you feeling?" Angelika asked Arlo from her seat beside the headstone.

She had tasked a clerk to bring her a chair as though spectatorship was to be reasonably expected, and she sat on the fine mahogany piece under a dome of night sky that bore ribbons of sunset pink. She looked every bit the fairy queen, seated beneath the yew tree clasping around her. She had dressed in a midnight-black gown, beaded with so many jet stones that she sparkled brighter than the cosmos. Beneath the skirts were long black boots, laced up to the knees.

Arlo decided he'd leave those boots laced up when he undressed her later.

"Are you all right?" Angelika prompted him. "You look a
little pale."

Arlo's physical exhaustion, the pain that shimmered across
his skin to grind deep into his joints, his icy-dead hands, the
astonishing mental toll it took to dig beneath a marble stone
bearing one's own name and birthday . . . none of that interested him now, because Angelika smiled down at him. A star
streaked across the sky above her.

His emotions overflowed.

"Angelika, no woman is as beautiful as you." Arlo knew
this to be absolute truth, because he now had every memory
his brain had decided to retain, from dropped-corncob moments to the life-altering losses of his grandparents and Michael. Waist deep in his grave, he leaned an elbow on the edge
and made a memory of this moment. "I love you so much."

In reply, she cooed and leaned down to cup his chin in her
palm.

"Keep digging, Sir Resurrection," Christopher interjected
in a complaining tone.

"Did you mention our news to the commander, my love?"
Recharged, Arlo sank his shovel into the ground and his news
like a dagger into Christopher's heart. "I asked Angelika to
marry me, and she said yes most emphatically. I am sure you
are very happy for us."

He hoisted both soil and broken heart at Angelika's feet,
with an unholy sense of retribution.

Christopher stood with a half-lifted shovel of dirt, shocked
to his core, but before he could say anything, a thin voice
urged, "Please, delay any thought of such a thing until we
understand what has gone on here."

It was Father Porter at the foot of the grave, inspecting their progress. If he was worried he would be found out for selling bodies to the morgue, he betrayed nothing. It was the same blithe expression Angelika and Victor wore. Wealth gave a person a certain inner strength. Perhaps he had no part in it? Mr. Thimms had not stopped pacing the path since their arrival.

Father Porter pursed his mouth at the scene. "Are you quite sure you would not like to wait in my office, Miss Franken-stein?"

"Quite sure," she replied. "It is a fine night to watch muscular men dig a hole."

"In that case, I'll take a turn," Victor said with a grin, and put a hand down to Arlo, pulling him out of the hole. It was an odd thing, volunteering to entertain his own sister, since Lizzie was at home with instructions to rest herself. But as Arlo regained his balance and straightened up, Victor whispered, "You look like you're about to faint. Rest yourself. Drink."

Father Porter was at Arlo's elbow with remarkable speed. "I really do wish we could speak privately."

"There's no need," Arlo replied, wiping his brow with his forearm, trying not to weave on the spot. Dizziness was giving the edges of his vision a swirling effect. Below, Victor and an exhausted Christopher were making a competition of it; dirt was flipping out faster and faster. "All will be revealed momentarily, and we will deal with the consequences then. We will open the casket, and either Arlo Northcott is there, or he is not."

Standing against the wall of the church, the magistrate heard this statement and nodded. "It's nonsense, but if it's what it takes."

Father Porter's eerie light eyes were intense on Arlo's face. "You have no memory of me?"

Arlo looked away. He had every memory now: the cries of the men who died defending him, the helpless slide of the carriage into the ravine, and the jarring pain in his knee as he kicked like a mule at the pinned door and screamed for God to save him. Then, wrenching off his sweaty robes, growing cold, and huddling under them. Throat dry, eyes stinging with salt.

He had been alone for most of his life in every way that counted, and as the days and nights wore on, he had accepted that he would die alone.

But as it turned out, he hadn't.

Broths and cold compresses still could not save him. This old man had been with him, holding his hand, reciting his last rites as he felt his entire essence drawing out, into the fireplace, dissolving into smoke, out the chimney, and into the night sky. Wouldn't the world be astonished to know that after death, one's spirit was caught in a star?

"You remember, don't you?" Father Porter whispered. "Don't lie to me, my child."

Arlo would have liked to take a step back, but it would have put him into the grave. "Let it be," he begged the old man in a whisper. "I am happy for the first time in my life. Whoever I am, let me walk away from here tonight, and let me go home."

"Home?" Father Porter inquired. "You will take up residence here, allowing me to finish my service before I collapse from exhaustion. I know you were dead," he said in a barely audible hiss. "I know who found your body afterward, and what he is rumored to do in the name of some unholy science. You are the work of the devil," he impressed upon him, with his eyes black and intense. "And the only way to convince me otherwise is to take your place at the pulpit of this church and resume your godly life."

Arlo shook his head. "I have sinned most terribly in my new life."

"You are forgiven."

Arlo's heart beat off-kilter with this next declaration. "I am possibly a father of a different sort, and I will never stop loving her. I will love her forever, beyond death."

Father Porter looked down at Christopher. "Sacrifices are required, and you have a willing replacement. Reapply yourself, young man."

Arlo's pulse was uncomfortable. "Let another take the role."

"There is no one else available. If I pass into the Lord's care before a replacement is installed, this village will leave civilization behind. They will not care that the Frankenstein family is the wealthiest of patrons. With no fear of God, and the rumors unchecked, the villagers will march on their wicked hill."

Arlo's stomach sank at the choice presented. "And this is what you require of me, in order to leave them be?" The Frankenstein siblings were arguing good-naturedly now. "Life would go on for them, just as it always has?"

"It would keep Victor Frankenstein from the gallows, and I would tell the archdiocese that Father Northcott is the product of the holiest of miracles, witnessed by the highest officials in this parish. It would reinvigorate the entire village, bringing positivity and renewed faith."

"And Angelika?"

The old man's stare cut to her, and it was so vicious that Arlo turned to block her with his body. "Witches have not burned in this forest for over two hundred years. But traditions are often revisited."

"Under no circumstances will you ever harm her," Arlo intoned darkly.

"Good boy."

They were interrupted by the sound of metal on wood. "It was me," Victor and Christopher shouted in unison, then began to squabble like schoolboys as they scraped at the coffin lid.

Nothing else that happened from there was a surprise.

They dug some more, fetched ropes, realized they were unneeded, and Victor and Christopher passed the coffin up with one-handed effort. A crowbar was procured. Everyone pinched their nose, the lid was opened, and nothing but a plushly upholstered interior was revealed.

"It looks rather comfortable," Father Arlo Northcott told everyone as they stared at him. "But as you can now see, it was not my time."

The smile was fading off Victor's face. "What the hell, Will?"

"I echo that sentiment," Christopher said. "Did you know about this?" This gobsmacked question was for Angelika. "If you knew about this, I think you very wicked."

Her pretty mouth dropped open in hurt.

No matter that she loved Arlo, she craved Christopher's approval all the same. It was a dangerous loose thread; one that the accomplished hunter would find, and pull on, until her faithful heart slowly unraveled. Weeks, years, the commander would never stop, because why would he settle for a sturdy widow and her son, when he could have this magical creature, this heiress, this trophy?

Would Father Northcott see a carriage pass by one day after his Sunday sermon, and see a married woman's silhouette, and die completely?

"Miss Frankenstein is a good and honorable Christian woman, is she not?" Father Porter slanted his eyes toward Arlo.

The magistrate found his voice. He was emotional, his eyes glassy with tears, apparently having a religious epiphany. "Father Northcott, I don't know how this has happened, but I believe now. Miracles do happen. Praise the Lord."

"I believe there is something more complicated at play," Christopher interjected, but he was interrupted.

"Amen," Father Porter said. "Thimms, please prepare a faithful record of these remarkable events. If you agree with us that a miracle has occurred here, Father Northcott, please lead us in prayer." No one else heard the threat in his tone.

Arlo opened his mouth, and badly out of breath, he managed: "Our Father in heaven, hallowed be Your name. Your kingdom come, Your will be done, on earth as it is in heaven."

Victor turned on his heel and strode off into the night.

"It's time to go," Angelika said to Arlo firmly. "What is happening to you? We are leaving now. Bring the carriage alongside," she shouted after Victor. They had all traveled in grandeur into the village today, as a reminder of their standing in society. Arlo had ridden Solomon alongside. Now he couldn't possibly get a foot in the stirrup.

"I cannot go," Arlo told Angelika. "I feel strange."

"Come now, of course you can," Angelika urged, pulling a face. "My goodness, don't you look pale."

Christopher observed it, too. "Perhaps you should sit down."

If Father Porter ruined them, the Frankensteins would not be able to set foot in the village ever again. Crowds bearing torches would advance on the manor, chanting, eyes gleaming at the prospect of a little comeuppance.

Sometimes, love required a sacrifice.

"I think . . . I think . . ." Arlo's heart was beating erratically, first gulping up in his throat, then dropping to his belly.

It must have been the exertion. "I think you must leave me here, Angelika. It might be for the best."

He was practically eight years old again, putting on a brave front, being left somewhere he didn't want to be, aching for the moment he could put his face into a strange pillow to cry. The one in the coffin would do at this point. He tapped on his chest now with his fist. Heartbreak felt different than how he imagined.

Angelika was flummoxed. "Stay here? Why on earth? Stop this nonsense at once."

Father Porter smiled benignly. "He has come to the realization that his church requires his ongoing devotion."

"Marry him," Arlo said, meaning Christopher. "Have a baby. Live your life. Promise me you will live."

"I will marry you, and only you," Angelika gasped. "Why are you saying this?"

"I—I don't feel—" Arlo's legs gave out, and he fell to his hands and knees. "My love, I think it is happening." The loose soil at the edges of his own grave crumbled and moved. Everything inside him began to draw outward, and he thought of chimney smoke. "But I don't want to go. Don't leave me here—"

As Angelika's frantic questions turned into screams, all he could think of was that he was so glad he had told her the truth: that she was beautiful, and he loved her.

And if he could tell her one more thing? He would be a star directly above Larkspur Lodge, her heart's true home, forevermore.

CHAPTER THIRTY-FOUR

Death was wise to recognize Angelika Frankenstein as a formidable opponent.

"He is stabilizing, for now, but things are . . ." Dr. Corentin searched for the right phrase before settling on, "Comme ci, comme ça." He began writing something down. In his heavy French accent, he continued: "The laudanum must be administered strictly as I write it here, as he appears to be in a great deal of pain. Mon Dieu, I have never seen injuries such as these. Was he at war?"

In their panic, the Frankensteins had forgotten about the scars delineating each of Arlo's joints. He was laid naked from the waist up in Angelika's four-poster bed, almost as white as her French linen sheets.

"He's lived quite a life," Victor said to the doctor. "But he is a survivor."

"His blood is brown when I do a pinprick. I am not sure enough to try bloodletting." It was becoming clear that the doctor wasn't sure of anything.

"He will not die." Angelika said this so adamantly the candles flickered around them. "I refuse it. I will bring him back, again and again. We haven't come this far to let him be overcome by exhaustion. That's all this is, of course."

"Calm yourself," Dr. Corentin warned. "You do not seem to comprehend the situation. This young man is close to death."

The man's pessimism was frustrating. "He isn't dying, he's just tired. What else shall we do?" Angelika's stress levels rose with each instrument that the doctor packed away in his case.

The doctor said, "Keep him warm. Pray for him."

"Our mother died from a prayer-related illness," Victor informed him acidly. "I expected more from you, sir. Give us real things to do. Science. Medicine. That is what we believe in this household. Got a goddamn leech somewhere in there?"

Angelika watched as the doctor became offended, and she searched for a solution; the best one she knew. "His return to health will entail a thousand-pound gift for yourself, Dr. Corentin, which should be easy money, because he will be fine after a good night's sleep. Please, may I entreat you to stay the night across the hall?"

It was midnight, and the wind outside howled. Dr. Corentin patted his pocket as he readily agreed. "I should be most interested to learn your method of resuscitation," he said as a peace offering to Victor as he was shown out. "To save a man's life in such a way is no small feat."

Victor and Dr. Corentin closed the door behind them. Angelika was alone with her love, and she promptly fell apart. She wept as she struggled out of her gown, undergarments, and boots, and sobbed as she put on her silky nightdress, placed in her drawer a lifetime ago by that old scamp Mary.

Mary would know what to do now, with her witchy folk remedies. She would put a green pine cone in the fireplace, or pack some damp yew leaves into his armpits or some such nonsense, but it would absolutely help, because it would mean she was here. Perhaps she was nursing poor Adam in a similar state? Angelika cried for Mary, and Arlo, and Adam, and her parents, and her own wretched soul.

With chattering teeth, she got into the bed and moved close to Arlo's side. He was as cold as a pane of glass. Rubbing his arms and chest, she called out loudly to her brother, "Ask Sarah for heating bricks. As many as we have. I'll save you again," Angelika told Arlo's sleeping profile. "I swear I will. As many times as it takes." She imagined his wry expression at this dramatic declaration. "I will even allow Victor to assist me, like I did earlier."

At the graveside, she and Victor had fallen to their knees beside Arlo's prone body and rolled him over.

"No pulse. The Persian book—the compressions," Victor had told Angelika. She'd read every book he had, and it was why she would always be his ideal assistant. It was advice from the fifteenth century, but it was all they had. Tearing Arlo's shirt open, Victor had begun pressing on his left-side rib cage.

When Angelika looked up at Christopher, he shook his head, helpless.

"No heartbeat, no breath," Angelika observed, kneeling at Arlo's head. *Improvise, experiment, use your brain, Jelly.* She put her mouth to Arlo's in a passionless kiss, and exhaled. When she felt air tickle her cheek, she blocked his nose and forced him, over and over, to take her air, her love, and her abundance of fussing.

Victor reentered the room now, interrupting the memory, loaded down with heating bricks wrapped in cloth, and more in Lizzie's arms behind him.

"I would swear it, Vic," Angelika told him absently as the bricks were packed in around them under the blankets, "when

I was breathing the air into him, I swear I felt his soul in my lungs."

Victor said briskly, "You're in shock. We don't believe in—"

She cut him off. "Never again tell me what I think. Never again attempt to convince me of what you think is true. He has taught me to believe in everything."

"I cannot believe you knew about this," Victor spat out. "A priest? Father bloody Northcott, in my own house? How long were you aware?"

"Who he was is not his fault," Lizzie said pointedly. "It is your fault, Vic, for experimenting on him in the first place."

"It is our fault," Angelika agreed. "Victor, we did this to him. We let him dig that hole, completely exhausting his life force."

Victor ignored her and kept at it. "Your complex reveals itself again—you do prefer those unattainable types. You truly believe a man would choose you, over his own God?"

With the confidence of an empress, Angelika replied, "Yes."

He choked laughing. "Then you are more delusional than I ever imagined. Well, if there are pitchforks and flames down below, you had better ready yourself for them."

"Happily."

"Vic, get out!" Lizzie snapped at him, and he stalked out, banging the door shut. Lizzie lay down on the top of the quilt, on the other side of Arlo. "Don't listen to your absolute pillock of a brother. I will always believe you. Tell me everything."

Angelika made a grunt that meant something like: *You'll tell Victor.*

Lizzie persisted. "I'm your sister now." She put her arm across Arlo's stomach, and the two women held hands. "How did it feel? His soul?"

The warmth in the bed was making Angelika drowsy. "Like

stars. I breathed it all back into him, and then Vic found his pulse again."

"What a pretty way to describe it. I may borrow that line." Lizzie mulled this over as they all lay there. "Funny, when I'm not vomiting into a chamber pot, that's what it feels like here." She patted her lower stomach. "Silvery and magic. Stars."

Angelika was somehow still able to smile. "That makes me happy. A little soul is swirling inside you." Inside herself, she only felt emptiness, and a true glimpse of her future was revealed. Now she was back to crying. "I'll be left alone. I can't go on."

Lizzie was firm with her. "He has lived twice for you now. Keep your faith in him. And you will never be alone. You have me."

"He seemed quite intent on crawling back into his own grave. You have to keep fighting," Angelika told Arlo with quiet urgency as she wiped at her tears. "Stop all of this dying nonsense. I beg you."

Lizzie wheezed in amusement. "I'm told you were rather insistent with Father Porter, when he tried to take him into the church."

"I screamed in his fishy old face until he crossed himself." Angelika let go of Lizzie's hand to rub Arlo's stomach for a while. "Why would Arlo tell me, just before he collapsed, that he had decided to stay at the church?"

"He was feeling unwell and was not himself."

Angelika did feel cheered by how certain Lizzie sounded. "I'm sure a nice night's sleep will restore him." She began to chatter mindlessly about the weather outside.

Lizzie tried her best to keep the doubt from her eyes, and they held hands over the almost-dead man once more.

Arlo died his third death right before dawn, but Angelika was highly persuasive. When he was resettled again into his body, she put her face into a pillow and howled.

Arlo was still alive at breakfast time. When Dr. Corentin assured her he would look after Arlo for a while, Angelika excused herself in search of Victor. "He's gone running," Lizzie had mumbled in her sleep.

"Running," Angelika repeated as she went downstairs. "Victor is running, in the pouring rain, when I need him?" Whatever she was hoping the doctor would produce from his leather valise did not exist. "He needs to invent a solution. Yes, yes, I will be back," she shouted over her shoulder at the gaggle of servants who slowly emerged from the shadows of the halls. "He lives, and I will be back."

To her intense irritation, Victor was not in the laboratory putting the finishing touches on an elixir to restore Arlo. "Time-wasting idiot," she seethed, and seized upon his notebook. "I will have to do this alone."

She began leafing through it backward from the most recent entry. It was, of course, in his secret shorthand code. "I can't read it," she complained out loud, in the exact tone from her childhood. "But wait, this is about Arlo."

There was a sketch of the wound on Arlo's hand, and the measurement. As she flipped back, she realized Victor had been measuring it every two days. It had not healed a fraction. "I have never listened to what Arlo was trying to tell me." She swallowed her rising panic, cast the notebook aside, and began lining up various compounds and glass beakers. It was here that Victor found her sometime later, hunched over the bench, alternately cackling and wheezing with panic.

"And they call *me* a mad scientist," he said. Then his smirk faded. "I think you should be sitting with him."

"I'm inventing a way to cure him."

With gentle pity, her brother replied: "You won't find it in here." He ignored her collection of foaming, poisonous previous attempts on the far bench. "Come inside."

She dipped a spoon at random into a jar of magnesium sulphate. "Do you have the monopoly on genius and talent? Did you achieve everything in your life alone? Am I mentioned even once in your notebooks? Does Herr Jürgen Schneider curse my name also? Will I be remembered in history?"

A speechless Victor was her favorite kind. She continued her rant.

"Everything you have ever done is because I helped you. Your conceit is exactly equal to my delusion. But despite these personal failings, we carry on."

Lizzie would definitely want to steal that entire monologue.

Angelika shoveled the powder into a fresh beaker, cast around for an additive, then hesitated. She was so tired she could not remember which reacted with what. But because Victor was watching, she filled the beaker with cold water and set it above a burning flame.

"You are thinking of giving him a warm magnesium tonic?" Victor pondered this. "It will have to be administered with a throat tube. But it may assist in keeping his joints and muscles softened. He said you have a marvelous salty bath solution that helps with the pain. Good thinking, Jelly."

Angelika was so relieved to have created anything at all, she wept all the way out the door, up the path, through the manor door, and up the stairs.

With one hand holding the beaker and apparatus, Victor patted her shoulder with the other, repeating, "I'm sorry, I'm sorry."

Dr. Corentin stood as soon as they entered. "I am called away for a childbirth."

"Absolutely not," Angelika countered, but Victor nodded to the man. She was aghast. "Victor, he is otherwise engaged, working here."

"There is a baby wishing to live who needs me more," the doctor replied as he picked up his case. As he passed them on his way to the door, he added sadly, "Ma chère, take my original advice. Pray for his soul and prepare yourself."

"Victor!" Angelika was unable to move her feet as her brother closed the door behind the departed doctor. "You're going to let him just leave? Offer him more! All that I have, take it!"

Victor's mouth was in a rueful line. "What if it were Lizzie one day, giving birth, needing him to come at once? He's right," he tried to impress on her, but Angelika was turning redder than an apple. "Jelly, he does not have the expertise. There's nothing more he can do."

"Shut up." She crawled up onto the bed and put her ear to Arlo's mouth. "He's still alive. Come on, help me." Hating Victor's reluctance, she wrenched the tube and funnel from him. "I have no idea how to do this." Arlo's body did not accommodate the intrusion willingly, but after several sweaty minutes she had poured the entire beaker into his stomach. "There," she said, rolling up the wet tube and thrusting it back at her brother.

"Good work" was his reply. "Can't hurt."

Arlo's body jerked. He vomited, and began choking. "Roll him," Victor directed, and they caught the expunged liquid with towels. "His body still has these kinds of base reactions," he told Angelika as they pounded his back. "I think this is a good thing."

"A good thing?" Angelika wiped Arlo's mouth. Her voice rose. "A good thing? You know what I see? You, standing about, being absorbed in yourself, jogging in the forest, working on your own precious body, doing absolutely nothing to improve this situation. Is it because he was originally a priest? Or is it because he loves me?"

"Jel—"

"You've never wanted anyone to love me. You've always laughed at my infatuations, and told me I am a fool, and nobody would ever want me."

"I never laughed at you," Victor said uneasily. "All right, maybe I did. But I was joking."

"You were never joking, and you weren't joking when you said it last night. But he loves me, and it's not for my fortune or my face. He loves my flaws. He makes me feel like I could be a better person. We are connected, at a blood level."

"I do not doubt the depth of your love."

She ignored that. "You are going to be right, as always. Being dead is the ultimate in unattainable, wouldn't you say?" In her rage, she was calmer than she'd ever been. "I will die of heartbreak. There's a plot vacant beside his grave. Put me there. That is my wish."

Victor's complexion turned ashen, and he said nothing.

She turned her back on him. "Get out, and don't come back until you can do something useful."

CHAPTER THIRTY-FIVE

The following morning, the foyer of Blackthorne Manor was well-occupied. "I can't get a word out of her," the cook, Mrs. Rumsfield, was saying like a complaint, before she jumped and clutched her chest. "Christ almighty, missus!"

Angelika was descending the stairs. She was gray, droopy, and her eyes were sunken into her skull. She smelled. If anyone had been able to look past this ghastly apparition, they would see that the portrait of Caroline was highly concerned.

"You look ruddy dreadful!" Mrs. Rumsfield hollered. Sarah appeared in the doorway to the kitchen hall, wiping her hands on a cloth. At the foot of the stairs, Angelika was surrounded by all the house servants, Jacob the stablehand, and even some of the garden laborers. She searched in vain for the face she ached for the most, and then dropped to sit on the bottom stair.

"He lives. Again." She wrung her hands. "We must all rally together these next few hours." She was touched by the worry in the faces looking down at her. Every single one of these people had been impacted by Arlo in some way; his kind leadership had brought them to Blackthorne Manor and, in turn, awoken the estate from its deep sleep.

Mrs. Rumsfield said, voice rich with self-importance, "I have some broth ready for when he wakes."

"Very good," Angelika replied, even though her hopes were fading. "But now, while he is asleep, we must make Arlo—ah, you know him as Will, but he is now called Arlo Northcott—we must make him proud, and do our best to run the house—"

She stopped when Mrs. Rumsfield tutted. "You are all done in, miss. Time for something to eat and some sleep."

"There is no time. Boys," Angelika commanded the ragtag crew, now knowing what needed to be done, "I want you all to begin planning the apple harvest."

"Will told us it's not something you do up 'ere," one nameless laborer said, confused. "Everyone in the village knows that."

"I am tired of waste. It's something I would like to do from this season forth. Is it possible? Are there more folk in the village who would like to be hired for this?" Angelika saw every head nod. "I know this seems like an odd thing to occupy ourselves with, given the circumstances, but I feel that Arlo would be so pleased to hear we had done this fine thing without him. He is the one who gets everything done around here, isn't he?" Again, more nods. "Let's show him that he has taught us well. Jacob, you shall be the organizer. Our neighbor may have a groundskeeper you could ask for advice."

The young boy nodded.

"What else?" She turned her face to the girls. "The remaining three cottages beyond the orchard require cleaning and whitewashing. One is for Sarah, one is for Jacob, and the last is for Adam. Mrs. Rumsfield, could you please keep everyone fed as they work?"

"'Course. But, miss, you need to eat, too," the cook entreated, and someone muttered, "Who's Adam?"

Angelika's stomach wasn't likely to hold on to a meal. "Let us make him proud." Tears began to threaten as she saw everyone straighten their spines, with fresh purpose shining in their eyes. She slipped out the front door, and then felt a hand on her sleeve.

It was Sarah. Blushing, she forced out: "I misunderstood. I'm to clean a cottage for Jacob?"

Angelika said, "You are to clean the cottage that will be yours."

Sarah took a step back, eyes huge and confused. "Like the ones where Will and Clara live?"

"Yes. Didn't I tell you that a long time ago? I've got to start telling people what is theirs. If it is comfortable enough, you can move there now. No more cold boardinghouse room. This is your home now if you wish it."

Sarah grabbed her, and hugged her hard, squeezing out Angelika's tears. The relief of this human contact was staggering, and Angelika babbled over the girl's shoulder. "If I organize everything just so, he will wake and be proud. He will be so proud of me, and us, Sarah. We must arrange everything."

Sarah rocked her employer in her arms, and repeated to the ivy-covered porch that everything would be all right.

Everything would be all right. Wouldn't it?

It was dawn again. Angelika didn't know how many dawns had tried to creep past her drawn drapes by this point; all she knew was Arlo had died twice more, and his breaths were so shallow she couldn't hear them over her own heartbeat as she lay beside him with her head on his pillow. She could no longer lift her heavy limbs, and she only sipped at water or broth when forced.

"Should I let you go now?" The question she asked Arlo broke her heart. "Am I being cruel to you?"

"Nobody has ever fought this hard," Lizzie said from the armchair. "And nobody has ever loved a man this much. But, Jelly." She choked up then, coughed, and wiped her eyes. "If he goes one more time, you need to let him."

Angelika knew there were no more arguments she could make. "Victor would call that natural science. But I will miss you," she said, putting her cheek into the wasting dip on his chest. "And I will join you soon," she added, too quiet for Lizzie to hear. Louder, she asked in a rasping voice, "Is it unscientific to request a miracle?"

"I don't think so," Lizzie said, and the door handle turned.

A miracle was speedily supplied.

"Dark as a tomb," Mary said with evident disgust from the doorway. "And the smell."

"Mary," both women gasped.

"I heard I'm required," Mary replied primly. She rounded the end of the bed, took ahold of the drapes, and threw them apart with violence, letting in the pale dawn light. Wiping at the condensation on the glass with her ragged sleeve, she continued. "I heard there's a young woman in this household dying of a broken heart."

"It's true," Angelika said. She felt herself being rolled by the shoulder, and now she was looking up at Mary. "You've been out in the forest, and I have cried every moment since."

"You're always embellishing," Mary countered, but she had a faint smile on her face. "So you've decided to just give up, and follow him? They tell me downstairs that you have stopped eating. And bathing." Her gaze flickered over to Arlo, and she winced at what she saw. The old woman thought for a minute, and then apparently made a decision. "My husband died on the eve of my thirtieth birthday."

"That's young," Angelika replied. "I didn't know you were ever young."

Mary ignored that. "And when my William died, I had a decision to make. Would I lie down and die next to him, too?"

"You obviously didn't," Lizzie said, when the pressure of the silence was too great. She winced under the stare Mary cut in her direction. "I will go and get Angelika some broth, and some more cloths . . ." She was gone in a blink.

"I have done nothing but keep him alive," Angelika confided, her parched throat barely able to finish the words. "I've kept him alive, and I've waited for you, Mary. I am more sorry than you'll ever know."

Mary put a hand on Angelika's forehead and smoothed back her hair. "I do know." She put a hand into her apron pocket and produced a brooch. "I took this, and you are within your rights to hang me."

"I don't care about a green stone." Angelika was out of tears. There was little liquid left in her body, but she allowed Mary to lift her up on the pillows to take a sip from a cup. "I don't tell people things in time. I say things in the wrong order, or assume that people know. The emerald is yours, and I was making you a cottage."

"I know. Adam told me."

Under the blankets, Angelika slipped her hand into Arlo's icy palm. "How is Adam?"

"He will follow Will in a few days, I think." The old woman was brisk, but Angelika could see a glassiness in her eyes. "We did our best, miss."

"I didn't." Even as she said it, Angelika realized it wasn't true. "No, actually, I did all I could."

"Did you tell him, then?" Mary nodded at Arlo. "You said you don't tell people things in time. Did you tell him everything you needed to?"

Angelika nodded. A sensation began to unfold in her chest: an easing of a tightness she had held and nurtured for days. "I did tell him, Mary. From the minute I brought him back that first time, I told him that I loved him, in different ways, and he knew it."

"Then you have done well, and it is time to lay him down." Mary cupped a hand on Angelika's cheek, just like she used to do when she was a child. "You will be all right. I'm here now. There's nothing to be afraid of." She glanced up, and her characteristic fierce frown formed. "Get that pig out of here."

"Mary. Jolly good, we may need a third hand for this." Victor stumbled into the room, looking every inch as exhausted as his sister. Belladonna was indeed in the doorway behind him. He set a tray of implements on the bed, where they slid around and clanged. "Oh, holy hell," Victor cursed, putting a hand into his hair.

Angelika's heart squeezed in sympathy. "Vic. It's time."

"Yes, exactly. I've only just gotten this finished now." He held up a long, strange strip of what appeared to be flesh. "I can't sew half as well as you, and I have failed so many times, but I think this is the one." He gave Lizzie a kiss on the cheek when she came to his side. "Hello, Lizzie. We are going to give him one more turn around the mortal maypole."

Angelika shook her head. "Listen to me. It's time to let him go. It's time to just . . . pray. We will be with him as he leaves, and we will let him rest in peace."

"You can do that," Victor said, and then held up a thick

sewing needle. "But you got me thinking, Jelly. You said you're connected at a blood level. That's what he needs. Not broth, not prayer. Blood. Do you want it to be me or you?"

Angelika lifted herself up onto her elbows with difficulty. "You've made a tube?"

"Out of a rabbit's intestine," Victor said. "The thinnest, most impossible thing to sew. I have gone through an absolute pile of them. So many times I almost came in here and asked you to do it. And that's when I knew how much I have taken you for granted in everything I have ever done." He was unbuttoning his shirt, but Angelika stopped him.

"Me."

Victor assessed his sister. "You don't look so good."

"It has to be me." The press of the needle into the bend of her elbow was so painful that she shouted, and beside her, Arlo's body twitched. They all watched with morbid fascination as the blood began to leak, spurt, and then fill the tube. Lizzie croaked. Mary fainted onto the bed. Angelika winced. "Wait, we should have put down a muslin cloth. Blood is so hard to soak out of linen."

But then the Frankensteins did not notice anything except the neat squiggle of red that charted a course across the bed, captured in a membrane thinner than an eyelash. One wrong stitch would undo it all, but Angelika saw that her brother had applied himself thoroughly.

"You always said you cannot sew," she said to him. "But you have done well. Whatever happens next, thank you for trying. I will never forget it."

"This is the only tube that I managed to completely suture, and I don't think I can reuse it. So you are going to have to hold on tight, Jelly. I just put this into him here." Victor plunged the other needle into Arlo's vein with detached calm.

"And we wait. And we pray." He held his sister's gaze and put out his hand to her. "I will pray with you, my beloved sister."

Mary was revived, Lizzie helped her into the armchair, and they both watched the impossible.

"Dear Lord," Victor said, with his eyes closed. "Dear Lord, save him. I will do anything. Whatever it takes, I will do it. I will bleed myself into him every day if it means my sister can live with her only true love. He is better than all of us put together, and I know that sounds like a strange thing to say about a man who is completely put together."

Everyone laughed.

Victor continued, still with closed eyes. "I have not prayed once, in my entire life. I did not pray for my parents; I did not pray to find Lizzie. I trusted the natural order of things. I trusted science, and I still do, clearly. But for the first and only prayer I will make in my life, I ask you to save him." His eyes opened and locked on Angelika's. "God, I am asking you to let us have him. One lifetime's worth will do, and when he is an old man, he can return to you."

Angelika felt a curious sensation: a sparkling, a pulling, a star sensation. She looked across the pillow. "Is he coming or going?"

"He's right on the edge," Victor said. Mary rounded to his side, still waxy from the sight of the blood, and her eyeline carefully averted. She assessed the man below. She put her hand on his forehead. She patted his cheek, and then put her thumb on his pulse, and was silent.

"Well?" Lizzie ventured timidly.

Mary replied with dignity, "I am praying, too." And in the silence that followed, they all thought of the life they wished for him.

Victor wanted a brother at last, to ride horses with at sunset, stomachs full of ale. He wished for a nephew or niece so hard that he brought himself to tears.

Lizzie prayed for Angelika's smile. She prayed for a blanket laid beneath an apple tree, and the faint buzz of bees. More than anything, she wished that a baby would look at her with Angelika's same tart, direct gaze.

Mary's prayers were not exactly centered on Arlo, but she prayed she would find the courage to say important words out loud. That was the fault Angelika had with herself, wasn't it? They were cut from the same cloth, because Mary had never once told either of these children that she loved them.

Angelika prayed for a heartbeat, and anything beyond that would be a bonus.

They were all so lost in thought, holding hands and making promises to themselves, that they did not notice the new tinge of pink on Arlo Northcott's cheekbones. And when they did, Angelika Frankenstein refused to let up; she drained herself into the only man she had ever loved, until he opened his exquisite eyes on a new day.

His head turned on the pillow. Everyone remained silent.

"Where am I?" His words should have been terrifying, but there was a dry humor in the question.

Angelika was so weak, the quality of her voice alarmed everyone. But she was smiling now, too. "You are in the bed of a spoiled, wealthy heiress who has realized her privileged position and will work for the rest of her life to deserve you."

His mouth twitched before he looked down at their linked arms. "What have you done for me?"

"She has at least halfway died for you," Victor interjected, efficiently pulling the needle from Arlo's arm, and then his sister's. The fragile tubing promptly disintegrated, and Mary roared at the mess it made on the bed. As Lizzie began to mop, and Victor began to crow about how Jürgen Schneider would take the news of this latest scientific breakthrough, Angelika used the last of her strength to put her cheek on Arlo's chest, the one she had personally selected.

"My dream man. The one I have waited for. The one I will live and die for. I think we have found a way to keep you with me forever."

"Forever?" Arlo's lips, growing pinker by the minute, quirked into a tired smile. "Forever is a long time, my love."

"I know." She tipped up her face to his, and they gave each other a kiss. "Do you doubt me? Have you forgotten who I am?"

"Angelika Frankenstein," Arlo said, "if forever is what you want, you shall have it."

He glanced up at the smiling faces that were beginning to appear in the room: Sarah, Jacob, the cook, and the gardeners. Mary was telling Sarah loudly how to soak a sheet. Mrs. Rumsfield was ladling out broth. Lizzie put her hand to her stomach, then laughed and took Victor's hand, pressing it to her side. "Like stars," she told him.

Dropping his voice to a whisper, Arlo said into Angelika's ear, "I think we will have some peace and quiet at Larkspur Lodge."

EPILOGUE

The change of season put Victor Frankenstein in a good mood.

"I've never seen apples like this," he enthused to Mary, who was digging a hole in the garden patch beside her cottage's front door. "There must be a hundred times the usual amount."

"It's the same number of apples as every year," Mary said as she pushed a flowering shrub into the dirt and began to press it in. "You're only noticing them because of the harvest. Every year they have fallen to the ground."

"Not this year," Victor said. "We are doing things differently around here. Now, why are you tidying up so vigorously?" He indicated the rug airing on her windowsill. "You're bustling around like mad when we want you to relax and enjoy your retirement."

"My grandniece is visiting me, which you should know, as I've told you at least ten times. She will be in Clara's old cottage."

"I've been distracted," Victor protested.

His every waking moment revolved around the growing protrusion on his wife's midsection. She was agreeable enough to cooperate in some baseline experiments, and the trip to the altar on the hill had been just in time. He grinned now at the memory. "Jolly good of Arlo to perform one last ceremony, wasn't it?"

"Focus," Mary scolded, and handed him a broom. "Sweep up. I want everything to look respectable."

"How old's your grandniece? How does that work? Is she your sister's granddaughter?" Victor didn't much care about some stranger, but he listened dutifully, and swept a path for the first time in his entire life. "Seventeen? Careful she doesn't fall in love with me. I am told that the girls in the village think me terribly handsome and rich, mysterious and refined. It's all truth, but I am now married, and a father in a matter of months. All the girls fall in love with me," he added to Belladonna, scratching her chin.

"I am sure you tell your reflection all that in the mirror every morning," Mary replied cuttingly. "Mary isn't a stupid girl; she won't fall for whatever charms you believe you have."

"Her name is Mary, too?" Victor smiled his particularly irresistible smile, and grudgingly Mary found herself smiling back.

"She is named for me. Put them on her bed," she said to Adam, who was walking up the path with blankets in his arms. "Good boy," she encouraged him. Mary had a grandson at long last, and it was delightful to see her dote on him in her way. "Do you feel all right?"

"Fine, fine," Adam said in his grumbling tone as he trudged past. "Victor won't need to top me up for another week, I'm sure."

"Just let me know," Victor replied, and patted his inner elbow firmly. "Plenty of blood to go around." Inventing a reusable blood transfusion tube was much more difficult than anyone knew. In truth, it was a task that had nearly broken him, but he had been determined to do it without his sister's assistance. Now that he thought about it, it was his first solo invention.

"It's a story nobody would believe," Mary said as they watched Adam bend down to fit through the cottage door. "Young Mary is a writer. She has a similar vivid imagination to you. You will get along with her. Ah, our little boy is here to visit old Aunt Mary."

Up the path, Edwin was being bounced along each stepping-stone. His hands were held by a very careful man, and he arrived at Mary's feet without injury.

Victor greeted them. "Commander. Clara. How lovely to see you both."

Christopher lifted the boy up. "We can't stay away. He loves it here."

"It's not the same here without you, Clara. I think you should move back." Victor said it to rile Christopher, but she answered earnestly.

"I've gotten rather used to the academy," Clara replied with a blush and straightened her son's trousers. "It wouldn't do for the commander's wife to live by herself, would it?"

"The troops might talk," Christopher agreed. "I shouldn't like to get a reputation as a bad husband."

"You could never do that."

Victor bit into an apple loudly as they kissed. "We're all taking coaches up to Larkspur as soon as Lizzie pops. She has an absolute insistence about lying on a blanket with Jelly. It makes no sense. And Jelly wants to plant her own apple tree. At least Arlo can keep it alive for her; she's got no green thumb. You all should come; there's endless guest bedrooms."

"That's a kind offer," Christopher said awkwardly, but Clara finished his sentence firmly:

"We should love to. We miss Angelika and Arlo very much."

"When Father Porter shuffles off his mortal coil, they can come back for a visit," Victor said. "There's no one left in the village who knows who Arlo really is. Thimms and the magistrate have moved away, thanks to some mysterious meddling." He jingled his pocket for effect. "He can come back then and walk about without looking over his shoulder. And if Belladonna could accept that she's a pig, Lizzie can walk around without a broom." Still, his face creased in amusement as his ever-present shadow put her head against his leg. Down to her adoring face, he said, "You must give up on me."

Belladonna made an impassioned squeal that meant, *Never.*

"I don't think Arlo has minded being holed up at Larkspur in the country," Christopher said with amusement. "I'm sure he's been well-occupied."

"Reading poetry," Clara said, and even Edwin laughed.

Mary wasn't in on the joke. "My grandniece, Mary—"

"I have never heard so much about a stranger as this new Mary," Victor complained.

"She writes and reads poetry. She wishes to write a book, but she cannot find a topic. That is why she is coming to stay. She will find inspiration here. She has torn her hair out with frustration, according to her letter."

"She will find your home positively charming," Clara encouraged with a smile. "You have decorated it to look so wonderful. I see Angelika has treated you to some fine furnishings."

Through the window, Mary's little cottage was a miniature palace, decorated in the finest French wallpapers. "She is a decadent young woman," Mary said, and then added in a voice like she was practicing: "But that is a reason we love her. Or, I should say, I love her."

Clara rubbed her arm. "Doesn't it all look so pretty. We might go and say hello to Jacob and Adam. Is Sarah here, too?"

Mary replied, "Sarah will be at school, but Adam and Jacob are here." The little family departed up the path. "Master Victor, I want to know something. Can I tell young Mary about the comings and goings of Blackthorne Manor? I think it might inspire her."

Victor thought, shrugged, and gave his apple core to Belladonna. "Why not? I'll send Schneider a copy. Won't that just burn his biscuits? We would have to ask Jelly if she consents to being a character. After all, I'm nothing without her."

Mary let out a bark of laughter. "I would strongly suggest changing every detail possible. If I know her, she'll say that under no circumstances will she allow her name in print to be attached to this scandalous tale."

"Shame. She was right there, next to me, achieving the same as me."

Mary squinted up at him. "She was. It's nice to hear you say it, too. But she's less vain about it than you."

Victor put a dramatic hand on his chest. "I submit to your grandniece that I am pure inspiration, through and through." He straightened the huge green emerald pinned to the old woman's cardigan. "Wouldn't it be fun to give Jelly a copy of this future book at some Christmastime? Perhaps Lizzie can adapt it for the stage."

"You are getting ahead of yourself. It's not written yet. And I doubt Angelika will have time to read it, what with all their traveling," Mary replied, and she watched Victor walk back to the house with her heart in her eyes.

Now free of the vines and cobwebs, and appreciated at last, Blackthorne Manor had regained the power of crystal-clear omniscience, and it had observed these exchanges. It knew that the apples would no longer fall, that visitors would be frequent, and that the stockpiled gold was now circulating in the villages. The hair-plaiting, bath-filling Angelika Frankenstein had moved away, but it wasn't something to be sad about. There was very little sadness left at Blackthorne. The regular evening-time routine that followed was as familiar to it as a heartbeat.

Chimneys threaded pale blue smoke into the dimming twilight; Adam's stomach rumbled at the smell of Mary's stew.

Victor climbed the staircase inside to kiss Lizzie breathless, but not before pausing beneath his new picture frame, hanging directly above the staircase. It looked ridiculously small, just a framed page, centered on the brighter rectangle of wallpaper, in Caroline Frankenstein's recently vacated space.

"I'm better than him," Victor said gently, and smoothed his hand over the letter from Herr Jürgen Schneider, which affirmed the sentiment. "I'm so much better than him. Lizzie, my duchess, guess what?" This he shouted, utterly invigorated.

"What, Bear?" she called from her nest in their bed.

"I'm going to live on in history, forever!"

Lizzie cackled. "I have no doubt. Now get in here and give me my kiss."

Miles away, at Larkspur Lodge, a similar evening routine was playing out, with a slight difference. "Are you sure?" Arlo was asking Angelika. He put another log into the fireplace, and then knelt down between her slippers. "Are you absolutely sure?"

"Do you believe I am incapable of counting the passing days?" She held her arched eyebrow a fraction longer, and then laughed. "Yes, I am sure."

"Then it's a miracle."

"I've always had faith in you," she replied as he began to kiss her stomach. "And you have put your heart and soul into it. Every room in the house, you have made an attempt. Over and over, just when I thought your inspiration had run dry, you surprised me."

"It's true." Arlo laughed, and when he put both hands into hers, she luxuriated in the warmth she felt in his fingers as she massaged his lingering aches away. She was the furnace that fueled and healed him. Her body was the giver of all life. She now had an extra reason to be smug about it.

Angelika sewed, night and day, creating exquisite garments for all she loved. Arlo had protested that a baby did not need a cloak and silver-beaded slippers, but his protests were cheerfully ignored. She occupied herself making hampers of baby clothes and food that were delivered to new mothers in the neighboring counties.

She funded a small army of midwives.

She was a benefactress to anyone she believed in.

Before the baby arrived, Arlo occupied himself in the evenings by rereading his beloved copy of *Institutiones Rei Herbariae* by Tournefort to make sense of the wild varieties of plants that grew across their estate. Blooms and weeds filled the intertwined courtyards and mazes that made up Larkspur Lodge's jaw-dropping grounds. He had found a strange little thistle in a hedgerow that required some research. He opened the cover and smoothed his fingertips over the inscription, never again allowing a single one of his wife's declarations to go unnoticed. It was perhaps a little sacrilegious to write in such a rare old book, but she had amended her annotation several times:

To my love: One day I will write your true name here.
Will, then Father Arlo, and then just Arlo, my husband,
and now a father!
With all that I am,
I am always,
your Angelika.

The seasons changed again, and the day came that Angelika Northcott gave her beloved Arlo what he had feared was impossible. She gave birth to the baby in her bathtub and cut the cord with her favorite sewing scissors. She wouldn't need them for a little while; at least until her new arrival required a wardrobe refresh.

From her new home above the mantel, the portrait of Caroline Frankenstein observed the scene below. Her daughter had made her perfect match, and it was that forever, Frankenstein kind of love. Larkspur Lodge held a similar view.

The baby boy looked absolutely *nothing* like his father.

They loved him more than any little boy had ever been loved before.

That much was certain.

ACKNOWLEDGMENTS

Before I thank some people, I want to acknowledge that this book surely contains historical inaccuracies. I know that men did not usually wear wedding rings in 1814, but I could not resist, for the sake of the story. Sometimes, when writing fiction, you take certain licenses and risks—and for me, this book was the best risk ever.

Next, I must acknowledge, and possibly apologize to, the genius Mary Shelley. There was a plague in my time, and I borrowed your characters for a short while.

Now, my thank-yous! Christina Hobbs and Lauren Billings, aka Christina Lauren, I have loved you two since the year 1814, and this book is dedicated to you both. When I write a book, it's done safe in the knowledge that you will understand the heart of it—even in this instance, when it's a heart from the morgue. Thank you, Roland, Tina, Katie, and my mum, Sue, for always being in my corner. I can't do this without my agent, my rock, Taylor Haggerty. Thank you, Root Literary. I gain a great amount of confidence from my editor, Carrie Feron, and the amazing team at Avon. The fact that so many people continued to work and try their best during a pandemic was inspiring and humbling. Publishing a book is a team effort, and I am a part of the best team there is.

Thank you to my readers and Flamethrowers, who have told me they'd read anything that I wrote. I clung to that as I unexpectedly began writing Frankenstein fan fiction. I hope you all meant it. Allowing me to have this incredible job is something I am grateful for, every day.

These last few years have had some wonderful moments, including the movie adaptation of my first book, *The Hating Game*, being released worldwide. But I have also cried an ocean of tears, and I finally understand Angelika completely.

I lost my horse on November 7, 2021. Louie, my special boy, to save you I would have bled myself dry. I have done some really astonishing things trying to turn back time. I hope you're a star above my house.

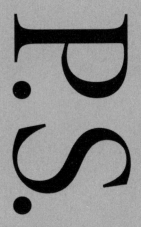

About the author

About the book

Insights,
Interviews
& More . . .

Meet Sally Thorne

Katie Saariklo

Sally Thorne is the *USA Today* bestselling author of *The Hating Game*, *99 Percent Mine*, and *Second First Impressions*. She spends her days climbing into fictional worlds of her own creation. She lives in Canberra, Australia, with her husband, in a house filled with vintage toys, too many cushions, a haunted dollhouse, and the world's sweetest pug.

A Letter to Mary Shelley

Dear Mary Shelley,

You are the rightful and revered author of *Frankenstein; or, The Modern Prometheus*, a seminal work that has been treasured by generations of readers and is hailed as one of the earliest examples of science fiction.

I feel the need to explain myself, and perhaps apologize to you. In the year 2020, I borrowed your characters with reckless abandon and used them most outrageously. My excuse is there was a new plague at the time, and I was rather bored.

I'm not sure how you coped with feeling creatively blocked in your time, but I know that you, Percy, and Lord Byron went on a holiday in Switzerland. After which, a group writing challenge was set and *Frankenstein* came to you in a dream. So perhaps a change of scenery, creative friends to spur you on, bad weather, and a bit of pressure helped spark something for you.
An aside: Please visit me in my dream tonight so I can know what happened on that vacation. Don't hold back on the details that may be lost to history, no matter how frank you must be.

A Swiss holiday was not possible for me in 2020. We weren't even allowed ▶

3

A Letter to Mary Shelley *(continued)*

to mix with people from other households, not that I know a Byron type. When I'm feeling like the well has run dry and my brain is coated in glue, I begin to write something random, and the worse it is, the better. I can write this way for pages, cackling at my own ridiculousness. These flowery little goof-offs contain too much detail, absolutely no *showing* and only *telling*, names are spelled inconsistently throughout, and there's some sort of silly danger. As an example, I wrote an argument between two lovers on a cliff, with many unneeded paragraphs about their clothing, and the heroine's ivory calfskin boots kept teetering too close to the cliff's edge, as she is repeatedly warned by a man (dressed in a denim three-piece suit) not to fall. This particular piece includes these lines of dialogue: " 'Frederick,' she cried. 'Frederic! I almost died!' " It's true. She almost did.

After I write something deliberately bad and am cheered up that I can do much better, I resume work on my *real* manuscript. One day, while working on the edits for my third book, *Second First Impressions*, and being strongly encouraged by the Australian government to not leave home unless it was absolutely essential to do so (on account of the plague I mentioned), I opened a blank Word document (parchment) and wrote the following:

Angelika Frankenstein knew what physical qualities her ideal man should have; unfortunately, she had to find those attributes at the morgue.

I was astonished by this sentence. I had never ever thought these particular words in this sequence before—let alone know who Angelika Frankenstein was, with her first name spelled with a *k* instead of a *c*. But it came over me in a hot, sure rush as I began to tell her story; of *course* Victor Frankenstein had a self-absorbed, spoiled, lonely sister, and of *course* she would ask for his help in creating her true love. And I was inspired another way, too. In my book, the Frankenstein's home, Blackthorne Manor, is modeled on my dollhouse. While I was at home writing, it sat behind me: a black slate roof, arched windows, mouseholes, and a gold-filled safe behind a painting. I'm glad it has now made its debut in fiction.

I played with Victor and Angelika like dolls. They argued and laughed and created together, in the shadow of the unspeakable sorrow of being orphaned. I grappled with the ethics of someone designing a lover, and with whether my modern audience would feel that ▶

A Letter to Mary Shelley (*continued*)

he had the appropriate agency and ability
to consent, given his limited options
and the brutal realities of being poor
and without title in that time period.
I realized how truly difficult it is to write
a character suffering from amnesia,
especially when no one else knows his
origin, either. Through Will, I learned
to admire the people who can truly live
in the moment.

And every time my hands froze, a
voice whispered that it wasn't my place
to try writing something set hundreds
of years ago—not when my best-known
book is set in the here and now and is
even on movie screens. (Cinema—
moving photographs—came after
your time, but I'm positive you would
have loved it.) Mary, I worried about
publishing this book. There are a lot of
Frankenstein experts out there. Really,
using published characters in new works
is what we call *fan fiction* today. It's fun
and freeing, and actually how I started
writing as an adult. (There was a book
published called *Twilight*—also written
from the writer's dream! Never mind,
I'll tell you later.) I was as careful
as I could be and researched topics
such as *when [candles, zippers, windows,
etc.] were invented* and looked up
the topographic maps of Salisbury.
I learned about common pig breeds,
types of trees in Britain, the history
of blood transfusions, and scoured

museum catalogues for examples of wallpapers and chandeliers so I could imagine everything correctly. I researched the etymology of almost every word I wrote. I forbade my characters to say *Okay*, even as their lips trembled with the need to blurt it.

In my book, there are many deviations from your tale, which I acknowledge and hope that you and my dear readers will forgive. For example, I knowingly placed a ring upon the resurrected Will's hand, which made Angelika think that he might be married. Wedding bands did not become common for men until much later. I didn't detail exactly *how* the resurrection procedure worked, and my story was influenced by classic movie portrayals. But my readers will not pick up this book hoping for a definitive medical explanation, and you didn't give us overly specific details, either. What I do know they will like is romance, and a mystery, and the fun of being tucked up in a gothic mansion in the chilly Salisbury countryside, with all the fires lit. I want them to walk in the fancy shoes of a girl with endless funds at her disposal, who realizes that money cannot buy what truly matters.

The journey with this book, *Angelika Frankenstein Makes Her Match*, showed me that big things can sprout from a single sentence or seed. One can never assume that writing something silly, ▶

A Letter to Mary Shelley *(continued)*

off the cuff, fan-fiction-y, or without any specific intention is not *real* writing. From the first word on the page, it's writing. It's creating. Even falling asleep in bed can produce a literary legacy.

Dearest Mary Shelley, what began as a flight of fancy became an actual book, one that I hope does not offend your esteemed, unforgettable spirit. I urge all my modern readers to read your book once in their lifetime, to carry your torch into the future.

Yours sincerely,
Sally Thorne ∾

Reading Group Guide

1. Have you read the original story of *Frankenstein* by Mary Shelley?

2. For those who responded no to the previous question, what basics of the storyline have you gleaned from just pop culture references and the general infamy of the book?

3. What are some romantic tropes in *Angelika Frankenstein Makes Her Match*?

4. This book was written during the COVID-19 lockdown. Are there any ways you feel that has influenced this book, its settings, or its characters, in particular Angelika?

5. What challenges can you imagine an author might face in writing a character with amnesia, especially one not known by anyone else, either?

6. Are there any elements that suggest magic exists in this book's world?

7. Christopher is introduced as a suitor for Angelika. What alternative possibility does he represent, and could he have been her soul mate? ▶

Reading Group Guide *(continued)*

8. Do you feel that it was faith or science that saved Arlo?

9. Who was the grandniece visiting the servant Mary at the end of the book?

10. Would you enjoy a story about how Victor and Lizzie met?

11. What would be your dream fan-fiction retelling of a classic novel? ᓄ

Discover great authors, exclusive offers, and more at hc.com.